CALL NO MAN
M•A•S•T•E•R

BY

TINA JUÁREZ

Arte Público Press
Houston, Texas
1995

This volume is made possible through grants from the National Endowment for the Arts (a federal agency), the Lila Wallace-Reader's Digest Fund, and the Andrew W. Mellon Foundation.

Recovering the past, creating the future

Arte Público Press
University of Houston
Houston, Texas 77204-2090

Cover design by James F. Brisson
Original art "Augustina of Aragón"
Oil on canvas, Anonymous, Circa 1820
Museo Lázaro Galdiano, Madrid, Spain

Juárez, Tina.
    Call no man master / by Tina Juárez.
      p.   cm.
    ISBN 1-55885-124-0
    1. Mexico—History—Spanish colony, 1540-1810—Fiction. I. Title.
    PS3560.U25C34   1995
    813'.54—dc20   94-24407
                                      CIP

To Joel

CALL NO MAN
M·A·S·T·E·R

I

When we were children and played Cristóbal's games on the grounds of his father's estate near Guanajuato, I did not think it was a curse to be a woman. Some of the maids in Don Esteban's household said it was a curse to be born a woman in the Viceroyalty of New Spain, a land the ancients had called Mexico. They said that only men and horses could be happy in such a place, but I did not see why it was so. I was a girl and I was happy. In all the games I could run faster, jump higher, and throw farther than any boy except Cristóbal and he was a year my senior. Of course, I never had a wish to be better at anything than Cristóbal. However, I always wanted to beat his brother, Humberto, and often did. The sons of the servants would not try against Humberto because he would get mad if he lost a contest. I would try to beat him and enjoyed it when I did. Most days I was very happy and I certainly did not think I was cursed.

Sometimes I would ask my aunt, Hortensia, what the maids meant when they talked about the burden of being a woman in the Viceroyalty of New Spain. Usually, they spoke of such things at mid-morning when the workers gathered around the big, hooded stone oven in the main kitchen to sample Hortensia's freshly baked *pan dulce*. My cousin, Teresa, and I were always first in line to get our share so we could race to the clay jars filled with cotton-seed honey and ladle the thick, clear sweetness onto the pastries, so piping hot they would blister our hands. My aunt would smile at my query,

7

stroke my hair, and say, "When you are older and have taken a husband, Carmencita, you will learn what they mean."

I would remind her that I had no intention whatsoever of taking a husband. Like my father and his father before him, I was going to be a soldier. My father was Baldemar Rangel, a captain in the Royal Dragoons and aide to Cristóbal's father, Don Esteban, the Marqués de Abrantes. Many times I had heard Don Esteban speak of how the men of the House of Abrantes had, always stood (since the days of Ferdinand and Isabella) first among the defenders of the Spanish monarchy. Beaming with pride, he would never fail to add: "And at their side, sword in hand, has always stood a Rangel!" Just because I was a girl was no reason for that tradition to end. My mother died before she could give my father a son, and so there was only me, María del Carmen Rangel, to stand at Cristóbal's side when it came our time to defend our king. It was my sacred duty. More than that, it was my destiny.

At first, Hortensia would listen patiently when I would detail for her the plans Cristóbal and I had made to go to Spain and offer our services to King Carlos. And it was necessary that we go to Spain. From our point of view, nothing of consequence had happened in the Viceroyalty of New Spain since Hernán Cortés and his *conquistadores* defeated the Aztecs almost three centuries before. The only opportunity for glory was in Spain which was usually at war with some country or the other. I thought my mother's sister would want to hear of our plans, but one day she said, "Carmen, women do not fight in wars. You are old enough to know this. Women do not become soldiers."

Hortensia, like most of the servants, could not read, and so she knew little history. I could easily show her where she was wrong. Don Esteban's library was full of books that chronicled the wars of Europe. There had been many women warriors. Had not Doña Sancha, a soldier of great courage and daring, rescued Fernán González, founder of Castile, from a Moorish dungeon? And did not Doña Jimena lead her husband's army when Rodrigo de Vivar, the Cid, died before completing his dream to unite all of the Spanish kingdoms against the Arab invaders? Of them all, the shining example of the woman warrior was Thalestris, Queen of the Amazons, who helped the great Alexander conquer the world.

That Thalestris was my favorite was due to the fact that Cristóbal, after reading *The Book of Alexander*, could think of little but the young Macedonian king who led a small band of warriors against mighty Asian armies. We would playact Alexander's victories. Waving wooden swords, Cristóbal and I would lead our imaginary armies up and down the winding marble staircases and through the cavernous hallways of the Marqués's great hacienda. We knew our parts well. In my case, I knew that Thalestris led a band of one hundred maidens, all of whom were, so the book said, experts in dealing precise blows, wounding shield-bearers, and shooting crossbows. Thalestris herself could behead a man with only a single swing of her sword, a feat I was certain I could duplicate if only presented the opportunity.

One afternoon, Don Esteban and my father came upon us just as Alexander the Great was about to win the Battle of Issus. They had been in Guanajuato at the intendant's palace to meet with an envoy from the viceroy in Mexico City, two hundred leagues to the south. King Carlos was concerned about the rise to power of a young French general by the name of Napoleon Bonaparte. Notables in the colonies were being asked for gold to strengthen the navy, so Spain would be prepared should war come. When he saw us, Don Esteban shouted, "Little soldiers! Come here, come here, my brave little soldiers!"

We rushed to his outstretched arms, and we were both hoisted high into the air. The Marqués was tall, a head taller than my father who was considered to be a big man. His hair was exactly the same shade of morning-sun red as Cristóbal's. It was a handsome color, and I had always wished my hair was similar in color to theirs, but it was not. My hair was raven black, the same as my Cousin Teresa's or Aunt Hortensia's, the same as most people who were *indio*.

His blue eyes sparkling, Don Esteban asked, "And who are my little soldiers today?" He looked back at my father whose stern expression betrayed that his thoughts were elsewhere, perhaps with the news brought by the viceroy's envoy. "Caesar and Anthony? Yes? Today, you are Julius Caesar and Mark Anthony!"

"No, *Papá!*" Cristóbal protested vigorously as we were returned to the stone floor polished so bright you could see your reflection. "I am Alexander the Great! You know that, *Papá.* Alexander the Great!"

"I see," Don Esteban said and stroked his beard. "And you, Carmencita? Let me guess. You are Ptolemy. Yes? Or...Hesphaestion! That's it! You are Hesphaestion, Alexander's loyal friend, his shield in battle, his—"

"No, Don Esteban," I interrupted. "I am Thalestris, Queen of the Amazons!"

"How interesting," the Marqués said, properly impressed. There was about him the manner of a thespian. When traveling actors came to the estate, Don Esteban would join them and recite lines he had committed to memory. His voice was deep and melodious. All the servants loved to hear him play his guitar and sing the ballads he had learned as a boy in Spain. The household of the Marqués de Abrantes was a happy one. "Thalestris, Queen of the Amazons. Indeed. You have come to fight at our young king's side?"

"I have come," I announced, "to bear Alexander's son!"

My father's jaw dropped and a strand of his greying hair fell over his brow. "What did she say?" he gasped, cupping his hand to his ear. He had begun to lose his hearing and seemed to have especial trouble with the sound of my voice. "Who told you such a thing, child? Tell me! Tell me now or," he drew back his hand, "I will—"

Smiling, Don Esteban raised his hand to silence my father, whose ruddy complexion was now flushed quite red. The Marqués would never allow my father to hit me. He would allow no one to touch me in anger, not even Aunt Hortensia. He knelt beside me and took my hands in his. "Carmencita," he said softly, "do you know what it means to bear a man's son?"

"No, Don Esteban," I admitted as tears came to my eyes. I felt confused and ashamed as though I had said something wrong. It must have been something very wrong, or my father would not have acted the way he did. Usually, he did not notice much of what I did, but now he was very angry. "It was in *The Book of Alexander*, Don Esteban. The book said Thalestris came to bear Alexander's son because he was a man of great courage."

Gently, Don Esteban wiped the tears from my cheeks. "Do not cry, Carmen. Soldiers do not cry. I will find you and Cristóbal another book." He laughed, apparently quite amused at what I had said. "But I think I shall read it first!"

✦

In time I learned what it meant for a woman to bear a child and a great deal more that had to do with that subject. As the years passed, Teresa became very interested in such matters and I have to confess was also curious. Cristóbal declared that it was not proper for boys and girls to discuss the topic and that Teresa and I should wait for her mother to tell us more than the fairy tales no one believed. The older girls were only too eager to tell us, yet what they said was too silly to be true. It was no wonder they giggled and talked in secretive whispers about certain things they claimed happened between men and women, about a thing they called love.

Finally, Hortensia had to tell Teresa about these things because her body was changing, and she had to understand what was happening. She decided to tell us both, and as odd as it seemed, much of what the older girls had said was accurate. Love, my aunt told us, was a wonderful thing, and some day it would become the most important thing in our lives, she said.

It was not long after Hortensia explained this matter to us that something quite unpleasant occurred. Humberto had begun to want to wrestle me. This was curious because he had frequently made light of our games. I would wrestle him even though he was much bigger. He was older and bigger than Cristóbal. But whereas Cristóbal was strong and agile, Humberto was just heavy. Without much difficulty, I could throw him to the ground. However, when I would try to pin his shoulders, he would grab me and hold me tight against him. He would grasp and squeeze my body with his hands in ways that were most peculiar and annoying. He did the same things with Teresa, and she did not even agree to wrestle him. He would grab her when she was not looking. Several times Cristóbal told Humberto not to wrestle with me or Teresa or any of the servant's daughters, but he kept on until Cristóbal boxed his nose and made it bleed.

One day, I happened to enter the carriage house and heard the muffled sounds of voices in one of the coaches, a closed-top landau. I prided myself on being able to move from place to place without being detected, and so I crept forward to investigate. In the coach I saw what I at first thought was Humberto once again wrestling with Teresa. I started to yell for him to stop, until I realized that he was attempting to do to Teresa what Hortensia said was a wonderful thing. Humberto had Teresa's mouth covered with his hand and from the way she was struggling what was about to happen did not appear to be wonderful at all. The sight of this so stunned me, I was not certain what I should do, so I did nothing but watch.

What I was witnessing confused and bewildered me. It reminded me of the time when, hiding in the hayloft, I observed the stablemaster bring a stallion to the corral where a mare in estrus was penned. After the gate was secured, the mare tried to leap over the railing, but the stallion pursued her, biting her neck and snorting furiously, until she became submissive and allowed him to mount her. For all I knew, the same thing was what was supposed to occur between men and women. I suppose I would have just stood there and allowed Humberto to accomplish what he was so desperately trying to do if Cristóbal, who had been looking for me, had not entered the carriage house. Even before I became aware of it, he had come up behind me and pushed me aside to get to his brother.

Cristóbal dragged Humberto from the landau and began to beat him. I did not mind seeing Humberto take a pounding, but after a few minutes, I could tell that Cristóbal's rage had overcome him, and he was on the verge of killing his brother. My efforts to prevent Cristóbal from slamming his fists into Humberto's unmoving body were to no avail. From the way Humberto's eyes rolled upward, I thought he might already be dead. It was only when Cristóbal had exhausted his strength that I was able to pull him away and explain to him that the proper thing to do was to tell his father what had happened.

When I made this suggestion, Teresa, who had managed to climb out of the coach, tearfully begged us not to tell anyone what had happened. She said people would think bad of her because of what Humberto had tried to do. Neither Cristóbal nor I understood what she meant, but so insistent was Teresa in her pleas, we finally agreed we would keep what had happened a secret among us. And when Humberto finally woke up, he seemed to understand that Cristóbal meant it when he promised he would kill him if he ever tried to do such a thing again.

✦

In the weeks and months that followed, none of us spoke of what transpired in the carriage house. Teresa seemed to want to pretend it never happened, so I did not talk to her about it. In fact, as we grew older, Teresa and I talked less about many things. My cousin was changing in ways I did not like. For example, though older, she had always followed my lead and had always participated in our games. When Cristóbal needed enemy soldiers I would assign the role to Teresa and Rubén Yepes, the stablemaster's son. Teresa began to make excuses not to be a part of our activities. At first, I attributed her reluctance to the fact she was having to assume more kitchen chores. However, I did not see why she could not participate in our Saturday evening contests.

For as long as I could remember, Cristóbal and I would stage the championship games on Saturday evening. The Marqués would award prizes to the winners. Because Cristóbal and I usually won, after a while our regulars began to make excuses to skip the contests; that left only the small children as participants, and it was no challenge to race babies. The problem was the older girls who loved to promenade about in brightly colored dresses, wearing flowers in their hair, and smiling at the boys who played their guitars and sang in the gardens on Saturday nights. When Teresa began to do these foolish things, Rubén forsook our games to join her, so she could stand in the gardens with him and giggle and whisper. I did not like this turn of events. I wanted things to go on as before, and somehow Teresa seemed responsible for the unwanted changes, so I decided not to have any more to do with her. If she would not participate in our games, I did not see why I should even bother to talk to her.

Had I not stopped speaking to Teresa, there was much I could have told her. For instance, I thought it was silly how she was constantly primping her hair and sticking flowers in it or fussing over the brightly colored cotton dresses she wore. Obviously, she thought she was pretty. People said she was pretty because of her large brown eyes and long hair. There were those who said she and I looked like sisters except I kept my hair cut short. After all, Alexander the Great had his men cut their hair short so it could not be seized by an enemy in battle. As we grew older, I was glad that I was turning out to be much taller than Teresa. I was proud of my height even though some of the maids clucked their tongues and said it was not good for a girl to be tall because a man would not marry a woman taller than he. I was shorter than Cristóbal and that was all that mattered.

It was inevitable, I suppose, that something unpleasant would happen between Teresa and me. The incident occurred at a time when Don Esteban and my father had gone to Mexico City to confer with the viceroy. Much to the Marqués's dismay, King Carlos had entered into a treaty with France against England. Napoleon Bona-parte had proclaimed himself emperor of France, and Spain was his ally. Cristóbal had gone with his father in order to visit his mother who lived in the capital. It was said the Marquesa's health was too fragile for frontier conditions in Guanajuato, where most of the colony's gold and silver mines were located. I was in the stables brushing down the Parisian barouche horses when Teresa came bouncing in with a basket of *pan dulce* for Rubén and his father. When she asked where they were, I was forced to break my silence to inform her they had gone to Guanajuato for supplies.

For a while she watched me curry the silver-maned horses, and then she asked, "Do you know Héctor Sandoval, Carmencita? He's a groom in the employ of the Conde de Sestos. Do you know him?"

I glanced at the birds embroidered in green and purple threads around the collar and sleeves of Teresa's dress. She worked endlessly on such things. Dresses made no sense to me. Like Cristóbal and his father, I usually wore leather breeches, a plain white cotton shirt, and boots. You could not ride a horse or swing a sword if you were wearing a dress and straw sandals.

"Yes," I said finally just so she would stop looking at me like a goose. "I know Héctor Sandoval. What of it?"

"Héctor likes you, Carmencita! He wants to ask your father if he can be your escort at the fiesta in Guanajuato. My mother said she would chaperon if you and Héctor go with Rubén and me. It will be so much fun and—"

"Enough!" I said. I did not want to hear about Héctor Sandoval or fiestas or chaperons. Did she not comprehend that if I went to a fiesta, which I never would, I would go with Cristóbal? "Is that all you can think about, Teresa? Fiestas and dresses and flowers and boys! How stupid!"

When I left the stall to retrieve sawdust for the mid-day bedding, she sniffed, "I don't think it's stupid."

I tried to ignore her but, after securing the rack-chain to prevent the horses from lying down in their fresh bed, I asked, "How can you think about stupid things at a time like this? We may already be at war with England. The English have the most powerful navy in the world. Don't you realize they might invade New Spain and force us to become protestants?"

As usual, when I spoke of such matters, Teresa had not heard a word I said. She could hardly wait for me to finish before she asked, "What about Héctor? Will you go with him to the fiesta?"

"I am a soldier!" I shouted. "Soldiers do not go fiestas!"

"Oh, Carmen," she huffed and turned to leave. "You're just a *juana gallo!*"

That did it! No one was going to call me a female rooster and get away with it. I grabbed the first thing in my reach, which turned out to be one of the pitchforks used to toss hay into the stalls. Raising it, I yelled, "Don't you call me that, you...you—" I could not think of something worse than *juana gallo* to call her.

At the stable door Teresa turned and her eyes grew so large I thought they were going to pop out of her head. "Carmen!" she screamed. "Don't stick me!"

Of course, I had no intention of sticking her with a pitchfork. All I was thinking about was what I could call her that would be the most insulting. Finally, I shouted, "Republican!" Don Esteban had told Cristóbal and me about the Paris mob who had used the guillotine to chop off the heads of King Carlos's cousin, Louis XVI, and his queen,

Marie Antoinette. There was nothing in the world, he explained, more disgusting than republicans, so I repeated, "Republican!"

Flinging the *pan dulce* to the sky, Teresa made a dash for the hacienda some distance up the hill from the stable and carriage house. I could almost walk faster than she could run, so it was no difficult task to chase her down. Unfortunately, just as she reached the door to the kitchen, Hortensia came rushing out like a wet hen and screamed for me to drop the pitchfork. In truth I did not realize I had carried the fork from the stable. I probably would have complied with my aunt's demand, except all of the household servants had come outside to see what the commotion was about. All eyes were on me, watching me, waiting to see if I was going to surrender. I did not want it to appear I was being forced to do something against my will, even something as reasonable as what my aunt had requested.

Several times Hortensia told me to drop the fork, and then she made a lunge for it. I held it above her reach, and like a matador, stepped aside each time she tried to grab it.

Finally, she placed her hands on her hips and shouted, "Who do you think you are, Carmen Rangel? Just who do you think you are to threaten your cousin with a pitchfork and to disobey me?"

For all to hear, I proclaimed, "I am María del Carmen Rangel, daughter of Baldemar Rangel, captain in the Royal Dragoons of Carlos IV, king of Spain! That is who I am."

"Oh?" Hortensia said. "Is that who you are? Is there nothing else?"

I did not understand. Slowly, I lowered the fork to the ground. What else was there to say?

"So you are a *gachupina*, Carmen? Nothing else?"

Gachupín meant "one who wears spurs," a term for people who were born in Spain such as the Marqués and Cristóbal. I shrugged. "My father is a *gachupín*. It is true."

I had never seen Hortensia's eyes so hard. "And your mother? Was she a *gachupina*? Was she a *criolla*?"

Criollos were those of Spanish blood born in the colony. Unlike the Spanish-born, the *criollos* were denied high military rank or positions of importance in the government or church.

"No," Hortensia said in answer to her own question when I did not respond. "She was an *india*!"

"You should know what my mother was. She was your sister."

"Yes," Hortensia said. "She was my sister. I am proud to say that. And I am proud, as was she, that I am *india*!"

At that moment, my uncle Anselmo came rushing ahead of several of the other ground keepers. He had heard Teresa squealing like a pig and wanted to know what was wrong. Anselmo had always been kind to me. He always made sure there were many brightly colored flowers in my room, and here I had chased his baby girl with a pitchfork. When Hortensia told him what had happened, he looked at me with genuine puzzlement while holding his high-crown straw hat in his dirty hands. He always removed his hat around me, the gesture of respect the servants made when in the presence of the Marqués or other notables such as Intendant Riaño. I told him many times he did not have to do that, but he always insisted on doing so.

Turning again to me, Hortensia reached into her dress pocket, retrieved something, and extended her hand, palm up. "I believe this belongs to you."

I saw that she was holding the blue jade pendant my mother had bequeathed me. It was a carving of a woman's profile. I was told it was a Mexican goddess. "Where did you get that?" I demanded. "Did you take it from my room? I told you to stay out of my rooms!"

"I found it on the ground outside your window. I guess you did not notice it was missing. You never wear it."

I had never much liked the pendant. Why should I? The *indios* were a defeated people. With less than six hundred men, Hernán Cortés had defeated thousands of Indians, tens of thousands. I had no interest in their gods and goddesses or, for that matter, anything else about Mexico. As for my mother, I had only the faintest recollection of her.

"Are you too good to wear it?" Hortensia asked. "Is that why you avoid your mother's people, Carmen? You are too good to talk to us? You are ashamed because we are not *gachupines*?" she added using the derogatory term *gachupín* used for Spaniards.

If my aunt's intention was to humiliate me before everyone, it did not work. I was no longer a child. It was true that I was not a *gachupina*, or even a *criolla*, but neither was I like Hortensia and Teresa. I was not born to be a cook or a maid. I was not a common servant. I was going to be a soldier in the army of Spain. I was going to be a captain like my father, or maybe even a general. Tossing the pitchfork to the ground, I told her to keep the pendant and returned to the stable.

From that day forward, I had little to do with Hortensia or Teresa. On several occasions, each tried to explain that what had happened had been a misunderstanding, that we had all said things we did not mean. I told them it did not matter, and it did not. I was convinced Cristóbal and I would soon leave for Spain, and what happened in the meantime was of small importance. If necessary, I would speak to Hortensia and Teresa. But they had their tasks to perform and I had mine.

✦

When word finally arrived that Spain and France were at war with England, Cristóbal begged his father to let us sail for Europe so we could participate in the battles. It seemed probable the war would be over quickly because Napoleon Bonaparte was proving to be a modern Alexander the Great, a general who knew only one thing: victory. Don Esteban said Cristóbal was still too young. However, as the weeks and months passed and other notables' sons departed for Europe, Cristóbal told his father that it was going to look as if the House of Abrantes was shirking its duty to the king. Humberto, who was old enough for military service, did not share his brother's enthusiasm. He began to spend more of his time in Mexico City.

Despite victory after victory, the Marqués remained mistrustful of the alliance with France. It was true that Napoleon put an end to the rule of the French republicans, but he had not restored the rightful Bourbon heir to the throne in Paris. Also, he had sold Louisiana–by all rights within Spain's domain–to the United States, the former English colony now an independent republic. Don Esteban did not like the idea of a republic on the same continent as New

Spain. He said it set a bad example. There were some in the Viceroyalty who secretly wished for the colony to declare its independence
from Spain and become a republic like the United States.

And then disaster struck. The combined navies of France and
Spain were destroyed by the English in the Battle of Trafalgar. Not a
single Spanish warship was left afloat. "It is," Don Esteban declared,
"a catastrophe! Without her navy, Spain is cut off from her colonies,
and we, the colonies, are her life blood!"

News of the terrible defeat at sea only strengthened Cristóbal's
resolve to go to Europe where Bonaparte and his enemies were
assembling the greatest armies the world had yet to see. "*Papá*," he
cried, "I must go! Please, *Papá*. Let me go!"

When Cristóbal spoke in such a manner, I assumed I would go
too. We would raise a company of men, perhaps a regiment. Naturally, my father would attend to the details of supply and organization. He had experience in such matters. It was of paramount
urgency, Cristóbal said, that we begin the preparations at once. It
was no small feat to assemble the weapons, the transport, and see to
the thousand and one details such an undertaking would involve.
Fortunately, the Marqués's gold and silver mines made possible
unlimited resources for the expedition. The major problem would be
to recruit enough men.

Don Esteban, however, would not give his consent to set the
process in action. The loss of the entire Spanish navy confirmed his
mistrust of the king's ministers who had recommended the alliance
with Bonaparte. Chief among those ministers was Manuel Godoy, a
man the Marqués detested. "No," he said in answer to Cristóbal's
impassioned pleas. "We will wait and see what develops. Besides, the
English control the seas. We will wait."

Cristóbal was certain great battles were coming, and he did not
wish to be an ocean away when it happened. His frustration grew
with every passing day. I witnessed it when we would practice the
skills my father and Don Esteban taught us. Each morning, we would
proceed to a hill some distance from the hacienda. In leather sheaths
attached to our saddle bows were *escopetas*, the light muskets favored
by dragoons. The drill we followed under my father's watchful eye

was to fire at a target, sheath the weapon, draw our swords from a scabbard attached to the left side of the saddle, and advance. Spurring our mounts to a gallop, we would charge and decapitate the enemy, a series of melons impaled on lances secured to the ground.

Though the course was rigorous, I could manage, but not with Cristóbal's speed and ferocity. He was magnificent. Brandishing a long and heavy double-edged walloon with both hands, he would negotiate his horse by flexing the muscles of his long legs wrapped tightly against the animal's flanks. The horse would leap over horizontal poles, around wooden barrels, or ascend rocky embankments as Cristóbal sliced through the imaginary English soldiers who had dared invade the sacred soil of Spain. One enemy after another fell to his furious onslaught. Long after I had tired, Cristóbal would run the course again and again, always striving to go faster and eliminate all mistakes. Watching him, my father would whisper, "He and the horse are of one mind. It is a thing of beauty. Truly, he is a dragoon!"

It was the highest compliment my father could pay. The dragoons, mounted infantry, were his passion. As far as I could tell, they were his only interest. On rare occasions, I would try to get him to speak of my mother. Why had he married a woman so much younger than he? (I had come to realize my father was old enough to be Don Esteban's father, and in fact he had served Don Esteban's father during battle in Europe.) When the Marqués came to the New World to claim the lands that had been awarded to men of his family by generations of grateful monarchs, my father, ever loyal to the House of Abrantes, followed. From everything I had heard, my mother was like Teresa, gay and fun-loving, someone who loved to sing and dance. Why would a humorless veteran of so many wars marry such a woman, a common household servant, an *india*? There were times when I wished my father had married a woman of his station, a *gachupina*. In any case, he would not speak of my mother other than to say I should try to be more like her.

While Cristóbal and I fought our mock battles on the hills above Guanajuato, France and Spain sent an army into Portugal to compel that country to keep its ports closed to English ships. Once conquered, Portugal was divided into three kingdoms, one of which

Napoleon gave to Manuel Godoy as a reward for his services. Enraged, Crown Prince Fernando, King Carlos's eldest son and heir to the Spanish throne, declared Godoy a traitor. This action gave Bonaparte what he apparently wanted, an excuse to turn on Spain. Old and weary, King Carlos abdicated, and for a brief time, Fernando was king. The Grand Army of France proved too powerful for the Spanish, and the House of Bourbon, the Royal Family of Spain, was forced to relinquish the crown, that Napoleon immediately conferred upon his brother, Joseph.

We were in the library when a viceregal courier came with the dispatch that a Bonaparte was now king of Spain. Immediately, Cristóbal shouted, "We must sail at once!"

To my surprise, the Marqués took the news calmly. After dismissing the courier, he began to unroll a map of the world onto the top of a mahogany table in the center of the room.

"*Papá*," Cristóbal pleaded, "let us begin the preparations. We will assemble an armada and sail for Europe. We will—"

Raising his hand to command silence, Don Esteban said, "We will waste no more of our resources in Europe."

Cristóbal looked at me, and for a moment he was speechless.

"*Papá*, I don't understand. What are you saying?"

"Come and look at this," the Marqués said, pointing to the map. "You too, Carmencita. Come. What do you see here?" His finger was touching the Iberian Peninsula. "Tell me."

"It is Spain?" Cristóbal said, puzzled.

"Spain." Don Esteban repeated and his eyes hardened. "A small and barren land." His hand swept across the map to the continent of North America. "And what do you see here?" He looked at me. "Carmencita?"

It was a beautiful map, a work of art. The cartographer's calligraphy was ornate like the lettering on viceregal documents. The different territories were designated in rich hues of red and blue. At the northern extreme of the great continent were the lands belonging to the czar of Russia and to the king of England. Below and to the east was the United States. Everything else, from the Isthmus of Panama to Canada, from the Mississippi River west across great plains and mountains to the Pacific Ocean, was New Spain. That was where the Marqués's hand rested. I shrugged my answer: "The Viceroyalty?"

"Yes," he said. "The Viceroyalty of New Spain. A land large enough to hold all of the kingdoms of Europe combined."

"But *Papá*," Cristóbal said and flicked his hand at the map as if brushing away flies, "most of it is a desert."

"That is what I once believed," the Marqués said. "My father believed it, and so did his father before him. That is why they did not come to claim the lands given them by their kings. Oh yes, there was gold and silver to be found, but little else. It is what we all believed. But we were wrong. I have studied chronicles kept by explorers and missionaries. In the provinces to the north—Texas, Nuevo México, California—are to be found the richest soils in the world. Moderate climates. Huge forests. Great rivers. Natural harbors. A desert, my son? No. It is an empire of unclaimed wealth. That is what New Spain is. An empire!"

I could see my own surprise reflected in Cristóbal's face. Never had his father spoken of such things. His words were always focused on Europe, not America.

"Here in New Spain," the Marqués continued, pointing to the map, "is something more important than gold. Land. We have land for people, land on which to farm, to ranch, to raise families. We have more than everything needed except for one thing."

From the way he was smiling at me, I thought he was waiting for me to say what that thing might be.

"A king!" he said finally. "What has happened in Europe is an act of Providence. It has been ordained by God that Fernando vacate the throne in Madrid so he could come to New Spain. Fernando will be our king!"

"Fernando?" Cristóbal asked. "Here? In New Spain?"

"Yes," his father replied. "But we must act at once. The plan will not be without opposition. We must proceed in secrecy. There are many things I must do before the king arrives. In the meantime, I will send Humberto to Spain to meet with Fernando and arrange for the royal family's passage across the Atlantic."

At the same time Cristóbal and I exclaimed, "Humberto?"

Don Esteban cocked his head. "Is there something wrong with sending Humberto?"

"I had hoped," Cristóbal said, "I would have the honor to escort the king to our shores."

Don Esteban placed his hand on his son's shoulder. "There will be much for you to do here at my side, Cristóbal. We will need to raise an army. There may be officers in the colony who will see the sad events in Europe as an opportunity to seize control of the Viceroyalty. There are young captains in the barracks who dream of becoming the Napoleons of the Americas." He shook his head. "And even now there are those who attempt to stir the Indians to rebellion. There is a priest in Dolores who has been making trouble of that sort for some time."

"A priest?" I asked. Why, I wondered, would a priest want the Indians to rebel. "What priest?"

"A man called Miguel Hidalgo. He is a priest with republican sentiments, I am told. There are many such men who will say that because a Bonaparte now rules Spain, there should be changes here, changes such as those made by the English colonists to the north." He placed his other hand on my shoulder. "I need both of my brave soldiers here by my side. Humberto will go to Spain. He is of age."

Humberto was of age, but as Cristóbal and I could have predicted, he was not of the inclination. Responding to his father's summons, he sent a message from the capital that he was ill with a malady physicians in Mexico City were unable to diagnose. He asked his father and brother to pray for him and vowed that if a miracle occurred and he did recover, he would dedicate himself to a life of service to the poor.

Cristóbal seized the opportunity. "Alexander was no older than I when he inherited his father's kingdom. I am seventeen years old. Almost eighteen. I am a man! I will bring the king safely to these shores. Please, *Papá*. Do not deny me!"

Finally, Don Esteban relented. He was influenced in part by the news that England now supported those in Spain who were resisting the Bonapartes. English warships were no longer a threat to Spanish shipping. The foe was now a friend. At least we would be safe on our passage across the Atlantic. "Maybe," I speculated, "the English will provide an escort on our return."

"Our return?" Don Esteban asked. "What do you mean?"

"When we return with King Fernando!" I explained, hardly able to contain my excitement. I was going to meet the king! It would be recorded in the books of history that Cristóbal de Abrantes and María del Carmen Rangel brought to the shores of New Spain her first king. I would be famous!

"Carmencita," the Marqués began and shook his head, "you cannot go to Spain. It is too dangerous. You are"—he gestured with his hand to my body and shrugged—"a girl, almost a woman."

At first I was not certain I had heard correctly. I could not accompany Cristóbal and my father to Spain because I was a woman? Cristóbal had cited historical precedent to convince his father that he was of age, so I attempted to do the same. "What of Doña Sancha?" I asked. "And Doña Jimena? Or Thalestris? They were women. They were warriors."

"Carmencita, those are just stories in books. Fairy tales. Women do not fight in wars."

I might as well have been talking to Hortensia. My arguments were to no avail. When I tried to appeal to my father, he not only said I could not go because I was a girl, he said, "You are just a girl. Do not be silly."

Worst of all, Cristóbal agreed with them. Each time I tried to get him to intervene with his father on my behalf, he would try to change the subject. He would talk about what a great empire New Spain would become under its own king. He had begun to read the reports on the provinces to the north, the lands called Texas and California. "New Spain will be the largest and richest empire ever," he said. "It will be greater than Alexander's!"

"It is not fair," I protested. "I should be able to go to Europe. I can use a musket and sword as well as any man, better than most. It is not fair, Cristóbal!"

"Carmen," he said, taking my hands. He looked into my eyes in a way he never had before. "We do not know what we will find in Spain. We may have to fight the French."

"That is why I should go! I will stand at your side. Like generations of Rangels, I will stand, sword in hand, at your side and—"

He touched my face with his hand. His eyes, his beautiful pale eyes, the color of the sky, were sad. "Carmen," he whispered, "I could not stand it if anything happened to you. I... I—" He looked away. "Please understand."

The only thing I understood was that I had to stay in New Spain while he had the chance for fame and glory. It seemed a betrayal, and I was angry. I ran away and hid in the hayloft above the stable. It was only with the greatest of effort that I did not cry. Again and again, I had to remind myself that soldiers do not cry.

Over the next several days, the hacienda was alive with activity as preparations were made for the departure. Because of the need for secrecy, the servants were told that Cristóbal and my father were going to Spain to join the fight against the Bonapartistas. Nothing was said of bringing Fernando to New Spain. In the carriage house, the men worked to ready the coach that was to be used for the journey to the port of Veracruz. In the main house, the maids filled chests with clothes and provisions. Cristóbal and my father spent time with the Marqués preparing documents to be conveyed to Fernando.

All the while, I avoided Cristóbal much as I had Teresa and Hortensia. Most of the time, I stayed in the hayloft or one of the other hiding places only I knew about. If I happened to go to the kitchen and Cristóbal saw me before I saw him, I would make an excuse to leave. I could see he was baffled. For some reason, he failed to grasp that he had betrayed me. He could have pleaded my case with his father, but he did not. Everything I had learned was for naught, and I was angry, angry at Cristóbal, angry at my father, angry at the Marqués. I was very angry.

Finally, the day of departure arrived. The great carriage never appeared more elegant, its brass trim gleaming and the corinthian leather panels spotless. I went to the kitchen for *pan dulce* while everyone was outside bidding their farewells. Presently, Teresa came to say Cristóbal was looking for me.

"Let him look," I said. "That is his privilege."

She stared at me a moment, and then, in a tone surprisingly harsh, she said, "You self-centered *niña*! For once in your life, think of someone other than yourself. You are sixteen years old, Carmen. You are no longer a child!"

Though her impertinence annoyed me, I did not take action because she seemed to have been crying. That puzzled me. Why, I wondered, would she be crying at such a time. It should be a time of great celebration and joy for everyone except me. If anyone had a reason to cry, it was me. I was being denied my rightful place in the history books.

"Don't you realize," she asked, "your father and Cristóbal are going to war? They may never come back. Cristóbal may be killed! He is just a boy."

The possibility had never crossed my mind. I looked beyond her to the yard where I could see my father climbing up to the driver's deck. No one was cheering. Suddenly, I had the strangest sensation in my stomach as though I had swallowed a cold rock. Cristóbal might be killed? The thought confused me. I ran from the kitchen and found him at the boot of the coach. He was very handsome in the Prussian-blue uniform. On it were no gold braids or the epaulets so favored by Spanish officers in the Viceroyalty. Its very simplicity made him look all the more noble, like a young Greek god. At his side hung a gold-hilted dragoon's saber in a black leather scabbard.

I tried to speak, to explain why I had avoided him, but my throat was tight. The maids were sobbing. I wanted to tell them to be quiet, to stop acting like donkeys, but there was no time.

"Carmen," Cristóbal said, "it will be only a few months and I will be back. And then, we will do all the things we planned." He swallowed hard and managed to smile. "When I return, we will go north to Texas where we will help King Fernando build an empire greater than Alexander's. Just a few months, no more."

Cristóbal gripped my arms tightly, drew me to him and kissed my cheek. I was startled. He had never done such a thing. Quickly, he strode to the carriage and climbed to the deck. My father cracked the whip and the team, their heads high, surged forward. High-stepping proudly, the big jobbers pulled the heavy carriage along the gravel roadway and through the gates.

After the coach was out of view, I watched the Marqués walk slowly back to the hacienda. Even he was not jubilant. Too late, I remembered I had not said good-bye to my father. He had left for Spain, perhaps not to return for months, and we had forgotten to say good-bye. I looked again at the maids sobbing like the world had ended. For the first time in my life, I thought I might understand what they meant when they said it was a curse to be born a woman in Mexico.

✦

There had never been enough hours in the day for the things Cristóbal and I had to do. For us dawn would not come soon enough and the sun would set far too early over the distant peaks of the Sierra Madre. But now, each hour was an eternity and the days were endless. My only consolation was that each passing day meant the moment was closer when Cristóbal would return. If the winds were right and the captain skillful, the Gulf of Mexico and the Atlantic could be crossed in two months. It did not seem unreasonable to anticipate Cristóbal's return in four. Each time I asked Don Esteban, he said it was possible, but he thought it more likely would take six months.

All I could do was be patient and hope there would be no unforeseen delays. It was a lonely vigil, but Don Esteban and I stood it together. He kept me informed of the latest news from Mexico City, most of which was discouraging. Various men began to claim authority over the colony. Some generals went so far as to position troops in rival camps around the capital without the authorization of the viceroy. They were waiting, poised like snakes, to make a bid for power if events were favorable. Even the legitimacy of the colonial government was questioned. It was said the king's abdication automatically dissolved his government in the colony. There was even a rumor that Joseph Bonaparte had named a viceroy for New Spain and was sending French soldiers to enforce his authority. Since the

English had destroyed Napoleon's fleet at Trafalgar, an invasion did not seem likely.

"Do you now comprehend," Don Esteban asked me on one of the strolls we took after dinner, "why we must have a king in New Spain? Without a monarch to chart the common good, there is anarchy. Do you understand?"

"Yes, Don Esteban," I replied as we entered the patio on the south side of the hacienda. It was one of my favorite places. Along the edges of the flagstone courtyard were all sorts of flowering vines and potted plants. There were azaleas, hibiscus, and fragrant roses. Winding around the limestone pillars supporting the arabesque archways were bougainvilleas heavy with vermilion blaze. My uncle Anselmo had created a place of enchantment. It was amazing that such a simple man, a man who rarely spoke, could make such beauty.

In the center of the courtyard was a tiled pool fed by a stream of water that gurgled out the mouth of a stone frog. Don Esteban sat at the edge of the pool and stared down at the glazed roseate tiles shimmering through the ripples of the water. "Men need a king," he said more to himself than to me. He was worried about his plan. "Without a king, there is chaos."

"Why not," I suggested, "announce your plan throughout New Spain? It would put an end to the dispute over who has authority to rule. It would—"

"No!" he said quickly and looked about as if someone might be listening to our conversation. "If it were known that Fernando is coming to these shores, there are those who would attempt to establish a government before he arrives. That priest to the north, Miguel Hidalgo, has called for the election of an assembly to write a constitution. He has gained the support of an artillery officer in Dolores, a captain by the name of Ignacio Allende. Such men are dangerous. We must proceed with caution."

Some of what he said I did not comprehend. I sat at the edge of the pool and dipped my hand into the cold water. "What," I asked, "is a constitution?"

Dismissing my query with a wave of his hand, he said, "We have little to fear from that quarter. The serious threat is in the capital. It comes from those *criollo* officers who dream of driving out the Spanish-born and taking our lands. They are the ones who…who—"

I glanced up when he stopped. He was staring at me, an odd expression in his eyes. "What is it?" I asked scanning the wrought-iron balustrades of the balconies above the patio. I thought perhaps he had heard something.

When I looked back, he smiled. "Your mother used to do that, what you are doing now, pulling your hand through the water in the pool." His gaze shifted to the balconies. "She loved this place. She would come here in the evenings and sing."

I withdrew my hand from the water and dried it on my shirt. There was a chill in the air.

"Cata Valeria had a lovely voice. So pure, so…beautiful."

"What will happen," I asked, hoping to bring his attention back to the subject at hand, "if the officers in Mexico City do not accept Fernando as king of New Spain?"

The smile faded from his lips. "That is why I must raise a force to place at his command." He got to his feet and for a moment massaged his temples with the tips of his fingers. Since Cristóbal's departure, he had suffered from headaches. "But it is proving to be more difficult than I anticipated. We have the resources. The problem is in finding men, good and loyal men, capable of putting down a challenge to the king's authority. Such men are difficult to find in the numbers we shall need."

I tried to think of something to suggest as a solution to the problem. There had to be an answer, though at that moment it eluded me.

Don Esteban said he was tired and that he was going to retire early. Before leaving, he turned to ask, "Did I mention I received a message from Humberto? He is planning to come to Guanajuato. He is bringing two men he met in Mexico City who wish to speak to me."

"He has recovered from his terrible illness?" I asked, making no attempt to conceal my sarcasm.

The Marqués did not seem to hear. His expression was one of bewilderment when he said, "The men are from the United States."

Few things Humberto did would surprise me, but this was different. *"Norteamericanos?"* Because of their location on the continent, the former English colonists were called *norteamericanos*. "*Norte-americanos* are republicans! Why would republicans come to New Spain?"

"I do not know. Humberto did not say. He only said they wanted to speak with me."

✦

I did not spend all my time with Don Esteban. Often he would confer with Juan Riaño, the intendant of Guanajuato, or other notables he trusted not to betray his plan. It gave me a chance to be alone and think about Cristóbal. I would climb to the third floor of the hacienda and perch in one of the *galerías* affording a view of Guanajuato below. From there you could see a sea of red-tile roofs and the tall, capped chimneys issuing forth the sweet aromas of firewood. In the middle of the city was the *Alhóndiga*, the massive stone structure where grains were stored. Cristóbal and I had always imagined it to be a great fortress, and we had played in its bins when our fathers went into the city. Now, I would stare at it for hours and remember those wonderful times.

There was, of course, my work to be done, and that helped to pass the time. Rubén's father died, and after an appropriate period of time, I convinced Don Esteban I should be in charge of the stable. When Teresa learned of the arrangement, she went to the Marqués to protest. She said Rubén had earned the right to assume his father's position of stablemaster. She and Rubén had declared their intention to marry, and I suppose for that reason Teresa wanted him to receive more pay. Rubén did not seem to care. Besides, Don Esteban increased his wages to what his father had been earning. However, he would not bear the position of stablemaster. Although Teresa had no further complaints, she was still unhappy that Rubén was to be my assistant and obey my orders.

Except for a thin mustache, Rubén had not changed all that much from the time when I would station him with the enemy soldiers against whom Cristóbal and I would mount our attack. His smooth face was that of the boy he had been, not that of the man he had become who could hoist and stack kegs of oats all morning. Sometimes, when he brought a fresh load from town, we would compete to see who could get the most kegs out of the wagon and into the loft. I liked Rubén. He did his work and said very little. He would have made a good soldier.

After I became stablemaster, Teresa no longer came to the carriage house with her little basket of *pan dulce*. I supposed it was because I was usually there. At mid-morning, Rubén would go to the kitchen for his snack. Before long, his time in the kitchen began to expand until it was evident he was being detained for reasons other than the *pan dulce*. I suspected what was happening and decided to investigate. I was able to observe Rubén when he left the stable without myself being seen. The servants paid little attention to anything but gossip, so I could easily move from place to place undetected. As I expected, Rubén and Teresa spent only a brief time in the kitchen before sneaking away when they thought no one was watching.

Removing my boots so as not to make a sound, I followed them down the hallway to Teresa's little room just above the wine cellar. At the door, I listened but was unable to make out what they were saying. Then I went outside and peeked in the window. Of course, I had some idea of what I might see. It was bad enough what went on in the gardens on Saturday night. They certainly were not getting paid to do such things during the workday, and I was prepared to jump through the window and tell them a thing or two.

To my surprise, however, they were seated across from each other at a small table in the middle of Teresa's tiny room. When I finally grasped what they were doing, I could not believe my eyes. Teresa was copying something from an opened book. From my position among some shrubs outside the window, I was unable to see what it was. And I was still unable to hear what they were saying. Rubén was using a small knife to trim the tips of goose quills. I was dumfounded to see Teresa writing. I did not even know she could read.

I decided not to confront them with what I knew. Instead, over the next several days, I continued to monitor their actions in hopes it would give me some clue as to what mischief they were about. Each day, the same thing occurred. Even at night this went on. By the light of a beeswax candle on her little table, Teresa labored at her task of copying. She was definitely up to no good. And then one evening, Teresa gathered a stack of the papers she had written, wrapped them in a serape, and carried them to the gardens where the servants were gathering for a fiesta. Hiding in the shadows, I watched as servants from surrounding haciendas arrived. Rubén and Teresa stayed apart from everyone. After a while several servants from the household of the Conde de Sestos joined them. Héctor Sandoval was among them. Seeing Héctor, I suddenly had an idea of what it was all about. What Teresa had made were copies of love poems. Strumming their guitars, the boys would sing love poems to their sweethearts. Teresa had made copies of poems for the boys to sing. She would sing with them, and people would gather around and say she had a pretty voice. She had copied silly love poems for her and the boys to sing.

Satisfied I had solved the puzzle, I prepared to leave until I noticed the servants from the Sestos hacienda were departing. They had been at the fiesta for only a few minutes and they were returning to their wagon. No one had sung. None of the boys had even brought their guitars or violins. There had been no carrying on in the gardens. And strangest of all, Héctor Sandoval was now in possession of the serape containing the papers Teresa had copied. As he walked hurriedly to the wagon hitched to a team of mules, he looked about as if afraid he was being watched.

That night I was unable to sleep. What was Teresa up to? I considered going to Don Esteban with what I knew. Teresa was not employed to scribble words when she was supposed to be in the kitchen scrubbing pans. Maybe she would be happier working at another hacienda.

By dawn I had made a decision. When Teresa and Rubén left with Hortensia and Anselmo for mass, I made my way to her little room. At the door, I hesitated. I did not feel comfortable invading Teresa's privacy. Nevertheless, it had to be done and I entered. I went to the little table on which were spread the books and papers. Looking first at the papers, I was baffled by what she had written. It made no sense and was certainly not a poem. In what I assumed was Teresa's handwriting were the words: "Man is born free, and yet we see him everywhere in chains. Those who believe themselves the masters of others find they are even greater slaves than the people they govern." There was more, but I stopped reading. Is this what she was copying to give to Héctor Sandoval? Why, I wondered, would she give him something that made no sense.

I picked up one of the books and opened it to the first page. The first sentence of the book was the same as what she had written. Wondering who had written such drivel, I turned to the title page. My eyes settled on the name: Jean Jacques Rousseau. It was a name I recognized. The author of the book was a Frenchman whose books had been banned in the colony. Possession of books written by this man was an act of treason, punishable by death. Quickly, I returned it to the table as I realized what I had uncovered. It was now abundantly clear what was going on, and I wondered why I had not thought of it sooner: Teresa, my own cousin, the daughter of my mother's sister, was a republican!

So engrossed was I in my discovery I did not hear the door to the room open. When I turned to leave, I was face to face with Teresa. Behind her, in the hallway, was Rubén. "Teresa!" I cried, startled. "What are you doing back so soon?"

Rubén followed Teresa into the room, and she closed the door behind them. For some time she stared at me as if I were a common thief before she answered, "I forgot my rosary."

I looked about, thinking that if I could find her rosary, she would take it and rush away so I would not have to explain what I was doing in her room. The bells were ringing in Guanajuato, and mass would soon be recited. Naturally, the rosary was nowhere in sight. Teresa made no attempt to search. While neither of us said anything, poor Rubén hung his head as if it had been him, not me, caught going through someone else's things."Well," I said and started toward the door, "I have to go to the stable and—"

Teresa moved to block the door. "Why, Carmen?"

"Why what?"

"Why are you in my room?"

"I have every right to be here!" I announced trying to think of at least one reason to back up my assertion.

"Oh?" she said before I had a chance to continue. "Even if you're just half Spaniard you think you can come in our rooms without permission? We don't matter. We are just Indians."

"Teresa," Rubén said softly. "We will be late. We—"

"I want to know," Teresa shouted, "what gives the *gachupines* the right to treat the *indios* as if we have no rights. Why, Carmen? Please tell me." Of course, she had no intention of letting me answer her question. Teresa was angry. I had never seen her so angry. Suddenly, this was a Teresa I did not know. "Is it the conquest, Carmen? The Spanish won and the *indios* lost and that settles that. Yes? To the victor belongs the spoils. Is that not what you taught us?"

I shrugged. She had said it.

"Three hundred years! It's been three hundred years since Cortés and his bandits conquered Mexico. Haven't we paid enough? Do you know how many thousands of *indios* have been killed by *gachupines* since that time, how many tens of thousands? They have taken our land, our language, our very lives. The *indios* mine their gold, grow their food, clean their houses, and what do we get in return?"

I could not believe she had called the *conquistadores* bandits. I myself had taught her about Hernán Cortés, and I certainly did not say his men were bandits.

"Taxes!" Teresa said in answer to her own question. "We get to pay tribute to the *gachupines*. They do not allow us to work for ourselves, to earn a decent wage, and yet they tax us. They tax our very existence! They hate us, but they tax our existence, and then they kill us if we are unable to pay the tax. Do you even know what is happening in New Spain, Carmen? You know every little thing that occurs in Europe, half a world away, but do you know what is happening in the land of your birth?"

It was ridiculous that I was being lectured by, of all people, Teresa. I supposed it was the price I had to pay for being caught in her room. Perhaps it was my punishment from God for not going to mass. Hortensia often said I would be punished for not going to mass.

"Our people are being killed," Teresa said almost as if she were pleading for me to hear what she was saying. She seemed about to cry. "They are being killed, Carmen! When a village cannot produce the tribute demanded by the *encomenderos*, people are executed as an example. All over the Viceroyalty, thousands are being killed!"

I had heard of the *encomienda*, an arrangement by which descendants of the *conquistadores*, the *encomenderos*, were entitled to tribute from Indian villages. "It is necessary that people pay their taxes, Teresa," I said in an effort to explain. "I suppose there is no one who likes to pay taxes."

"But we have no say in it, Carmen. The *indios* have no say about taxes or any of the laws we must obey. We have no rights. None! All rights and privileges go to the *gachupines*. Even the *criollos* have a few rights, but we have none. That must change, Carmen. We must elect an assembly and write a constitution that recognizes there are certain rights all people have."

I stepped away from the table and pointed to the papers and books. She had tried to make me feel like I was the person who had done something wrong, when all the time it was her conduct that was at issue. I had begun to gather my wits. "You make copies of this... this treason so it can be distributed throughout the colony. That is what you are doing, is it not?"

She was a small person, but she drew herself up as though she were ten feet tall and said, "We are letting our people know that all people are created equal and are entitled to live in freedom!"

I had heard enough, more than enough. I stepped to the door and reached for the leather pull.

"Carmen," Rubén said. "What are you going to do? You are not going to tell the Marqués, are you?"

Teresa was making a brave attempt to appear unconcerned, to act like she did not care what I did, but she was waiting for my answer, and I saw the fear in her eyes. "Tell the Marqués you are plotting against the king, Rubén?" That, I suspected, would take the wind out of Teresa's sails.

Without the slightest hint of contrition, Teresa's eyebrows arched. "Plotting against what king, Carmen? Spain's king is Joseph Bonaparte. Therefore, if we are plotting against a king, it must be Joseph Bonaparte. Is it treason to plot against a Bonaparte, Carmen?

Was it not you who told us these Bonapartes are no good? Have you not told us this...endlessly?"

For a moment, I was speechless. Strictly speaking, she was correct. Joseph Bonaparte was king of Spain. The laws against reading republican literature had been made by a viceroy under the authority of King Carlos.

"Carmen," Rubén said, "please do not tell Don Esteban. He will go to Juan Riaño. The intendant executes those who have books such as these!"

Rubén was exactly right. Juan Riaño was quick to execute anyone he thought guilty of treason. What was I to do? I had never lied to Don Esteban. On the other hand, Teresa was my cousin.

We all turned when we heard Hortensia, outside the window, call for Teresa to hurry.

"Carmen?" Rubén whispered. "Please do not tell Don Esteban."

I could see in Teresa's eyes she would not ask. Rubén could ask that I not disclose to the Marqués what I had found, but she would not. She was too proud. I thought of making her wait for my decision, but I knew Rubén would worry if I did not say what I intended to do. I did not want that. I liked Rubén. "I will not tell Don Esteban." Before either could move, I added, "But you must get rid of all of these books. No more of this republican rubbish. Get rid of these books. Burn them!"

Teresa's expression did not change, but Rubén, relieved, answered, "We understand." Then quickly he led Teresa from the room.

✦

It was difficult to know what angered me more, the discovery that Teresa was a republican or the fact I had to conceal it from Don Esteban. It was not a matter of my lying to him since he knew nothing of what I had seen. Nevertheless, I did not feel comfortable. Besides, Don Esteban knew my moods too well for me to hide anything from him for long. It was for that reason I was glad that Humberto arrived at the hacienda with his guests. I never thought I would see the day when I was happy to see Humberto, and I was not happy to see him. But it meant the Marqués would be busy for a few days, and that would afford me a chance to get over the shock of what I had uncovered.

As might be expected, Humberto made his appearance in the dead of night. Everyone had retired, all candles and lanterns extinguished, when the commotion began. From my bedroom window, I could see the men making their way in the darkness along the gravel pathway to the stable. Three were on horseback, and another, traveling behind, was riding a mule. From the moment I heard the laughter and vulgar language, I knew it was Humberto. Who else would make noise when other people were trying to sleep? Most likely, he had visited the *pulquerías* in Guanajuato before coming up the hill. Humberto had developed quite a taste for *pulque*, the alcoholic beverage distilled from the maguey cactus. He and other lazy sons of notables wasted much of their time in the *pulquerías* where they could drink *pulque* and do other things too unspeakable to mention.

When they reached the stable, Humberto shouted for Rubén's father to come outside and tend to their animals. He did not know that Señor Yepes had died. As the new stablemaster, it was my duty to assist in bedding the horses of any guests at the House of Abrantes, so I was glad when Rubén, carrying a lantern, came rushing from the carriage house where he slept. As far as I was concerned, the less I had to do with Humberto, the better. I resolved to stay out of his way until he returned to Mexico City which, I suspected, would not be long since the *pulquerías* in the capital were more luxurious than those in Guanajuato.

In the dim glow cast by Rubén's lantern, it was hard to see the men with Humberto. I had never seen *norteamericanos* and I was curious. One of the men was as large as Humberto, if not larger. After dismounting, he untied from his saddle the longest musket I had ever seen. The third man, a smaller fellow, dismounted and handed his reins to the man riding the mule. There was something unusual about this last man, but in the faint light, I was unable to determine what it was.

Humberto continued to talk loudly, and then I saw him shove Rubén. There was no reason I could see for Humberto to be abusive except to demonstrate his importance to his friends. When he cursed and pushed Rubén a second time, I started to climb out my window until I noticed Anselmo with a torch illuminating the way for the Marqués to the stable. It was not long before Humberto quieted down. More than once, Don Esteban had taken a buggy whip to his oldest son for striking a servant. I had never seen Humberto so drunk he would not become subdued in his father's presence.

I watched as Humberto introduced two of the men to the Marqués. Ever the gentleman, Don Esteban bowed and gestured for them to follow him to the hacienda. The man with the mule was not introduced, and he remained at the stables. It seemed logical to conclude that he was a servant. Stepping into a shadow on the balcony outside my bedroom, I strained to get a closer look at the men as they approached the house. So intent was I to get a better look, I almost did not draw back when I noticed Humberto glancing up at my balcony. He lingered for a moment at the doorway before following his guests into the house. Though he could not see me, I could tell from his ugly grin he knew I was watching him.

II

At the first light of dawn, I hurried to the stable to find out what Rubén may have learned from talking to the *norteamericanos'* servant. He had already herded the stock to the corral and was removing the soiled bedding in the stalls when I entered. "Rubén," I said eagerly, "tell me about the *norteamericanos*! What did their servant have to say?" Servants loved to gossip with other servants so I was certain that by now Rubén had the answers to any and all questions I may have. "Rubén?"

He continued to remove the hay. There was anger in his eyes and he said nothing.

"Rubén, what's wrong?"

Staring in the direction of the hacienda, he said, "He had no right to push me."

I felt ashamed. As stablemaster, I should have confronted Humberto the night before and told him he was not to abuse anyone who worked for me. He did not do such things when his father or Cristóbal were present. He was not going to do them around me either, I decided.

"He used to shove my father," Rubén continued. "One time he hit him and knocked him to the ground. And my father was an old man." His eyes narrowed. "He had no right to hit my father."

Never before had Rubén expressed such anger in my presence, and it surprised me to the point I almost forgot why I had come. Remembering, I urged, "The *norteamericanos*, Rubén; did they say

39

why they are in New Spain? Did you see that big man's musket?" I could not get my questions out fast enough. "Did you talk to their man-servant? Did he—"

I stopped because Rubén was looking behind me and, from his focus, I could tell someone had come into the stable. Turning quickly, I drew back when I saw the man at the door. Momentarily, I was startled because I had never before seen a black man. I knew it was not polite to stare, but I could not help it. It was not so much that his skin was black; he really was not all that much darker in complexion than I. Because I was outside so much, the sun had turned my skin quite brown. It was not even his unusual hair that gripped my attention. What gave me pause were his eyes, his dark eyes that peered right through to the back of my head.

Recovering my wits, I stepped forward, nodded, and said, *"Buenos días, señor."*

In a low voice, Rubén explained, "He does not speak Spanish, Carmen."

Of course not, I realized. As he was from the United States, he would speak the language of the English. He could not comprehend my words, but he must have understood I was trying to be civil. You would think he would sense what I had said and reciprocate. His expression, however, had not changed from the moment our eyes met. Though he did not appear hostile, neither was there the slightest indication of a desire to communicate with me. His clothes were those one would expect of a servant: breeches, shirt, jacket, all cut from a coarse-woven, unbleached cloth. On his feet were ankle-high, laced leather boots.

The lack of any response to my attempt to be friendly made me uncomfortable. I was relieved when he looked at Rubén and nodded his head toward the hay and then back toward the stalls where the *norteamericanos'* animals had been bedded. Rubén made a gesture to indicate the stable was at his disposal. Gathering an armful of hay, the black man went to the boxes and began the task of replacing the night bedding.

"Rubén," I whispered, "the men who arrived last night with Humberto, he is their servant?"

"He is their slave."

I looked back at the man. His muscular body was evidence of the fact that he was by no means unfamiliar with physical labor. "A slave?" I repeated, not certain I had heard correctly. I had never before seen a slave.

"That is what Humberto told Don Esteban." He returned the pitchfork to the rack and began to open the ventilation shutters so the stable would dry out.

When the black man finished his work in the stalls, he went to the saddle room. A peculiar thought occurred to me. "Rubén, there is no one looking over him. If he is a slave, why does he not run away?"

It was near the time when Hortensia usually served breakfast to all the workers, and Rubén was washing his face and arms in a metal basin. "I do not know, Carmen." He dried his hands. "Why do we not run away?"

I looked at him. His question made no sense.

"Those of us who are *indio*," he said and paused, "we do not run away."

"What are you saying? *Indios* are not slaves."

Rubén shrugged and left the stable. Not wanting to be alone with the man who was a slave, I quickly followed.

For most of the morning I remained in my room until I realized I was doing so to avoid Humberto. I was not afraid of Humberto. Why should I hide because of him? I was about to leave when there was a knock at my door, and the Marqués called my name. When I opened it, he said, "Where have you been, Carmencita? I've been looking for you everywhere. You are never in your room at this time of day." He placed his hand to my forehead. "You are not ill, are you? Should I summon the physician?"

I assured him I was not sick.

"In that case," he said, smiling, "I would like for you to accompany me to the firing range. Humberto and his guests arrived last night and the *norteamericanos* wish to demonstrate a new weapon. I thought you would enjoy seeing it. They have gone ahead."

My impulse was to decline. Again, I was thinking of Humberto and it angered me. He had never had such an effect on me before.

And then it occurred to me that always before, Cristóbal had been near. Humberto had never been at the hacienda when Cristóbal was absent. "Yes, Don Esteban," I said with resolve. "I would like to see this new weapon."

When we arrived at the range, Humberto came rushing forward to help me dismount. I tried to push away his hands. He knew I needed no help in getting off a horse. He was the one who had trouble getting on and off horses. "Be careful, Carmencita," he said, reaching for my waist. "You might fall."

I freed myself quickly from his grasp and stepped back. It was disconcerting how similar in appearance he was to Cristóbal. They had the same golden red hair and blue eyes. Both, like their father, were tall. But there the resemblance ended. Humberto's fondness for food and drink and the life of comfort in the *pulquerías* of Mexico City was evidenced by his thick waist and broad posterior. He attempted to conceal his corpulence through his choice in clothes. His blue morning coat, heavily padded at the shoulders, sloped back from waist level to form two short tails. He wore a yellow vest that hung low over the high waist of his brown strapped-pantaloons. A lavender silk cravat was knotted around his neck.

"Carmencita," he said, extending both hands, neither of which I took in mine, "are you not going to greet me? It has been a long time! Have you not missed me?"

In as formal a tone as I could manage, I said, "Good day, Humberto." I scanned downrange where the *norteamericanos'* slave was setting up the targets.

Humberto's eyes shifted toward one of the *norteamericanos*, the smaller of the two, and then he looked back at me. "You are no longer a little girl, Carmencita. You have become a woman." The Marqués escorted me to where the smaller *norteamericano* was standing and said, "Carmen, this gentleman is Colonel Latham Barnet." His tongue stumbled over the strange sounding words of the man's name. "Colonel Barnet, please allow me to present María del Carmen Rangel. Carmen is my..."—he paused and looked at me as if, momentarily, he had forgotten who I was—"Carmen is the daughter of my aide, Captain Rangel."

Removing a wide-brimmed, beaver-skin hat, the man bowed crisply. "It is my pleasure, Señorita Rangel," he said in a correct but accented Spanish. "The Marqués speaks highly of your skills with the musket."

I acknowledged his greeting with a nod. Like Humberto, this Colonel Latham Barnet wore the expensive clothes of a gentleman. His buff-colored frock coat fell below his knees to just above highly polished, black top-boots. He was clean shaven, and his copper-colored hair was trimmed short. Though small in stature, he had the bearing of a military officer, his back rigidly straight and his arms held tightly against his body. I noticed a slight tremor at the corner of his mouth which may have been caused by the fact that he pursed his lips tightly together into a small straight line.

Gesturing to the big man that came stepping to his side, Colonel Barnet said, "Señorita Rangel, allow me to introduce my associate, Coalter Owens."

Until that moment, I had paid little attention to the man who now stood before me with his right hand extended as if he expected me to take it in mine. It was not the custom for men and women to shake hands in New Spain, and I drew back a step when I looked up at the fellow. I do not know what made me catch my breath. Perhaps it was because his handsome face reminded me somewhat of Cristóbal. "*Buenos días, señorita,*" the man said as he reached to take my hand which I suppose I had involuntarily raised. "It is my pleasure."

He really did not resemble Cristóbal all that much, though, like Cristóbal, he was tall and I guessed they were about the same age. Although his eyes were blue, they were darker than Cristóbal's, more the blue of a mountain stream than the color of the sky. His hair, too, was darker, almost as black as mine. Really, they were quite different, Cristóbal and this man. This Coalter Owens had a big easy, open-mouthed grin, and Cristóbal rarely so much as smiled. I was not sure what made me think of Cristóbal at that moment.

The man's hand was strong and calloused like that of someone who had done much labor in his life. His long fingers completely encasing my hand, he seemed reluctant to let go his firm grip, but I pulled away as I mumbled something like, "Welcome to New Spain, Señor Coalter Owens." It was not an easy name for me to pronounce.

"Please," he said, his grin growing even wider, causing deep creases to form in his rugged, sun-burnt face. "Call me Coalter." Of course, I had no intention of calling him 'Coalter.' This fellow assumed too much.

Quickly, I turned back to Colonel Barnet. He was older and I was more comfortable looking at him even though his expression was not nearly so friendly as Coalter Owen's. There were so many questions I wanted to ask these *norteamericanos* I hardly knew where to begin. "Colonel Barnet," I said, my tongue twisting over the unfamiliar sound of his name, "you are from the former English colonies to the north. Yes?"

"Yes, Señorita. I am from a place called Virginia."

He seemed to be a gentleman and I felt more at ease. "Can you explain to me why the people in your colonies rebelled against their king?"

He glanced at Don Esteban. "As I explained to the Marqués, Señorita Rangel, not everyone in the English colonies was in support of the rebellion. The men who led the revolution did so for private gain. These men were traitors to their king."

As the colonel elaborated his point, I was aware that Coalter Owens continued to stare at me. From the corner of my eye, I glanced toward him and noticed, for the first time, his clothes were not of the quality worn by Barnet or Humberto; they were not custom-tailored garments. The cloth of his shirt, trousers and jacket were of a coarse weave, not so very different from that worn by the slave who stood by the targets some distance away. And he wore heavy boots that bore scuffs and cuts, more signs that he was a man of labor. If Colonel Barnet had not introduced him as his associate, I would have concluded that this young man was little more than a servant, a field hand or perhaps a stableman or blacksmith. His broad shoulders and muscular arms were certainly not those of a gentleman of leisure.

It was evident from Don Esteban's expression that he approved of Latham Barnet's response to my query. I had many more questions but knew the Marqués was anxious to get on with the demonstration of the weapon the *norteamericanos* had brought from their country. Colonel Barnet made a gesture toward Coalter Owens who retreated to his horse and withdrew from his saddle-sheath the unusually long musket. Returning to where we stood, he placed it in Don Esteban's hands.

After inspecting the weapon, Don Esteban said, "It makes our muskets look like toys,"—he looked at me and smiled—"like those wooden muskets Anselmo made for you and Cristóbal when you were little. Do you remember, Carmencita?"

"Yes, Don Esteban," I said without taking my eyes from the weapon. It had none of the ornate beauty of an *escopeta*, but in every way it was obviously a better crafted weapon. The octagonal barrel was made of thick metal and was secured to a drooped wood stock with heavy brass hardware. Eagerly, I took it in my hands when the Marqués offered. It was easily three times the weight of the weapons Cristóbal and I used.

Laughing, Don Esteban said, "It is as long as you are tall, Carmencita. Never have I seen such a musket!"

"We do not call it a musket, Don Esteban," Colonel Barnet said. "This is a Pennsylvania long-rifle, sometimes called a Kentucky rifle."

"A rifle?"

"With your permission," Colonel Barnet said to me and retrieved the instrument from my hands. He inverted it so Don Esteban could see the inside of the barrel. "The barrel has been rifled, Don Esteban. See the spiral groove? That causes the bullet to discharge with a spin, an action that will propel it farther, with more force, and with greater accuracy than a ball discharged from the smooth bore of a musket."

"Yes, I see. Quite different from our Spanish muskets."

"I can assure you, Don Esteban, the Pennsylvania long-rifle is the finest weapon in the world."

The mystery was solved. The *norteamericanos* were gun merchants. They had heard of the Marqués's wealth and were hoping to sell him this new weapon. I was not convinced. I did not see how a rifled barrel would make all that much difference from an ordinary musket. Our Spanish *escopetas* were light in weight, easy for a dragoon to fire and reload from the back of a horse, something I did not think possible with this long-rifle. From the way Don Esteban folded his arms, I could tell he shared my skepticism.

Twisting his lips into something resembling a smile, Colonel Barnet offered the rifle once again to me and said, "Perhaps, the Señorita would care to demonstrate her skills with this weapon and—"

"No!" Coalter Owens said firmly before I could take the rifle in my hand. He grasped the long gun from the colonel, and there was an expression of fierceness in his deep-set eyes that was chilling to behold. This was not a man one would want as an enemy. The two men may have been associates in their business of selling guns, but it appeared they were not necessarily friends. They exchanged words in what I assumed was the language of the English. It was the first time I had heard that language spoken, and it was harsh to my ears, flat and sharp like the sound of dogs barking.

When I recovered from my surprise at the young man's abrupt action of intercepting the gun before I could take it, I steadied my gaze on him and said, "I would like to fire the weapon, Señor Owens. If you do not mind."

Once again the boyish smile returned when he looked down at me and explained, "The rifle has a strong recoil, Señorita Rangel, one much stronger than a musket. It would knock you to the ground."

"I can assure you it would not knock me to the ground," I protested, more than a little miffed by the suggestion that I was too weak to fire his cumbersome rifle. But as I continued to explain my familiarity with weapons, I detected something in Barnet's expression that conveyed he might have liked to see me thrown to the ground by the rifle's kick. He glanced at Humberto who was grinning to himself. The two men were silently communicating, and I suspected I may have been the subject of some previous discussions between them.

Finally, Don Esteban suggested the young man demonstrate the weapon, and that later, both he and I might try it.

Coalter Owens turned to look in the direction of where the slave had set up the targets. When I followed his gaze downrange, I saw that the black man had set the targets—a row of five clay jars—too far away, and I said so to Don Esteban. They were triple the distance of where we usually placed the targets when firing *escopetas*. They would have to be brought closer.

"No, Señorita Rangel," Colonel Barnet said. "Jeb has placed the targets exactly where I told him."

The slave's name, I assumed, was Jeb. He may have been instructed to place them where he had, but it was an impossible range. I could hardly see the jars. I watched as Coalter Owens poured powder into the barrel from a horn and used a long metal ramrod to pack the wadding. He then wrapped a small bullet in a waxed patch and rammed it into the tube. He pulled back the cock on the flintlock and took aim.

"He is aiming," the colonel explained, "at the jar on the left."

The young *norteamericano* waited until a lull in the breeze, braced himself, and gently squeezed the trigger. The explosion of the powder made a sound more like a small cannon than the crack of a musket, and I was able to understand why the weapon's violent recoil would very likely have knocked me down had I been making the shot. The jar on the left shattered. Quickly, he reloaded and fired at the next target and continued to do so in rapid succession until none of the jars remained intact.

Don Esteban glanced at me, and I could see my own amazement reflected in his expression. Coalter Owens straightened, lowered the rifle and smiled. He was proud of his marksmanship as well he should be. In five shots, he had not missed one jar, something that was virtually impossible with a musket, which would often fire off mark when the barrel became hot. I tried to conceal my astonishment because I did not want the young man to know I was impressed. For some reason, I was not inclined to want to like this fellow even though there was something about him that made it difficult for me not to keep an eye on him. He had a very handsome face and, for a big man, he was very graceful in his movements.

"Colonel Barnet," Don Esteban said, stroking his beard, "this rifle,...would I be able to purchase weapons such as this rifle?"

Barnet shrugged. "I suppose you could, Don Esteban. You would have to travel to the United States or Europe to do so. You will not find them in New Spain."

Clearing his throat, the Marqués said, "Would you be able to sell me rifles like these?"

"I could," Colonel Barnet said. He removed a handkerchief from his jacket and wiped his face. The sun was rising and it was becoming quite warm. "But I will not."

I was as stunned by his words as Don Esteban. A gun merchant who would not sell guns?

"I am not in the business of selling guns," the colonel explained. "Besides, Don Esteban, what good are weapons such as this if you have no men to use them?"

Don Esteban glanced at Humberto whose fine clothes were now soaked with perspiration. Obviously, he had told Colonel Barnet of his father's problems in obtaining men.

"From what I understand," Colonel Barnet continued, "you will soon have a new king who, alas, has no army. That is not a happy prospect in the best of times."

Humberto, under his father's stern gaze, focused his eyes on the bare earth. He knew of the secrecy necessary to successfully execute the plan to bring King Fernando to New Spain. It was no surprise to me he had betrayed a trust.

"The army you need," Barnet said dryly, "I can supply. Your new king will have a force at his command unequaled in this hemisphere."

Don Esteban cocked his head. "You have men, Colonel Barnet?" He looked at Coalter Owens and then back to the colonel. "I do not understand. How many men?"

"Give the word, and I will have thirty-five hundred men here in Guanajuato by the time your king arrives, each with a Pennsylvania long-rifle exactly like the one you saw demonstrated this morning." He removed his hat and used it to knock the dust from his coat. "Inside a year, I can easily raise ten times that number."

The Marqués stepped back. "These men, why would they come to New Spain? Are they mercenaries?"

Colonel Barnet's cold eyes were steady. "They will not come for your gold, Don Esteban, if that is what you are asking."

"Then why, Colonel Barnet," Don Esteban pressed, "would men from the United States come to New Spain? Are they so anxious to be the subjects of a Spanish king when they would not support the one they had in England?"

"It depends," Colonel Barnet answered. "There are a great many men in the United States who will be loyal subjects to your king if..."—he rubbed his fingers over the brim of his hat— "...if your king will provide them with what they need."

"What," Don Esteban asked, "is it that your men need?" I could tell from his tone he was growing impatient.

"Land, Don Esteban," the colonel said. "The lands in the northern provinces of New Spain are the richest in the world. My men will settle that land. They will bring their families. And they will fight to protect the man who will allow them to settle that land. They will fight for your king."

"Land?" the Marqués said, more puzzled than before, as I was. We both looked from Barnet to Coalter Owens and back. The young man was no longer smiling. It did not appear that he might agree with what his partner was saying. "I do not understand, Colonel Barnet. Is there not an abundance of land in the United States, readily available, free for the taking?"

"Yes," Colonel Barnet answered. "But there is one thing not readily available in the United States. It is the thing required if New Spain is to prosper and take its place among the great empires of the world."

"And what is this thing, Colonel Barnet?"

"Cheap labor, Don Esteban." He straightened. "Slaves. That is what is needed. That is what will bring the men you need to New Spain. Free land and cheap labor. If your king will provide this, we will make him the most powerful monarch on earth."

"I see," Don Esteban said, nodding his head. "I am beginning to understand. You want to bring slaves to New Spain."

"The importation of slaves from Africa is forbidden in the United States," Colonel Barnet explained. "Of course, those who already have slaves are allowed to keep them. And what happens when a commodity is made scarce? The price rises. In the United States, only a wealthy man can afford to keep slaves. If we import slaves to New Spain, we can make them available at a price all men can afford.

Thousands will come here. Tens of thousands, not only from the United States but from Europe. Slaves are what will bring men to New Spain, men who will take the land from the savages and make it productive."

"And you will be able to import these...these slaves? I gather you have had experience in such matters?"

"I have letters which will verify my competence in the trade if that is of concern to you. I will be able to—"

Coalter Owens interrupted Barnet, and they began to talk in English. I, of course, had no idea of what they were saying, but it was not difficult to grasp that the two men were not in accord. I glanced downrange to where the targets had been and noticed the slave standing with his back toward us. He seemed to be studying the distant peaks of the Sierra Madre to the east. "Perhaps," the Marqués said, waiting for the men to end their dispute and look at him, "we should return to the house, gentlemen. It has become quite warm and I am sure you wish to rest from your long journey."

"My proposal?" Colonel Barnet asked before we could move toward our mounts.

"I will consider your proposal, Colonel Barnet," Don Esteban replied. "And after I have made a decision, I will give you my answer. You are welcome to remain as our guests until then." There was no smile on his face when he turned to Humberto. "I would like to see you in the library before dinner."

✦

Never had I seen the Marqués so enraged. He had asked me to come to the library, and so I was there, sitting in one of the scallop-backed chairs, as he explained to Humberto how careless he had been to share with strangers the plan to bring Fernando to New Spain. Pounding his fist on the table, he demanded, "Who else did you tell of our plan? Who else knows Cristóbal has gone to Spain to persuade King Fernando to come to the Viceroyalty?"

Humberto's hands were trembling. "No one," he said wiping the perspiration from his face. "Only Barnet and Owens. I believed they could be trusted."

"Do you not realize that if word of Cristóbal's mission found its way to Madrid, his life would be in danger? Captain Rangel's too. The Bonapartes would not hesitate to have them shot! You placed their lives in peril! And why? Because you believed these men could be trusted, men about whom you know absolutely nothing except that they are former slave traders!"

Humberto glanced in my direction, obviously displeased that I was in the room. "What of Colonel Barnet's offer? Thirty-five hundred men, each with a long-rifle!"

The Marqués put the tips of his fingers to his temples. "But at what cost?" His voice was hoarse. "Do we wish to build New Spain on the backs of men and women taken from their homes against their will and forced into bondage?"

"Thirty-five hundred men," Humberto repeated, choosing to ignore the question. "Ten times that number within a year! Who in New Spain could stand against such a force?"

The Marqués drew a deep breath. He was considering the point, as was I. Humberto was right. Thirty-five hundred men with long-rifles would be an invincible force in New Spain. This would especially be the case, I considered, if the men were like the man named Coalter Owens. I had watched him on the ride back. A man of his obvious strength and agility was a natural warrior. Thirty-five hundred such men would make a splendid army for King Fernando. These were the soldiers of the army Cristóbal and I had always dreamed of leading.

"The *criollos* hate the Spanish-born," Humberto continued. "Given the chance, they will hang us all and take our land, our mines, everything! Need I remind you, Father, there are less than twelve thousand Spanish-born in all of New Spain? There are two hundred thousand *criollos* and at least two million *indios*. We must have an army!"

"But slavery," Don Esteban said. "Our religion forbids it. Spain has always been the defender of Christendom. That is the reason for its existence. New Spain can be no less."

"This slavery," Humberto said, "it is not so bad. Colonel Barnet says the Africans in his country are well treated. They never complain. The one Colonel Barnet brought with him from the United States never complains. He does what he's told and rarely says a word."

I turned to the Marqués. "This slave, Don Esteban; the one called Jeb, no one watches over him and yet he does not run away. If he were unhappy, would he not run away?"

Wrinkling his forehead, Humberto stared at me. He was as surprised as I that we seemed to be taking the same side. "That's right," he agreed. "Carmen's right. If he were unhappy, would he not run away? Of course he would. He has plenty to eat and a dry place to sleep. He has not a worry in the world. He knows he has a good life. Very good, Carmencita!"

I knew Don Esteban well enough to understand he valued the observation. He stroked his beard the way I had seen him do so many times when my father gave him advice. I was proud that I was able to contribute something that would help. Cristóbal was doing his part in this grand adventure, and so was I.

"These slaves from Africa," Humberto said, "are good workers. Colonel Barnet says they can labor from sunup to sundown. That is what we need in New Spain. That is why we have failed to make progress in our colonies. We have not had good workers. The Indians are lazy, and they die easily if you make them do very much. We need these Africans to—"

The Marqués raised his hand for silence. He said nothing and then rose from the chair. "We will speak more with our guests at dinner tonight. Before I can make a decision, I need to know more about this slavery in the *norteamericanos'* country." He looked at me. "Carmen, I want you to be there. You will listen to what they have to say and help me decide."

"Yes, Don Esteban," I replied and turned to leave the room all the while thinking what a great story I would have to tell Cristóbal when he returned with our monarch.

Before I reached the door, the Marqués said, "And Carmen?"

"Yes, Don Esteban."

"Please..."—he cleared his throat—"...please wear a dress."

✦

Wearing a dress was not something I had counted on having to do. After some consideration, I realized it was a sacrifice I would have to make if I hoped to assist the Marqués in making his decision regarding Colonel Barnet's proposal. Unfortunately, it was customary for the notables to dress in formal attire when serving dinner to their guests. Normally, Don Esteban and I ate in the kitchen, the same as the servants. But this was a special circumstance. So special, in fact, the Marqués sent word for Intendant Riaño to join us that evening. He and the other notables who supported the plan to make Fernando king of New Spain would want to know about the *norteamericanos'* offer.

Since I had no experience in wearing the kind of clothes appropriate to this occasion, I summoned Hortensia to help me select one of the many dresses Don Esteban had purchased for me in Mexico City, none of which I had ever worn. Several dozen of them hung in my closets and I had little idea of how to put one on, much less which was suitable. Hortensia was knowledgeable about such things.

Hortensia brought Teresa with her when she came to my suite. Before I could dismiss my haughty cousin, Hortensia explained that Teresa would have to help me with my dress because she had to return to the kitchens to supervise the preparation of the meal. There was not much I could do about it because the garment my aunt chose before she left looked to me like so much shiny blue cloth, all bunched up and stitched in the strangest of places. It was called a tunic dress and consisted of a tunic wrapped around a trained frock. It was supposed to resemble the kind of garment worn by women in ancient Greece, and I felt naked with the tunic worn so low over my shoulders. Worst of all, the waist was stitched high, just below my breasts, so it looked for all the world as if I were with child.

"I cannot wear this," I told Teresa after she had managed to get me in it. "It's too flimsy."

"You look lovely in it," she said in a voice little more than a whisper. She kept her eyes averted from mine, and I assumed she was still angry that I had made her burn her treasonous books.

There was no time to change into another dress as the hour for dinner was nearing. Besides, the other dresses looked just as ridiculous. If this was what was considered to be the high fashion for women of the aristocracy, I was for once in my life happy I was not a *gachupina*. I slipped on the flat-heeled sandals that went with the dress and began to tie the criss-cross lacing around my ankles.

"Carmen?" Teresa said meekly.

"What?"

"How...how long is Humberto to remain at his father's hacienda?"

I glanced at her. She held ready the frilly white lace mob cap I would have to wear on my head. "Not long, Teresa. You know how he much prefers Mexico City to Guanajuato." She seemed relieved to receive that news. "Give me that stupid thing. Hurry!"

I pulled on the cap and started to the door. Before I could open it, Teresa said, "Carmen, the *norteamericano*? The young one?"

"Yes?"

"He was in the kitchen earlier. He asked about you. He asked many questions about you. I think he likes you." She smiled weakly. "He is very handsome."

In a few days, Teresa and Rubén were to be married, so I supposed she was back to her old habit of thinking about nothing more consequential than such matters as she was now raising. At least it would keep her out of the kind of trouble she would get into copying from books by French republicans. I ignored her silliness and rushed out the door, down the winding marble staircase and into the corridor that lead to the dining hall.

It was awkward having to run in the dress, the hem of which touched the floor, so I raised it over my knees in order to have more freedom of movement. This proved embarrassing because I was still grasping the dress in that manner when I rushed into the hall and almost collided with Humberto who stood next to the *norteamericanos* and Juan Riaño, the intendant. I saw that the Marqués had not yet arrived. He was probably attending to some detail in the kitchen, and I wished I had thought to go there first. I was very uncomfortable with all these men looking at my bare legs and I quickly lowered my dress.

Humberto and Barnet exchanged glances. I looked from them to Coalter Owens, and it would be impossible to describe the young *norteamericano*'s expression as he stood there in a gentleman's suit of clothes, complete with a long-tailed maroon coat and shiny black boots that rose to just below the knees of his grey trousers. He was really quite handsome. His mouth half-open, he stared at me with the same wide-eyed expression I remember Cristóbal had the time his father presented him with his first saber. The look on his face made me feel quite strange. I did not know if I was pleased or displeased.

So engrossed was I in what the young man was thinking, I did not notice that Intendant Riaño had taken a step toward me. When I turned to face him, I saw a menacing scowl across his thin face. "Intendant Riaño," I said with a slight bow of my head to acknowledge his office. "Good afternoon."

He did not acknowledge my courtesy, this sour-faced man who was all arms and legs. When we were little children and the intendant used to visit the Marqués at the hacienda, Cristóbal and I used to giggle and secretly call him Campamocha, praying mantis, because he so resembled the slow-moving predator insect that clasped its prey in forearms held as if in prayer. Something about me was obviously not to his liking, and I had no idea what it was until, in a rasping voice, he said, "Do you not know it is against the law for Indians to wear the clothing of Europeans?"

Of course I knew of the law that only the Spanish-born and *criollos* could wear the clothes of a European, but I had not remembered it until that moment. There was a severe penalty to be inflicted upon an Indian, or even someone part Indian—a mestizo—who wore such garments. For a moment I was confused by this unexpected outburst of anger on the part of the intendant. He started toward me, his bony right hand extended, and I think he may have entertained the idea of grabbing my dress. It was at this point that Coalter Owens stepped between us and said, "You are being rude, Señor Riaño."

Colonel Barnet said something in English, but the young *norteamericano* ignored him and kept his gaze steady on the intendant who, quite clearly, was alarmed at the challenge of such a powerfully constructed fellow. At that moment, Don Esteban entered the hall in great haste. The smile on his face faded quickly. "Gentlemen," he asked, "what is happening here? What is wrong?"

Sputtering with indignation, Juan Riaño explained that I was in violation of the viceroy's injunction against *indios* wearing European clothing.

The Marqués's face grew red with anger. "Need I remind you, Intendant Riaño, Carmen is...is..."—his hands trembled—"...she is the daughter of my aide. She may wear any style of clothing she chooses! Is that understood?"

Juan Riaño stared at the floor like a scolded schoolboy. As intendant of the wealthy province of Guanajuato, his office in the colony was second in importance only to that of the viceroy, but like the King's regent, he owed his office to Don Esteban's friendship and influence with King Carlos.

"We will hear no more talk of clothes," Don Esteban said conclusively and gestured toward the great table beneath the massive chandeliers. These held dozens of candles that bathed the entire dining hall in a golden light. "Let us dine," he added.

Before anyone could move, Coalter Owens put his hand on the intendant's shoulder, and in a low voice he said, "Your apology, Señor?"

Juan Riaño swallowed hard, and without looking at me, muttered what sounded like an apology. The words were inaudible.

We proceeded to the table where the young *norteamericano* held my chair until I was seated. At first, I did not know what he was doing. I needed no help sitting down and started to tell him so until I realized it was an act of courtesy. From the corner of my eye I could see Hortensia, along with others of the servants waiting to serve the meal, smile at my awkwardness.

The meal was served and soon the former unpleasantness seemed forgotten, though the intendant sat glumly in his chair and said little as he picked sparingly at the meal of seasoned pork, wild turkey, rice, and a number of green and yellow squashes mixed with corn, tomatoes, and peppers. Undoubtably, he was thinking of what had happened, as was I. He had insulted me and I was angry. That anger, however, was tempered by my surprise that the young *norteamericano* had come to my defense. I was no longer certain what to make of this boyish man who sat across from me looking as uncomfortable in his expensive clothes as I felt in my flimsy dress. I could not help but smile as he repeatedly tugged at the black silk cravat wrapped around his neck and knotted in a generous bow at his throat. Obviously, he was no more used to wearing such clothes than I was a dress.

Soon, my attention was absorbed by what Colonel Barnet was saying about events in his country. It turned out he was a man of no small knowledge of military matters. He described how the president in the United States had created "the mosquito fleet," an assortment of small coastal craft, most of which had only one gun. When Don Esteban asked why the United States did not build an ocean armada, the colonel explained that this president, a man called Jefferson, did not wish to protect his country's merchant ships because the owners of those ships were not of his party. The ship owners were what were called Federalists while Jefferson was the leader of an opposing rabble called Democrats. It was yet another confirmation of Don Esteban's contention that a people without a monarch would always plunge into anarchy.

Eventually, Don Esteban turned the conversation to the subject of slavery in the United States and Colonel Barnet was quick to assure the Marqués that the Africans were well treated. He related stories of how many of them would tell of how hard their lives in Africa had been and how they preferred their new homes on the cotton and tobacco plantations in America. He told of a black woman who had been like a second mother to him, who had nursed him as a baby, and who always, in her prayers, gave thanks that her own parents had been taken from a tribe in Africa where they practiced a religion in which human sacrifice was common. Without slavery, Barnet said, the Africans would never have been introduced to Christianity, and their souls would have been lost to eternal damnation.

I knew this last point would weigh heavily in Don Esteban's decision whether to accept the colonel's offer, which I desperately hoped he would. The vision of an army of thousands of magnificent men like this Coalter Owens, each equipped with a Pennsylvania long-rifle,

thrilled me, and I could barely sit still. And yet, I could tell the Marqués remained unconvinced. So, with the intention of resolving any
lingering doubts he may have had, I asked, "Colonel Barnet, do any of
the slaves run away?"

For me, this was the test. If they did not run away, it was a sign
they were receiving just treatment. "Do any express a desire to return
to Africa?"

Barnet's eyes flicked toward Humberto who, I suspected, may
have told him I was in favor of their plan. "It is very strange, Señorita
Rangel. Of course, when they first disembark the ships, it is not
unusual for some to exhibit rancor. They are by nature a childlike
and primitive people. However, they soon learn the constraints of civ-
ilized behavior just as any other servant."

"Then," I said by way of drawing the logical conclusion, "your
slaves are like servants. Yes?"

"Indeed, Señorita Rangel. In most cases, they are like members of
the family, not unlike your servants in New Spain."

For me, the issue of slavery was now clarified. The word "slave"
was simply another way of saying "servant." The words meant essen-
tially the same thing. That was what Jeb, the black man who accompanied the *norteamericanos*, was: a servant; and, from what I could
see, he was a well-treated one though somewhat surly. I saw no reason to reject Colonel Barnet's generous proposal and said so to Don
Esteban. Smiling, I looked at Coalter Owens, thinking that he, too,
would be pleased. But he was not. His face somber, he was staring
down at his largely untouched plate of food.

After dinner, the Marqués suggested we retire to his library so
the men could smoke and sip brandy, a custom I did not relish. When
I quietly reminded him of my aversion to cigar smoke and suggested
that, instead, we go outside, Coalter Owens stepped forward to say he
did not smoke or drink spirits and would enjoy seeing the patio.

Don Esteban said, "Carmen, why don't you show Señor Owens
the patio? Humberto and I will continue our discussion with Colonel
Barnet in the library and join you later."

Since I could not readily think of a way to gracefully extricate
myself from this assignment, I led the young man to the courtyard

filled with Anselmo's plants and vines, now in bloom releasing their sweet fragrances. We walked to the fountain where water gurgled from the mouth of the stone frog. Not far away, some of the servants had gathered to gossip and strum their guitars. With the presence of our exotic guests in the hacienda, I knew they had much to occupy their tongues, and most certainly, the maids were having a happy time clucking about how I had had to wear a dress. Since the moon was full, I could easily observe them gawking to see what we were doing.

"This is a lovely place," Coalter Owens said, scanning the wrought-iron balustrades above us. He looked at me and smiled. "Very lovely."

I pulled my fingertips through the icy waters shimmering above the glazed tiles. Oddly, my thoughts were disordered, and I could not think of anything to say though I wanted to ask him many questions about his country, especially about the soldiers and the long-rifles. Even though I avoided his eyes, I could sense that he continued to watch me. This made me uncomfortable in a way I had never quite experienced before. Most of the time I did not like it if someone stared at me. But I did not mind this young man staring at me. I rather enjoyed it, in fact. Finally, the silence became too much to bear, so I said, "Señor Owens? You did not—"

"Please," he interrupted. "I would be honored if you would call me Coalter."

Men and women simply did not call each other by their first name in New Spain, especially young men and young women, but I supposed he, being a stranger to our land, did not know this so I shrugged and said, "Coalter." It was not such a hard name to pronounce. "And you may call me Carmen." I looked back toward the house. "Except in front of other people, you should call me Señorita Rangel, and I will call you Señor Owens."

He smiled his understanding with a funny twist of his head that was most appealing.

This taken care of, I knew we must now get on with more important things. "Coalter," I said. "You did not speak at dinner about this slavery. Why did you not tell the Marqués that it is not a bad thing?

He will accept Colonel Barnet's proposal if he believes this slavery is not a bad thing."

The smile faded from his lips and he turned his face from me as if he did not wish for me to see the hardness of his expression. For a moment, I thought he was going to say something, but he did not and his silence seemed to say things I did not want to hear. More than anything, I wanted men like him and their rifles in New Spain. And yet, try as I might, I could not vanquish the unwelcome thought that possibly this slavery might not, after all, be right. I was afraid that Coalter was going to confirm that suspicion, and then I could not honestly urge Don Esteban to accept Colonel Barnet's offer.

Perhaps in order to prevent his saying what I did not want to hear, I decided to change the subject. "Your Spanish is very good, Coalter," I said, surprised at how quickly I found it easy to speak his name. I liked saying his name. "How did you acquire facility in a language not your own?"

It may have been that Coalter, too, did not wish to have to contemplate this slavery because his smile quickly returned and he appeared eager to respond to my query. "I learned to speak Spanish in Texas."

"Texas?" I said, recalling what Don Esteban had said about that northern province of the Viceroyalty and how Cristóbal had spoken of our going there upon his return. "How did you come to be in Texas?"

His eyes sparkled as he told me of how his family had come to Louisiana soon after the United States purchased that territory from France. So enthusiastic was he, I decided against reminding him that Louisiana legally belonged to Spain and would some day have to be returned. His father, he said, was a merchant of farm tools and practiced his commerce along the Camino Real from Natchitoches to San Antonio de Béxar. Coalter had traveled with him and learned Spanish from the ranchers and farmers who traded with his father. "Texas," he said, "is the most beautiful land in the whole world!" He tugged at the silk cravat, loosening it from around his throat. "The richest soil in the world is in Texas!"

For a moment I thought his knowledge of Spanish had failed him. He must have chosen the wrong word. "Soil?" Why would someone talk about soil in such glowing terms.

"*Suelo*," he said and repeated the word in what I assumed was English: Soil. "Did I say it correctly?"

"Do you mean..."—I pointed to the ground—"...dirt?"

He laughed. "Yes, Carmen. Dirt! Dirt that you can grow things in. Beautiful, rich, black dirt!"

Now I was completely baffled. "Why would a soldier wish to grow things in dirt?"

"A soldier?" He cocked his head. "I don't understand."

"You are a soldier. Yes? And soldiers do not grow things in dirt." The mere thought of it made me frown. Only peasants worked the soil. "You must be using the wrong words in Spanish."

"Carmen, you misunderstand. I am not a soldier. I am a farmer. I grow things." Mimicking with his hands, he said, "I plow. I plant. I harvest. This is what I do. I make things grow, things that people can eat and wear."

What he described would certainly explain why he had such broad shoulders and powerful arms, I thought. He was a simple *ranchero*, one who did things only a peasant would do. It was incredible. And he acted as though he was proud to do these things no gentleman would think of doing. To work with horses, even to care for and feed them, was acceptable because only a *caballero* could afford a horse, but to plow the ground was not the occupation of a man of station. Recalling how he had demonstrated his skill with the rifle that morning, I said, "You fired the weapon with such precision. I assumed you were a soldier. I thought you were perhaps an officer in the dragoons."

He responded that most men on the frontier of his country were adept at using the rifle to hunt game. He then proceeded to explain how his father, in association with Latham Barnet and several other men, had hoped to obtain permission from the viceroy to settle *rancheros* from the United States in Texas. In the confusion following Joseph Bonaparte's ascension to the throne in Madrid, they had had no luck in even obtaining an interview with the viceroy or any of his officials. When they met Humberto and learned his father was a man of influence with the viceroy, they made the decision to come to Guanajuato.

I was about to inquire again about the issue of the slaves when Don Esteban entered the patio ahead of Colonel Barnet and Humberto. "Ah, here you are!" he said cheerfully. "How nice it is out here tonight." Stopping at the fountain he looked down at me and smiled. "Carmencita, tonight, in that dress, you look so like Cata Valeria." He pronounced my mother's name with great tenderness. "You are truly beautiful! Do you not agree she is very beautiful, Señor Owens?"

"Yes," Coalter said and blushed. "I think she is very beautiful."

All this made me feel most awkward.

Clearing his throat, Colonel Barnet said, "We shall be on our way, Don Esteban." He turned to Coalter. "Intendant Riaño has invited us to return with him to Guanajuato for..."—his eyes darted from Coalter to me and back—"...entertainment."

From the sly grin on Humberto's face I knew they were on their way to the *pulquerías*. For some reason, I was pleased when Coalter said he was tired and would prefer to retire to his room for the night. Barnet and Humberto excused themselves and headed for the stable. I remained with Don Esteban by the fountain when Coalter, bowing awkwardly, bid us a good night and returned to the hacienda.

After a while, I inquired of the Marqués if he had reached a decision on Colonel Barnet's proposal, and he said he had not. He asked if the young *norteamericano* had said anything about the slaves in his country, and though I was truthful in saying he had not uttered a word about the subject, I was not happy with myself for not volunteering my suspicion that Coalter was not in accord with his associate's report that the slaves' lot in the United States was a happy one. I did not disclose my impression because I knew that if the Marqués refused the colonel's offer, the army of men with long-rifles would not be forthcoming. I did not want to say anything that might prejudice Don Esteban against the offer.

Furthermore, I was not unaware that a refusal would also mean Coalter Owens would return to his country, and it was likely I would never see him again. My concern over this prospect puzzled me because I told myself it was of no consequence to me whether Coalter Owens returned to his country or whether I ever saw him again. It was absolutely of no consequence to me whatsoever.

III

That night I found it impossible to fall asleep. Several times I got out of bed and went to the arched window on the east side of my room in hopes of detecting signs of dawn. Over and over, I rehearsed the words of Colonel Barnet's plan to support King Fernando with men and long-rifles in exchange for permission to open New Spain to the slave trade. What would Don Esteban decide? Would agreeing to Barnet's terms be the right thing to do?

In truth, Barnet's proposal and the Marqués's decision were not the primary reasons I tossed and turned and climbed in and out of bed. What would not allow my repose were the images in my mind of Coalter Owens. Try as I might, I could not banish from my head the memory of the way he smiled or the way his eyes seemed so alive and eager when he looked at me. I pretended that I could not stop thinking of him because he was an example of the kind of soldiers Cristóbal and I would lead in battle against Fernando's enemies. I would try to think of Cristóbal at the head of that mighty army, but when my effort relaxed, I would again be thinking of Coalter Owens. It was ridiculous. I could not force this man's image from my mind.

Finally, just as the roosters began to crow, I drifted off into a fitful sleep and, to my chagrin, I did not awaken until well after daybreak. I was more tired than I had been upon retiring, but I forced myself out of bed and dressed. At least I was back in my leather breeches, cotton shirt, and boots, not in some flimsy dress. Downstairs, one of the maids informed me Don Esteban had instructed her

64

to tell me he had left on a tour of his mines. He always asked if I wanted to accompany him when he made the rounds of the mines, so I supposed he had found me asleep when he came to my room and had not wished to disturb me.

In the kitchen, Hortensia told me that Humberto and Barnet had not returned from Guanajuato, but that the young *norteamericano* had breakfasted early and gone to the stable to help Rubén with one of the mares that was about to foal. The slave was with them. I thought of going there. After all, I was the stablemaster and should be present to direct their activities even though seeing a mare give birth was not something I especially enjoyed. I asked Hortensia why Teresa was not in the kitchen, and she said it was because my cousin was not feeling well and had decided to remain in her room for the day.

It occurred to me to go to Teresa's room. She had said the young *norteamericano* had asked many questions about me, and I wanted to know what she had told him. There was no telling what had been said about me. Moreover, perhaps Coalter had said some things to her about himself. It might be of passing interest to know a little about him.

I went instead to the library because I convinced myself I did not want to know what the young *norteamericano* had asked about me or what Teresa had told him. Who cared what she told him? What concern was it to me? I decided to read a book and selected the well-worn copy of *The Book of Alexander*. That, I knew, would make me think of Cristóbal. He was the one I should be thinking about because when he returned with King Fernando, we would go to Texas. We would not go there to plow and plant and grow things, but to conquer that land for our monarch. We would lead the army of men with long-rifles and tame Texas for King Fernando who, in his gratitude, would give Texas to Cristóbal to rule. I would become Cristóbal's wife and rule Texas at his side. It was really the first time the notion of being Cristóbal's wife had occurred to me, but it made sense. Why should I not be Cristóbal's wife?

With the book in hand, I stepped to one of the windows and happened to see Humberto and Barnet returning from Guanajuato. From the way Humberto was struggling not to slide out of the saddle, I knew they must have had quite a night in the *pulquerías*. I wished very hard he would fall off the horse, but somehow he managed to stay mounted until they reached the corral.

Returning to a scalloped-back chair, I made a grand attempt to become engrossed in *The Book of Alexander*. It was to no avail. I could not read a single sentence without the image of Coalter coming to my mind. It made me angry with myself that I could not sustain my focus on Cristóbal. It was absurd I could not get Coalter Owens out of my thoughts, and it made me angry with him. He was trying to take Cristóbal's place. He had made such a big show of his skill with the long-rifle. I was certain Cristóbal could do just as well, and probably much better. Coalter Owens had no right to come to Cristóbal's house and try to take his place. Nobody could take Cristóbal's place. My entire life had been centered on Cristóbal and my future was with him. I would become his wife. It was my destiny. Nothing or no one could change that.

Finally, I tossed the book aside and made the decision to go to Teresa's room. I had to know more about this man from Louisiana. I had to know what he had asked about me and what he may have revealed about his life in the United States. I ran down the stairs to my cousin's room above the wine cellar but stopped before knocking because I heard strange sounds on the other side of her door. They were muffled noises like those made by someone unable to summon help. Quickly, I grasped the pull and rushed inside.

I was both shocked and not shocked by what I witnessed. Teresa was frantically struggling with Humberto who held her down on her bed with his hand over her mouth. It was quite obvious what he was attempting to do.

"Let her go!" I ordered. I knew I had little chance of taking on Humberto with no weapon but my bare hands, though I was prepared to do that if necessary. I thought a firm voice would coerce his compliance. "At once, Humberto! Now!"

He stared at me. "Get out of here, Carmen. This is none of your concern."

Taking a step toward the bed, I repeated, "Let her go!"

Slowly, he removed his hand from Teresa's mouth and, with great effort, gathered his bulk from the bed. His wrinkled and stained clothes were a filthy looking mess and the room reeked with the disgusting odor of *pulque*.

"Come, Teresa," I said, extending my hand.

She did not comply but remained, sobbing, on the bed. She would not even look at me.

Humberto's wet mouth shaped into an ugly grin. "Teresa's not going anywhere, Carmencita. She wants to stay with me." He staggered backwards as he fumbled with the fastens on his trousers. "Maybe you'd like to stay with me too, Carmencita. Yes? Would you like to stay with me?"

My throat had tightened, but I was able to whisper, "Get out of this room immediately, or I'll kill you!"

"You will kill me, Carmencita?" He laughed. "All by yourself, you will kill me? I don't think so. You don't have Cristóbal here to do your dirty work anymore. Cristóbal is very far away from you now. You don't have Cristóbal to cater to your every whim."

It infuriated me that he would say such a thing. I wanted to take that smile from his ugly face and I knew exactly what would do it. "Yes, Humberto," I said and narrowed my eyes. "Cristóbal is far away doing what you are too big a coward to do. But his father is not. Don Esteban is in Guanajuato. And what do you think he is going to do when I tell him what you were trying to do here today? What is he going to do to you when I tell him of this foul thing?"

Humberto did not even flinch at my threat. Smiling even more broadly, he said, "He will do nothing, Carmencita, because you are not going to tell him what I was doing here today." He looked down at my cousin who was trembling violently. "Is that not right, Teresita? Carmen will say nothing to my father about what we were doing."

Without looking up, Teresa whispered, "You must not tell Don Esteban what happened here, Carmen."

I could not believe my ears. "Not tell him? What do you mean? I am going to tell him!"

"No!" Teresa shouted and glanced up at me before again turning her head away. "You must not."

"But why, Teresa? He will be punished."

"No."

"Tell me why!"

Her trembling had subsided and she looked at me without flinching. "Because he knows, Carmen."

What she meant by that became immediately apparent when I looked at Humberto and saw that he was holding the book by Rousseau. Obviously, Teresa had not done what I told her. She had not burned these materials by the French republicans and Humberto had found them.

"Oh yes, Carmencita," Humberto said, correctly discerning I was off balance. "I know. I know that Teresa and Rubén are supporters of Miguel Hidalgo. And what will my father think when he learns of this? More importantly, what will Indentant Riaño think?"

Holding her torn blouse in place, Teresa rose from the bed and faced Humberto. "No one is a supporter of Miguel Hidalgo except me."

For a moment, I was stunned by the revelation that Teresa had disobeyed my order to burn the books. My anger at her, however, was nothing compared with what I wanted to happen to Humberto.

"It does not matter," I said. "Come, Teresa. Don Esteban will soon be home, and I will tell him what happened. It does not matter about these silly books. They mean nothing."

"No!" Teresa repeated and rushed to take my arm. "You must not tell Don Esteban, Carmen. Humberto will tell the intendant and we will be shot!"

Despite my vigorous protestations that the Marqués must be told, Teresa continued to insist that I divulge nothing of what happened. And so I was forced to stand aside as Humberto, carrying the book, swaggered out of the room and slammed the door behind him. It enraged me that he was going to get away with what he had done, and that he knew I would not tell. Again, I tried to convince Teresa to let me tell Don Esteban what happened, but she was adamant in holding to her position that if I did, Humberto would go to Riaño, and she and Rubén would be shot.

I had to admit I could not guarantee that this was not exactly what in fact would happen. Riaño had never been reluctant to use the firing squad for even the smallest transgressions against viceregal law. Moreover, I was not at all sure what the Marqués's reaction would be to the revelation that Teresa and Rubén were republicans in support of the traitor, Miguel Hidalgo. After beating Humberto to within an inch of his life, he might himself turn Teresa and Rubén over to Intendant Riaño. He despised republicans. Teresa was a silly girl, but she was my cousin.

When I started to leave the room, Teresa took my arm and begged me to stay. She was terrified that Humberto would return. I stayed with her the remainder of the morning. At least now my thoughts of Coalter Owens were no longer my singular preoccupation. There was plenty more to think about as we sat in that tiny room and waited for the day to drag on.

Late in the afternoon, I rushed to the window because I recognized the sounds made by Don Esteban's mount coming up the path from Guanajuato. Listening to the hurried pace of his golden palomino, I inferred that he was eager to return home. It occurred to me he might have news of Cristóbal. Maybe a letter had finally arrived telling us when he would be arriving with King Fernando. Don Esteban was hurrying back to share this wonderful news with me. I so wanted Cristóbal to be home. I could confide in him, and he would know what to do about Humberto. He would himself deal with Humberto, and he would do so severely. So that Teresa would be safe, I took her to my suite and told her to bolt the door shut behind me when I left.

After running to the stable, I found Don Esteban talking to Coalter Owens. The young man appeared quite serious and he offered only a quick smile when I approached. By contrast, the Marqués seemed unusually happy, lending credence to my theory he had heard from Cristóbal and my father.

"Don Esteban!" I cried. "You have news of Cristóbal! You have received a letter?"

"No, Carmencita," he said sadly. "No message from Cristóbal. But I do have good news. Come with me to the library while I pack. I must leave immediately for Mexico City." He turned to Coalter who was wiping his hands on a soiled cloth. "Señor Owens wishes to speak with me, Carmen. Perhaps he will be so kind to join us in the library."

A look of resolve hardened in Coalter's face when he said, "I would like what I have to say to you, Don Esteban, to be heard also by your son and Latham Barnet."

"As you wish," the Marqués said summoning my uncle who was walking the winded palomino in the corral next to the stable. "Anselmo. Go and tell Humberto and his guest that I request their presence in the library. And Anselmo, tell Rubén to harness the Parisians to the barouche coach."

While waiting for Humberto and Barnet to arrive in the library, Don Esteban assembled and packed various documents in a leather pouch.

"Don Esteban," I asked, "why must you go to Mexico City?"

He looked up and smiled. "Carmencita, I have received a message from one of our supporters in the capital. He informs me there is reason to hope that some of the *criollo* leaders in Mexico City will support our plan. They understand that the anarchy in New Spain is as bad for them as for the Spanish-born. They want to talk with me."

"You are leaving now?" I asked as he resumed the assemblage of the papers on his desk. "Today?"

"There is no time to lose. I will leave immediately after I hear what Señor Owens has to say."

I looked at Coalter who had stood silently in the corner of the big room while Don Esteban and I talked. He stiffened when Humberto and Barnet stepped inside and looked warily about. The sudden alarm in Humberto's eyes when he saw me made it evident he had leapt to the assumption I had revealed to his father what he had tried to do to Teresa. He seemed to relax when he saw how Don Esteban busied himself with his packing, but he stood close to the doorway as if prepared to make a quick exit should the need arise. I did not take my eyes from him and strongly entertained the idea of reneging on my pledge to Teresa and exposing Humberto for what he was.

Before I could make up my mind as to what to do, the Marqués put aside his materials and explained that he had asked the two men to join him in the library at Coalter's request.

Barnet watched as Coalter stepped closer to where the Marqués stood behind his desk. He began to relate some of the things he had told me the night before about how his father had wanted to obtain the viceroy's permission to bring *rancheros* from the United States to Texas. He explained that there were many families who would come to Texas if given the opportunity to farm the rich lands of Texas. Some of the smile returned to his lips as he spoke of this, but his expression once more turned somber when he said, "The plan to open New Spain to the slave trade was not part of my father's agreement with Barnet. It was not something that was discussed between them, and had it been, my father would have had nothing to do with it."

For a moment Coalter and Barnet stared at one another, and though the older man's expression did not change, it was evident that he was not pleased with what he was hearing.

Don Esteban asked, "And why, Señor Owens, would your father want nothing to do with opening New Spain to the slave trade?"

Without shifting his gaze from Barnet, Coalter said, "Because, Don Esteban, slavery is evil. Against their will, many tens of thousands of people in Africa were taken from their homes, by men like Barnet and made to cross the ocean in the most horrible circumstances. Many perished of diseases and others were thrown overboard to drown because they tried to escape. Once ashore, many were maimed or killed because they tried to break free and find a way back to their homes."

Barnet said something in English which, though I did not understand the meaning, sounded like a threat.

Ignoring him, Coalter looked to Don Esteban. "If you allow the slave trade to be reopened in New Spain, Don Esteban, this horror will be repeated. Many thousands of Africans will be taken by force from their homes, and they will suffer in ways that words cannot describe. Do not accept Barnet's proposal. Do not allow him to bring the evil to your land that men like him have brought to mine."

"Father!" Humberto shouted from his position near the door. "Don't listen to him. We need Colonel Barnet's men and their long-rifles. Without them, Fernando will have no kingdom to rule! What this man is saying is a lie!"

The Marqués ignored Humberto's frantic appeals to disregard what Coalter had said. Quietly, he inquired, "Why, Señor Owens, did you not speak of this until now? Why did you say nothing when Colonel Barnet made his proposal yesterday? Even though you knew your father had not agreed to such a thing, you remained silent. Why?"

Coalter walked to one of the windows that afforded a view of the city of Guanajuato in the valley below. "I said nothing, Don Esteban, because I saw you as the last hope to allow immigrants from my country into Texas. Part of what Barnet told you is the truth. If New Spain is opened to the import of slaves from Africa, thousands of men from the United States will come. They will come with rifles and they will support your king or any man who will enable them to obtain free land and cheap labor. I thought that might be the only way to gain permission for our people to settle Texas.

"But I was wrong. If my father were not ill and had been able to come here, he would never have agreed to what Barnet proposed. The kind of people my father would bring to Texas are simple farmers. They do not want to force other people to do their labor. They are not the kind of people to form an army to fight for a king they do not know. I was silent about what Barnet told you because I wanted to realize my father's dream of establishing a colony in Texas, and I thought offering you an army for your king might be the only way to do it. But what Barnet wants to do is wrong."

When I heard Coalter's words, I thought of my own willingness to ignore my suspicion that slavery was a bad thing. I had no desire to open Texas to farmers. That had no appeal to me whatsoever, but I did want the thousands of men with their long-rifles for the army Cristóbal and I would lead on behalf of King Fernando. It was not difficult for me to understand what Coalter was saying about why he kept silent.

Don Esteban stepped to where Coalter stood and patted his arm. "I am glad that you told me this, Señor Owens. Now I know that my decision with regard to Colonel Barnet's proposal is a correct one." Facing Barnet, he straightened and said, "There will be no slavery in

New Spain. Our kingdom will not be built on human suffering and misery."

Barnet abruptly turned and left the room. Humberto scurried after him.

As Don Esteban resumed packing his papers, I scanned the contents of the room. My thoughts were confused. Nothing was happening as I had anticipated. For some reason, my eyes settled on a double-edged walloon mounted on the wall. The long broadsword had been handed down from father to son in the House of Abrantes since the time of the great Cid. Once, Cristóbal had removed it from the wall. It was almost too heavy for him to swing and he was strong. I could barely lift it, much less swing it. Suddenly, surprising myself, I said, "Don Esteban, take me with you to Mexico City."

The Marqués was tying the last cord to a leather pouch in which he had placed documents and other papers. He shook his head. "It is too dangerous. There have been reports of fighting between troops loyal to one or the other of the several factions attempting to gain the upper hand in the capital." Returning to his task, he added, "And besides, Carmencita, who will look after things for me while I am gone? I am leaving you in charge. Until my return, you are the head of the House of Abrantes!" He looked at Coalter and smiled. "Come. Both of you. See me off. I must be on my way."

No sooner had the wrought-iron gates been secured behind Don Esteban's departing carriage than I realized I had committed a serious error in not telling him what Humberto had done to Teresa. What was to prevent Humberto, in his father's absence, from attempting to do the same thing again? Who was to prevent it? So engrossed was I in my thoughts on this matter, I did not at first realize that Coalter, who stood beside me at the gates, had spoken.

"I'm sorry," I said. "What did you say?"

He was smiling. "I asked if you would like to go for a ride with me, Carmen. I have been wanting to explore the countryside around Guanajuato. I will saddle your horse."

At that moment, I would have liked nothing more than to go for a ride in the countryside. Riding always cleared my head and made me feel good. And I wanted to go with this young man. Something in me wanted very much to be with him, to talk with him and learn more about him, but I knew I could not. What had happened to Teresa made it impossible for me to leave the hacienda.

"I cannot," I said. "I do not feel well."

There was concern in his face. "Then I will stay here. Perhaps there is something I can do. I will—"

"No," I said. "You go for your ride. See the countryside. It is a good day for it. Please, excuse me." I turned and walked quickly to the house and went to my room.

After unlatching the door, Teresa took my arm, pulled me inside and anxiously inquired, "Are the *norteamericanos* leaving? I saw Humberto and the one called Barnet leave earlier. They are returning to their country?"

"I do not know," I told her truthfully though I suspected they would be back since they had not taken the time to pack their things. Most likely, they were going to Guanajuato to the *pulquerías*.

Teresa decided to return to her own room to change her clothes. I told her to come right back and started to go with her but did not because I was starting to have a deep pain in my head. I decided to lie down and rest for a while. Before I did, I stepped to the window in time to see Coalter riding out of the corral. Beside him, riding his mule, was the slave. It occurred to me to run after them. If Humberto returned and tried to do something to Teresa, I could use some help. I decided against going after them. My problem was not their problem.

As tired as I was, I could not sleep because I began to think that Humberto might come back at any moment. He and Barnet may not have gone to Guanajuato. They might have ridden off in anger and, after discussing the Marqués's decision, decided to come back to the hacienda. What would I do if Humberto came back and attempted to finish what he had started earlier? It was not difficult to imagine that he might do that. Thinking about this made it impossible to rest so I got up and paced the floor, which only served to make my head hurt more.

If necessary, I would fight to protect Teresa, a prospect that gave me pause. It was not that I was afraid of Humberto. I was not, but I knew I could not defeat him with my bare hands as I once could. It was prudent to prepare for the worst so I removed a short-barreled fusil from my gun-rack and began to load a charge. And then, I began to wonder if I was, in fact, prepared to use a firearm against Humberto? He was, after all, Don Esteban's son, Cristóbal's brother. As disgusting as Humberto could be, was I really capable of shooting him?

For some time, I paced my room and thought of this matter. Finally, I returned to my bed and closed my eyes. I was tired and my head was about to split open. Maybe, I thought, if I could get just a few moments sleep I could refresh myself and plot a course of action. I was not thinking clearly. I needed rest. I knew if I fell asleep Teresa would wake me up when she returned from changing her clothes.

✦

When I opened my eyes, I realized I had dozed. I raised my head. It was past the horses' feeding time. Hearing no noises from the corral, I relaxed. If the stock had not been fed, they would be letting everyone know it. And then I heard a terrible commotion outside and jumped up with a start. It was the sound of horses, many horses.

When I got to my feet, I realized I had been asleep for some time because it was now dark outside. Stepping to the window, I looked down to find the grounds between the hacienda and the stable filled with several dozen men on horseback. Some of them were carrying torches. They were riding destriers, the Spanish war-horse favored by the Royal Dragoons. I recognized the blue, red and black uniforms of dragoons and their distinctive two-cornered, plumed sombreros.

And then, a magnificent coach was drawn at a brisk pace through the gates by a team of brougham-horses. Several men with torches dismounted and ran to open the door as soon as the driver of the elegant carriage reined the team to a halt. On a shield beneath the driver's deck was emblazoned a coat-of-arms consisting of two red lions on a white field, two gold castles on red, and in the center, three gold fleur-de-lis on blue. My hand went to my mouth. The coat-of-arms on the shield was that of the Spanish House of Bourbon. Cristóbal had returned with the king!

Upon reflection, I knew it was impossible for it to be the king. Cristóbal had not been gone long enough. Very soon, I had my answer for I saw, emerging from the coach, Intendant Riaño. I should have remembered that all vehicles of high officials in the Viceroyalty bore the Royal Crest. Suddenly, there was a knock at my door which turned into a pounding. Quickly, I dressed and pulled on my boots.

"Carmen!" Teresa shouted and tried to open the door. "Carmen, hurry! Let me in!"

I ran to the door and threw back the latch-bolt. "Teresa," I said. "What is it? What's wrong?"

"They're going to kill Rubén, Carmen! You must stop them!"

"Calm yourself, Teresa. What are you saying? Who is going to kill Rubén?"

Gripping my arm, she pulled me into the hall and down the corridor to the main foyer where stood Hortensia, Anselmo, and the other servants, all dressed in their nightclothes. They looked at me like frightened rabbits when I paused before going outside. In the yard, the soldiers fell silent and watched as I came out of the house. Teresa was behind me. And then I saw Rubén. His hands tied behind his back, he was standing near one of the caldrons used to wash clothes. Ten dragoons, muskets at the ready, were in a line some fifteen yards from where he stood. When I saw Humberto near the intendant's coach, I knew immediately what had happened. Even though I had not told his father what he had done to Teresa, Humberto had carried through with his threat.

When Teresa ran to embrace Rubén, I turned and found myself facing Juan Riaño. His thin face was twisted into a furious scowl. "Intendant Riaño," I said. "What is the meaning of this? Why are—"

Before I could react, the intendant slapped me. "Do not question me, you filthy *india!*"

He drew back his hand to strike me again and I instinctively raised my arms to fend off the blow. When I did, I felt hands, strong grasping hands, all over my body and I was thrown to the ground. On my stomach, my face in the sand, I was held down by several of the dragoons. Thus restrained, unable to move, I watched the intendant walk toward the house and order everyone brought out. Quickly, his men complied, rushing into the house and returning behind the servants who cowered before the bayonets affixed to long-barreled muskets.

Riaño pointed a trembling finger toward Rubén and exclaimed loudly, "This man is a traitor to our king! As an example to others who may contemplate similar treason, he will be executed!" He turned toward the line of dragoons holding their muskets. "Proceed!"

"No!" Teresa screamed as two soldiers pulled her from Rubén and forced her to stand with the other servants. Hortensia and Anselmo held her to prevent her attempting to escape past the soldiers who encircled them. Frantically, she looked at where I was being held down. "Carmen!"

Everything was happening too quickly. I wanted to remind the intendant that he seemed to have forgotten that Don Esteban was a personal friend of King Carlos. The Marqués would be enraged if he knew what was happening. Riaño did not know what kind of trouble he would be in if he carried out his threat. I needed to tell him these things, but I was unable to so much as open my mouth before those holding me applied more pressure, making it almost impossible for me to breathe.

A lieutenant raised his saber and the men in the firing squad took aim. Rubén, his eyes blinking from the sweat running down his forehead, peered in the direction from where he could hear Teresa's screams for me to do something. The officer whipped his sword down and the muskets cracked. Rubén lurched backward but he did not immediately fall. For an instant he seemed to straighten as if preparing to walk. I had never seen anyone shot, and so I looked on with horror as Rubén suddenly went limp and his body collapsed. It was an awful thing to see. There was something particularly ugly about how his body sprawled to the ground in such a twisted, unnatural way.

I do not know when in the silence that followed I was released from the soldiers' grasp. All I could do was stare at Rubén's body. I kept waiting for him to move. And when Teresa was allowed to run to where he had fallen and she gathered him into her arms, I kept thinking he would respond to her embrace and would say something to still her sobs. Slowly, I rose to my knees as I became aware that I was no longer restrained. My arms were numb from being held so tightly.

Humberto walked to where Riaño stood. "Allow me to offer your men food and drink."

Riaño directed his officers to grant the men permission to enter the house and soon there were shouts and the sounds of celebration. Rubén lay dead in the dirt and these men were having a fiesta. The intendant looked down at me and said, "This one has always been a troublemaker. She too should be punished."

Just as I was managing to get to my feet, Humberto put his hand on my arm, squeezed tightly and forced me back down. "I will tend to her, Intendant Riaño. I have in mind an appropriate punishment for her treachery."

Humberto was the reason for the grotesque nightmare I was witnessing. What he had done was the cause of this horror. I tried to force my way up, thinking only of what I could do to make him pay for Rubén's death, but he tightly clamped his fingers into my flesh until my stomach sickened and I had to sink to my knees. I wanted to scream out for him to release me but could not. Any movement intensified the pain. My head was spinning at the throbbing ache in my arms. My hands were numb. Finally, Humberto jerked me to my feet and, Riaño at his side, led me up the steps to the front doors of the hacienda where Barnet stood.

Gesturing to the door, Barnet smiled and said, "Please join me in the library, Intendant Riaño. There is an excellent brandy there we can sip while Humberto tends to his wench."

Rubén's death meant no more to these men than if they had just squashed an insect. The sounds of Teresa's sobs affected them not in the least. Her pain was of no importance and meant nothing to them. Two of the dragoons holding a torch opened the doors to the hacienda and Humberto started to force me in. I resisted and he gave me a powerful jerk which caused me to once again fall to my knees on the stone stairway.

And then I heard a voice: "Let her go!"

It was Coalter. I looked up just as he dismounted and bounded toward the steps. Several of the dragoons raised their muskets and trained their sights on him.

"No," Barnet said to Riaño. "Don't shoot him. I'll handle this."

Coalter was prevented from coming up the stairs by the dragoons but again he repeated, "Let her go! Now!"

Though Humberto loosened his grip, I was unable to get up. He had hurt me severely. When I looked up, I saw fear in his eyes despite the fact Coalter bore no weapon and was surrounded by a score of dragoons holding muskets with fixed bayonets.

"What is happening here, Barnet?" Coalter demanded.

"We've uncovered a plot to overthrow the viceroy's government," Barnet said. "As a consequence, Intendant Riaño and other of the notables of Guanajuato have requested that we bring our army to New Spain. And, I might add, they have agreed to our proposal regarding the slave commerce."

Although I continued to strain to fill my lungs with air, I managed to gasp, "Don Esteban did not agree to your proposal!" I looked up at Humberto who had not taken his eyes from Coalter. Juan Riaño also appeared nervous. I thought I might be able to bluff them into letting me go. Since Coalter had no weapon, I saw no other way to prevail. "The Marqués will have you both shot for what you are doing here. When he returns, he will—"

"When he returns," Humberto interrupted, "Colonel Barnet's men will have arrived from Louisiana." He had apparently concluded he was in no danger from Coalter. "Who does my father have to follow him? *Criollo* merchants in Mexico City? Who will King Fernando turn to for support, me or my father?"

His words gave me pause. If Barnet brought his men to New Spain, who would there be to stop him? Riaño and the other notables would welcome him with open arms. All this passed through my mind, but my problem was more immediate. I had to get away so I made another effort to find my feet and when I did Humberto brought his fist down onto the back of my head and knocked me to the stone staircase.

Coalter charged up the steps. I saw Barnet make a gesture to the dragoons not to discharge their weapons. So intent was Coalter in reaching Humberto, who had drawn his hand back to strike me again, he did not see that Barnet had reached inside his coat to withdraw a large knife from a scabbard attached to a belt strapped around his waist. Before I could cry out a warning, Barnet plunged the long blade into Coalter's abdomen. He withdrew the knife and stepped back.

"No!" I screamed as Coalter reeled backward and fell down the stairs. In the flickering light of the torches, I saw the blood ooze out on the front of his shirt and jacket. He collapsed on the cobblestone walkway and lay motionless.

Barnet removed a handkerchief from the lapel pocket of his coat and wiped the blade of the knife before returning it to the scabbard. "His father will be quite distraught when he learns of this tragedy. When he learns his son was killed by primitives in revolt against their king, he will be broken-hearted. It will fall my sad lot to tell him." He smiled. "Come, Intendant Riaño. Let us go to the library. We must not keep Humberto from his work of punishing the wench."

Dragging me inside, Humberto followed the two men down the corridor leading to the library. They both laughed and made lewd comments when he parted their company and began to climb the stairs to the second floor. I had neither the strength nor the will to fight him. My arms throbbed with pain and I could not even feel my hands. The blow to my head had addled me. But more than all else, I was devastated by what had happened to Rubén and to Coalter.

Humberto forced me into his bedroom and closed the door behind us. Though there was a window open, the stench of tobacco and *pulque* was overwhelming. The room was as filthy as a pigsty. Clothes, empty wine bottles and *pulque* jars were scattered about on soiled rugs.

"Well, Carmencita," he said. "You and I have some unfinished business to attend to."

Recovering my wits in some measure, I saw the possibility of making a move to the window. There was a balcony outside. It would be a long drop to the ground, but I would risk anything to get away from Humberto and what I knew he was planning. As if reading my thoughts, he quickly positioned himself between the bed and the window. Now my only path of escape was the door.

He picked up a bottle of *pulque* on the table next to his bed and removed the cork. "All these years, you've lived like a princess at my father's house. I've never understood why he treated you that way. An *india*, that's all you were, a servant's daughter, and he treats you as if you are a princess."

Upending the bottle, he took a long drink and I looked again at the door. If I could get out and make it to my room, I could load the muskets and pistols I kept there. Certainly, I would be killed. There were at least three dozen dragoons drinking and celebrating on the floor below us. I could not kill them all, and they would surely kill me but not before I paid these men back for what they had done to Rubén and Coalter. Riaño. Barnet. Humberto. I would kill them all if only I could get to my room.

"But it's all over now, Carmencita," Humberto said and wiped his mouth with the sleeve of his coat. "Soon, I will be the Marqués de Abrantes. This will be my hacienda. The gold and silver mines will be mine. All will be mine because I was smart enough to accept Barnet's offer."

I edged toward the door.

"And now, Carmencita, I am going to teach you a lesson you will never forget."

When he paused to take another drink from the bottle, I saw my chance. I started toward the door. Unfortunately, my body was stiff and I was unable to reach it before Humberto grasped my hair and slung me to the bed. Before I could roll away, he was on top of me, tearing at my clothes and I could not move under his heavy bulk. I was unable to draw a breath. He was crushing me and I could not fill my lungs with air.

Suddenly, I felt his weight lift. He came off the bed rapidly, and before I knew what was happening, he was on the floor. I heard a noise like that of a ripe melon being thumped. When I was able to focus my vision, I saw that Humberto was stretched out and someone was standing over him.

It was the slave. His hand grasping an ax-handle, he stood over Humberto who was motionless.

Gasping to recover my breath, I asked, "Is he dead?"

"No, Señorita. He is not dead."

The black man had understood my question and replied in Spanish, so it was evident he had only pretended not to understand when I had tried to speak to him in the stable. I watched as he knelt beside Humberto and began to tie him to the legs of the bed with ropes he had brought with him through the window. I assumed he had come through the window because Humberto had latched the door. Then he tore off a piece from the bedsheet and arranged a gag around Humberto's mouth. "This will give us a chance to get away before the soldiers come. Come Señorita, we must leave this place. Quickly!"

I tried to get to my feet but the blow Humberto delivered to my head had made me lose all sense of balance. "I cannot," I said after several failed attempts to stay upright. "Something is wrong with my head."

He quickly gathered me up in his arms and carried me to the balcony. "Can you hold on to me, Señorita?"

"I think so," I replied and wrapped my arms around his chest and locked my hands together. He had strung a rope from the balcony and I could feel the strength in his body as, hand over hand, he made the descent. Even with my weight on his back, he accomplished the task effortlessly, and once on the ground, gently helped me to the grass.

Peering into the darkness, I saw someone approaching from around the corner of the house and started to sound a warning. I thought it might be one of the dragoons. Before I could utter a word, the slave placed his hand over my mouth and whispered, "Señorita, do not make a noise. We must be very quiet." His deep voice was gentle, reassuring, though the tone was one of urgency.

It was Teresa. Behind her was Anselmo and several of the other servants. They had with them three of the mules used for the supply wagons.

"Teresa," I said when she rushed to my side and knelt. I did not know what to say to her to convey my sorrow at Rubén's death, or my regret I could not save him.

Obviously, Teresa had planned my escape with the black man. Looking at him, she asked, "Will she be able to ride? She has been hurt."

"I can ride," I answered for myself and somehow managed to get to my feet. My assumption was we were going to Mexico City. We were going to Don Esteban, and he would take care of the men who did these awful things. "Where is my horse?"

"A mule is best," the slave said, "for where we are going. A horse cannot negotiate mountain trails as well as a mule."

"Mountain trails?" I whispered. I had never been to Mexico City, but I did not think it was necessary to go over mountains to get there. "There are roads to Mexico City. We will need horses!"

Teresa said, "You are going to Dolores, Carmen."

I looked at her and then her words registered. Dolores was the village where Miguel Hidalgo lived. She wanted us to go to where the republicans were. "No!" I protested. "We must go to Mexico City. We must find Don Esteban!"

"He cannot make it to Mexico City, Carmen. Dolores is much closer. If he is to have a chance to survive, you must take him to Dolores."

"He?" I asked. I did not know who "he" was. And then, peering through the darkness, I saw Anselmo and the other servants helping to lift Coalter Owens to the back of one of the mules. "He is not dead!"

"No," Teresa said calmly. "But he will die if he is not helped. You cannot go to Mexico City because the soldiers will catch up with you. When Riaño learns you have fled, we will tell them you have gone for Don Esteban. They will follow. By the time they discover you have gone the other way, you will be in Dolores. They will not go there. They fear Ignacio Allende. They do not wish to fight him."

There was not much I could say. I saw the blood on Coalter's shirt and pants. He seemed barely conscious. I certainly did not want to go to where these republicans were, but I knew Teresa spoke the truth.

"Are you not coming with us?" I asked.

"We will stay and send the dragoons to Mexico City. After they have left, we will follow. Also, we must stay to..."—she lowered her head—"...bury Rubén."

The black man helped me to mount one of the mules. He then mounted the other and took the reins to the one Coalter was riding.

Teresa handed him a piece of paper. "I have drawn a map. It will show you the way to Dolores. Father Miguel will know what to do."

Bringing his heels to his mule's flanks, the slave urged the animal to a walk. Though I had never ridden a mule, I did the same, and it responded as a horse would. When I looked back, I saw Teresa watching us. She seemed so alone.

✦

It was dawn before the black man reined his mule to a halt and dismounted. I helped him lower Coalter from the mule he was riding and carry him to a place on the ground near a red granite boulder. All night we had climbed, going higher and higher. Now we were in the foothills of the Sierra Madre where the terrain was barren and rocky. The pain in my head had subsided to a dull ache. I was still dizzy, but no longer did everything appear to be spinning. The slave placed his hand to Coalter's head and said, "He is very hot."

Kneeling at his side, I touched Coalter's face feeling the heat. I spoke his name several times, but he did not respond. In his partially opened eyes there was no recognition of who I was. His teeth were chattering in the manner of someone cold. "He seems cold," I said. "Why would he be cold when he feels so hot?"

"It is not a good sign."

It suddenly occurred to me that this black man had risked his life to save me from Humberto. He had jeopardized his own life for a stranger.

"Señor...you are called Jeb?" I asked.

"That is what the slave traders called me. In Africa, my name was Lebe Seru. It was the name given to me by my mother and my father."

"Lebe Seru," I whispered in order to familiarize myself with the pronunciation. If it was the name given to him by his parents, I felt

that was what I should call him. It was a name easy for me to pronounce. The first light of day was illuminating the great mountains
which towered above us. The air smelled cold and sweet. A dozen
yards from where we had stopped was a stand of tall pines.

"Señorita, we must—"

"Please call me Carmen." I interrupted, "My name is María del
Carmen Rangel." It did not seem right for him to continue calling me
Señorita. He was old enough to be my father.

He nodded and smiled. There was kindness in his eyes. "We must
continue on, Carmen. I know it is difficult, but we cannot stop. We
must get help for Coalter Owens, or he will die." He looked at the map
Teresa had drawn. "We are still some distance from this village called
Dolores."

I helped place Coalter on the back of the mule, but he was too
weak to stay upright. He began to slide out of the saddle. Lebe Seru
climbed on the back of the mule behind Coalter and held him steady.
Securing the reins of the now riderless mule, I followed behind.

Slowly, we continued our climb, moving always to the north.
From time to time, Lebe Seru would stop, consult the map, look for a
landmark, and then we would advance. The mules were sure footed,
and I found the one I was on as easy to ride as a horse. After a while,
I began to doze. The mule seemed to know to follow, caravan style,
without my guidance. My body was in need of sleep. Occasionally, I
would awaken with a start and look around, unsure of where I was,
disoriented and wondering why I was riding on the back of a mule.
And then, the memory of what had happened flooded my thoughts.

So abruptly it had happened. Rubén had been alive and healthy
and happy, and now suddenly he was dead. His life had been extinguished as easily as the flame of a candle. And I had been helpless to
stop what had happened. I had failed in my duty. Don Esteban would
be disappointed in me. He had left me in charge, and I had failed.
Cristóbal would not have failed had he been in my place. Of this I had
no doubt, and I was very ashamed.

At dusk, Lebe Seru halted at a mountain stream crossing. He
helped me to place Coalter at the base of a huge tree and then, wading into the stream, removed his shirt and soaked it in the water. I

saw scars on his back. They were old scars but they were terrible and deep. He returned to apply the cold compress to Coalter's face and I saw worry in his eyes. Coalter was not moving and all color had drained from his face.

An awful thought seized me, something that had not occurred to me despite the severity of the wound. "Is he dying?"

"I am afraid he is."

I knew that what had happened to Coalter would not have occurred if he had not made the attempt to help me. He had been foolish to charge ahead with no weapon. He should not have tried to help me. What was I to him?

"I do not want him to die," I whispered. And I did not. Of course, I had not wanted Rubén to die either, but in a strange way, this was different. There was something about this man that made the thought of his death as terrible as if it were my own life that were in peril. "Maybe we should wait for Teresa and the others. My aunt will know how to help him."

"We cannot wait. If they do not come soon, it will be too late. We must go on."

Once more, I helped with the difficult task of raising Coalter to the mule's back and we pressed on. After a while I again began to doze. This time, I started to have horrible dreams. Over and over, I saw soldiers in a firing squad raise their weapons. I saw Rubén, frightened and confused, look to me for help. He raised his hand to me. He needed my help. When the muskets made that awful noise, I would scream out as Rubén crumpled to the ground, his body coming to rest all twisted and misshapen like an animal in the slaughtering pen. The sound of my own voice would awaken me and I would desperately try to stay awake because I could not stand the horror of these images. As soon as my head fell forward, the dream would repeat, and it seemed to go on for hours.

Finally, the dawn broke in the east, and we stopped at the edge of a field of maize. The long leaves on stalks taller than a man made a dry, scratchy sound in the cool morning breeze. There were roosters crowing in the distance. After helping to place Coalter's limp body on the ground, I knelt at his side and looked up at Lebe Seru. He was obviously tired and exhausted. Having to hold Coalter all this way had taken its toll. Unlike me, he had been unable to nap.

"We are lost, Carmen," he said as if making an apology. "I tried to follow the map but I must have misread it."

I could see he was discouraged. Again, I thought of what he had done for me. He had saved me from a horrible fate. I wanted to take his thoughts away from our predicament, so I asked, "How did you come to speak Spanish so well?"

He sat beside Coalter. "I learned as a child. After I was taken from my home and made to cross the ocean, I was sold to a man in New Orleans. It was many years ago at a time when Louisiana was owned by Spain. Even today, one hears Spanish spoken in New Orleans more often than English."

It was a strange thing to hear a man speak of being sold to another man. "Did you...belong to his father?" I asked tentatively, looking down at Coalter.

"No," Lebe Seru said. "Señor Owens does not own slaves. He is opposed to slavery. The man who owned me was an associate of Barnet. Last year, he sold me to Barnet so I could teach him Spanish in preparation for his trip to New Spain."

"You helped Barnet learn to speak Spanish? He was a slave trader and wants to bring more of your people from Africa to New Spain. Why would you help him with anything?"

"Barnet did not confide his plans to me, Carmen. Only at the Marqués's hacienda did I learn of his plan to reopen the slave trade."

There was such sadness in his face. "Lebe Seru," I asked, "why did you not run away?" It was the question that had puzzled me from the beginning. "You have had chances to run away, but you do not."

He touched the damp red dirt and stared across the field of maize. "You have seen my back, Carmen. I saw you watching me. I ran away many times when I was younger. But I found there was no place to run. Can I swim the ocean to my home? Each time I ran away, I was found and whipped. At first, I would try again and again. I wanted so much to return to my home. I wanted to see my mother and father, my brothers and sisters, all my family. But the beatings grew worse. Other slaves died of the beatings. I realized that I would never go home if I died, so I quit trying to escape. I learned never to take risks, thinking that someday I would be given a chance to return to Africa." He looked at me and smiled. "That is why I did not speak with you or anyone else at the hacienda. Barnet told me to talk to no one, and I obeyed." He nodded at Coalter. "You have seen what Barnet is capable of doing. Life means nothing to him."

"Then why did you take a risk in helping me? You would risk your life just to help me or Coalter?"

"No, Carmen; not just to help you and Coalter. If it were just you and Coalter, I would have looked the other way. Over the years, I have learned to do that. I helped because I must do something to stop what Barnet is planning. The trade in slaves must not be reopened. I must find a way to stop it. I—"

I saw that his gaze had frozen on a spot behind me. Quickly, I turned and saw, some twenty feet away, hidden among the stalks, a little girl. She was watching us.

"Don't scare her," Lebe Seru cautioned, getting slowly to his feet. "We need to ask her if we are close to this Dolores."

The little girl's dark eyes remained on me even when Lebe Seru called out if she knew the way to Dolores. I judged her to be six or seven years of age. She wore the white cotton pants and shirt common among peasant farmers, and her feet were bare. She was some distance away but I could discern she had a deep scar running across her forehead.

"Carmen, you had better ask. She has probably never seen a man who looks like me."

"Muchacha!" I called. "We are on our way to Dolores. Can you tell us how far we have to go? And which way?"

She said nothing, but gestured for us to follow. Lebe Seru lifted Coalter into his arms and hurried after the girl through a narrow lane between two rows of maize until, suddenly, we came upon a stand of mulberry trees. There were a dozen or more children laughing and shouting near the base of a tree. When they saw us, their voices grew silent. Dark eyes followed our every move as Lebe Seru carried Coalter closer to where they were standing, and I followed. Looking up, I saw an old man in the lower branches of the tree around which all the children had gathered. He was bald, but the hair around the edges and back of his head hung to his shoulders in a long mane of the whitest hair I had ever seen. He was tending silkworms. He wore white pants and a white shirt, the same as the children.

For a moment, we all stood staring at one another. And then, the old man shimmied down the tree and approached us. "Good morning," he said looking down at Coalter.

When he drew closer, I suspected I may have misjudged the man's age. Though his hair was white, his face was unwrinkled, almost youthful. He was not as old as I had at first thought. He had large, forest-green eyes that sparkled in a manner not unlike the children who had formed a circle around us.

"Señor," I said, "we have come from Guanajuato. We are trying to find Dolores. Can you tell us the way?"

"Dolores is just beyond that rise." He stepped closer to Coalter. "This young man seems to have been hurt, Señorita." Turning to one of the boys, he said, "Saturnino, run ahead and tell the women we have someone who is ill. Tell them to prepare a bed and heat water. Hurry, muchacho!" He stood next to the little girl with the scar, and put his hand on her shoulder. She continued to stare at me. She had yet to say a word though the other children had begun to whisper among themselves. "Why have you come to Dolores?"

I was uncomfortable with how the little girl looked at me. There was something haunting in those eyes. "We are seeking a man, a priest called Miguel Hidalgo."

The man stroked the little girl's hair. "Then you will seek no longer." He shrugged. "I am Father Hidalgo."

IV

Carrying Coalter in his arms, Lebe Seru followed the priest down a dirt path between fields of bronze-headed maize. I led the mules and walked at the side of the little girl with the scar on her forehead. Over a gentle hill, the village of Dolores came into view. Surrounded by an escort of excited children, we entered a gravel street along either side of which were thatched-roof houses. Several men stepped forward to assist Lebe Seru with Coalter, and soon dozens of people joined our advance toward the town square. Shaded by thick-trunked oaks whose spreading limbs were laden with streams of blue moss, the plaza contained many flowering bushes and vines that climbed over limestone rubble walls. In the center of the square was a weathered stone wellhead, surmounted by a pulley-standard topped by a wrought-iron cross.

Father Hidalgo led us past a stonewall church toward the front door of a wood-frame house. Before we entered, he turned when several men in military uniforms rushed forward, and one called his name. Never in my life had I been afraid of soldiers, but now all I could think about was what had happened at the hacienda. Looking at Lebe Seru, I knew we shared the same thought. Were these troops sent by Intendant Riaño? Had they been dispatched to apprehend us for what we had done to Humberto? These men were wearing simple white cotton field uniforms, not the elaborate parade dress of the royal dragoons who had accompanied Riaño, but we had no idea from whence they came or their mission.

The priest explained our appearance to one of the soldiers on whose uniform was the insignia of a captain of artillery. The officer, a man of middle-years, had golden hair and a beard similar in color to the Marqués's. Resting his hand on the officer's shoulder, Father Hidalgo looked at us and said, "This is Captain Ignacio Allende."

I recalled Don Esteban's mention of Ignacio Allende, a *criollo* officer who had become a supporter of Miguel Hidalgo. It was hard to imagine that here, standing before me, were the leaders of the republicans in the Viceroyalty of New Spain. Somehow, neither was what I expected. The captain nodded politely and said, "You have come from Guanajuato. Perhaps you would be able to tell us if there have been recent movements of troops from the capital. There have been reports of—"

"Ignacio," the priest scolded. "Can you not see the young man has been hurt? There will be time enough for questions later."

Captain Allende directed one of the soldiers behind him, a sergeant, to help Lebe Seru carry Coalter into what I assumed was the parish house. In the narrow hallway, a band of some dozen or so old women eagerly pointed the way to a room they had prepared. The little women's energy and alertness to every detail belied the age suggested by their grey hair and bent backs.

Once in the room, which was brightly lit with amber beeswax candles, the women proceeded to remove Coalter's clothes and boots, after which they bathed him with steaming water in ceramic basins. At first I turned away in modesty but when I looked again, I was horrified. Coalter's muscular body was drained of all color. He looked like a corpse. The flesh around the deep wound in his side, made by Barnet's long-blade knife, was dark and swollen.

Father Hidalgo entered the room with a clay jar from which he scooped a green salve to work into the wound. His long fingers went deep into the gash. The sight of this made my stomach upset. I tried to look away, and in the hallway I saw Lebe Seru talking with Captain Allende and the sergeant. My stomach churned violently, and before I knew what was happening, I sank to my knees. I heard one of the comadres cry, "Catch her!" The room seemed to go around in a circle. Before I closed my eyes, the last thing I saw was the little girl with the scar.

✦

Each time I would awaken, I had to think to remember that I was not in my own bed. I kept hoping that by closing my eyes and going back to sleep, I could somehow change what had happened and wake up to discover that Rubén was alive and all that had happened had been a bad dream. Several times, I heard voices, and once I thought Cristóbal was standing next to the bed. He was calling my name.

"Cristóbal?" I whispered. He had come to take me home. "Cristóbal!"

"It is me, Carmen," a gentle voice said. "Miguel Hidalgo. Go back to sleep. Rest."

At first I did not recognize him because he was now dressed entirely in black except for a Roman collar at his neck. I wondered if I was dying and a priest had been summoned.

Another time, I awoke with the need to attend to nature's call. I struggled to get out of the bed, but I fell back. Gasping for breath, I looked up and there, beside the bed, was the little girl. She handed me a porcelain chamberpot. There was absolutely no change of expression in the dark eyes when I thanked her. Several times, I was in need of the chamberpot, and each time, she brought it to me, emptied and cleaned.

Finally, I awoke and could not make myself go back to sleep. There was a faint glow at the only window in the small room. The white walls of the chamber were bare except for a simple wooden crucifix above the tiny bed which was little more than a cot. I assumed it was dusk, and that I had slept away the day. Looking about, I did not see the little girl, concluding she had gone home for the night. A terrible thought seized me. This looked just like the room where Coalter had been taken. He must have died. They had removed his body and placed me in the bed where he had lain.

I jumped from the bed and my feet felt the smooth coldness of a wood floor. Looking down, I saw that my boots had been removed. I was barefoot. Not only that, my breeches and shirt were gone. All I was wearing was a cotton gown. Quickly, I removed the woolen blanket that had been my covering on the cot and wrapped it about my shoulders. There was a bracing chill in the thin air. Outside, the fragrant pines made a whispering noise, and an owl called.

Grasping the blanket tightly to my throat, I crept to the door and peered up and down a hallway that ran between a series of doors. The house reminded me of a convent. Across from me was a room and the slightly open door revealed the flickering light of a candle. I stepped across the hall and looked in. Coalter was on a bed next to the window, and I recognized this as the room to which he had been taken. The small candle next to his bed yielded just enough light for me to see that he was breathing. The steady in-and-out motion of his chest was of one in deep and peaceful slumber. I drew closer to the bed and saw that color had returned to his face. A great feeling of relief swept over me.

I started to go to him. I saw then the little girl with the scar, sitting between the bed and the window, and I stopped. Those large dark eyes were focused on mine. Of course, I wanted to ask her how he was, to hear confirmation of my assessment that he was much improved and would survive. There was, however, something in the girl's countenance that made me draw back. Somehow, she seemed to convey that all was taken care of, that he needed his sleep, and that it would be best if I withdrew, so I did.

Back in the hall, I jumped when someone whispered, "He is doing much better."

It was the priest, Miguel Hidalgo. He was carrying a tray of food.

"I did not mean to startle you," he said with a smile. "I was just bringing you something to eat. Shall we go inside?"

Inside my room, he placed the tray on a table next to the bed. Striking a flint to a tinder box, he made a flame and used it to light a beeswax candle on the table. He rubbed his hands together briskly over the ivory glow. "Quite cool this morning!"

"This morning?" I looked out the window. The light had increased, illuminating the mist-covered dark trees between the house and the church building next door. "I thought it was dusk. I slept all day?"

"And all night," he added with a broad grin. "I'll bet you are hungry! Eat before it gets cold."

I stared at those sparkling green eyes. "Thank you...Father." I had never been comfortable around priests, and the sight of one serving my breakfast made me nervous. I sat down on the corner of the bed and pulled the table with the food toward me. I still felt a little unbalanced and disoriented. The aroma from a steaming bowl of rice and milk brought me to my senses. I soon discovered it had been sweetened with a generous portion of what could only be cottonseed honey. While I ate, the priest went to the window and waved at some children who were now shouting outside. The area between the house and the church seemed to be their playing field.

A shrill voice called, "Come outside, Father Miguel. You can be on Hermalinda's team!"

"In a little while, Saturnino. And this time we will allow no cheating!" He laughed along with the children. Then he turned to me. "Do you like games, Carmen?"

I told him I enjoyed games. There was about this man a look of intelligence. Perhaps it was the long mane of white hair beneath his ample bald dome. White hair, I had been told, meant wisdom, and bald men were supposed to be smart. There was also a touch of mischief in the boyish face that reminded me of a fox. Maybe it was his long, thin nose that made him look like a fox. As he continued to watch the children at their game, I said, "Father Hidalgo?"

"Call me Father Miguel, Carmen. Everyone does except the viceroy." The smile deepened. "That one has other names for me."

"What did you do for Coalter? You have restored his health. I thought perhaps he was going to..." I could not bring myself to say it.

"To die?" He shrugged. "He was near death, but he is fine now. He will be as good as new. He is a strong young man."

"What did you do?"

"I applied some herbs to his wound. But that was of small value. It was Lupita who saved him. He was too far gone for it to be anything else."

"Lupita?"

"The little girl who found you and brought you to the mulberry orchard. Do you remember?"

"The girl with the scar?"

He nodded and smiled. "Yes. Lupita. At least that is what we call her until she tells us her given name. She has not spoken since she was found."

I was thoroughly confused. How could a child so small save Coalter's life? She could not be more than six years old, seven at the most. "Since she was found? Who found her? Where?"

His was a face made for smiling or laughing, but now it dissolved into sadness. "Lupita was found in a village north of here. Everyone had been killed except her. People from a neighboring village found the child and brought her here."

"Everyone in her village was killed? Who killed them?" I thought of bandits.

"The viceroy's soldiers," he said in a tone that seemed to indicate I should have known. "When they couldn't pay the *encomienda* they were all destroyed, even the children. The soldiers were ordered to use their swords because the viceroy does not want to waste money on bullets. You have seen the scar on Lupita's head. She was struck by a sword and left for dead. The people who found her said they did not know how the wound healed so quickly. Judging from the scar, the cut must have been very deep. It must have penetrated the skull. The people who found her came as soon as the soldiers rode away. There was much blood on her clothes, but the cut had already closed." He crossed himself. "That is why she has the gift of healing."

"I do not understand."

His eyes brightened. "I believe she was healed by Our Lady! She closed Lupita's wound but left the scar as a sign to others. When someone is touched by the Virgin, that person often has the gift of healing. Many people have overcome illness when they are in Lupita's presence."

"Why was Lupita brought here? Does she have family in Dolores?"

He walked to the window and looked out at the children playing in the yard where the mist was burning away. "All of these children are like Lupita. Their parents were killed. Grandparents. Aunts. Uncles. Their entire families. Throughout New Spain, people are killed for failure to pay taxes even if they have nothing of value. The viceroy's intendants demand what does not exist. And the people are killed when they ask for a government that is just. Many times, as in Lupita's village, the children are killed. Other times they are spared, either because the soldiers take pity on them, or perhaps, they do not want to make the effort to destroy them. Some of the children have no relatives and these are sent to Dolores."

When he turned back to me, I asked, "Why do the soldiers not come to Dolores?" If what he said were true, and I was not at all certain it was, it seemed the soldiers would come to Dolores, the place where the leader of the republicans dwelled.

"The soldiers do not come here because of Captain Allende. Men who will kill children, men who will beat women"—he looked at the bruise on the side of my face—"are cowards. Such men are rarely eager to confront someone who will stand up to them."

Though I had not finished all the food on the tray, I pushed it away. His words disturbed me. What he was saying was the opposite of everything Don Esteban had told me. It was the soldiers of the king who fought for what was right. It was republicans who were evil. However, the one thing I knew for certain was that it was not republicans who had killed Rubén.

Taking the tray, Father Hidalgo said, "I had better let you get more rest. Perhaps later this morning, you will be able to visit Coalter. He called for you often."

"He called for me?"

"You did not hear him? As he began to come to his senses, he called your name many times. It was only when we assured him you were all right that he took a little nourishment and was able to sleep."

"Do you know what was done with my clothes?" I asked, knowing I did not want to go to Coalter's room wearing only a cotton gown. "They seem to have been taken."

"They were burned."

"Burned?"

"They were soaked in Coalter's blood. Your boots too. I will try to locate some clothes for you."

As he was leaving, Lebe Seru and a man in uniform appeared at the door. The priest greeted them warmly and excused himself. Smiling, Lebe Seru entered the room ahead of the man whom, I recognized as the sergeant who had helped carry Coalter into the house. He was a thick-shouldered fellow and wore a mustache that drooped over his mouth. There was something peculiar about the top of his head, but not wishing to stare, I could not identify what it was.

"How are you this morning," Lebe Seru asked, smiling when I told him I was better. He turned toward the soldier. "Carmen, I'd like you to meet Sergeant Guerra."

The sergeant nodded.

"Sergeant Guerra and I are going to ride out this morning to see if we can locate your cousin and the others."

"Teresa!" I whispered. I had forgotten about my cousin. She and my aunt and uncle and the other servants were supposed to follow us to Dolores. They should have arrived by now. I tried to get up, but when I did, I grew dizzy and I had to sit down again. My head throbbed and I assumed the blow Humberto had delivered was responsible for my difficulty in maintaining balance.

"We will find them, Carmen," Lebe Seru said. "You rest and get your strength back."

"Yes," Sergeant Guerra said. "You rest, Señorita Rangel. We will find them. And the men who did this to you,"—his eyes hardened—"they will be punished."

As they started to leave, I noticed the African was wearing different clothes than he had worn at the hacienda. "Lebe Seru," I asked, "Why are you wearing...a uniform?"

He looked at Sergeant Guerra and then back to me. "The people here, Carmen, are opposed to slavery." He straightened himself up. "I have accepted Captain Allende's invitation to be in his army."

After they had left, I continued to feel tired. Although I had slept through an entire day and night, I dozed off and on until the *comadres*, the old village women, showed up with their basins of hot water and insisted I take another bath. They brought fresh clothes which turned out to be an ankle-length, white cotton dress, a pair of straw sandals, and a wool rebozo dyed a dark shade of blue. I hesitated to put on the dress, but realized it would have to do until I was able to get back to my room at the hacienda. There I had many pairs of leather breeches and boots. More importantly, there I had my muskets, pistols and swords.

After dressing, I went to the room across the hall where several *comadres* were in each others' way serving Coalter a meal. When he saw me, he flashed a big smile and started to get up. The women were having none of that and forced him to lie against a big pillow propped against his back while they arranged a tray in his lap. He was wearing white cotton pants and was bare from the waist up except for a bandage wrapped around his stomach. Before drawing closer to the bed, I glanced about and saw that the little girl, Lupita, was no longer in the room.

"Carmen," Coalter said when I stood beside his bed. His voice was strained and weak. "Are you all right?"

I found it impossible to hold back a smile of my own. Despite his powerful arms and shoulders, he looked like a helpless little boy in that bed. "Yes, Coalter. I am all right."

The women seemed to be in a competition as to who would assist Coalter in eating, and there was something of a dispute until one of them, a rotund little lady whose hair was pulled back in a severe bun, handed me a spoon and announced loudly to the others: "The señorita will feed him. He is her man."

I suppose I must have blushed at the woman's statement because the others laughed as I took the chair next to the bed. They watched anxiously until the plump lady waved them from the room with a swish of her apron.

"You eat everything!" she instructed Coalter with a wag of her finger and looked at me. "Make him eat everything, little daughter. And if you need more, you call for Alamar."

After Alamar left, Coalter started to talk, but I scooped up a spoonful of what appeared to be rice and corn cooked into a soft broth and held it to his lips. He swallowed and nodded his approval of its flavor. I had never fed anyone, so it was difficult getting the food to his mouth without spilling. He took several more spoonfuls before holding back his head to express a desire to speak.

"Carmen," he whispered anxiously, "your cousin and your aunt..." His voice trailed.

I explained what had happened, and how Lebe Seru and the sergeant had gone to look for them.

"Lebe Seru?"

"He is the one you called Jeb. Lebe Seru was his name before he was made to be a slave."

"Jeb's name..." he said and hesitated, "I did not know." I fed him a few more spoons of the broth and offered him some of the pan dulce on the tray. Smiling, he shook his head signaling that he could take no more food. Then he reclined on the pillow. I placed the tray on the small table and started to get up. He took my hand, and I saw that he wanted me to stay. I sat back down and watched as he lost his battle to stay awake. His breath slow and measured, he soon entered a deep sleep.

For a long while, I stayed in the chair, my hand still in his as he slept. Carefully, so as not to awaken him, I raised my other hand to touch his face. Slowly, my fingers traced a path down his neck and across the contours of the muscles of his broad chest. I stroked the smoothness of his bare arms. Truly, this was the body of a warrior. It was too bad, I thought, he was only a *ranchero*. What he needed was someone to teach him the arts of war.

There was no use pretending. Something about this man fascinated me as no man ever had. I tried to think of Cristóbal, and my memory of him was one of great fondness and a profound longing to see him. But my thoughts of him were of a whole different kind than what stirred in me as I brushed back the locks of Coalter's thick, dark hair.

I slipped my hand from Coalter's grasp, rose from the chair and walked to the window which afforded a view of the town plaza. For a while, I watched the people crossing through the square, some of them stopping to visit, and then I looked back at Coalter. The woman called Alamar was wrong. This was not my man. I had never said he was and, most certainly, had never wanted him to be. In an effort to reinforce that fact in my mind, I endeavored once again to think of Cristóbal. He was the one I should be thinking about. I should be thinking of his safe return from Spain and the things we were going to do once Fernando was king of New Spain.

Cristóbal was more of a warrior than this *norteamericano*, this *ranchero*, turned out to be despite his skill with the long-rifle. Certainly, Cristóbal would never have been so foolish as to charge up those steps at the hacienda without a weapon. Moreover, Barnet would never have been able to stab Cristóbal. Cristóbal would have killed him. He would have killed him and Riaño and Humberto just as I should have if only I had been better prepared. All my training, all the things my father and Don Esteban had taught me, had gone for naught.

Turning this over in my mind, I began to see what would divert my thoughts away from this peculiar obsession I seemed to be developing toward this man called Coalter. I would do what I should have done in the first place. Barnet, Riaño, and Humberto must die! It was necessary that they pay for what they had done. Riaño would pay for what he did to Rubén. Barnet would pay for what he did to Coalter. And Humberto? He would pay most of all. No one could attempt to do what he did to me and live. No one! It did not matter that he was Don Esteban's son and Cristóbal's brother. He must die.

I lingered in Coalter's room the remainder of the afternoon and, gazing out that window, tried to devise an appropriate plan of action for what I should do next. Most assuredly, I would extract my revenge on Humberto, but I concluded, that would have to be deferred until somehow I found a way to Mexico City. There I would tell the Marqués what Humberto and Barnet were planning. Barnet must not be allowed to return to his country and assemble his army of men with long-rifles. But I had a problem. How was I to get to Mexico City and warn Don Esteban when in fact I had no real idea of where I was? I knew Dolores was north of Guanajuato, but that was the extent of it. I had never been to the capital. And even if I knew what direction to take, what was I to do: ride a mule to Mexico City? How could I manage that if I became dizzy just by walking across the room?

Some soldier I had turned out to be; I was helpless. I was weak and powerless, totally at the mercy of strangers, people who were, I had to keep reminding myself, republicans, opposed to kings and would, given the opportunity, cut off a king's head and, maybe, the heads of his supporters. It was true, these republicans were not what I had always imagined. Their leader tended silkworms and laughed and played games with children. None of the republicans appeared to be different than anyone else. Nevertheless, I kept telling myself, they were dangerous people. They were traitors to their king and thus were enemies of Don Esteban, which, I guessed, made them my enemies as well.

By the time Coalter awoke and Alamar brought a tray containing the evening meal for us both, I was no closer to formulating a plan of action than I had been when I started. I had no clear idea of what I was going to do. Just as I started to feed Coalter, we heard a commotion in the plaza.

"Carmen," Coalter asked when I rushed to the window, "what is happening?" His voice was stronger. "What do you see?"

"It's Lebe Seru and Sergeant Guerra," I said, running to the door. "They've returned! I'll be back in a minute."

In the plaza, a crowd of soldiers were gathered around Lebe Seru and Sergeant Guerra, both of whom had dismounted. I eagerly looked about for Teresa, Hortensia, Anselmo, and the other servants from the hacienda.

Sergeant Guerra was reporting to Captain Allende. "We rode as close to Guanajuato as we dared. There was no sign of the señorita's people." He glanced at me. "I am sorry, Señorita Rangel."

Something had happened at the hacienda, something terrible. I knew it. Humberto had done something awful. I should have made Teresa and my aunt and uncle come with me when we left. When I looked over my shoulder, I saw Father Hidalgo had joined us. The little girl with the scar on her head, Lupita, was at his side.

Seeing the priest, Captain Allende said, "Tell Father Miguel what else you learned, Sergeant."

Sergeant Guerra said, "On the way back, we encountered people who had fled the village of Atotonilco. They told us that in that place more of our people have been arrested by Riaño's dragoons. They are being executed. Men, women..."—he shook his head—"...and children!"

By now a large crowd had assembled in the street.

"Father Miguel," Captain Allende said, "we can wait no longer."

"It is not yet time, Ignacio. We must—"

"But they are killing our people!" Allende shouted. "This madness must cease!"

The breeze blew strands of Father Hidalgo's white hair. "I know, Ignacio," he said and closed his eyes. "I know what they are doing to our people. But it is not yet time." He turned and walked slowly to the church. Lupita followed him.

✦

Over the next several days, Coalter's strength returned. Soon, he was able to feed himself, although I probably continued helping him with his meals after it was no longer necessary. And I helped with such things as shaving. I knew how to put an edge on a knife. With Lupita ever at his side, he progressed from taking a few steps in his room to going outside for short strolls. The little girl seemed absolutely devoted to Coalter, and without her, I am convinced, he would not have made such a rapid recovery.

After a while, I felt guilty I had nothing with which to compensate the people for the food and services they were so freely rendering to Coalter and to me. I had, of course, brought no gold with me when we had been forced to depart the hacienda so suddenly. Several times I assured Alamar, who seemed to be in charge of Father Hidalgo's household, I would make restitution as soon as I was able to return to Guanajuato. Don Esteban had always provided me with however much gold I needed for anything I wanted. Alamar said it was not necessary that I make a payment but when I persisted in reassuring her I would, she surprised me by suggesting that if I wanted to pay for our food and lodging, I could do so by helping with washing dishes and clothes.

Washing dishes and clothes were the last things I wanted to do, but I could think of no gracious way to avoid it after I had made such a fuss over paying my debts. And so I spent a part of each day in the kitchen or at the edge of a stream behind the parish house engaged in the menial work of scrubbing pans and pots or pounding clothes on a rock.

In the kitchen, which I visited often, alone or with Coalter, I had an opportunity to listen to the *comadres* chatter and gossip. I hoped I could learn more about Father Hidalgo, this priest who was the leader of the republicans in New Spain. It was not unusual for him to come to the kitchen and assist in the preparation of food. He was nothing like the arrogant bishop in Guanajuato or his flock of pinched-mouth priests who were always trying to influence the Marqués to give them gold for their lavish accommodations. Miguel Hidalgo puzzled me greatly and I wondered how a simple priest in a frontier village had come to be a republican.

One morning, after helping to serve breakfast to the orphaned children, I managed to set Alamar to talking about Father Hidalgo and learned she had been his housekeeper since the time he was rector of New Spain's only seminary at San Nicolás Obispo. When I expressed surprise that a simple country priest had occupied a position of such great importance in the Viceroyalty, the portly little woman's bright eyes grew wide and she said, "Father Miguel came from an important family in New Spain. The Hidalgo's and the Costilla's owned much land."

"Was his family Spanish-born?" I asked. Normally, only the priests from Spain occupied the highest offices of the church.

"No. If he had been a *gachupín*, Father Miguel might today be the archbishop of New Spain." It was obvious Alamar adored the man. "In fact, he might have become Archbishop if not—" She was diverted by the need to clean a little boy's face with a wet napkin and then forgot what she was going to say.

"If not what, Alamar?"

"Father Miguel was brought before the Inquisition on the charge of heresy. If that had not happened I think he would have been the Archbishop even though he is not a *gachupín*."

"Heresy?"

Her grin conveyed that she was about to tell me something she found most amusing. "The bishops said Father Miguel was a heretic because he said there was no hell. But at the same time they said he was also a heretic because he said one of the popes..."—she rubbed her chin—"...I forget which one. Anyway, Father Miguel said one of the popes had gone to hell." She threw back her head and laughed.

Though Alamar thought this was hilarious, I was quite shocked. "Father Miguel said there was no hell?"

"Yes," Alamar continued after swatting a little boy's bottom to send him out to play. "At his defense, Father Miguel made the bishops look like donkeys. He asked how they could charge him with being a heretic for saying there was no hell when they also charged him with saying a pope had gone to hell! He made them look like donkeys!" She pointed to her head. "Father Miguel is very smart. They had to drop the charges." She sat down for a rest and folded her stubby fingers together on her lap. "Of course, he was forced to resign as the rector of the seminary, but it was not so bad. We got to come here to Dolores. The bishops thought they would never hear from Father Miguel again in a little village like Dolores. But they were wrong. They will hear from him again."

Alamar's story disturbed me the more I thought about it in the days that followed. I knew that the one thing Don Esteban despised more than republicans were heretics, and Father Hidalgo seemed to be both. I did not know what to think about him, and I did not know what I would tell the Marqués about him when I finally got to Mexico City.

One thing for certain, there was no denying Miguel Hidalgo was a man of learning. Often, Coalter and I went to a room where Father Hidalgo taught music to the children. We would listen to them play their violins and cellos and take turns on an old clavichord that somehow had made its way from Spain. They were all quite good. While listening, I would survey the dozens of books on shelves lining the room. The priest's collection was by no means as large as the Marqués's, but it was impressive.

On one occasion, I delayed our departure after a recital until Father Hidalgo and the children left the study. I wanted to get a closer look at the books. Coalter was sitting on a chair by the window, and his eyes followed my every move as I took one after another of the books off the shelves. Not unexpectedly, I found the book by the Frenchman, Jean Jacques Rousseau, the treasonous book Teresa had failed to burn. Father Hidalgo's copy was in the French language. Many of his books were in languages other than Spanish.

"Carmen," Coalter asked as I flipped through the pages of one of the books, "what are you doing?"

It seemed obvious. "I'm looking at this book."

"Can you read?"

The question annoyed me. "Of course I can read! Don Esteban secured the finest tutors in all of New Spain for Cristóbal and me. Some of our tutors came from Spain and others from Italy! Did you think I could not read?"

He lowered his head like a boy scolded for doing something he did not understand was wrong. "I did not mean to insult you. I am sorry."

"You think I cannot read, don't you? You think that. Let me show you." I reached for one of the books on the shelf, the biggest one I could see. "I'll show you I can read. There's nothing I cannot read!"

Naturally, the book I selected was not in Spanish. Nor was it in Greek or Latin, two languages our tutors forced us to study and which I could read in limited measure. I did not know what language I was staring at on the pages of this book.

"What's wrong?" Coalter asked. He got up and looked over my shoulder. When I glanced at him, he smiled. "The book is in English, Carmen."

I shrugged and handed it to him. "Then you read it."

"Do you want me to read it to you?"

"No."

He opened the book. "This book is called *The Pilgrim's Progress*. We could read it together. I could teach you English!" His eyes grew wide. "You can follow along as I translate and—"

"I have no need to learn English."

"As you wish," he said quietly.

"I may not be able to read English," I said, "but I can read Spanish and Greek and Latin. Cristóbal and I spent many, many hours together reading the books in his father's library. I would read to him and he would read to me."

Coalter walked slowly back to his chair. The cotton shirt he was wearing was too tight across his chest and his trousers were several inches above his ankles. The *comadres* had had a difficult time finding clothes the size he could wear while they were making him new ones. He looked funny when he walked and I wanted to laugh.

After sitting down, he said, "You and Cristóbal did many things together."

"We did."

"You must miss him very much."

"Yes," I said truthfully. But then a strange thought crossed my mind. "I miss him very much because..."—I straightened to my full height—"...because he is my *novio*. We will be married when he returns from Spain with King Fernando. So it is only natural that I miss him. Do you not agree?"

"Cristóbal is your *novio*?" He pronounced the word as if uncertain of its meaning. "You and Cristóbal are to be married? I did not know."

From the expression on Coalter's face, he was as stunned by my words as I was surprised I had said them. Cristóbal and I had no plans to be married. Immediately, I wanted to take back what I had said. But I did not. Instead, I continued: "It is difficult when the one you love is so far away." I narrowed my eyes to focus on him. "As I am sure you understand."

He had fixed a blank gaze on the floor, but now he looked up. "As I understand?"

"Have you no one in Louisiana waiting for your return? Perhaps, a *novia*?" I shrugged. "A wife?"

He looked away. Staring out the window, he did not seem to hear me.

"Coalter?" I hated to be so direct but, for some reason, I wanted to know. "Do you have a wife?"

"No."

"Then a *novia*?"

"There is," he began and hesitated, "someone."

"And you miss her." I selected another book from a shelf and pretended to be interested in its contents. "Yes?"

He nodded.

"It is natural," I said and cleared my throat. "You miss your *novia*, and I miss Cristóbal." I put the book back in its place wrong side up and two books fell off the shelf as I fumbled to get it right side up. I picked up the books from the floor and forced them into their places. "But we have much to occupy us, and we shall not have the time for our thoughts to be so far away. There is much that we must do, you and I."

He wrinkled his brow, puzzled. "What is it we must do?"

"We must avenge the wrongs done to us. We shall return to Guanajuato. I will kill Humberto. You will kill Barnet. And Riaño? I suppose it does not matter which of us kills him. We will—"

"What are you saying?" he interrupted. "Kill Humberto? Kill Barnet? I don't understand."

I wondered why he would all of a sudden have a problem with a language he had seemed, until that moment, to have mastered. I repeated my words, this time with more conviction as I realized that what I was saying was the answer I had been seeking. Why, I wondered, had I not thought of it before. I did not have to run to the Marqués in Mexico City, nor did I have to face the three men in Guanajuato alone. It was unrealistic to expect that I should or could battle them alone. Coalter would assist me. He was healing rapidly and with my guidance he could be an effective soldier. He might be little more than a *ranchero* but I could show him what to do.

When I finished, he said, "You are angry about what was done to you, and you are going to Guanajuato to take your revenge."

"Yes," I said. The word had not occurred to me. Revenge. "I am going to Guanajuato to take my revenge. I think I am entitled to it, don't you?"

"I suppose."

Something in his tone conveyed disapproval, so I inquired: "What is wrong with wanting revenge?"

"What purpose does it serve?"

"Purpose?" His question baffled me. "What do you mean, 'purpose?' It will make me feel better."

"You would kill so that you will feel better?"

"And what is wrong with that?" He had no ready answer, so I
continued. "Would you not feel better if you killed Barnet? Look what
he did to you." I gestured to his wound. "He almost killed you! You
would have died if Lebe Seru had not helped us. Do you not want Barnet to pay for what he did to you?"

He studied my question. "I would like to see justice."

"Justice?"

He nodded.

"What is that?"

"It means to see that right prevails. If we simply go to Guanajuato and kill Humberto and Barnet, we will be no different from them.
It is justice we must seek."

This discussion was getting us nowhere. "Will you or will you not
go with me to Guanajuato? That is all I need to know."

He drew a deep breath, apparently wearied by our debate. "I will
go with you, Carmen, wherever you wish."

✦

As the days passed and I waited for Coalter to recover fully so we
could go to Guanajuato and kill Humberto, Barnet, and Riaño, I came
to understand that I might have underestimated the difficulties of
achieving that objective. Certainly, I could not take on three men by
myself. With Coalter by my side, I believed it could be done, but I had
neglected to take into account Riaño's dragoons. We needed help. And
then one morning, as I was returning from washing clothes in the
stream, a possible solution occurred to me. Over the clamor of the
children playing in the field between the parish house and the
church, I heard another noise. Someone was shouting a cadence and
men were marching in unison. It was the unmistakable sound of soldiers in training.

The sounds were originating from beyond the buildings on the far
side of the town plaza. Lebe Seru had joined these republicans, so he
was likely training with their army. Thinking of that, it occurred to

me that maybe he was the answer to our dilemma. Like Coalter and me, Lebe Seru had reason to seek his revenge on those who had mistreated him. The three of us could return to Guanajuato and extract our revenge. Lebe Seru had proven he had the stealth and daring to be a warrior. I went to Coalter's room and told him of my plan. He agreed to go with me to talk to Lebe Seru whom he had not seen since our arrival in Dolores.

The army was training in a pasture just outside the village. We took a position at the edge of the activity near a clump of small pines. The soldiers were engaged in various drills. Some were marching while others were simulating firing their muskets in ranks. It was not unlike what I had watched with my father many times when we went to visit the garrison outside Guanajuato, except at Guanajuato, there were no women soldiers. Here, there were many women in each platoon. Most were girls no older than I, some younger. Although I had long dreamed of being a soldier, I must admit it was odd to see women in uniform doing the same things as the men.

Turning away from the drill field, I saw Captain Allende walking briskly toward where we were standing. On either side of him, running to stay up, were two younger men wearing the insignia of lieutenants. Behind us, the sergeant whose platoon we had been observing brought his soldiers to attention at the officers' approach.

Captain Allende told the sergeant to carry on. Then looking at Coalter, he said, "I see you are up and about, Señor Owens. Father Miguel and Lupita have worked another of their miracles. I am happy to see that you are better."

"I am feeling much better, Captain Allende," Coalter said. "Thank you."

The Captain turned to me. "And you, Señorita Rangel. You have come to inspect the troops?"

"I have come to speak with Lebe Seru, Captain Allende. Can you tell us where he is?"

"He is at the blacksmith shop. Please allow me to show you the way." The lieutenants trailed behind as we walked in the direction of a row of huts near the edge of the drill field. On the way, we went past several platoons of soldiers clustered around various size cannon. Captain Allende must have noticed my interest because he asked, "You are familiar with artillery, Señorita Rangel?"

"In small measure."

Laughing, he looked at Coalter and said, "I think she is being modest. I would be very surprised if the daughter of Baldemar Rangel did not know a great deal about artillery." He stopped near one of the platoons that was in the process of moving an eighteen-pounder siege gun. It was no meager task, since the eleven-foot bronze tube would easily weigh in excess of three tons. "Few men in the Viceroyalty have a knowledge of Spanish weaponry to match that of your father's, Señorita."

"Do you know my father, Captain Allende?"

"Not personally. But I have heard many things of his distinguished career. Had he been born a notable, he would likely have been one of Spain's great generals, and perhaps, a Bonaparte would not today sit on the throne in Madrid."

It was strange to hear a republican pay such a high compliment to my father. I think he was about to say more, but at that moment, the men moving the cannon began to lose control of the carriage, and the captain and his lieutenants rushed to their assistance. The carriage upon which the cannon was mounted, though painted with a fresh coat of red paint, was old and coming apart at its bracing, making it difficult to move. If it was as old as the cannon itself, it was ancient, for on the tube was engraved the royal monogram of Philip IV, a Hapsburg, the dynasty that had not ruled Spain in over a century.

Wiping his hands with a rag, Captain Allende returned, and we resumed our walk. "Well, Señorita Rangel," he asked, "what do you think of our artillery?"

"They are interesting pieces," I replied truthfully. "There was a time when such guns were most effective in knocking down castle walls, or so I've been told."

He smiled. "But they are not of much use in the field against an army."

He had said it. Guns that lobbed nine-, twelve-, eighteen-, or twenty-four-pound balls were too heavy to move except with great difficulty. At the garrison in Guanajuato were smaller field artillery which fired two- or four-pound balls. They could be moved rapidly from place to place as the character of battle changed. "There are few castles in New Spain," I said, not intending my observation as sarcasm, but as a simple statement of fact.

"There are few castles in New Spain," he repeated. "Yes, Señorita Rangel, there are few castles in New Spain."

"Why," I asked, "do your men not fire the cannon?" I had heard no sounds of big guns since we had arrived in Dolores. The noise they made would be hard to miss.

"For the same reason we do not fire our muskets. We have little powder, certainly not enough to waste in drills."

One of the lieutenants said, "We will use our powder in Mexico City!"

"We will take our practice on the National Palace!" the other added.

Neither of the young officers looked older than Cristóbal, and both had his eager confidence. Their attitude reminded me of a thing Don Esteban often said: an army could be judged by its discipline and the enthusiasm of its officers. Scanning the field, I could see the evidence of discipline. And if these young officers were an indication, here was an army led by men not afraid to fight. All this spoke well for Captain Allende's leadership. It was too bad, I thought, his equipment was little more than what might be found in a scrapheap.

"Here we are," Captain Allende said when we reached the hut. I could hear the sounds of a billowed fire and smell the aroma of burning wood, indications that we were at the blacksmith shop. "Sergeant Guerra?"

The sergeant stepped outside and saluted his captain. Lebe Seru followed and also executed a crisp salute. Captain Allende wished Coalter a continued recovery and excused himself. The lieutenants hurried after their leader who was already on his way back to the drill field.

Lebe Seru and Sergeant Guerra expressed their pleasure that I appeared to have fully recovered. I wanted to get on with why I had come to visit, but before I could begin, Coalter, who had been staring at the ground, looked at Lebe Seru and said, "I want to thank you for what you did. You saved my life."

Folding his arms, Lebe Seru scanned the field where the soldiers were drilling. He said nothing.

Coalter was struggling for words, and I realized there was a tension between these two men, one of whom had been forced to be a slave in the other's country. After clearing his throat, Coalter said, "Carmen told me that your name is Lebe Seru."

"That is right," the African said as he finally looked at Coalter. "My name is Lebe Seru."

"I would like..." Coalter began and stopped. "I would like, if I may, to apologize to you...Lebe Seru. I would like to apologize for not knowing your name."

Lebe Seru placed his hand on Coalter's shoulder and gave him a gentle shake. What was conveyed by the gesture meant much, I think, to Coalter.

I glanced inside the hut and could see that they had been working on the repair of muskets. Several dozen in various stages of disassembly lay on worktables. "I did not know you are a blacksmith, Lebe Seru," I said.

"Lebe Seru is a very good blacksmith," Sergeant Guerra said warmly. He was not wearing his hat, and I saw more clearly in the daylight the unusual marks on his forehead, the marks I had noticed when Lebe Seru had brought him to my room that first day after our arrival. Again, I tried not to stare.

"My people in Africa," Lebe Seru said, "are wellknown for their metalwork. My father was a *dyemme na*, one who practices the craft of metalwork." We stepped away from the heat coming through the open door and walked past another hut from which came the sounds of hammering. Inside, I saw men working on carriage wheels. "But Carmen, you and Coalter did not come to watch us repair broken muskets."

Deciding it best to speak directly, I said, "We want you to go back with us to Guanajuato, Lebe Seru. As soon as Coalter has regained his strength, we are going back and we want you to come with us."

Lebe Seru rubbed his chin with his fingertips. "You wish to find your people."

I told him I did and then explained what we intended to do to Humberto, Barnet and Riaño. "Come with us, Lebe Seru. Kill Barnet for how you have been treated."

The African walked away a few steps and looked again across the field at the soldiers. "Carmen, do you not think I have had the opportunity many times to kill Barnet?" Before I could respond, he turned to face me. "I would have done it if it would have ended slavery."

"If you kill Barnet, there will be no slave trade in New Spain. That is what you said you wanted to stop. That is why you helped me."

He looked at Coalter. "Coalter can tell you there are many more men like Barnet, Carmen. If he is killed others will take his place. The lands in the northern provinces of New Spain are rich, and the profits in slavery would be very great. Others will come if Barnet does not succeed. The only way to prevent men like Barnet from bringing slaves to New Spain is to make a government in which laws are written that guarantee liberty for all people. That is what Father Miguel wishes to do, Carmen. That is why I have joined Captain Allende's army."

"Laws will do no good," I said. "There are laws against slavery in the Viceroyalty today. What good will—"

"Señorita Rangel," Sergeant Guerra interrupted. He had stood by silently while we spoke. "Please excuse me, but there are no laws against slavery in New Spain."

My inclination was to tell him there were, but since I really did not know and his tone was one of certainty, I was willing to concede the point. "Perhaps not, Sergeant, but there are no slaves. There will be if we do not act to stop what is being planned by this man Barnet."

"No slaves, Señorita?" He glanced at Lebe Seru and then back at me. He raised his hand and touched his forehead. "See this, Señorita? You are too polite to stare. I do not mind. Do you see these scars? Look at them."

I looked at the thick welts of scarred tissue on his head. Portions of his hair were missing above his forehead. I had never seen anything like it.

"Do you know what a trumpline is, Señorita? Have you ever seen one? No? It is a harness, a leather harness, except it is made for a man to wear, not a horse or an ox. It is fitted around the chest, and a strap is placed over the front of the man's head. To the back of this harness is attached a sack. For many years I was made to wear a trumpline, from before dawn until after dark. And the sack, it was filled with rocks in the mines, and I was made to take those rocks out of the mines where I dumped them only to return for another load. I was made to do this all day, every day for twenty years. It was the trumpline that gave me these scars."

Lebe Seru lowered his head.

"Yes, Señorita Rangel," the sergeant continued, "I was a slave. When the people of my village could not pay the *encomienda*, the man who owned the fields sent soldiers to our village, and they took the men and the boys to work in his mines. There was a priest in our village who went to the intendant to ask him to make the landowner let us go. But the intendant said there was no law against slavery in New Spain. He said *indios* have been made to labor for the *gachupines* since the time of Cortés."

Though I had never heard of such things happening, I had no reason to doubt the sergeant's words. And the scars on his head seemed to be proof of what he was saying. When he did not continue, I asked, "Were you allowed to go home when the *encomienda* was paid?"

"No one was ever allowed to go home. I escaped because one night the men who were supposed to keep us from running away became drunk. When they fell asleep, we ran away. It was then I heard of Father Miguel and joined Captain Allende's army." He stood up. "And now, if you will excuse me, Señorita Rangel, I must return to our tasks."

I watched the sergeant walk to the blacksmith shop. Of all people, he should have understood what I wanted to do and why. He should have been anxious to go with me to Guanajuato and mete out punishment. If someone had made me wear a trumpline for twenty years until it wore the hair off my head, I would not rest until that person was dead. I turned to the African and pleaded one more time, "Lebe Seru, go with us."

"Carmen," he said, "what was done to you was bad but killing the men who did it will solve nothing."

"It could prevent this slavery."

"There are many kinds of slavery," he said and looked at Coalter. "Not all slaves are in chains."

I did not know what he meant by that.

"Carmen," Lebe Seru said, "Miguel Hidalgo is a man of rare wisdom. Let us follow him. He will help us put an end to slavery in all its forms. Follow him, Carmen. He will show us the way to freedom."

✦

That evening after dinner, I went to my room to think. I was not at all happy that Lebe Seru had not volunteered to return with us to Guanajuato, and I needed to consider how that might affect my plan. It was growing dark so I lit the beeswax candle on the table next to my cot. As I stared at the flame, I began to ponder the advisability of returning to my original plan of going to the capital and telling Don Esteban what had happened. He would know what to do about Humberto, Barnet, and Riaño. This was, I realized, probably the more realistic course of action, but I wanted to settle accounts with Humberto on my own. If I did not pay him back for what he had tried to do, I suspected I would never be able to hold my head up again.

I heard the noise of people outside. It was too late for the children to be playing, so I went to the window to take a look. In the plaza I saw the yellow glow of lights from lanterns. People were gathering there. I heard the sound of guitars and violins. They were having a fiesta. Girls in brightly colored dresses with flowers in their hair were dancing. Some were the women soldiers I had seen earlier on the drill field. They were swirling about, making their skirts sway from one side to the other. What foolishness, I thought. Soldiers should not be doing such things. I watched them for a short while and decided to return to my cot. I had more important things to think about. No sooner had I sat down then there was a soft knock at the door.

"Yes?" I said, thinking it might be Alamar. She was always bringing me things to eat because she thought I was too thin.

The door opened and Coalter peeked in. "Carmen?" he asked. "Are you awake? I hope I am not disturbing you."

He looked quite handsome in the blue silk shirt the *comadres* had made for him, a present he received just that afternoon. I told him he was not disturbing me. "In fact," I said, "we need to talk more about our plan to return to Guanajuato."

He stepped into the room. "Is it possible that it could wait until tomorrow?" He nodded toward the window. "The people of Dolores are having a celebration. I thought you would like to go."

When I glanced out the window, I happened to notice Lebe Seru with Sergeant Guerra. They were talking with Captain Allende and several other soldiers. If I could talk to Lebe Seru one more time, I was sure I could convince him to go with us to Guanajuato, I thought. I might even convince Sergeant Guerra. Therefore, I told Coalter we could go to the fiesta for a short while.

He said it was cool outside and picked up my shawl from the bed and wrapped it around my shoulders before we left the room.

The night was more than cool. It was turning cold, and there was a mist in the air. We entered the square just as the music stopped, and all eyes were focused on us. I was not born yesterday, so I knew what these people with their grins and knowing looks were thinking. They assumed that since Coalter and I had come together to the fiesta, he was my escort. This usually meant a man and a woman were more than just friends.

Before long, the musicians began to play again. It was a group of about a dozen or so young students with violins, mandolins, tambourines, and a variety of guitars. They were dressed alike in black jackets and knee breeches. They wore white stockings. Brightly colored green, red, and white ribbons were pinned to their sleeves and flashed wildly as they vigorously played their instruments.

Soon, people started to dance. Every person in Dolores must have been in the plaza, including all of Captain Allende's soldiers. They were dancing or joking and laughing with the *comadres*. The old women in turn went about offering sweets to everyone there. Children were running in every direction, eating and playing games.

And then people began to clap their hands as Father Hidalgo stepped to the dance area and joined in a promenade. The *caballeros* and señoritas moved back to make room for him to join in a jig with Alamar. Father Hidalgo was as light on his feet as the young people, and Alamar was quite agile in her turn considering her heftiness. After the dance, Father Hidalgo borrowed one of the students' violins, leading the musicians in a fast-paced polka as couples rushed once again to dance.

I looked at Coalter. "Do you dance?"

Because of the noise, I had to repeat my question. He smiled and said, "Yes. Do you?"

"No," I admitted. "Cristóbal and I never had—"

Before I could explain that Cristóbal and I had never had time for such nonsense, he had taken my arm. "I'll teach you!"

Not wanting to appear a complete goose, I watched some of the other girls and tried to imitate how they jumped about holding the hem of their dresses off the floor. It seemed to me we must have looked like donkeys hopping about on one foot and then another, spinning around and around. However, it was not an entirely unpleasant thing to do.

Eventually, the music stopped and the dancers, myself included, were ready to take a rest. Coalter escorted me to a stone bench at the edge of the plaza.

After we sat down, he asked, "Did you go to fiestas in Guanajuato, Carmen?"

"Cristóbal and I had more important things to do."

He smiled and studied his hands for a moment, but he said nothing.

"And you?" I asked. "You seem to be very good at this dancing. You must have had much experience at it. I suppose you and your fiancee went to many dances. Yes?"

His smile faded.

"What is her name?" I asked. I was not interested, but at such times one is expected to make conversation.

At first, he seemed not inclined to answer. Finally, he looked at me and said, "Her name is Rhoda."

Some of the people were starting to drift away from the plaza. Families were strolling up the streets to the rows of houses. The *comadres* were attempting to coax the children to the parish house. Young men and women, reluctant to leave, remained in the square, quietly talking.

"Have you known her long?" I asked when it was apparent he was not going to volunteer more information.

"Since we were children. My father sometimes worked for her father when times were difficult. Rhoda's father is the one who would provide the financing for the colony we wished to establish in Texas."

"I see."

Before I could ask another question, he said, "I know nothing of you, Carmen. Your father is a captain in the Royal Dragoons. He went with Cristóbal to Spain. I know that. But what of your mother? You never speak of her. Where does she live? Is she—"

"My mother died when I was a baby."

"Was she an *india*?"

I nodded, though I was not at all sure I liked being asked questions about my mother.

The smile returned to his lips. "She must have been very beautiful."

I rose from the bench. I did not want to talk about my mother. "It is getting cold. We had better return to the house."

We had taken only a few steps when I heard a faint rumbling noise. "Listen."

Coalter turned in the direction of the sound. "Thunder?"

"No. Horses. Riders are coming this way."

We were not the only ones to notice the noise, which was rapidly growing louder. A short distance from where we were, Lebe Seru called to other soldiers who were still in the plaza. Several of them ran to notify Captain Allende who had already departed with his wife and children. We walked quickly to where Lebe Seru was standing.

Shortly afterwards, soldiers were running from the barracks with their muskets. Sergeant Guerra came with two guns handing one to Lebe Seru. "How many riders?"

"Two," Lebe Seru said. "Perhaps three."

Suddenly, emerging from the darkness, a man on horseback raced into the plaza and reined his mount to an abrupt halt. He was followed by a second horseman and then a third. Foam dripped from the horses' nostrils and white lather covered their coats. They had been ridden hard. Seeing a dozen muskets aimed at them, the first man shouted, "Don't shoot! I am a friend!"

Captain Allende and his lieutenants came running to the plaza. "Lower your weapons," he ordered. "I know these men. They are with us."

The third horseman was in a priest's garb. The other two were both wearing frock coats and knee-boots. All were having a problem bringing their horses to bay. Finally, with the help of soldiers who held the reins, they were able to dismount and, in haste, follow Captain Allende and his officers to the parish house. Father Hidalgo was at the doorway, and after embracing each, he escorted them inside.

Lebe Seru asked, "Do you know who they are?"

"Yes," Sergeant Guerra answered. "The priest is Father Miguel's brother, Mariano Hidalgo. The others are Juan Aldama and Ignacio Pérez, both friends of Captain Allende. Señor Pérez is the Chief Magistrate of Querétaro Province. Something must have happened, something important."

It surprised me that one of the men was a Chief Magistrate. I had no idea Father Hidalgo's supporters included officials of the government of New Spain.

We walked to the parish house. Gradually, people who had retired to their homes joined us, and it was not long before everyone who had been at the fiesta gathered in the area between the house and the church. Each new arrival inquired about the riders and was told what little was known. Soldiers walked the riders' winded horses before taking them to the stables. Alamar came outside with nothing to report except that the men who had come were meeting with Father Hidalgo and Captain Allende.

Presently, Father Hidalgo emerged from the house, followed by Captain Allende and the other men. He paused a moment in the doorway to survey the crowd and then walked slowly across the yard to the steps leading to the front door of the church. He climbed to the top step and turned to look down at the up-turned faces. Torches had been lit making a hissing noise as droplets of the night's mist fell upon the flames. Finally, he said, "My children, the time has come."

Alamar bowed her head.

"We have received news," Father Hidalgo continued, "that Viceroy Villegas has ordered Intendant Riaño to dispatch troops from the garrison at Guanajuato to Dolores." The people whispered to one another, and the priest waited until they were silent. "We had hoped to hold a constitutional assembly before the end of the year. Already, representatives throughout New Spain have been elected to attend the assembly. Many have sent messages directing me to establish a provisional government. Acting on that authority, I do hereby proclaim that government.

"My first act will be to send messages to all duly elected representatives throughout New Spain ordering that they proceed to Mexico City where they will convene to write a constitution for the people of Mexico. In order to guarantee that the constituent assembly be able to discharge its duty, I am hereby establishing an army whose mission it will be to protect the constituent assembly. I name Ignacio Allende general of that army."

At this announcement, the soldiers in the crowd began to cheer. Father Hidalgo gestured for his newly appointed general to join him on the steps of the church. Allende signaled for his men to be silent.

"My children," Father Hidalgo said. "We must bring an end to bad government. Will you follow me?"

"Yes!" the people around the church shouted.

The priest cried, "Long live liberty, equality, and justice!"

The people responded, "Long live liberty, equality, and justice!"

Immediately, General Allende began to issue orders. The soldiers were told to return to the barracks, pack their gear, and prepare to depart Dolores within the hour. "Our destination," he said, "is Guanajuato!"

People scurried off in every direction. I stood at Coalter's side, stunned for a moment and not at all certain of what I had just witnessed. Only the king's regent could establish an army and commission officers. Miguel Hidalgo was exercising the power of the viceroy.

I looked at Coalter. "Did you hear what Allende said? They are going to Guanajuato."

"Carmen," he said as I turned to leave, "what are you planning to do?"

Those carrying torches had departed. "We must go and pack our things. We are going with them. We are going to Guanajuato." In the darkness I could barely see his face. "The time for our revenge is at hand!"

V

During the night, General Allende's army negotiated the narrow lanes separating the fields of maize south of Dolores and finally advanced into open country. In the darkness it was difficult to see more than a few feet in any direction, but the noise conveyed that we constituted an army of considerable size on the march. There was the clang of metal against metal, the rumble of caissons groaning beneath their heavy loads, the squeak of leather harnesses, and the tromping of feet upon the hard earth. Sergeants barked commands, and from time to time, soldiers would break into a marching song or shout playfully to one another up and down the line. It was something I had never experienced except vicariously from the books Cristóbal and I had read. It was easy to envision ourselves as soldiers in Alexander's brave hosts off to conquer Asia.

For the moment, I was able to overlook the fact that this was a rebel army, that it was led by men who had openly proclaimed their opposition to the viceroy of New Spain and intended to usurp his authority. All I knew, all I needed to know, was this army, whatever the intentions of those who led it, was on its way to engage the garrison under the command of Juan Riaño. That Riaño was the duly appointed intendant of Guanajuato no longer mattered to me. I did not care. He would pay for what he had done to Rubén as would Barnet for what he had done to Coalter. And Humberto would pay for what he did to me. They would pay with their lives. I may not have shared a common purpose with this army of revolutionaries, but we

122

had a common enemy, and for the present, that was all that mattered.

At dawn, wispy clouds on the eastern horizon glowed a pale red, and the jagged, blue peaks of the Sierra Madre loomed on the horizon. With the light of day, what I saw seemed different from what I had heard in the night. It was true that what was descending from the foothills of the great mountain range was an army. It was less than an army, however, because of its size and weaponry. There were no more than four hundred soldiers in uniform, and I knew for a fact that there were three times that number in the garrison at Guanajuato and that their troops were not equipped with discarded muskets and cannons so ancient the tubes might explode when fired.

Still in the light of day I could also perceive that we were more than an army because trailing behind the soldiers—as well as ahead of them and among them—were the townspeople of Dolores. Under the direction of Alamar, the grey-haired *comadres* distributed bread and cups of milk or juice to one and all. Running and screaming as if they were back at their playground at home, the children from the parish house scampered in and out among the gun carriages in games of hide-and-seek. The band of student musicians, still carrying their instruments, were walking together, chatting amongst themselves or with the soldiers, with the *comadres*, with the children, with Father Hidalgo, with anybody and everybody. It was as if the fiesta of the night before had not ended but had simply moved down the road. What kind of army, I wondered, included old women, little children, and school students who played violins and guitars.

When a *pan dulce*, a sweet roll, was slipped into my hand, I turned to thank the person I assumed was Alamar. But what I saw by my side was the small form and the large dark eyes of Lupita. "What are you doing here?" I cried out to her.

There was, of course, no answer.

I caught up with Coalter, who was a few steps ahead, and said, "Coalter, look. Lupita has followed us."

He glanced back and smiled.

"Lupita," I repeated, "has followed us. She must be sent back to Dolores. An army marching into battle is no place for a little girl!"

"Who is there in Dolores to look after her, Carmen?" he pointed out patiently.

His point was welltaken. I had begun to wonder if anyone had remained in Dolores. And, as the morning progressed, it was evident that few were being left behind in the surrounding countryside as people along the way joined our ranks. They came in small groups: five or six, a dozen, sometimes more. There were men and women, children, the young and the old. Somehow, the word of what had been spoken on the steps of the church at Dolores—Father Hidalgo's *grito*, his cry for freedom—was spreading. With each new arrival there were shouts of greeting, much embracing, and cries of "Long live liberty!"

And though few who joined us carried muskets, each had something in his or her hands that would, I suppose, qualify as a weapon. Most commonly they brought a machete, the short flat-bladed sword that was the *ranchero's* most important tool for clearing brush and cactus or preparing firewood. Others carried shovels, pitchforks, and axes. By noon our ranks had expanded to at least twice the number that had left Dolores. The soldiers in uniform were almost lost among the people in the white cotton garments of the peasant farmers. Some who came to us brought along ropes, and soon, dozens of men and women joined the soldiers on the lines attached to the gun carriages to help the mules pull them up the hills or brake their descent as they made it down the other side.

At a mountain stream General Allende called a halt so that we could eat. The women had brought along more than enough, and all shared from the bowls of rice and beans, tortillas, cheeses, fruits, and juice. Coalter, Lupita, and I ate with a group of soldiers that included Lebe Seru and Sergeant Guerra—Sergeant Guerra who by now had been promoted to Lieutenant Guerra. General Allende had been reorganizing his army and assigning promotions even as they marched. In the colonial army, a man like Lieutenant Guerra, an *indio*, could never have become an officer. This was not the case among the new order that hoped to replace the Viceroyalty.

This new order, however, encompassed a variety of viewpoints. Lieutenant Guerra said New Spain had declared its independence from Spain and was now the Republic of Mexico. Alamar, who joined us briefly to offer freshly prepared tortillas, said that independence had not yet been declared and that Father Hidalgo had done no more than call for a constitutional assembly, which would decide the future of the colony now that Joseph Bonaparte was king of Spain. Some of the soldiers sided with Lieutenant Guerra and others with Alamar. The only point upon which there was agreement was the need to end the corrupt government of the viceroy and his intendants. I listened in silence to the discussion and wondered what all this might mean when Cristóbal returned with Prince Fernando de Borbón, the man Don Esteban had chosen to be the first king of New Spain.

Following lunch, Lebe Seru and Lieutenant Guerra set about to repair a broken wheel on one of the caissons. Coalter and I went with Lupita downstream to wash the utensils used in the preparation of the meal. On the way we passed a stand of cottonwoods under which Father Hidalgo was meeting with General Allende and other leaders of the insurrection. Mariano Hidalgo was there along with Juan Aldamo and Ignacio Pérez. Father Hidalgo smiled and waved when we walked past. I noticed Coalter was somberfaced. Everyone else appeared jubilant and excited as preparations were made to resume the advance upon Guanajuato. Some were even singing, and the students were gaily playing their instruments. "Coalter," I asked, "what's wrong? Is it your wound? Is it bothering you?"

He stopped and shook his head. "Do you know what will happen if what was begun in Dolores last night fails, Carmen?"

"Fails?"

"If Father Miguel fails in what he is doing, do you realize what will happen to him? He will be stood before a firing squad and shot."

I glanced back at the white-haired priest standing serenely among the men now waving their arms and shouting at one another in vigorous debate. And then I looked again at Coalter. "Why would you care what happens to Miguel Hidalgo? This is not your country. Why should what happens in New Spain be of concern to you?"

"Last night, Father Miguel spoke of liberty and equality. When my father was a young man, he fought in the revolution against England. He told me he fought for liberty and equality. Until now, they were just words to me, but I think I am beginning to understand what they mean. I don't think it matters in what country you happen to be. It is liberty and equality that are important." He looked again at the leaders before we continued on our way to the stream. "Father Miguel is a brave man. He is risking his life so that the people of Mexico can enjoy freedom."

What he said about his father troubled me. Don Esteban had said that the most terrible thing men could do was to overthrow their kings. "Your father was a revolutionary?"

"Yes," he said as he knelt at the edge of the stream to begin the cleaning of the pots we had carried. "My father was in the army led by General Washington."

Though Coalter's words disturbed me, I began to realize it was not so much what he had told me about his father that was of concern, but his statement that Miguel Hidalgo would be stood before a firing squad if he failed. I was not at all certain of what this priest was attempting to do, but I knew that whatever it was, it was doomed to failure. I wondered why I should care what happened to Miguel Hidalgo. He was a republican and probably should be shot. Quickly, I returned to our task when one of the buglers signaled the order to assemble for march.

✦

Sometime in the late afternoon, I realized we were not moving in the direction of Guanajuato. We had traveled far enough that I was beginning to recognize certain peaks in the Sierra Madre as familiar landmarks. By then I realized that we were moving in a direction away from my home. Had it not been a matter of such importance, I might have laughed. These people planned to supplant the viceroy's government, and they did not even know the way to Guanajuato.

"Coalter," I said, "this is not the way we should be going."

"Are you sure?"

"Of course, I'm sure!" I quickened our pace until we caught up with Lieutenant Guerra and Lebe Seru and told them of my concern. Before either could speak, I raised my hand and pointed. "Look! On the hill!"

Men had suddenly appeared on the crest of a hill we were approaching. There were a hundred or more on horseback; they were in red and blue uniforms and wore low-crown, flat-brimmed sombreros. Juan Riaño's soldiers had found us!

As the riders spurred their horses to a gallop down the hill, I looked about to see what General Allende was doing and, to my astonishment, discovered he was doing exactly what I was: watching the horsemen as they descended the hill. The artillery needed to be positioned, anchored, and powder packed into the tubes, I realized. The musketeers and grenadiers should have been assuming ranks and loading charges into their weapons. There was no time to lose. But Allende was doing nothing, absolutely nothing.

Again, I looked up the hill. Behind the line of dragoons was the infantry. They were running behind the riders and I could see that each carried a spontoon or a halberd. The spontoons were lances seven feet in length, tipped with thin blades a foot and a half long. Halberds were also lances, but were shorter than a spontoon and were mounted with crescent-shaped ax blades. In the hands of soldiers who knew how to use them, these weapons were deadly in close fighting. If nothing was done to break their advance they would be upon us in a matter of seconds, and we would be like sheep in the slaughter pen. And still, Allende was doing nothing.

"Lieutenant Guerra!" I cried, but even he did not seem alarmed by what was happening. I started toward General Allende. He had to take some action immediately or we would be doomed.

Grasping my arm, Lieutenant Guerra held me back. "Carmen," he said. "There is no danger."

Behind the infantry, more people were coming over the hill, among them women and children. All were yelling. The people on our side had begun to run forward, straight toward the cavalry and they, too, were shouting. But on both sides, the cries were not those of battle; they were the joyful sounds of greeting. When the men on horseback drew near, they jumped from their mounts and ran to embrace Allende's soldiers who were running to meet them. Everyone was smiling or laughing, eager to embrace those coming down the hill. On the spontoons and halberds were green and white and red streamers, and they were being waved like flags in celebration. Despite their protests, Father Hidalgo and General Allende were lifted to the shoulders of some of the soldiers who had come down the hill.

"It is the people of Atotonilco," Lieutenant Guerra explained. "Their village is just beyond that hill. They have come to welcome us!"

We entered Atotonilco as if we were Caesar's army returning to Rome after the conquest of Gaul. Our arrival had come as no surprise. The news of what had happened in Dolores had preceded us. The contingent of dragoons and infantry garrisoned at this village were eager to join General Allende's army, and their officers were prepared to serve under his command. The village priest embraced Father Hidalgo as if he were his long lost brother. It was evident his sympathies were with the insurrection being mounted against the government of the viceroy. The bells of the small church on the plaza rang as people continued to embrace one another and celebrate.

Soon, there were shouts of "Long live liberty!" and more people joined in the cry of, "Long live Hidalgo!" And then, some in the crowd took up the chant of, "Long live Hidalgo, King of Mexico!" Everyone— the people of Dolores, those who had joined us on the way, and the people of Atotonilco—took up this chant, shouting again and again, *"¡Viva Hidalgo, rey de México!"*

Father Hidalgo stood on the steps of the church and raised his hands to silence them, but they only shouted louder.

Alamar joined Coalter and me at the edge of the crowd, which now filled the town plaza. Coalter held Lupita on his shoulders so she could see. Alamar was distraught over what the people were saying.

"They do not understand," she said. It was almost impossible to hear her over the noise. "It is liberty we seek, not another king. Father Miguel did not take the action he has so that he can become a king."

Finally, after failing to quiet the crowd, Father Hidalgo entered the little church, which, like his own church in Dolores, was facing the village square. The chant grew louder. The people were in accord. They wanted Miguel Hidalgo as their king. If they had a crown, they would have forced it upon his head right then and there.

Suddenly, there was a hush. All shouting came to an abrupt halt. At first I did not understand what had happened. People near the church began to kneel and make the sign of the cross. And then I saw that Father Hidalgo had returned to the steps of the church and was holding aloft a pole upon which was mounted a banner. Embroidered on the banner in blue and reddishbrown pastels was the image of the Virgin of Guadalupe. Everyone in the plaza knelt, and those wearing sombreros removed them.

I touched Coalter's arm for him to lower Lupita to the ground. Though he complied quickly, I could see from his puzzled expression he did not understand the significance of the banner. In a whisper, I told him of how the Virgin was said to have appeared to an *indio*, Juan Diego, in 1531 at a place called Tepeyac Hill near Mexico City. She expressed to him her wish that a church be built on the hill. So that the bishop would believe his story, the Virgin caused her image to be formed on flowers she had told Juan Diego to gather in his serape. He showed the image to the bishop and they built the church. Since that time, the Virgin of Guadalupe has been considered to be the protectress of the *indios*. I explained this to Coalter so he would know why the people became silent.

"My children," the priest said, "do not ask for Miguel Hidalgo to become your king. Invoke the name of the Holy Mother of the only true King. She is the one to lead us to freedom!" He held the banner higher. "Stand fast, and do not be caught again under the yoke of slavery."

When Father Hidalgo finished speaking, General Allende mounted the steps, called for an assembly of his officers, and issued the order that we would spend the night at Atotonilco.

After the evening meal and after the utensils had been washed and put away, the people celebrated. Musicians from Atotonilco played their instruments joyfully for their guests from Dolores and the many surrounding villages. There was dancing and singing and everyone was of great cheer.

Coalter and I found a place to sit under a tree a short distance from the church where Lupita had gone to be near the banner of the Virgin of Guadalupe now mounted in front of the building. Other people came from time to time to kneel, cross themselves, and offer a prayer before returning to the festivities. I could see that Coalter was tired and that occasionally he would rub his hand across the place on his stomach where Barnet had thrust the knife. When I asked him if it hurt, he said it was just a bit sore after the day's march.

"I suppose," I said, "after we do what we must in Guanajuato, you will be ready to return to your home. You will return to Louisiana. Yes?"

"I suppose," he shrugged. He removed his sombrero and rubbed his face. The locks of his dark hair fell loosely around his ears. I remembered how soft they felt the times I touched them while he was asleep. "And you, Carmen? What will you do after Guanajuato?"

"I do not know." It was not something I had anticipated. My thoughts were focused on what I would do in Guanajuato. "I suppose I will wait for Don Esteban to return to the hacienda. Together, we will wait for Cristóbal's return with the king."

"And then you will be married."

"Yes," I said without hesitation. A lie becomes easier the more times it is told. "Cristóbal and I will marry." I located the North Star in the night sky. "And then we will go to Texas. That is what Cristóbal wishes to do."

Coalter smiled. "You will love Texas, Carmen. It is beautiful."

I rested my back against the tree trunk. "Cristóbal and I used to believe the northern provinces were nothing but desert. We thought Texas was a vast desert."

"It is far from being a desert," he said, and he began to describe Texas. He spoke of rolling hills and green valleys where crops could be grown, of great forests and rivers, rich and fertile plains. He told me all the things that could be planted in these lands. From his expression, I could see that he loved this place called Texas.

As Coalter talked on, describing things he had seen in Texas, an idea occurred to me. "Perhaps," I said, "Cristóbal and I can help you with your plan to establish a colony in Texas. We will secure permission from King Fernando for you to bring settlers to Texas. And then we shall build Texas into a mighty empire!"

At first, he seemed to like this idea. He smiled, but then he simply nodded his head as if he may have thought I was speaking of what could not be done or, worse, that I was a child making things up. "You and Cristóbal," he said without much enthusiasm, "want to make Texas into an empire?"

"Yes! We can do it together. Cristóbal and me. And you and...and Rhoda...after you are married. We could do it together. We could build an empire..."—my idea no longer seemed so good—"...together."

Coalter stared off into the darkness of the night. He seemed very far away. By speaking of his fiancee, I had reminded him of his home, and I saw the sadness in his eyes. I suspected he was thinking of the woman he left behind, and that bothered me though I knew it should not. He had a right to think about the world he had left behind.

And that was what it was, I thought, as I turned my eyes again to the sky. Coalter's was a whole different world from mine. He may as well have arrived from one of those stars sparkling above us. We came from two entirely different worlds. He had stumbled into mine, and soon, he would go back to his own.

That night we slept under the open sky which was yet another new experience for me. Never in my life had I so much as slept with another person in my room, and now I was in the midst of hundreds of people. Everyone used their shawl or serape as a wrap after finding a spot on the soft grass. I chose a place near Lupita who had placed her serape right next to Coalter's. She seemed to be quite attached to him. The little girl had no one to look after her. As long as she had made the mistake of coming along on this journey, I thought I might as well keep an eye on her. She might wake up frightened in the night, and I would be near to calm her.

It was not uncomfortable, sleeping on the ground. At first it was somewhat difficult to fall asleep because there were so many distractions. The children whispered and giggled far into the night even after the *comadres* told them to be quiet. General Allende posted guards, and I watched them patrol beyond where we slept. Some of them were smoking. Husbands and wives slept holding each other. Babies slept in their mother's arms. People, who had to attend to nature's call, would make their way to a designated area far away from the village. It was hard for me not to notice all the things that were going on.

When I finally dozed off, I woke up several times, disoriented, not certain where I was. Once, I must have said something because when I looked around to see if Lupita was all right, I found Coalter looking at me. He smiled, and I recovered my bearings. After a while, I moved my shawl closer to Lupita because it had turned cold.

✦

The next morning, the army broke camp before sunrise. At the head of the column, ahead of even Father Hidalgo and General Allende, a soldier marched proudly holding high the pole bearing the banner of Our Lady of Guadalupe. There were some who shouted "Long live Hidalgo" as the day's trek began, but none called him king anymore.

The army had more than doubled in size. It now included a contingent of some one hundred dragoons as well as three hundred infantry armed with spontoons and halberds. This number, however, was only those in uniform. As had been the case in Dolores, the people of Atotonilco—hundreds of men, women, and children—joined the march, and they too carried machetes, shovels, pitchforks, hoes, knifes, axes; anything that might be used as a weapon. And no sooner had we passed beyond the cultivated fields south of Atotonilco, than we were met by more peasant farmers ready to join the ranks of the insurrection. People even came from remote tribal villages in the mountains. They spoke in strange dialects and carried bows and arrows, spears, and slingshots.

Over the next several days, we continued on a southeasterly direction, well past the city of Guanajuato, before turning to the west and moving north. In village after village, the army was met with the same enthusiasm as had been demonstrated by the people of Atotonilco, Chamacuero, Apaseo, Celaya, Silao, Salamanca, Irapuato, Burras. The people in each of these towns hailed Father Hidalgo and General Allende as liberators. There was but isolated resistance. Some of the *criollo* officers in the village garrisons, as befit the first generation born in Mexico of Spanish parentage, did not care to join a revolution against the viceroy and his intendants, and so they did not volunteer to surrender their swords to General Allende. Their troops, however, were eager to cast their lot with an army led by officers, many of whom were, like themselves, *indios* and mestizos. The *criollo* officers who did not surrender were placed under arrest along with Spanish-born landowners who had failed to flee before the advance of the insurgent army.

Although impatient because of the delay in reaching Guanajuato, I understood General Allende's strategy. His wide maneuver around the city enabled him to build strength and train his citizen-soldiers for battle. There was a never-ending stream of new arrivals that included the thousands of men who toiled in the many gold and silver mines of the region. Gripping the picks and sledges that were the tools of their trade, the miners marched shoulder to shoulder with the peasant farmers who made up the bulk of the insurgent force. It seemed to me Intendant Riaño had committed a grave error in not taking the field to challenge Allende immediately after Father Hidalgo's proclamation against bad government. He had allowed himself to be surrounded by an army that now greatly outnumbered his own. In effect, his garrison was under siege.

Finally, General Allende began to move his soldiers into strategic locations on the hills above Guanajuato. He positioned his artillery in the narrow passes which were the only way in or out of the city. He knew exactly where to place his dragoons and cavalry so they would be most effective in the event Riaño's soldiers tried to escape or mount an attack. And the thousands of farmers and miners who had joined the insurgency were arranged behind the artillery and the musketeers. Watching the deployment proceed methodically like the moves of a chessmaster, I realized I had been correct in my initial assessment of Ignacio Allende. He was an outstanding commander, a supreme strategist whose skills my father would have admired.

✦

It was late in the morning when I rushed ahead of Coalter and Lupita up the hill upon which sat the Hacienda de Abrantes. Seeing it and the stable and the carriage house after so long a time, I had to pause. Part of me wanted to cry out in joy at the sight. Another part had to struggle against tears. It was my place of birth, the site of so many happy memories. I could almost see Cristóbal race across the yard pretending to be Alexander the Great charging up the hill to personally capture the Persian king, Darius. But I had no time for remembrances. The day of reckoning had come. I would soon settle accounts.

And then I saw people around the hacienda, many people. It was with a measure of disappointment that I soon recognized them as soldiers under Lieutenant Guerra's command. I saw Lebe Seru. The hacienda had already been secured. Humberto and Barnet, I assumed, were already dead or under arrest. For a moment, I was angry at Coalter. He was responsible for the fact that we were among the last to reach Guanajuato. On the way he had stopped to assist an insurgent dragoon whose mount had gone lame. Despite my protestations, he would not proceed until he had found something with which to bandage the horse's leg. And, since we were going to deal with Humberto and Barnet together, I had had to wait for him, even help to steady the horse while the wrap was applied.

My mind was engrossed in these annoying thoughts when suddenly something much more important occurred to me. "Teresa," I said and started racing towards the house. "Hortensia! Anselmo!"

We were met by Lebe Seru and Lieutenant Guerra. From their expressions, I knew something was wrong.

"Carmen," Lebe Seru said, "I am sorry to have to tell you but...your uncle is dead."

My legs grew weak and my hands began to tremble. My uncle was dead. Gentle Anselmo, who never hurt anyone and had created such beauty with his plants, was dead. All I could think about was that it was my fault. I should have made him and Hortensia and Teresa come with us that night. Or I should have stayed. I had failed in my duty to protect them.

"The servants told us," Lebe Seru explained, "that Humberto blamed your cousin for our escape. He caught her before they were able to follow us that night. She had just returned from burying

Rubén. Your uncle went to her defense. Barnet killed him. He cut his throat."

"Teresa?" I whispered. "And my aunt?"

"Teresa is in her room with her mother. She has been hurt very badly. She was beaten and..."—he closed his eyes—"...and raped." He looked down at Lupita. "Father Miguel is with her. He has asked that the small one come to Teresa's room."

"Humberto and Barnet; where are they?"

"The servants said they left for Mexico City when word reached Guanajuato of what happened in Dolores."

"And Riaño?"

Lieutenant Guerra said, "The intendant and his troops have barricaded themselves inside the granary."

I looked down into the city. There it was, like some great fortress: the Alhóndiga. So many times over the years I had looked down at that massive stone building where the city's supply of grains was stored. Cristóbal and I had pretended it was a great medieval fortress, and now a fortress was exactly what it had become. Lifting my gaze, I could see General Allende's army on the hills around Guanajuato. There were thousands of people on those hills, tens of thousands and more. Riaño was trapped. He would pay for what had happened. Humberto and Barnet would have to come later. First, it would be Riaño's turn.

"Carmen," Coalter reminded, "your cousin?"

In the hallway outside of Teresa's little room, we found my aunt standing with Father Hidalgo. I embraced Hortensia, and over her shoulder, I saw the sadness in the priest's eyes. He patted my hand, and looking down at the little girl, he asked, "Lupita, would you please come with me?"

Coalter and I remained in the corridor with Hortensia while Father Hidalgo and Lupita went into Teresa's room. "Tía," I whispered, "I am so sorry!"

For some moments, I tried to comfort her the best I could and then she stepped back. She managed a weak smile as she looked up at me and reached into her pocket to retrieve the pendant that had belonged to my mother. "I kept this for you, Carmencita." Her voice was weak. "It was Cata Valeria's. She wanted you to have it."

Of course, I was not going to refuse the jade pendant even though it struck me as odd Hortensia would think of it at that particular moment. I did not know if she remembered I had once refused to take it from her.

"Thank you, Tía," I said and took the pendant in my hand.

Brushing back the loose strands of her hair with her hands, Hortensia looked up at Coalter and smiled. "I had better get to the kitchen and prepare food. We have many guests."

When she turned to leave, I started to reach for her, but Coalter touched my arm. His eyes conveyed that it was best to let her go. I supposed it was, for I did not know what else to do or say.

As we stood alone in the hallway, I thought again of Humberto, Barnet, and Riaño. It angered me that I had allowed myself even for one moment to forget the revenge I would take on them. I remembered the night I danced in Dolores and the nights I sat with Coalter listening to the musicians in the villages we had come through. I had allowed myself to deviate from the one and only thing I must do. "They will pay for this, Coalter," I said. "They will pay with their lives!"

I started to say more about what I was going to do to them, but Father Hidalgo opened the door and said that Teresa wished to see me.

It was the saddest sight I had ever seen when we entered that room. I was almost unable to recognize Teresa. Her eyes were swollen and there were terrible cuts and dark bruises all over her face and arms. More than that, she seemed somehow smaller than I had remembered, sitting there at that little table where she had once so eagerly copied her books. She whispered my name and slowly raised her hands to me. I knelt, took her in my arms, and as I held her, I tried to think of what I should say. It would do no good for me to tell her she should have come with us, or I should have stayed. All that was too late, and it was not something she needed to hear. I started to tell her what I was going to do to those who had killed Rubén and her father, but even that did not seem appropriate.

We sat with Teresa for a long time in the room until she decided to lie down and rest. When we left, Lupita stayed.

Outside, aides to General Allende were waiting with a carriage to take Father Hidalgo to where a headquarters post had been established on a hill closer to the city. Before entering the carriage, the priest looked down at the jade pendant Hortensia had given me and that I now held in my hand. I had the leather cord on which it was strung wrapped around my fingers. He asked to see it, and after turning it over in his hands, inquired, "Do you know what this is, Carmen?"

"A pendant."

"A very old pendant." As he held it to the sun's light it seemed to glow as if the stone had ignited into a green fire. "This is a carving of Chimalma." He looked at Coalter. "Do you know about Chimalma, Coalter?"

"No, Father."

"Do you, Carmen?"

I had to admit that I did not, though I did not bother to add that I did not care. Obviously, he did.

"Chimalma," he explained, "means 'Shield Hand.' She was the protectress of the Toltec people." He returned the carved stone to me. "This pendant is very old, Carmen. See the cross beneath Chimalma's head? It is an ancient symbol for self-abnegation."

"Then it cannot be so very ancient," I said, looking at the stone really for the first time. "The *indios* have known of Christianity for less than three hundred years."

"The cross depicted here does not represent the Crucifix, Carmen. The Toltec Cross is older than the Crucifix."

I looked at the cross on the pendant. It was a series of dots arranged to form a cross.

"There was a Toltec civilization long before the Europeans came to this hemisphere," Father Hidalgo said. "The Spanish forbade the practice of the ancient religions. But many Mexicans continued practicing their old ways of worship along with Christianity. There are many similarities. Even today, you will find representations of Chimalma and of the Virgin side by side on altars in the homes of those who are descendants of the Toltecs."

I studied the pendant. The feathered headdress upon the goddess was carved in exquisite detail. For the first time, I noticed it was actually rather beautiful.

"Among the Toltecs," Father Hidalgo continued, looking at Coalter, "pendants of Chimalma were handed down from mother to daughter. They were given for protection."

After he climbed into the carriage and settled back, I asked, "Father Miguel, when will General Allende order the attack on the Alhóndiga?" The sooner I could deal with Riaño, the sooner would I be able to confront Humberto and Barnet. "It will be today?"

He looked in the direction of the city below. "We hope we will not have to attack the Alhóndiga, Carmen. We hope that Intendant Riaño will surrender."

"Surrender?" Even to hear the word infuriated me. "Riaño must not be allowed to surrender. He and his men must be put to the sword!"

"Many lives will be lost if we are forced to take the Alhóndiga by force, Carmen. The soldiers in the garrison have mounted their artillery on the roof and have trained their guns on a square we would have to cross to get to the doors."

"You have siege guns! Blast them out!"

"The walls," Coalter said, "are too thick for even General Allende's guns."

"Let us pray this will all be resolved peacefully," Father Hidalgo said and then signaled the driver he was ready. The carriage lurched forward and, surrounded by an escort of dragoons, made its way slowly toward the big gates to the estate.

Coalter and I walked to the stable only to discover that Humberto and Barnet had taken the horses with them to Mexico City. All that was left were four mules which Coalter proceeded to feed and water. While he attended to the animals, I returned to the hacienda and went to my room where the first thing I did was heat water and bathe, something I had been unable to do for days. And then I put on a pair of leather breeches, boots, and a cotton shirt. It felt good to get out of a dress and back into my own clothes. I selected a gun from the musket case and located my powder horn along with the leather pouch containing wadding and bullets. Never again would I be defenseless as I had been on that terrible night. The next time I met Humberto, Barnet, or Juan Riaño I would be prepared.

✦

For the next several days, Father Hidalgo sent emissaries to the Alhóndiga to entreat a surrender. Riaño refused to even open the doors to admit the insurgent delegations. Barricading his forces inside the granary was not turning out to be the fatal blunder I had at first believed it would be. Coalter was right. The walls were too thick for General Allende's siege guns, and the doors to the building faced an open courtyard which was an easy target for the artillery on the roof. Before our arrival, the garrison had stocked the massive structure with provisions. The troops, and the Spanish-born citizens of Guanajuato who had entered the Alhóndiga with them, could hold out for months if necessary.

Lieutenant Guerra, whose troops camped on the grounds of Hacienda de Abrantes, attended General Allende's daily staff meetings. These often lasted long into the night. When he returned, his soldiers were eager to hear his report of what was being planned. I always went with Coalter and Lebe Seru to listen to what he had to say.

A difference of opinion as to how to proceed had developed between Father Hidalgo and General Allende. Father Hidalgo wanted to continue the siege. Hundreds more people were arriving each day to take up positions on the hills, and he thought this fact would make Riaño realize he did not stand a chance. He would consequently surrender. General Allende said Riaño was holding out until troops from the capital arrived. It would be better, he argued, to have a victory at Guanajuato before taking on the viceroy's army. Winning control of the second largest city in New Spain, he said, might persuade Viceroy Venegas to recognize the right to convene a constitutional convention.

While the stand-off continued, I busied myself with supervising the servants in maintaining the estate, which I saw as my responsibility in Don Esteban's absence. Hortensia prepared meals for the soldiers who were encamped on the grounds. The storehouses and granaries at the hacienda were wellstocked with sacks of grains, beans, sugar, and many other provisions. There was more than enough for Lieutenant Guerra's soldiers. Every other day or so, Coalter and I loaded the supply wagon and drove it to Alamar who was in charge of preparing meals at the headquarters camp. Sharing the food was a way of repaying my debt for what had been done for me in Dolores.

Alamar always thanked me for the foodstuffs and, when she had more than she needed, directed us to other camps where food might be in short supply. On these excursions, I was able to show Coalter the countryside around Guanajuato, including the mines that belonged to the Marqués. He was more interested in some of the farmlands that had been irrigated by a system of dams and aqueducts built in ancient times by the *indios*.

One evening, upon returning from the camps, we went to Teresa's room where we found her sitting in the chair at her desk while Lupita braided her hair. The swelling had gone down around her eyes and the cuts and scratches were almost healed. We visited awhile, and then Coalter said he was tired and thought he would turn in for the night. Though I had several times told him he could use one of the many guest rooms, he had chosen to sleep outside with Lieutenant Guerra and his soldiers. They all slept outside even though I had placed the hacienda at their disposal. Before Coalter left, I told Lupita I would stay with Teresa if she would care to go outside for a while. The little girl had been cooped up inside all day.

"She is an unusual child," Teresa said after Lupita and Coalter had left. "What do you know about her?"

I told her what Father Hidalgo had said about Lupita when we were in Dolores.

"There is something very unusual about her." Rising slowly from the chair, Teresa walked to the window. She limped, but at least she was able to walk. For a few minutes she looked outside before she asked, "You like Father Miguel, don't you, Carmen?"

"It would be difficult not to like Father Miguel."

She smiled, the first time I had seen her smile since my return. "Has my cousin become a republican?"

"No, Teresa, I have not become a republican."

"Then why are you still here? Why have you not gone to Mexico City to be with Don Esteban?"

"I have not gone because I want to see the man who killed Rubén die just as I want to see Humberto and Barnet die for what they did to me and for what they did to your father. Is that not what you want?"

She sat down in the chair and placed her hands on the table. "No," she said finally. "That is not what I want."

"You don't want to kill the men who did this to you?" It was not something I could comprehend. "Then what is it you want, Teresa? Tell me."

"What I want is for what happened to me and to you, to my father and to Rubén..."—she bowed her head—"...I want what happened to all of us to never happen to anyone else."

"It won't if we kill the men who did these things."

She shook her head. "It will happen again and again, Carmen. Other men will do similar things to other people unless we have a constitution that guarantees the rights of all people. We must have a government that is chosen by the people and serves all of the people, the weak and the strong. These are the things Father Miguel is trying to achieve for Mexico. If we simply kill those who have wronged us and do it only to satisfy our desire for revenge, then we are the same as Riaño or Humberto and the *norteamericano* called Barnet."

Teresa had been hurt badly. She was tired and was not thinking clearly. In time, I was certain, she would feel as I did. She would want her revenge. It was only natural.

"You need to get some sleep," I said smiling. "I'll come back in the morning."

✦

That night I was awakened by the sound of noise in the yard. For a terrible instant, I remembered when Riaño and his soldiers came to the hacienda to execute Rubén. Was it possible it was happening again? Maybe while I slept General Allende had been defeated and now Juan Riaño was coming for me. Rushing to the window, I looked down into the yard, and when my eyes adjusted to the darkness I saw that Lieutenant Guerra's soldiers were moving the artillery. They were preparing to leave. Quickly I dressed, grabbed my musket, and ran outside.

It was dark and no one held a lantern or torch. It was a few moments before I located Lebe Seru. He was hurriedly working to repair one of the gun carriages that had just collapsed. I asked him what was happening.

"General Allende has issued the order to take the Alhóndiga. He convinced Father Hidalgo that it was necessary."

Knowing that Teresa and Hortensia must have heard the commotion and might be alarmed, I went back inside to tell them the time had come and that I was going with the army. They tried to convince me to remain at the hacienda. I told Lupita to stay with Teresa and her mother and returned to the yard where I found Coalter helping to harness a team of mules to a wagon containing kegs of gunpowder.

I asked, "Are you ready?"

He looked at the musket in my hands. "Carmen, you cannot go down there."

"It is why we came. If you do not wish to go with me, that is your choice." I turned to join the soldiers moving toward the road leading to Guanajuato.

Coalter caught up with me. "Carmen, you could be killed!"

I ignored his pleas to return to the hacienda as we continued to the road and began the slow descent toward the city. I refused to listen to what he said. All I knew was that somewhere in that darkened valley, in the city, inside the Alhóndiga, was Juan Riaño. He and I had something to settle. I would not be denied.

Lieutenant Guerra passed along General Allende's order that there were to be no lanterns or torches. We would enter the city under the cover of darkness. We were to be as quiet as possible, speaking to no one as we advanced. It was a strange sensation. I could not see the thousands of people silently streaming down the hills to converge on all sides of Guanajuato, but I could feel their presence. I could feel it as surely as I felt my own heart pounding harder and harder in my chest. Though we were for the most part strangers to one another, we shared the same resolve and drew from each other's strength. It was at once something both wonderful and frightening.

When Lieutenant Guerra's soldiers entered the streets at the edge of town, we merged with other units converging from all directions and quickly moved toward the center of the city where the Alhóndiga loomed. It was not long before soldiers in the granary detected the sounds of gun carriages being wheeled up the cobblestone streets and began to fire from positions on the roof. At first there was only the isolated crack of musket fire. The soldiers were firing blindly at the noises. And then they began to use their artillery, lighting up the sky to reveal what must have been to them a terrifying sight: twenty thousand people, most carrying machetes, surrounding them, moving ever closer.

At the sound of the cannons' roar, everyone scurried for cover behind stone buildings. Coalter and I took refuge behind a high masonry wall near an inn. We were in no danger because we were out of range of the two- and four-pounder field artillery mounted on the roof of the Alhóndiga. However, the insurgent army's advance had been halted just short of the square, which would have to be crossed before reaching the big wooden doors to the granary. Realizing they had us pinned down, the artillerymen on the roof ceased fire.

Suddenly, a great cheer went up from among the insurgents. It was for General Allende who was arriving to command the assault. He began to position his heavy siege cannons at the edge of the square, just beyond the range of the garrison's artillery. The big three-ton guns could easily lob twenty-four- and thirty-pound balls to the Alhóndiga. The artillerymen anchored the carriages, packed the twelve-foot tubes, and adjusted the elevation of the muzzles as the officers calculated the precise range for each gun.

As big as they were, I knew the siege guns could not knock down the thick walls of the Alhóndiga. I soon understood Allende's intent when the order to commence firing was given and the siege guns blazed forth their charge. His target was not the granary's walls but the artillery on its roof. The ground trembled and the sky was lit as bright as day as the cannonade continued. The artillerymen worked diligently to reload as round after round was launched. It was not long before a series of explosions on the roof told that a hit had been scored on a store of gunpowder. Kegs exploded sending sparks that set off still more explosions. For a few moments, the Alhóndiga looked like an erupting volcano.

The artillery on the roof of the granary had been destroyed. General Allende then directed the siege guns be moved onto the square so they could be used to blast open the doors of the Alhóndiga. The guns had not been advanced more than a few feet, however, before musketeers appeared on the roof and opened fire. Their movements were silhouetted by blazes that had continued to burn after the explosions had ceased. Allende again fired his cannons at the roof, but after each barrage, the musketeers reappeared to prevent the siege guns from being moved close enough to be effective against the doors which, recessed in the thick stone walls, were difficult targets.

After a conference with his officers, Allende dispatched a squad across the square to attempt to break open the doors with sledges. He moved forward his own musketeers to return the fire of those on the roof who were now shooting at the soldiers approaching their walls. Just as the insurgents reached the doors, the area they now occupied was lit up by the flash of explosions. The soldiers on the roof were dropping something that exploded upon impact with the stone floor of the plaza.

"Quicksilver!" several people cried in unison. Quicksilver was often used as an explosive in the mines. I had seen its use in Don Esteban's mines. The soldiers in the garrison were using it as a weapon to drive away those attempting to gain entry to the granary.

With his own soldiers beneath the walls, Allende could not resume firing the siege guns. Until the doors could be forced open, those positioned on the roof had a decided advantage. The fires made by the quicksilver were like torches, making the soldiers with the sledges easy targets. They were forced to abandon the effort to break open the doors and return carrying comrades who had been hit by musket fire or the explosives. The insurgent musketeers fired at the roof to cover the retreat. As the soldiers came off the square with the wounded, Allende directed them to the inn next to where Coalter and I were standing. The general told the proprietor of the inn and his family to light as many lanterns as they had and to build up the fire in the hearth.

Father Hidalgo and several other priests arrived along with physicians who had cast their lot with the insurgency. I lay my musket next to the stone wall, and Coalter and I began to help carry the wounded inside the inn where they could be helped. Once inside, I was stunned by what I saw. As many times as Cristóbal and I had listened to Don Esteban or my father describe battles, neither had ever told us what it was like for bodies to be torn apart by metal and explosives. And if they had, I do not think it would have been possible to portray such horror in words. Even to say it was horrible in no way begins to describe the suffering I saw in that room. How do you describe the plight of someone who has lost a leg or an arm, and no one is able to do anything to stop the pain?

Those of us who lifted the wounded onto tables watched as the physicians and priests labored to do what they could to help those who had been hurt the worst. Many we had to hold down to prevent them from twisting away from what was being done to try to stop the loss of blood. Others sat quietly, their eyes focused on nothing in particular. It was if they were asleep with their eyes open. They were the fortunate ones. And there were those whose eyes took on a flat vacant stare which, I soon came to realize, meant they were dead. Some we brought into the inn with that dreadful look, and a physician would shake his head at those of us who carried them. Others died while being tended to. Some of the soldiers, tears streaming down their face, would plead for one of the physicians, or a priest, or anybody, to continue to try to help their comrade even when the body was being removed to make room for those yet alive.

Coalter and I made trip after trip, in and out of the inn, to bring in the wounded who were carried from the square where the fighting continued to rage. Each time we ran outside, I tried to determine what was happening. It was not only soldiers crossing the square. There were farmers and miners—men, women, and children—fighting the battle. From time to time I would recognize someone we were carrying into the inn. We lifted several of the women soldiers I had seen on the drill field in Dolores. I tried to stop because I was horrified by what I was seeing. I had not come back to Guanajuato to carry the dead and dying; I had come to kill Riaño. I wanted to say this to Coalter, but there was no time to talk. We could not even pause to catch our breath.

And then, coming out the door, we passed Lieutenant Guerra who was carrying someone in his arms. My hand went to my mouth when I saw who it was. I ran after him as he lay the person on a table. I was watching when Father Hidalgo turned and looked down. I saw his hands go to his head.

"No!" the priest cried.

It was Alamar. The physician who was at the table shook his head and motioned for Coalter and me to remove the body. I could not do it. The sight of this little woman, who had cared for us all, lying on that blood-soaked table, unmoving, her eyes staring vacantly at nothing, was more than I could bear.

Backing away, I watched Coalter help Lieutenant Guerra lift Alamar from the table and place her gently on the floor next to the body of one of the women soldiers. I turned away, but everywhere I looked there were bodies. It seemed as if the room was filling with bodies, and for a terrible instant I thought I might suffocate beneath a sea of dead bodies.

Rushing outside, I stopped at the edge of the square to catch my breath. Looking up, I saw men using picks to break apart the flagstone. I could tell from their manner of dress they were miners. While those loosening chunks of stone labored, others loaded knapsacks with pitch and combustibles. Slinging the sacks around their necks, the miners picked up the flagstones, raised them above their heads, and began to run across the square to the Alhóndiga. The stones deflected the bullets fired at them by the musketeers on the roof. Allende's soldiers returned the fire. More quicksilver was thrown from the roof, and the flames it caused made it possible to see what was happening. Using hand-axes, the miners gouged out cavities in the wooden doors, filled the holes with pitch and combustibles, and set them on fire. Since the doors could not be broken open, the miners had contrived to burn them down.

It was not long before the doors were ablaze. Seeing this, the insurgents gave forth a cheer and began to surge across the plaza. Many were felled by the musketeers on the roof but that did not deter thousands more from storming the doors, pushing through the still-flaming embers, and entering the Alhóndiga.

I now had a decision to make. I could go back to the inn and help with the wounded, or I could proceed with what it was I had returned to Guanajuato to do in the first place. There was no time for deliberation. Now that the granary had been breached, the battle would soon be over. The garrison was outnumbered fifty to one. There was no place for them to run. What had afforded them protection, the thick walls of the Alhóndiga, was what now prevented their escape. Their refuge was now their tomb.

Returning to the wall, I found my gun and loaded a charge. I made the decision there was no need to involve Coalter. This was not his fight, and more importantly, I did not want to risk his life. I began to run across the square. I could not run very fast because the plaza was choked with people. They carried machetes, pitchforks, lances, shovels, bow and arrows, every kind of weapon one could imagine. Some clutched only stones and bricks.

There were still musketeers on the roof firing at us. When I looked up and saw them aiming their weapons, it was most strange to know I was among those they were hoping to kill. Stranger still was the fact I was not afraid. No one seemed to be afraid even though we could hear the bullets hit the pavement beneath our feet. We each knew we might be hit, we might be killed, but that was only a matter of chance. What was certain was that those men on the roof, those men desperately trying to kill us, would themselves soon be dead.

Like a stick in a raging river, I was swept through the charred doors of the Alhóndiga and into the interior courtyard filled with the sounds of battle. I could not have turned back if that had been my wish. It was several minutes before I was able to break away from the crowd, step back against a wall, and try to get my bearings. The courtyard was well lit by timbers that had been set ablaze, but there was so much smoke it was difficult to see. Sulphurous fumes made it difficult to breathe and caused my eyes to water. Peering through the haze, I saw bodies everywhere. Bodies were piled upon bodies like cords of wood.

And then, just as I looked up a stairway leading to the second floor level, I saw several garrison soldiers in their blue and red uniforms. They were aiming their muskets in my direction. Before I could get down, they were shot by insurgents. Men with machetes were on them in an instant, hacking at those not yet dead and then continuing to hack at the bodies until there was little left to indicate those men had ever existed.

Moving out of the courtyard and down a corridor past a series of rooms, I witnessed the same thing again and again. The garrison soldiers, once they fired their muskets, had no time to reload before they were set upon and hacked to death. The screams of those being killed combined into one loud continuing shriek that I shall never forget. I am certain that in the darkest pits of hell there occurs nothing more ghastly than what I saw happening in those rooms. No devil could ever inflict on men what men are capable of doing to each other.

Nowhere did I see Riaño. He was in none of the rooms. The fighting was moving to the higher levels of the granary where, I suspected, Riaño had gone. Probably, he was on the roof where the final stage of the battle would be fought. If that were the case, I had little chance of finding him because there were hundreds of people ahead of me on the stairways. As I watched the insurgents fight their way ever higher, it occurred to me that the intendant might not have gone to the roof. He would know that his soldiers were going to be forced to retreat ever higher. What would make more sense than to hide below and try to escape while the battle raged?

Many times Cristóbal and I had played in the granary as children. We had played games of hide-and-seek in its maze of storage bins. The thought came to me that Riaño was hiding in one of the bins. Somehow, I knew that was where he was. I ran in the opposite direction of the stairways to a corridor which led to where the grain was stored. As the passageway was dark, I stopped to pick up a torch someone had dropped. When I did, I heard a noise in one of the bins.

Holding the torch in one hand and my gun in the other, I slowly approached the small door to the chamber. Of course, I had no idea what I would find inside. It might have contained a dozen of the garrison soldiers, each holding his musket ready to fire at anyone foolish enough to come through the door.

But I knew there were no soldiers in that room. The soldiers of the Royal Dragoons were not the kind of men to hide while their comrades were being slaughtered. I tossed the torch into the bin from which I had heard the noise. I assumed it would draw the fire of anyone standing ready with a loaded weapon. And then, bracing the butt of my musket to my shoulder, I jumped inside. My calculations proved correct. There he stood: the man Cristóbal and I had called Campamocha.

Riaño looked more like a cornered rat than a mantis. He was at the far side of the bin, bent down as if trying to make himself smaller. I kicked the torch closer to him so I would have a clearer view. He had removed his fine European clothes, the kind of clothes I was forbidden to wear. He had on a white jacket and white pants which, judging from the bloodstains, had probably been taken from the body of a fallen insurgent. The intendant was hoping to disguise himself. I framed the sights of my musket on the center of his chest, exactly the spot my father had taught was the place to aim when you intended to kill a man. I touched the trigger of the gun.

"Please," Riaño whispered. "Please!"

Preparing to squeeze off the shot, I tautened my finger ever so slowly.

"I do not wish to die! Please! I beg you, please!"

It should have been very easy. As clearly as I now saw this man's desperation, I could also picture his arrogance that night he ordered Rubén executed. The same hand which he now held out as an appeal for mercy was the hand that had knocked me to the ground. I hated him more than ever. I had no pity for him.

So what was stopping me?

Sinking to his knees, the intendant, sobbing, continued to plead for his life. "Please!" he cried. "I want to live! I do not want to die! Mother of God, please let me live! Blessed Mother, I want to live!"

I do not know why I was unable to kill him. All I know is that at that particular moment, however much I wanted to kill Riaño, thirsted to kill him, I could not bring myself to do it. Something about the finality of death seized me to the depths of my very soul. He must have discerned my confusion because he looked up and his crying stopped. Slowly, he got to his feet. I took a step back toward the door.

"Señorita," he said, holding forth his hand. "Give me the weapon." Once again, he reminded me of a *campamocha*, a praying mantis. He was a predator reaching for his prey. "I will not hurt you, Señorita. Just give me the weapon. That is all you have to do."

What was I to do? Of course, I was not going to give him my gun. I was still giving serious thought to blowing out his wretched heart. But at the same time I was also thinking about taking him to General Allende. That might be the best thing to do, I thought. The soldiers might stop fighting if they saw one side's leader had been captured. It was an ancient and honorable rule of war that soldiers would stop fighting when the leader of one side or the other was captured. I would take Riaño to Allende, I concluded. Lives would be saved and that was more important than my revenge. I lowered the musket from my shoulder.

When I did, Riaño suddenly produced a saber. I do not know from whence it came. In the darkness of the storage bin, I had not seen it. Maybe it had hung at his side all along. All I knew was that he now gripped a curved single-edged saber. The hilt-guard, made of silver engraved in floral designs, reflected a crimson glow from the flame of the torch on the floor. Raising the saber above his head, he stepped toward me.

Quickly, I aimed the gun at his chest.

Riaño must have known I could not bring myself to fire the weapon. The mantis sensed weakness in his prey. Drawing the saber back to strike, he shouted, "Do you think I do not remember you? I should have killed you that night, you filthy *india*! You are nothing but a filthy *india*, an animal! All of you are animals!"

Someone pushed me from behind, and I fell to the floor just before the blade whipped by within inches of my head. It was Coalter. He had knocked me out of the way and now, kneeling at my side, shielded me with his body. Riaño raised the saber again and prepared to bring it down a second time. I tried to aim the gun which I still had in my grasp, but there was not time, and Coalter was in the way. The blade was coming toward us, and I could not get the musket in a position to fire.

For a terrible instant I thought Coalter had been struck because I heard the hideous sound of metal against bone and a man gasped. But when I was able to look up, I saw the intendant staggering backwards, his hands touching the base of the long blade of a spontoon which had been buried deep into his chest. Holding the shaft of the spontoon was Lieutenant Guerra. He let it fall when Riaño's limp body crumpled to the floor.

Coalter held me tightly. "Carmen, were you hurt?"

I looked into his eyes and realized he had crossed the plaza and entered the Alhóndiga to search for me. Somehow, in all the confusion of the battle, he had he found me.

Touching his face with my fingers, I said, "I am not hurt." I looked up at Lieutenant Guerra. "The battle? How goes the battle?"

"The Alhóndiga has fallen. Guanajuato is ours. And now"—his face hardened—"we go to the capital."

VI

Teresa insisted she was strong enough to make the journey to Mexico City. I had wanted her to stay with her mother and look after Lupita and the orphaned children. The Hacienda de Abrantes would have made a wonderful place for them to live. But, as Teresa pointed out, the children had found homes among the people who had come from throughout Mexico to follow Father Hidalgo. They were going with their new families, wherever that might eventually lead, and no one could make them stay behind.

So on the day of our departure, Teresa was packed, ready to go, and at her side was Lupita who seemed to have selected my cousin, Coalter, and me as her family. Hortensia and other servants of the hacienda walked a ways with us on the road out of Guanajuato before they had to turn back. We waved to them until they were no longer in sight. Once again, I was leaving the place of my birth but under far different circumstances than before.

I used one of the hacienda's supply wagons to haul our belongings together with a supply of grains, beans, honey, and other provisions for Captain Guerra's soldiers. He had again been promoted by General Allende as had Lebe Seru, who was now a lieutenant and second in command of Captain Guerra's soldiers. Our wagon, pulled by the mules that had been left at the stable, was just one of a long line of vehicles that stretched as far as the eye could see, flanked on either side by dragoons and infantry. I taught Teresa to drive the team, so from time to time, I could climb down and walk with Coalter and Lupita. It was not comfortable riding all day on the hard deck of a wagon with no springs.

The army which advanced along the road leading to Mexico City was different from the one that had left Dolores the night Father Hidalgo stood on the steps of his church to openly denounce the viceroy's corrupt government. The men and women of this army had tasted battle. They knew what it meant to kill. They knew what it meant to see their comrades die at the hands of an enemy, to leave behind others who could not travel, and in many cases, were mortally wounded. And so the mood those first days on the trek south was no longer that of a fiesta. There were no happy marching songs. No one shouted jokes up and down the line. Everyone was lost in thought about what had transpired at the Alhóndiga, and few words were spoken.

It was not long, however, before spirits were lifted, for we were soon joined by those who had arrived too late to participate in the victory at Guanajuato. Daily, soldiers in the frontier garrisons continued to make the decision to cast their lot with the insurgency. As before, those in uniform were only a small number of the men and women who came by the thousands from the villages and the countryside. Farmers, miners, masons, *rancheros*, teamsters, *indios* from the mountain tribes, even people from as far away as the northern provinces of Texas and California; all these and more never ceased coming. From the far corners of the Viceroyalty, wherever people heard of Father Hidalgo's cry for freedom, they hurried to join Allende's army. These new arrivals had not been present at the fall of the Alhóndiga, and so they were jubilant. They wanted to celebrate. There was once again song and laughter. We became like a great medieval pageant slowly moving south behind the banner of the Virgin of Guadalupe, moving confidently to what everyone believed was the final victory against the viceroy and his intendants.

After several days, I had to admit I was not unhappy Teresa had come with us. It reminded me of the time when we were little girls and we were like sisters, a time before I was angry at her for calling me a *juana gallo*. And she was a great help. Each evening, after the army had set up camp for the night, I would go with Coalter to help tend to the mules and horses used to transport soldiers and materials. Inevitably, there were animals that had come down sick or lame, and between Coalter and me, we would usually come up with a remedy. While we were gone, Teresa supervised the preparation of food for Captain Guerra's soldiers. When, as was usually the case, Coalter and I were late returning to camp, Teresa always had a meal waiting. And she would also awaken before dawn to have breakfast prepared for when the rest of us reluctantly left our warm beds for another day's march.

✦

One morning, unable to sleep, I arose early and sat with Teresa while she waited for the fire to burn down so that she could begin cooking. In the high altitude it was cold and we sat, wrapped in our *rebozo* shawls, close to the dancing flames and held our hands to its warmth. The stars sparkled brightly in the clear sky, making it easy to identify the constellations. I glanced back to where Coalter was sleeping under the wagon. Perhaps it was the time of day, or the silence, or the stars, or the sight of Coalter asleep, but I decided to ask Teresa about something which had troubled me since even before leaving Dolores.

"Teresa," I said hesitantly. It was not a question I had ever asked anyone. "What does it mean to be in love?"

Immediately I wished I had not made the query because, though her expression did not change, I could sense she was thinking of Rubén. I had been insensitive not to realize what I asked would remind her of the man she had planned to marry. But she looked at me and smiled.

"Do you not know what it means, Carmen?"

I scanned the field beyond us which was aglow from hundreds of campfires being stoked by those preparing the morning meal. "Teresa," I began hoping I would choose the right words, "how..."—I was not sure what I wanted to ask—"...how does one know when one is in love?"

Teresa stood up busying herself with a green branch to break the logs into a bed of glowing red embers. She then suspended a cast-iron kettle from a tripod, filled it with water, and added coffee. Finally, she returned, sat down next to me and took my hand in hers.

"Carmen, you do not have to ask another to tell you if you are in love." She smiled and nodded toward where Coalter was sleeping. "Do you not know that you are in love with this man?"

How often I had asked myself that question. I felt very strange when I was with Coalter. There were times when I wanted to embrace him and hold him in my arms. Many times, I had wanted to lie down beside him at night and sleep close to him as did the husbands and wives who were traveling with us. I often had a deep yearning to do this. When these impulses came, I would put them out of my head by forcing myself to think about other things such as what I was going to do to Humberto and Barnet when we reached the capital. It was all very confusing to me.

"I do not know if I am in love with him or not," I admitted truthfully. "Besides, it would not matter. Coalter is promised to another woman in Louisiana."

She smiled. "Coalter loves you, Carmen."

This, too, had been much in my thoughts. "If he loves me, why does he not tell me? If a man loves a woman, is it not customary for him to tell her? Coalter has never said he loves me." Until that moment, I did not think it mattered. But all of a sudden it did. I was much troubled by this issue, more than I had thought, and I did not understand why it could not be resolved in a straightforward and forthright way. "We are always together, but he never speaks of love to me."

"How can you expect him to tell you he loves you, Carmen? You told him you were going to marry Cristóbal. Coalter is an honorable man. He will never speak of his love for you if he thinks you love another." She shook her head. "What I do not understand is why you would tell him you are going to marry Cristóbal. You know it is not true. Why did you say it?"

Coalter and Teresa had become good friends, and I often saw them talking. Sometimes they would walk together when I drove the wagon, and they would lag behind. He had, I supposed, told her what I had said to him about Cristóbal. I did not know then why I had told him that, nor did I now. Cristóbal had never said he loved me. We had never talked of marriage.

"I love Cristóbal," I said weakly after unsuccessfully trying to think of an explanation for what I had said. "You know how we were always together, Teresa. You must have known that I loved him."

"You do not love Cristóbal."

"I do!" I exclaimed, angry that she would say such a thing.

"You have great affection for Cristóbal, Carmen. Affection is not love. It is completely different from what you feel for Coalter."

For a moment, I thought she was being unkind, but I could see in her expression she was not. Teresa had changed. Despite all that had happened to her, the loss of Rubén and her father, the terrible thing Humberto had done to her, there was about her a serenity that made it impossible for Teresa to be mean.

The sun was breaking over the horizon, a sight I always enjoyed, so I got to my feet and moved away from the fire. What Teresa had said disturbed me. I suspected she might be correct in saying that what I felt for Cristóbal was not the same as what I had begun to feel for Coalter. This made me feel I had become disloyal to Cristóbal somehow, as if I no longer cared about the things we had planned to do when he returned with King Fernando. I still wanted to do those things. Even if I did not daydream about them as much as before, I still wanted to do them. At least, I thought I did.

As the eastern sky began to faintly wash in gold, I could see in the distance, gently waving in the morning breeze, the banner of the Virgin of Guadalupe atop a hill just beyond where the army had encamped. As my eyes adjusted to the light, I noticed a small figure at the base of the staff. Someone was kneeling in prayer. And then I recognized who it was.

"Lupita," I whispered and turned toward my cousin. Teresa was now grinding corn for the meal on a *metate*. "Look, Teresa. Lupita is on that rise over there." There was no one with her, no *comadres*, no other children, no one. "Alone."

Teresa did not seem particularly alarmed. "It is not unusual."

"She is just a little girl. What if a puma is prowling over there?" We were in rough, uninhabited country. I had heard soldiers speak of seeing pumas, and one of them had said he had seen a wolf, though another had argued it had been nothing but a coyote. A coyote was bad enough. It could kill a child. Teresa, Coalter, and I were responsible for Lupita. "I'll go get her," I said.

"Leave her alone, Carmen. Lupita goes every morning to pray to Our Lady."

"What if something attacks her?"

"Nothing can harm Lupita."

I did not know what Teresa meant by that, but seeing the child so absorbed in prayer, I decided against disturbing her. Just the same I retrieved my musket from the wagon and kept an eye on her until I saw Father Hidalgo leave his tent and go to kneel beside the little girl.

✦

Some three weeks after our departure from Guanajuato, Captain Guerra and Lebe Seru returned from an officer's call one morning to report that the army was going to make a detour from the march to Mexico City so that Father Hidalgo could meet with Father José Morelos in a town called Valladolid. Father Morelos, who had been a student in the seminary at San Nicolás Obispo when Father Hidalgo was rector there many years before, had become the leader of the insurgency in the south of New Spain. He had raised an army. Father Hidalgo and General Allende wanted to confer with him before they continued on to Mexico City.

In Valladolid there was much cheering when the two priests met in the town square and embraced. Father Morelos was a tall, barrel-chested bear of a man, with raven black hair. He was an imposing figure in his black frock coat and Roman-collar. He was the first *indio* priest I had ever seen, and though he and Father Hidalgo were quite different in appearance, they were, in many ways, like father and son. Father Morelos and Father Hidalgo retired to hold a meeting with General Allende and the officers of the republican armies. While the soldiers in both armies visited and sang songs, the leaders talked long into the night.

The next morning, Captain Guerra and Lebe Seru returned to our encampment outside of town and shared with us the distressing news that Father Morelos had brought from the south.

"Many of the garrisons in the villages in the south of New Spain," Captain Guerra explained, "have remained loyal to the viceroy. They have been told that Father Hidalgo and Father Morelos are working on behalf of Joseph Bonaparte. The viceroy's generals have moved these troops to the capital along with hundreds of their best cannon."

"Most of our cannon," Lebe Seru said, "were damaged during the siege of the Alhóndiga. Many of the tubes cracked and are too dangerous to fire. Most are beyond repair. We have no more than a dozen that are reliable."

"We may as well have none," Captain Guerra added. "Our supplies of gunpowder were exhausted in Guanajuato, and the prospects of capturing more between here and the capital are slim. If the Spanish do not surrender, we will be forced to take the city armed with little more than our own bodies, numerous as they may be. It will be a terrible and bloody battle, much worse than what occurred at the Alhóndiga. There, hundreds were killed. In Mexico City, the dead will be counted in the thousands."

For over a week, Father Hidalgo and General Allende met with Father Morelos. Not all of their discussions, however, concerned military strategy. Though a constitutional assembly had yet to be convened, the greater part of New Spain was now under the control of the insurgency, and there was a need to provide guidance to local authorities on matters such as public health and the administration of courts of justice. Many of the delegates chosen to attend the constitutional assembly were at the meetings held by the two priests. For that reason a number of laws were enacted during these sessions.

At the conclusion of the meetings, before the two armies assembled in a field south of Valladolid, Father Hidalgo and Father Morelos stood side by side under the banner of the Virgin of Guadalupe to proclaim the first law of the new government, an edict making slavery illegal in New Spain. A cheer went up after the text of this new law was read. Teresa, Coalter, Lupita, and I were standing with Captain

Guerra and his soldiers. Overcome with emotion, Captain Guerra was unable to speak.

Lebe Seru said, "It is the first law enacted against slavery in the Western Hemisphere."

Following the reading of the laws, there was a great celebration to mark what many regarded as the creation of the government of the Republic of Mexico. Others continued to insist that the fate of New Spain would not be decided until the constitutional assembly met in the capital, but all were united in the jubilation of the moment. Food was prepared, musicians from all parts of the land played an assortment of exotic instruments, and soon there was dancing and singing.

In the midst of the festivities, I went to sit under a tree near a pond. I felt the need to be alone. We would soon be in Mexico City and I was wondering what I would say to Don Esteban. There was a possibility Cristóbal had returned with the king. How would I explain why I was with this army of insurrection? I could have made my way to the capital long before now; nothing was stopping me. In Guanajuato, Teresa had asked if I had become a republican. I had not. All this talk about a constitution and liberty and equality made little sense to me, although I liked the idea of a law against slavery. But I still believed what Don Esteban had always maintained about the need for a king who would govern his people like a father. At least, I thought I still believed this.

Just as I was preparing to return to the encampment, Coalter appeared. Immediately, I surmised where he had been and what he had been doing, for he was now wearing a soldier's uniform.

"You have joined the army," I said, not at all sure I approved. Despite the fact the uniform was cut from a simple unbleached cotton, he looked at that moment more handsome than ever.

"Yes," he said and held out his arms to demonstrate that someone had managed to find a shirt big enough for him. "How do you like it?"

"Why, Coalter? Why was it necessary for you to join Allende's army? You were helping with the animals. Was that not enough? Are you going to carry a musket now? Are you going to fight?"

"Captain Guerra wishes for me to continue doing what I have. He said tending the horses and mules is important."

"Then why join the army and wear a uniform?"

He walked a few steps to the pond and gazed across the bright sheen of its mirror-like surface. "These people here," he gestured toward the celebration," are risking their lives for what they believe, Carmen. I, too, believe in liberty and equality. I believe in justice. So I guess I want to take a stand with them. Joining General Allende's army seemed to be a way of doing that. Lebe Seru joined and I wanted to do the same."

"But this is not even your country!" I protested, not entirely clear in my own mind why I was opposed to what he had done. "You weren't born here. What about your own country?"

"I am in my country, Carmen. Ever since I was a boy, I wanted to live in Texas. Texas is a part of this new land Father Hidalgo is creating. I want to help him with what he is doing. I want Texas to be a place where people can live in freedom." He picked up a pebble and tossed it in the pond, creating a succession of ever-widening circles in the water. "I may never return to the place of my birth. I am where I want to be."

"Never return?" I asked. "What of Rhoda? Will you not return for her? Will you not...marry?"

"I think you know the answer to that, Carmen." He drew closer to me. "When this is over, I will write to Rhoda. I will explain that, while I believed what we knew was love, I now realize it was not. And the reason I realize this is because, for the first time in my life, I know what love means."

Before I knew what was happening, he had taken me in his arms. His lips touched mine and we kissed. It was something I had never done before but it seemed as natural as the beating of one's heart. I touched his face and looked up into those beautiful eyes.

"Carmen," he said softly, "it is you I love. It is you I wish to marry."

We kissed a second time. Never had I suspected such joy was possible. I did not want to stop, but as wonderful as it was, I was certain that something about it was wrong. For a moment I could not imagine what could possibly be wrong with something so pleasant, and then I remembered Cristóbal and backed away. I saw the confusion in Coalter's eyes. He continued to hold out his hands as if to beckon me back even as I backed away.

"Coalter," I whispered. "I-I cannot love you. I..."—every instinct within my being was fighting what I knew I must say even though it was not the truth—"...I love Cristóbal. We shall be married when he returns from Spain." Only with great discipline did I manage to control a quiver in my voice. "I am sorry. I cannot love you. I cannot marry you."

He awkwardly began to apologize for what he had done as if what had happened was a bad thing. He said he had not meant to offend me. I assured him he had not. In truth, I had kissed him as much as he had kissed me, though I did not say that. I told him it was best that we forget what happened and go about our tasks as though nothing had changed. And then, I turned and walked as quickly as I could back to the encampment. What had happened was, of course, something I knew I would never forget. It was not something I would want to forget.

✦

It was decided Father Morelos would not accompany Father Hidalgo to the capital. Rather, he would return with his smaller force to the south and do what he could to prevent more of the Spanish garrisons from reinforcing the viceroy's armies in Mexico City. This would impede royalist power from being concentrated in one place. On the day the armies separated, there was much sadness as friends, old and new, realized the uncertainty of what lay ahead. There was no guarantee that those going their separate ways would ever meet again. The parting of Father Hidalgo and Father Morelos was especially sad. Father Morelos knelt before the older man and for a long time could not bring himself to release his teacher's hands. Somehow, I think they knew they would never see each other again.

There were several skirmishes before we reached the capital. The entrance to the Valley of Mexico was through a chain of tall peaks, which included several great volcanic cones. At a mountain pass called Monte de las Cruces the advance elements of the insurgent army were ambushed by Spanish artillery. General Allende, at the head of the main force, raced to the scene of the fighting and after a fierce battle forced the royalists to retreat.

It was a costly victory. Over two thousand insurgents were killed. The physicians worked desperately to help the wounded. As we had at Guanajuato, Coalter and I, assisted by Teresa, did what we could to help. And as at the Alhóndiga, I was overwhelmed by the absurdity of human beings slaughtering one another. I saw no glory in it, not even in what was supposed to have been a victory. I knew then that those who wrote books saying there is glory in war were either liars or they had viewed a battle from a far distance, if at all.

Finally, the day came when we arrived to the heights above Mexico City. General Allende deployed his forces around the capital, quickly placing it under siege. It reminded me of what we had seen when we arrived in Guanajuato, except that the capital of the Viceroyalty was much larger. It was a city of magnificent smooth-stone buildings, wide boulevards, lakes, tree-shrouded parks, and dozens of churches. Everywhere one looked there were churches and cathedrals including the Basilica (on Tepeyac Hill), that had been erected on the exact spot where the Virgin of Guadalupe had appeared to Juan Diego.

As we stood in awe of what we surveyed, Coalter asked, "Have you never been here, Carmen?"

I told him I had not. I did not even know where the Marqués's hacienda was located, and I wondered how I would ever find him in this city of hundreds of streets and thousands of buildings. "I've got to find Don Esteban, Coalter. I have to convince him to speak with Father Miguel."

"Speak with Father Miguel? I don't understand."

"If I could arrange for Don Esteban and Father Miguel to meet, I believe a battle could be avoided. Both are reasonable men and want what is best for New Spain. I have to enter the city and find Don Esteban."

"Carmen," he said and pointed to the city. "Look below. What do you see?"

Located all around the city were gun emplacements. Behind buildings, behind stone walls, amongst fortifications partially camouflaged by trees and shrubs, were cannon, hundreds of them. The National Palace and the government buildings were ringed with artillery and soldiers. Mexico City was an armed camp. I could not help but think that if all these weapons and all these soldiers, thousands of the king's finest, had been in Spain rather than its American colony, Joseph Bonaparte might not be on the throne in Madrid at that very moment. It was apparently more important to the Spanish to maintain their grip on the Viceroyalty than to drive foreign invaders from their own land.

"How long," Coalter asked, "do you think you would remain alive if you were to go down there?"

"If I go unarmed, they will not harm me."

"Carmen, the soldiers in the city are frightened men. Try to look at things from their perspective. They are surrounded by two hundred thousand people, maybe more." He gestured to the hills around the capital where the insurgent army was positioned. "They have heard of what happened at Guanajuato. They know that if we enter the city they will die. They will kill thousands of us, but they will certainly die. They will shoot at anything that comes down from these hills."

Coalter was correct. I did not know how I had expected to find Don Esteban when we arrived in Mexico City. I suppose I thought I would simply stroll down a street, call his name, and he would magically appear. That was not going to happen. And yet, I knew I had to do something. A terrible battle was approaching, one in which many thousands of people would die unless something was done.

Father Hidalgo sent emissaries led by Captain Guerra to request a meeting with the viceroy and his generals. Viceroy Venegas refused to receive the delegation and ordered them to return with the message that anyone else dispatched would be shot unless they came with a message of surrender. He was as stubborn as Riaño had been. Captain Guerra said the viceroy and many of the Spanish-born aristocracy had barricaded themselves inside the National Palace. Everything was happening as it had at Guanajuato, and we all wondered if it would end the same.

After Captain Guerra had completed his report to Father Hidalgo and General Allende, I took him aside to inquire if he had heard anything of Don Esteban while in the city.

"The Marqués de Abrantes is in personal command of the defense of the city." He shook his head. "He will be a formidable opponent."

✦

That night, as we looked down at the sparkling lights from thousands of torches and street lanterns burning in the capital, I pondered what Captain Guerra had said. I was with an army preparing to do battle with a force led by the head of the house I was born to serve. The heads of the House of Abrantes had been patrons, to my father's family for centuries. I recalled what Don Esteban had said so many times: "Men of the House of Abrantes have always been protectors of the Spanish monarchy, and at their side, sword in hand, has always stood a Rangel." What would Cristóbal say if he knew I was with an army that was in opposition to his father? I knew what he would say. And yet, was I supposed to fight on the side of those who had killed my uncle and Rubén? I was supposed to fight with those who killed children? Never in my life had I been so confused.

Teresa, Coalter, and I stood near where Father Hidalgo was meeting with General Allende and his officers beneath the Banner of the Virgin of Guadalupe. A great bonfire had been lit so the citizens in the capital could look up to the hills and see that the insurgent army was led by the Virgin of Guadalupe. From time to time, we could hear the sounds of distant musket fire and the rumble of artillery as skirmishes broke out along the lines stretching for leagues around the city.

General Allende was arguing for an immediate invasion of the capital. Though it would involve massive losses, he knew his numbers would almost certainly insure the defeat of the Spanish in street to street fighting. He wanted to avoid an open field battle where the royalists would have an advantage with their field artillery. Father Hidalgo was reluctant to give the order that would mean the end of so many lives on both sides. Their debate was interrupted when the general was forced to take personal command of a skirmish on the far side of the capital where the Spanish were threatening to overrun the insurgent positions. Coalter and Teresa left to assist with the wounded. I told them I would catch up. It had become clear to me what I must do, and I did not want either Coalter or my cousin to stop me. I approached Father Hidalgo and asked if I could speak with him.

He was staring down at the lights of the capital. He looked at me and smiled. There was weariness in his eyes. "Yes, Carmen. Please join me."

"Father," I said, "the viceroy refused to meet with you. And he would not hear your emissaries."

"That is correct."

I explained how my father's family had always been associated with the House of Abrantes and how Don Esteban and I were close. "If I could reach him, I believe I could convince him to speak with you. The viceroy would listen to what the Marqués has to say."

"If you could get to Don Esteban, Carmen, what would you tell him? How would you convince him to meet with me?"

Again, I reminded him that my father was the Marqués's aide and added, "Don Esteban has always valued what I have to say."

"Yes, Carmen. I understand. But what will you say to him? That is what I am asking."

Truthfully, I had not considered what I would say to Don Esteban. The important thing was reaching him and the rest would take care of itself. "I will tell him,..." I began hesitatingly. There had to be a basis for a compromise, but I could not think what it might be. I did not know what I would tell him.

"What is it that the Marqués wishes for New Spain?"

"He would like for New Spain to have its own king, Father. He wishes for Fernando de Borbón to become king of New Spain."

"Fernando? Here in New Spain?"

Suddenly, I remembered the issue upon which I knew the Marqués and Father Hidalgo could agree. "Don Esteban would never bring a king to New Spain who would allow slavery. He is as opposed to slavery as you are, Father Miguel. I know he would support the

law you and Father Morelos made against slavery." I knew I had
found the basis for a compromise. "In return, could you not support a
king for New Spain? Would you agree for Fernando to become our
king?"

"Carmen, I have never opposed a king. What I oppose, and will
continue to oppose, is tyranny. It is wrong for one man, or a group of
men, to rule a people. People must have a choice as to how they are
governed. They must be able to freely choose their government and
have a voice in what laws they should obey. Only in this way can we
hope for justice."

I recalled what had happened in Atotonilco where the people had
almost forced Father Hidalgo to become king. "What if the people
choose a king? If the people freely select Fernando de Borbón to be
their king, would you agree?"

He pondered my query. "I suppose that if that is the will of the
people, I would agree."

"Then I will go to Don Esteban!" Somehow I would get to him.
There was no need for more fighting. Not one more person need die.
There was a basis for a compromise. The Marqués wanted a king and
Father Hidalgo wanted the people to choose their leader. If the people
chose a king, which I was certain they would, everyone would be sat-
isfied. "I will tell him what you said!"

"It must be understood, Carmen; even should the people choose a
monarch, that individual must abide by a constitution which guarantees the rights of all people."

There was that word again: constitution. I was still uncertain
what it meant. "Rights? What do you mean? What rights?"

"There are certain fundamental human rights that a king must
not abridge. The right to life and liberty are given by God and no one
else,"—his eyes narrowed—"not a king, not a president, not even a
congress, has the authority to withhold those rights."

"I do not understand, Father Miguel. If the people choose to be
ruled by a king, he must rule as he sees best. He must have authority. Is it not true? You have spoken of the will of the people. If a king
is what a majority of the people wish, then... I do not understand."

His expression softened. "Carmen, there are rights that even a majority of the people cannot withhold from even just one person. For example, if a majority of the people decide to enslave one man, it would be wrong. A constitution will safeguard our freedom against tyranny whether the tyrant is one man or a majority of men. That is what we are seeking, Carmen, and this is what you must tell the Marqués. Do you understand?"

What I understood was that Father Hidalgo was agreeing to my finding the Marqués and arranging a meeting between them. This is what I heard, and I was anxious to get started. But I thought I did grasp some of what he was saying.

"Yes, Father," I said, "I believe I do."

"Good," he said and smiled. "If you can convince Don Esteban to arrange for me to meet with Viceroy Venegas, you will have performed a valuable service to Mexico, Carmen." He looked below into the city. "But how will you find him? It will be dangerous. You may be—"

"Do not worry, Father," I said quickly. "I will find a way. He will be at the National Palace. I will go there."

"I will pray for your safe return."

Remembering Coalter's words about how the Spanish soldiers were nervous and might fire their muskets at anyone coming down the hill, I reasoned they would be less likely to shoot at a woman than at a man. Most men would not regard an unarmed woman as a threat. They were mistaken in such an assumption, but it was a matter of custom. However, dressed as I was in leather breeches and boots, I might be mistaken for a man, especially in the darkness. For this reason, I hurried to the wagon and changed into one of the cotton dresses Alamar had given me in Dolores. Donning a pair of straw sandals, I looked no different than the wife or daughter of a peasant farmer. Though I did not like wearing such apparel, it would, I hoped, keep me alive.

I scurried down the hill and, crouching, followed a gulch that ran in the direction of the city. Suddenly, as I stopped in a stand of mesquites, I heard a noise behind me. My heart began to pound so hard I thought it was going to leap out of my chest. Someone was coming. And then I saw who it was.

"Lupita!" I whispered as loud as I dared. "What are you doing here?"

The little girl stopped a few feet short of where I was and stared at me.

"Go back, Lupita!" I ordered. I had a feeling she understood much more than she let on. "Do you hear me? Go back. Now!"

There was no indication she did or did not comprehend. I thought of taking her back up the hill, but there was no time. Any moment now, the skirmishes around the capital might escalate into full battle, and the opportunity to arrange a meeting between Father Hidalgo and Don Esteban would be lost. I had to press forward. After again telling Lupita to return to the camp, I hurried on. Looking back, I could see she had not obeyed, but at least she was not following.

I reached the edge of the city without encountering Spanish soldiers. I advanced down a street I thought might lead in the direction of the palace. Several times, I hid in recessed doorways or behind foliage when I saw soldiers in the blue, red, and black uniforms of foot infantry. They did not see me. I had begun to feel a little smug about my ability to elude the viceroy's best soldiers when I heard someone shout, "You there! Halt!"

Even though I did not see anyone, something told me not to move a muscle. From behind a masonry fence a soldier emerged, and then another, and another. Before I knew what was happening, I was facing a line of five soldiers, each with his musket aimed at me. They all appeared to be *indios*, and except for the uniforms they wore, were no different than the soldiers in General Allende's army on the hills. They stared at me and I at them. Finally, one of them, a corporal, said, "It is a woman!"

Hearing his words, I was able to take a breath. For once, I thought, something I had planned was working. It was good I had changed into the dress. My luck was changing.

But then another one of the soldiers, a sergeant, said, "There are many women in Allende's army. She may be one of them. Kill her."

"She is unarmed," the corporal said.

"Everyone in the city was told to stay inside tonight," the sergeant countered. "Why is this one on the street alone? Take no chances. Kill her."

A heated discussion ensued as to what to do with me. Unfortunately, the sergeant who wanted to kill me turned out to be the most persuasive. No one could think of a reason to rebut his query as to why a woman would be out on the streets alone at night unless she was with the insurgent army. The case was settled in minutes. I was to be shot on the spot. I heard the click of flintlocks being cocked.

Just as I was about to bolt away in what I knew would be a futile attempt to escape my fate, one of the soldiers pointed behind me and cried, "Look, a child!"

Following his gesture, I looked down and saw, stepping calmly to my side, Lupita.

"She is your child?" the sergeant demanded.

At first, I did not grasp what he was asking, but then I realized he thought Lupita was my child. Without thinking, I blurted, "Yes! She is my baby." I swept Lupita into my arms and kissed her. "I have been looking for her everywhere! She ran away when she heard the cannon. The noise frightened her. That is why I am in the streets. I had to find my baby!"

The corporal looked at the sergeant and asked, "Are there babies in Allende's army?" He was being sarcastic. Some of the other soldiers laughed. "You would have us kill unarmed women and their babies? Are we Frenchmen?"

"Where do you live?" the sergeant asked.

Again, I had to act without thinking. I did not know enough about Mexico City to even make up a good lie but I knew I could not appear to waver, so I said, "I live in the palace."

"Oh?" the sergeant said with a sneer. "Are you the viceroy?"

"I am a servant in the House of Abrantes. I came with the Marqués de Abrantes from Guanajuato. He is a guest of the viceroy," I replied.

One of the soldiers said, "The Marqués de Abrantes is in command of the defense of the city. We cannot kill one of his servants. We would be shot!"

Apparently, the sergeant agreed with this assessment. "Then hurry and go to the palace, woman. There will soon be a battle, and anyone out in these streets will die."

The corporal said, "Come with me, Señora. I will escort you to the palace. Otherwise, you may be mistaken for one of Allende's soldiers and you may not be so lucky next time. I will take you because your master is a brave man. He is not like the other notables. He does not hide in the palace. When Allende comes, he will die with the rest of us, fighting like a man."

Carrying Lupita in my arms, I followed the corporal. On the way, I realized it would have been impossible for me to have made it to the palace alone. The closer we came to the palace, the more soldiers we encountered. Most were in charge of field artillery. There were scores of four-pounders, their bell-shaped muzzles aimed down the wide streets the insurgents would have to traverse to come near the center of the city. Closer in, the cannon were heavier, nine- and twelve-pounders, all the way up to 24-pounder fortress guns.

As we drew near the palace, the corporal said, "Please tell the Marqués that we will fight for him, Señora. We will not allow Joseph Bonaparte to come to New Spain and kill our people."

I looked in this man's determined face. He had the appearance of one who could give a good account of himself in battle. It occurred to me he was no different from the thousands of young men and women on the hills surrounding us. The one difference was he believed he was fighting to prevent Father Hidalgo and General Allende from delivering New Spain to the French.

"You are a brave man," I said. "Tell me your name. I will tell Don Esteban you helped me."

He looked surprised. "My name is Santiago Montemayor."

The courtyard in front of the National Palace was filled with soldiers. It was lit by hundreds of torches and lanterns. "There is the Marqués de Abrantes," the corporal said when we walked past a large bronze statue of King Carlos astride a rearing stallion. "There, with General de Flon."

I thanked the corporal and turned to look at where he had pointed. Whereas before my heart had pounded like a drum, now it stood still. The Marqués was leaning over a small table on which a map was spread. He was pointing something out to the red-faced man whose name, Flon, I recognized. General Manuel de Flon, the Count of Cadena, was known in Spain as "the butcher."

But I hardly saw the officer whose red and blue uniform was covered with braids and metals. All I could see was Don Esteban. Letting Lupita down, I took her hand and walked slowly toward him. As we approached, General de Flon looked at us and scowled. He was about to say something when Don Esteban turned. I could see the disbelief in his eyes. His lips parted but there was no sound. Finally, he whispered, "Carmencita, is that you?"

I, too, had no voice, so I nodded eagerly.

"Carmencita!" he shouted and rushed to sweep me off the flagstone pavement and raise me above his head the way he had hundreds of times when I was a girl. Over and over, he exclaimed, "Carmencita! My Carmencita!"

It had been so long since I had been called little Carmen. I touched his hair and, seeing its golden color, was reminded of Cristóbal.

"Don Esteban," I whispered. There were so many things to tell him and there was, of course, the reason I had come, but first I had to know. "Have you received a message from Cristóbal?" He continued to hold me in his arms, and I noticed the general and all those around us watching. My hand touched the Marqués's jacket where I felt the pistol he carried inside his coat. He did not answer my question, and I wondered, if in the excitement, he had heard. "Don Esteban. Cristóbal and my father? Have you—"

"No, Carmencita," he said, lowering me to the ground. "There has been no word."

For just a moment, I forgot everything else. I forgot the urgency of my mission. There had been ample time for Cristóbal and my father to arrive in Spain and for a message to be received. Something was wrong. I had the most horrible feeling that something was wrong.

Holding my hands, the Marqués said, "Carmencita, I was afraid you were dead. Humberto said you—" He stopped because General de Flon was repeatedly clearing his throat. "General, forgive me. This is...this is my aide's daughter, María del Carmen Rangel. She was taken against her will in Guanajuato and...and she has escaped! Please excuse us. I will return shortly."

He led me away from the table in the direction of the palace. We stopped under a covered walkway leading to the main entrance. Hundreds of kegs of gunpowder were stacked on either side of the walkway.

"Carmen...," Don Esteban began and then looked behind me. "Carmen, who is this little girl? Is she with you?"

I told him who she was.

Kneeling, he brushed Lupita's hair with the tips of his fingers. "Look at these eyes. There is much wisdom in these eyes for one so small."

"Don Esteban," I said, glancing about to confirm our privacy, "I must speak with you on a matter of great importance. I have a message for you."

He rose and gripped my arms. "Oh Carmencita, I am so happy to see you, but I wish you had not come here. Soon, there will be a terrible battle. Thousands will die! We must find a way to get you out of the capital." He raised his gaze to the hills and then looked back at me, his expression slowly turning to puzzlement. "How did you get here? How were you able to get through the enemy's lines?"

From where we stood, I could see the Banner of the Virgin of Guadalupe on the hill. The bonfire made the image of Our Lady seem to hang suspended in the dark sky. It was too great a distance to see the people there, but I knew Father Hidalgo would be somewhere near that banner. He said he would pray for my safety. It served to remind me of why I had come. And though I knew there was not much time to lose, I realized I would have to explain to the Marqués what had happened or he would never understand what I had come to ask.

As rapidly as possible, I told him what had happened at the hacienda that awful night. I told him of Rubén's execution, of how Barnet had stabbed Coalter when he tried to rescue me from Humberto. I told him of how Lebe Seru saved us both and took me to Dolores. I related how Father Hidalgo and the people in Dolores had nursed Coalter back to health and helped me. Finally, I told him what Humberto and Barnet had done to Anselmo and Teresa.

When I finished, I saw the fury in his eyes. "I should have known Humberto was lying! I suspected as much. Never in his life has he told the truth. Never!"

"What did he tell you?"

"He said Rubén had become a revolutionary. He said Rubén convinced Barnet's slave to join their cause, and when he was found out, they took up arms and the young *norteamericano*, Owens, was killed. He said the African escaped and forced you to go with him against your will."

It came as no surprise that Humberto would have made up such a lie. What else was there to expect? "Where is Humberto?"

For a moment, the Marqués was too angry to answer. Finally, he said, "He is in the palace with his mother. They think they will be safe there."

I knew better. The stone walls of the palace were not nearly as thick as those of the Alhóndiga, nor were they as tall. If the insurgent army could get past the Spanish artillery and set up the two or three siege guns still able to fire, they would knock down these walls in minutes. "And Barnet? Has he returned to his country?"

"Barnet is also in the palace." His eyes narrowed. "I will kill them both for what they did. I swear it!"

"Don Esteban," I said, eager to take his mind away from Humberto and Barnet. They were not important. They could be dealt with later. "This battle can be avoided! No one need die. I have a—"

"Carmen," he interrupted, "you're wearing Cata Valeria's pendant! I have not seen it in years."

With all that was happening, I did not see why he would at that moment notice I happened to be wearing my mother's pendant. It even seemed to have dissolved his anger with Humberto and Barnet. "The battle can be avoided," I repeated in hopes of returning his attention to matters at hand. "I have a message for you from Father Hidalgo."

Slowly, his gaze drifted from the pendant. "A message from Hidalgo? What are you saying? That man is a traitor! What message could a traitor possibly have for me?"

"Don Esteban, he is not a traitor. He is a good man. He is—"

"He is a traitor! He is a traitor to his king! How can you say he is a good man? Has he bewitched you? He is not only a traitor, he is a heretic! The archbishop excommunicated him and that other traitor-ous priest...that...that José Morelos!"

I waited for him to calm before I said, "Father Hidalgo and Father Morelos are not traitors, Don Esteban. They only want what is good for the people of Mexico. They want—"

"And Allende," he interrupted, "is even worse! He swore an oath to defend his king. He violated his sacred duty to his monarch! There is nothing worse a man can do! Nothing!"

I thought of reminding him that both King Carlos and Prince Fernando, his son, had renounced the Spanish Crown in favor of Joseph Bonaparte. Had they not violated their duty to their people? But I knew such talk would do no good. There was no time for a debate.

"Don Esteban," I said when he paused to draw a breath, "Father Hidalgo is not opposed to a king for New Spain."

That brought his tirade to an abrupt halt. "What did you say?"

"It is true. He told me himself. Father Hidalgo will not oppose a king for New Spain."

He stroked his beard. "Hidalgo said he was not opposed to a king? He told you this himself?"

"He said it, Don Esteban! He said that if the people of Mexico choose a king he would not oppose it." I could not get it out fast enough. "He said that if it is the will of the people to have a king, he would abide by that will." While anxiously awaiting a response, I remembered what else Father Hidalgo had said I must tell the Mar-qués. "All he wants is a constitution which guarantees certain rights of the people. As long as there is this constitution, a king may rule if that is what the people decide."

"Carmen," he said, shaking his head. "This priest has tricked you. He has made you play the fool, and he thinks he can trick me as well. He is a sly and cunning man."

I looked down at Lupita. "Tricked me? What do you mean? I do not understand."

"Of course you do not understand, Carmencita. You are still a child. These things Hidalgo talks about are republican nonsense. The people cannot choose their king. There cannot be a king and a constitution restricting his power. The will of the people? The only will a king must obey is God's. It is God who selects the king, not the people. This Hidalgo tricked you, and he wants to use you to trick me."

The force with which he spoke his words silenced me. I wondered if I had been tricked. Perhaps I had. Father Hidalgo did have a clever way with words. And then I remembered what had happened in Valladolid.

"Don Esteban, Father Hidalgo and Father Morelos made a law against slavery in Mexico. Is this not a good thing? You are against slavery. I know you are because you refused Barnet's offer to bring slaves to New Spain in exchange for his *norteamericanos* and their long-rifles. Do you not agree a law against slavery is good?"

"You do not bring an end to slavery by making a revolution against your king. The *norteamericanos* overthrew their king and they have slavery."

Now I was thoroughly confused. If only I could get the Marqués and Father Hidalgo together, I knew they would find a way to avoid the terrible battle that was now all but inevitable. "Don Esteban, would you meet with Father Hidalgo? His followers will not harm you. You would be safe."

"I am not afraid of Hidalgo's rabble."

"Then you will come? You will—"

I paused because a lieutenant had stepped from the palace and, seeing us, rushed to where we stood.

"Don Esteban," the young officer said, "the viceroy is preparing to make an announcement, and he wishes for you to be present."

At the Marqués's bidding, I took Lupita's hand and we followed the lieutenant through the huge mahogany doors and into the palace.

The palace was breathtaking in its grandeur. We walked along a corridor whose stone floor reminded me of a cloud-streaked sky. On the walls hung enormous paintings mounted in ornate gilded frames. Reflecting the light from a series of oil lamps mounted in gold fixtures cast a soft red glow over the long hallway. It was if the air itself was made of gold.

We came to a ballroom crowded with hundreds of finely dressed men, women, and children. They were dwarfed by the enormity of the high-ceilinged room which contained several dozen crystal chandeliers so immense they looked like the tall masts of square-rigger galleons. Judging from their clothing, I assumed the people were the notables who had taken refuge inside the palace. Most of the men wore strapped pantaloons, frock coats, and high-collared shirts. The women were attired in draped tunic dresses made of thin fabrics, similar to the one I had worn at the hacienda the night the Marqués had arranged the dinner for Barnet and Coalter.

As we entered the room, all eyes shifted to Lupita and me. Everyone seemed to draw back as if the presence of a solitary woman and a little girl, both dressed in cotton dresses and straw sandals, was a threat.

And then I saw them. In the rear of the room stood Humberto and Barnet. Humberto shifted his position in an attempt to conceal himself behind a woman I assumed was the Marquesa. There was hatred in the woman's face as she stared at me through eyes as narrow as slits.

The lieutenant said, "I will tell the viceroy you are here, Don Esteban." He stepped to a door guarded by two soldiers.

I knew that now was not the time for me to confront Humberto and Barnet. At that moment, they were very unimportant. Thousands of lives were at stake.

"Don Esteban," I said, "you must speak to the viceroy about what Father Hidalgo said. You must make him understand that there is no need for a battle!"

Don Esteban rubbed his temples. Suddenly, he looked very tired. "Carmen, I'm afraid it would do little good to speak with Viceroy

Venegas even if what Hidalgo told you was not a trick. The viceroy is—"

He stopped because men were exiting the room the lieutenant had entered and the people in the ballroom anxiously pressed forward. When I looked up at the Marqués, I saw that perspiration was running down his face. His hand was trembling.

"Don Esteban?" I whispered. "Is there something wrong?"

He struggled to catch his breath. "I am fine," he said and patted my arm. "Here comes the viceroy."

A portly man in a burgundy-colored frock coat was approaching us. Several other men in uniform marched by his side and slightly behind. Extending both hands, he said, "Don Esteban, thank you for coming! I am sorry to take you away from your duties, but I have made an important decision, and I wanted you to be here when I announce it to our friends."

Bowing slightly, Don Esteban said, "Excellency, may I present the daughter of my aide, Señorita María del Carmen Rangel. And this is Lupita."

The viceroy acknowledged my presence with a quick nod of his head but then, after glancing down at Lupita, narrowed his focus to take note of me a second time.

"What are..."—he looked once more at Lupita and then back to me—"...what are these...*indias* doing in the palace? Why are they here?"

"Carmen and Lupita are with me, Excellency," Don Esteban said and gripped my arm. At first I thought he was merely demonstrating his affection, but I realized he was holding on to me for support.

A smile replaced the viceroy's expression of displeasure. Lupita and I had been quickly forgotten. "Don Esteban! I have made a decision as to who will be in command of our forces defending the capital!"

Removing his hand from my arm, the Marqués straightened his back. "I was under the impression you wished for me to command the defense of the capital, Viceroy Venegas."

"Oh yes, Don Esteban, I do! You are doing an excellent job, and you will continue to command the troops. It is just that you will now have a commander above you!"

"I am afraid I do not understand."

Whirling about, the viceroy gleefully clapped his hands and more men emerged from the room he had exited. One was carrying a flagstaff, but as the man cleared the doorway and raised the pole, it was evident it was being used to hoist not a flag, but an enormous banner. There was a gasp from the people in the room when we collectively recognized who was depicted on the banner.

"Behold!" Viceroy Venegas shouted. "Here is our new commander, the Supreme Commander of the armies of New Spain!"

The Marqués made the same mistake I did because, turning to the viceroy, he said, "You are naming the Virgin of Guadalupe the commander of your forces?"

"No, no, no!" the viceroy said, jumping from foot to foot as if performing a jig. "It is not the Virgin of Guadalupe, Don Esteban. Do you not see?"

Don Esteban looked again at the faded image on the banner. The cloth was quite old.

"It is Our Lady of Remedios!" the viceroy announced with a flourish of his hand.

Though they were similar, I had begun to detect the differences between the two images of the Holy Mother. Our Lady of Remedios was shown clad in a golden cape decorated with many jewels and with a crown on her head. The Virgin of Guadalupe on the banner carried by the insurgents was depicted in simple garments. She wore no jewels or crown.

Facing the crowd, the viceroy shouted, "This is the banner carried by Hernán Cortés into battle against the *indios* almost three centuries ago. It is the exact same banner! And just as she led the *conquistadores* to a great victory over the heathens, Our Lady of Remedios will lead us in an even greater victory! Miguel Hidalgo has convinced his followers that he is invincible because they are led by the Virgin of Guadalupe. When they see that we are led by Our Lady of Remedios, they will run away. We will pursue them and punish them for what they did in Guanajuato. Long live Our Lady of Remedios!"

The officers around Viceroy Venegas drew their swords and shouted, "Long live Our Lady of Remedios!"

Some in the crowded ballroom began to join in an unenthusiastic chant of "Long live Our Lady of Remedios!" Others stared at one another in disbelief.

The viceroy ordered that the banner be taken outside and a bonfire built so that the insurgents on the hills could see who was the supreme commander of his army. The people in the room followed as the banner was taken down the corridor to the front doors to the palace.

"Carmen," the Marqués said, "this way."

He escorted Lupita and me along a hallway leading in a direction opposite from where the crowd had gone. We entered a room lit only by a solitary candle. After closing the door, Don Esteban went to a chair and sat down.

I crossed the room and knelt by his side. "Don Esteban, you must tell the viceroy what Father Hidalgo said. If a battle comes, thousands will lose their lives. Tens of thousands. It will not be a battle. It will be a massacre!"

"I know," he said and started to get up. "That is why we must get you out of the city, you and the girl. You must not be here when—"

"Don Esteban," I said, placing my hand on his knee to prevent his rising from the chair, "tell the viceroy what Father Hidalgo said. There is no other way to avoid this battle! You must tell him. You must arrange for them to meet!"

He took my hand in his. "Carmen, you saw the viceroy. He has lost touch with reality."

The truth of this statement had not escaped my notice. It was impossible to envision the viceroy meeting with Father Hidalgo. "Then, Don Esteban, you must assume his authority."

For a long moment, he stared at me before he asked, "Do you know what are you saying?"

Excited by my own idea, I got to my feet and paced across the room. "It is the only way. You must assume his powers and meet with

Father Hidalgo and General Allende. The soldiers will follow you." I was thinking of the corporal who had escorted me to the palace. "Why should they die to defend cowards like Humberto who hide in the palace? Don Esteban, declare yourself viceroy of New Spain! The soldiers will recognize your authority."

"Yes," he said. "If I declare myself viceroy, the soldiers will support me. But if I did such a thing, I would be no better than Hidalgo and Morelos. It would be an act of treason. Only the king can appoint a viceroy. Carlos or Fernando would have to approve my becoming viceroy."

"Don Esteban!" I shouted. "The king of Spain is Joseph Bonaparte!" Never before had I raised my voice to him in such a way, but I had to make him understand. "Carlos and Fernando both abdicated the throne of Spain. It is time to face this fact. New Spain has no king!"

Rising from the chair, he looked at me as if I were a stranger. "What would you have us do, Carmen? Surrender? We should capitulate to Hidalgo and Morelos? We should allow one of these men to become the king of New Spain?"

"What they want is for the people of New Spain to choose their leader. That is what they are seeking." I could see that I had only managed to confuse him. "They want the people to elect the leader of New Spain."

"Elect?" he asked. "Whom would they elect, Carmen?"

"The best person."

"How would they know who that is?"

This was not something for which I had a ready answer, but a peculiar thought came into my head. "They might elect someone like...like Cristóbal! The people would elect Cristóbal to be our king." I thought I detected a favorable reaction in his expression so I continued. "No one who has ever known Cristóbal fails to proclaim what a great leader he will be. Once the people of New Spain come to know him, they will certainly want him to be their king. They will demand that he accept the crown of New Spain. I know it, Don Esteban!"

He stroked his beard. "Cristóbal? King of New Spain?"

"Why not?"

He smiled.

"Cristóbal would make a great king for New Spain!" I cried and looked down at Lupita who gave no indication she understood a word we were saying. "He will be the king of New Spain, and I will be his queen!"

The Marqués's eyes narrowed as I continued to talk about how certain I was Cristóbal would be selected to be our king. Finally, when I paused, he asked, "What did you say? About your being the queen. Why did you say that?"

In truth, I did not know why I said it. I was speaking in the manner I did when Cristóbal and I were children and acted out the stories we read in the histories. I shrugged and repeated, "Cristóbal will be the king of New Spain, and I will be his queen."

"A king and a queen are married."

"Yes."

He seemed quite disturbed by that idea. "You cannot marry Cristóbal."

For some reason, I did not like hearing that. I meant nothing by my remark, but I did not like hearing that I could not marry Cristóbal. "Why not?"

Raising his hands, he shrugged, "You simply cannot."

It is strange how one's emotions can change so abruptly. At that moment, I completely forgot my mission to arrange a meeting between the Marqués and Father Hidalgo. My thought turned to something that I suppose I had thought about many times but had never voiced. "Is it because I am half *india*? I cannot marry Cristóbal because my mother was an *india*?"

"No," he said, shaking his head vigorously. "That has nothing to do with it. You must never think that. Your mother was a wonderful person! It makes no difference if she was an *india*. Never think such a thing."

"Then why should I not marry Cristóbal?" It was because I was half *india*; I was certain, and I wanted him to admit it. All my life I had tried not to think about the fact that I was part *india*. I thought it made no difference to me. My father was European, and that was all that mattered. But I was wrong. The *gachupines* looked down on anyone who was part Indian, and Don Esteban was no different. He thought I was somehow inferior because I was *india*. "I want to know why I cannot marry Cristóbal. Tell me! Now!"

"You cannot marry Cristóbal...," he began and then hesitated. "You cannot marry Cristóbal because...because he is your brother."

VII

If I had received a blow to my head, I could not have been more stunned. All I could do was stand there as the Marqués took my hands in his. "Carmencita," he said softly, "I had hoped that when you were older I would be able to explain." I wanted to pull away but could not. "Captain Rangel is not your father. I am."

It would have been easier if I had been struck in the head. Such a hurt can be understood. Now I felt a different hurt, one much worse than mere physical pain. And I was angry, though it was an anger I did not understand.

"I loved your mother very much," he continued, "but our religion made everything impossible. Captain Rangel agreed to marry your mother and give you his name. He had never married, and at his age, it was unlikely he ever would. He was her husband in name only. We did not know what else to do, Carmen. We were helpless. What else could we do?"

I wanted to cry out that what he was telling me was a lie, but I could not. Though I had never allowed myself to consider it, I think I may have known for some time that Baldemar Rangel was not my father. He had never acted differently toward me than he did toward any of the other children of the servants at the hacienda: cold and aloof. And, of course, I in no way resembled him. Like Cristóbal, I had always been taller than the other children. And why not? We shared the same father. It was a strange thing to think that Cristóbal and I were brother and sister.

183

The Marqués continued to talk, but I did not listen. Suddenly, this man standing before me, this man I had admired more than any other person in the world, the man now telling me he was my father, was an enemy. And I hated him. I hated him more than I had hated Juan Riaño, even more than I hated Humberto and Barnet. Don Esteban had lied to me. He had made my life a lie. I was not María del Carmen Rangel, the daughter of a captain in the Royal Dragoons, and most certainly, I had never been Carmen de Abrantes. I had no heritage. I was nothing. That is what he was telling me. Carmen Rangel was a nothing, a lie. I managed to pull my hands from his and back away.

"Carmencita," he said, "please."

"Stay away from me!" I warned when he stepped toward me.

"Please, Carmen. I—"

Shoving past him, I grabbed Lupita's hand and ran out of the room. Of course, I had no idea where I was, but I knew I did not want to go in the direction from whence we had come because I had no desire to encounter the viceroy and the other notables. I now knew who these people were. They were my enemy too. They had always been my enemy, and I had been too stupid to realize it. The Spanish-born, the *gachupines*, were my enemy. And so, dragging Lupita, I ran down the corridor until I came to a door. Reaching for the pull, I turned and saw that Don Esteban had followed. He was calling my name. When I opened the door, I found, to my surprise, it led outside. The front doors were barricaded, protected by artillery, and yet here was a door leading into the palace that was guarded not even by one man, inside or out. It was not even bolted.

Before leaving, I looked back one last time and saw the Marqués standing in the hallway, slumped against the wall. He was holding one hand toward us and the other was clutched to his head. Lupita seemed to want to go to him, but I jerked her through the door and raced across a darkened courtyard.

From that point I did not look back, so I had no idea if Don Esteban was following. I looked neither to the right nor to the left, but ran straight ahead. All I wanted to do was get away from where I had been. Instinctively, I ran toward the darkness, knowing it would afford some measure of protection. Several times, I heard the voices of men shouting, and I heard muskets being discharged. Whether they were warning me to stop or even firing at us, I did not know. Seeing a wooded area, I gathered Lupita into my arms and ran for it. Her little legs would not carry her fast enough. Also, I wanted to place my body between her and the soldiers if in fact they were firing at us.

The wooded area was, I soon discovered, a park. Incredibly, in the middle of the city was this park which now became our refuge. When I no longer heard voices or the sounds of muskets being fired, I stopped to catch my breath and tried to get my bearings. For a moment, I thought I was lost. I knew nothing of Mexico City. The park was like a huge forest, and for all I knew, I might have been running in circles. I might even be headed back to the palace. And then, Lupita raised her hand. She was pointing toward the hill on which the banner of the Virgin of Guadalupe was displayed. There she was, the Blessed Mother, suspended in the sky, shining like a beacon. I knew which way to go.

After what seemed an eternity, I got beyond the city and climbed the hill. At the crest, I was met by men aiming their muskets at us. At first, I thought they were Spanish soldiers until I saw they were not in the elaborate red, blue, and black uniforms. They were insurgents. And then I realized they had no way of knowing who I was. They might think I was the first of many soldiers coming from the capital to fight them. I heard the sound of flintlocks being pulled. How ironic, I thought, if after eluding the *gachupines*, I was shot by General Allende's soldiers.

"*Muchachos!*" I yelled. "Don't shoot! I am one of you!"

And then a familiar voice cried, "Carmen!"

Never had I been so thrilled to hear my name called. It was Coalter. He came sliding down the loose rocks, and before I knew it, I was in his arms.

"Oh, Carmen!" he said. "Why did you go down there alone? I was so worried!"

It felt good to have his arms around me again. I had yearned for his arms to be wrapped around me. Even though he squeezed me with such force I could hardly breathe, it was wonderful. I did not ever want him to let go. However, looking above to the crest of the hill, I saw Father Hidalgo. I could see him in the glow of the bonfire that shone upon the banner. Standing behind him was General Allende. With him were his officers, including Captain Guerra and Lebe Seru. They were all watching me. Father Hidalgo must have told them of my mission, and they were anxiously awaiting for me to report. When I let go of Coalter to climb up the hill, Father Hidalgo reached to help me. Teresa was at his side, and she took my arm.

"Carmen," the priest said, "we heard shots. Were you hurt?" He knelt beside Lupita and touched her face. "Lupita?"

As my cousin embraced me, I assured everyone that neither of us was hurt. When Teresa looked into my face, I averted my eyes.

"Carmen," she whispered, "what's wrong? Have you been crying?"

"No," I said and walked to where Father Hidalgo was now standing next to the general and his officers. "I spoke with the Marqués de Abrantes."

I think Father Hidalgo read my expression because he closed his eyes and bowed his head even before I was able to relate what had happened. I did not, of course, speak of what had transpired of a personal nature between Don Esteban and me, but I spoke of the Marqués's opposition to a constitution or a king chosen by the people. When I finished, Father Hidalgo, his hands clasped tightly behind his back, walked slowly away a few steps and peered down at the city. I, too, gazed at the palace where I had been only a short time before. The image of Don Esteban leaning against the wall lingered in my head.

For a time, no one said anything, and then General Allende asked, "Carmen, can you tell us how the palace is fortified?"

I eagerly detailed to the general how the Spanish artillery was deployed. His officers moved closer as I told of how far apart the light field artillery, the two- and four-pounders, were arranged on the streets and where the fortress guns were located in relation to the palace. I described how kegs of powder were stacked in great quantities near the palace entrance.

Captain Guerra said, "We have one 24-pounder that is not cracked. If we score a direct hit on those kegs we could destroy their heavy cannon in front of the palace and, at the same time, knock down the doors."

"Exactly!" I said. "And there are other doors to the palace that are not even guarded! I know where they are." I began to suggest a plan for taking the palace. Considering how I had come through the park unopposed, I recommended that a platoon of musketeers move through the park and attack the palace immediately after the gunpowder at its entrance was blown. And there were other means I had devised to counter the Marqués's strategy of ringing the palace with artillery. It would still involve the deaths of many people, but the palace would be taken and the *gachupines* destroyed. And that was all I wanted. I wanted every single *gachupín* in Mexico dead. Exactly why I wanted this, I did not stop to ponder. It was what I wanted and that was all that mattered at that moment.

When I stopped talking, Father Hidalgo, still gazing over the city, said, "Carmen?"

We all turned to look at him. "Yes, Father?"

"The banner in front of the palace..."—he glanced at me—"does it display the Crest of the House of Bourbon?"

From where we were situated on the heights above the city it was difficult to discern what was on the banner even though the area around it was well lit with bonfires. It would be natural to assume it was the standard of the royal family.

"No, Father. It is a banner of Our Lady of Remedios. It was the banner carried by Hernán Cortés when he conquered the Aztecs. Viceroy Venegas ordered it placed there."

General Allende asked, "Why would he do that?"

I related what the viceroy had said.

The officers scoffed at the idea that Cortés's banner would frighten their soldiers. They returned to a discussion of how best to stage the invasion of the capital. I listened with great interest. They were using my ideas. Their plans were based on information I had obtained. I had known what to look for and how to analyze that knowledge. For a moment, I found myself thinking how proud Cristóbal would be of me until I remembered that the invasion would almost certainly mean his father would be killed. That gave me pause. Cristóbal's father was my father. An invasion of the capital meant our father would be killed. Part of me was happy that the contest was about to begin, the decisive battle that would mean the defeat of the *gachupines*. Another part was sickened and confused. How could I want my own father to die if I did not even know what I wanted? It was as if I were possessed by a demon.

General Allende approached Father Hidalgo. "We are ready to begin when you give the word."

Father Hidalgo continued to gaze down at the banner and said nothing. All I knew was that if a battle was about to begin, I was not going to fight in a dress, so I went to the wagon where I had left my clothes. After retrieving my leather breeches and boots, I remembered they were just like those the Marqués wore. They were the clothes of the Europeans, the kind of apparel Juan Riaño had said I was not entitled to wear. It was against the law for an Indian to wear such clothes. I threw them aside. I would not wear their clothes, but neither would I wear a dress. I knew what I must wear and why.

I ran to where Captain Guerra was standing and demanded, "Where can I find a uniform?" From his expression, I knew he did not understand. "I want a uniform!"

Coalter was behind me. "Carmen," he asked, "what are you doing? What is wrong?"

There was nothing wrong, and it seemed obvious what I was doing. I turned to face him. "You made your commitment, Coalter, and now I am making mine. All my life I have trained to be a soldier. Now I will be one. I will be a soldier in the army of the Republic of Mexico! We shall fight together."

With some reluctance, Captain Guerra told me where I could obtain a uniform. I retrieved it and returned to our wagon to change. Coalter followed, asking me over and over what was wrong or what had happened in the city. I told him I had no time to explain and that what had happened did not matter.

The uniform was not a particularly good fit. It was necessary to tie a knot in the waist to make it stay up and it was too short, both in the pants and in the shirt sleeves, but it would do. I grabbed my musket, my powder horn, and my knapsack of bullets and wadding.

Quickly, with Coalter on my heels, I raced back to where the officers had gathered at the top of the hill.

To my surprise, they were walking slowly away. I had expected to find orders being given to begin the advance down the hill. Reading the expressions of those moving away from the bonfire, I knew no such action was being taken.

When I saw Lebe Seru and Captain Guerra, I ran to them and asked, "Are you ready to move the twenty-four-pounder? It will have to be moved closer to the palace. I will show you where to position it just beyond the *gachupines'* artillery so you can hit the kegs of gunpowder in front of the palace."

"Carmen," Lebe Seru said. "There will be no battle. We are withdrawing."

"Withdrawing?"

"Yes," Captain Guerra said. "Father Hidalgo has directed that we go to Guadalajara. It is controlled by those loyal to our cause."

On all sides the officers were directing their troops to break camp. Wagons and caissons were being hitched to teams. *Comadres* were removing the banner of the Virgin of Guadalupe. I could not understand what was happening or why. This made no sense at all.

"We are retreating?" I looked from Lebe Seru to Captain Guerra and back. Neither answered. "But why?" I gestured to the city below. "They are beaten. They are trapped like rats! We cannot retreat. We must attack!"

"Thousands will be killed," Captain Guerra said.

"Of course thousands will be killed!" I shouted. I was tired of hearing that excuse. "Is that not what happens in war? People are killed! Such it has always been. Such will it ever be. What do you expect? Why else do we fight wars? Do you expect to fight a war and have no one killed?"

"Carmen," Lebe Seru said, "it is for the best. The cause of liberty is not served by—"

"What do you know?" I interrupted and stared at the African who had saved me from Humberto. Only I was not thinking of that now. My anger continued to grow. "Perhaps you were a slave so long, you do not know how to fight. Is that what it is? You are afraid to fight the *gachupines*?" I looked at Captain Guerra. "Is that what is happening? General Allende's officers are afraid of the *gachupines*? Is General Allende a coward too? Cowards! All of you are cowards!"

Turning to Captain Guerra, Lebe Seru said, "I must help with the loading of our wagons."

After Lebe Seru left, I stared in disbelief at the activity around me. These people were retreating from certain victory. It was absurd. No one in the entire history of warfare had ever retreated from a victory. I could not believe my eyes.

"Señorita Rangel," Captain Guerra said, "you were wrong to speak to Lebe Seru the way you did. He is not a coward. He is a brave and honorable man. You were very foolish to speak in such a way."

Of course I knew what Captain Guerra said was true. Lebe Seru had saved my life at great risk to his own. He had saved Coalter's life. He had fought in Guanajuato. He was no coward, neither were General Allende or any of these people who were preparing to withdraw. They had proven their courage a thousand times over. I do not know why I said what I did, or why I was so angry. None of what was happening made sense. It seemed very wrong to throw away a victory.

When Captain Guerra walked away, I turned to Coalter. "We must attack the Spanish. Tell them, Coalter! If we do not attack them, all will be lost!"

"Carmen," he said, almost in a whisper. "Let's return to the wagon. We must prepare to leave."

He took my arm and in a daze, I walked with him back to the wagon where we found that Teresa and Lupita had already harnessed the team and hitched them to the wagon. They were on the deck, ready to go. "Teresa!" I cried. "Tell them. We must attack the *gachupines* or all is lost!"

"Carmen," she said, "Father Miguel has made the right decision. We will go to Guadalajara. There we can write our constitution and establish a government. The Spanish will know we spared their lives. They will realize we mean them no harm. When they do, we can live together in peace."

"They will not care that we spared their lives!" I shouted. "They will see it as a sign of weakness." I knew how the *gachupines* thought.

It would never occur to them their lives had been spared, and even if it did, they would not care. "Teresa, they will—" Suddenly, all that had happened seemed to weigh down upon my shoulders. I felt terribly weak and fell to the ground.

Before I knew what was happening, Teresa had climbed down and was helping Coalter and Lupita stretch me out in the wagon. I tried to protest and continued to attempt to explain to them why Father Hidalgo's decision was wrong, but I had no strength. The wagon began to move, and when I looked up, I saw Lupita by my side, wedged in amongst the bags of corn and rice. She was looking in the direction of where she and I had been only a short time before. There was a pale light cast against the clouds by the fires in the capital. As we moved to the north, that light slowly faded on the southern horizon, and soon there was nothing behind us but darkness.

✦

In the days that followed, as we turned to the west and pressed on toward Guadalajara, I was not the only one to question the wisdom of Father Hidalgo's decision. At night, councils were held around campfires, and some argued that we should return to the capital and finish what had been started. This kind of talk increased when reports were received that units of the Spanish army had left Mexico City and were following us. They were careful to stay several days behind, but like vultures, they were trailing us, stalking our every move. And when further reports arrived to confirm that the Spanish were putting to the sword people in the villages that had hosted the insurgent army, many advocated we reverse our course and engage the viceroy's troops in open field.

I listened passively to the debates. I did not want to think about what had happened or what might happen. The only way I knew to deal with the unpleasant was not to think about it. And so when we pushed on, I insisted on driving the team, morning to night. It gave me less time to think, fewer opportunities to remember. It also tired me so that in the evenings, I could wrap myself in my *rebozo*, crawl under the wagon, and go to sleep. Sometimes, I wished I could go to sleep and never awaken. I felt hollow, like a tree that had died and was slowly rotting from within. There were days when, unless Coalter and Teresa insisted, I would not bother to eat, and when I did, the food had no taste.

Of course, I continued to assist Coalter when he was called to help with the animals. I wanted to be with him. Being near Coalter was the only thing that prevented the rage I felt from erupting into something beyond all control. Thankfully, he did not ask what had happened in the capital. Certainly he knew, just as Teresa did, that something had occurred there to disturb me, but like Teresa, he never pressed for an explanation. Sometimes in the evenings, we would sit together for a long while and Coalter would put his arms around me and hold me. I wanted to tell him what Don Esteban had said. I wanted to share what was now a terrible burden, but how could I tell him the truth? I was ashamed. I could not tell either him or Teresa that my entire life had been a lie. More than that, much more than that, I could not tell them I had been conceived in sin.

As we traveled across the eastern Sierra Madres and time passed, it began to occur to me what it now meant to know that Cristóbal was my brother. Certainly, I could not marry my own brother. There was no longer a need to pretend. I was free to admit my love for Coalter. And, despite my anger at Don Esteban and the *gachupines*, this made me very happy. It made me happy because I knew I loved Coalter and he loved me. Teresa was right. There was no need for words. Love could not be explained in words. I needed no words to realize that Coalter and I loved each another. He had said he loved me from the first time he saw me, and I knew the same was true for me. Though I had pretended otherwise, I had to admit I had loved him from the first time I saw him as well. From the very depths of my soul, from a place beneath all the lies and pretensions, I loved him.

The problem was how to convey my love to him, how to let him know the situation had changed without divulging what had happened in Mexico City. Day after day, he comforted me, but said nothing. As far as he was concerned, I was still planning to marry Cristóbal, and so he said and did nothing other than try to lighten my passage through a time of troubles. I remembered what Teresa had

said about his being an honorable man and how this would prevent
him from speaking of his love for me. I recalled how he had apologized the time he thought I had been offended by his kiss. More than
anything, I wanted him to express his love to me again, but I did not
know what to do. I could not talk to Teresa about my quandry
because I would have to tell her the ugly truth about me, and I did
not want to do that.

One evening, we set up camp in a grove of cedars near a bend in
a river. After dinner, Teresa said she was going with Lupita to a
neighboring camp where musicians were going to play. People often
asked Teresa to come to their camps because she sang so beautifully.
I had grown to enjoy listening to her, and I told her Coalter and I
would come later because it was necessary that repairs be made to
one of the wagon wheels.

She looked at me strangely and then touched my hand. "This
camp we are going to, Carmen,"—she paused—"Lupita and I will
spend the night there. Captain Guerra and his men are on patrol
tonight and will not return until tomorrow."

I helped her find extra blankets and told her again we would be
along later.

It took longer than expected to make the repairs and by the time
we finished, it was dark and it had begun to rain. Thinking it would
be just a passing shower, we crawled under the wagon. It was not
long before we realized the rain had set in for the night, and it was
turning cold. I sat down next to Coalter. I very much wanted him to
hold me, and after wrapping his serape around me, he did.

Soon, I understood what Teresa had been trying to tell me. Coalter and I were alone, and from the way the wagon had been situated,
we were not in view of the other camps. It was the first time since we
had met that we had had a measure of privacy. I looked up into his
eyes and touched his face. He smiled but looked away. Gently, I
pulled him closer, turned his face to mine, and kissed him.

"Carmen," he whispered. "We must not—"

I placed the tips of my fingers to his lips to hush him. I kissed
him again.

He asked, "What of Cristóbal?"

"I have come to realize I do not love Cristóbal as I love you, Coalter." It was the truth. Despite what had happened, my affection for Cristóbal had not lessened. It was the natural affection a sister has for her brother. That was what it had always been even before I was aware that Cristóbal was my brother. But it was not the love I felt for Coalter. "I will not marry Cristóbal. It is you I love."

"Carmen!" he whispered and hugged me so tightly I thought my ribs might break. And then, he looked at me. "Why? What happened? Is it... is it because of something that happened in Mexico City?"

I did not want to lie to Coalter, so I ignored his question and said, "What happened is that I have come to know that I love you, Coalter. I love you with all my heart."

"Then," he began, and his beautiful smile deepened, "we can be married! Let us go to Father Miguel. Tonight! He can marry us. Let us go at once!"

It was not without difficulty that I restrained him from rising and dashing out into the rain which was coming down in a torrent. I held him close to me. "No, Coalter. We cannot be married."

"I do not understand. You said you will not marry Cristóbal. Why can we not be married? Let us go to Father Miguel."

The disappointment and confusion in his eyes saddened me. I did not want to hurt Coalter, this man who was more precious to me than my own life. However, neither could I tell him the real reason I could not marry him. I could not tell him I was conceived in sin and not worthy of becoming his wife. It occurred to me there was an answer I could give and not have to lie.

"Father Miguel cannot marry us, Coalter."

"He is a priest."

"Father Miguel has been excommunicated by the archbishop. He is no longer a priest." It pained me to say this, not only for Coalter's sake, but for Father Hidalgo's as well. Everyone knew how devastated he had been when the news of his excommunication became known. "He is forbidden to perform the sacraments of the church. He would be unable to marry us."

It took a moment for Coalter to assimilate this fact, and then he said, "There are other priests in camp. There is Mariano Hidalgo, Father Miguel's brother. He is a priest. He could marry us."

"No," I said and rested my head to his chest. I could hear his heart beating. "The archbishop excommunicated all priests who follow Father Miguel. They too are without authority to perform the sacraments."

"It is not right, Carmen. Father Miguel and the priests who follow him have tried to stay the hand of those who kill the children of New Spain. For this, he is excommunicated? It is not right!"

"I know, my love," I said and placed my hand beneath his shirt.

"I know a priest in San Antonio de Béxar. He is a good friend of my father's. He would not have been excommunicated. We shall go to him. He will marry us."

"Yes," I said. All I knew was that San Antonio de Béxar was a town in Texas, and Texas was a long way off. I would deal with that when the time came, if it came. "This priest in San Antonio de Béxar will marry us."

He brushed my hair back from my face. "You will go with me to Texas, Carmen? You will go north to Texas and become my wife?"

"I will go with you anywhere you wish."

Coalter wanted to wait until we were married to consummate our love, but I did not. I loved Coalter deeply, more than I ever thought possible. It was time we gave expression to our love for one another. It was as natural as the beating of our hearts.

✦

In the days following, people seemed to sense there was now a special relationship between Coalter and me. They treated us as husband and wife and respected our need for privacy. There were many young couples like us whose lives had been disrupted by the revolution. Life could not stop because the archbishop in Mexico City had chosen to side with the Spanish and excommunicate Father Hidalgo and the priests who followed him. We would all carry on and try to adjust as best we could until life could return to normal. Everyone prayed it would be soon. Eventually, this conflict would be resolved. However, no one could predict when this would come to pass.

✦

General Allende's army was received with great enthusiasm by the citizens of Guadalajara, a lovely, sun-bathed city of brightly colored buildings and lush tropical foliage. I was surprised to learn we were not too far from the Pacific Ocean. Entering the city, Father Hidalgo, as was his custom, went first to the church where a Te Deum was sung. Wherever this man went, there was bound to be music. He then spoke to the people and explained why he had come to Guadalajara. He renewed his pledge to support the principles of liberty, equality, and justice.

In answer to those who faulted him for not choosing to decide the issue of independence in the field of battle, he said, "A single drop of Mexican blood weighs more, in our estimation, than the success of a single battle."

With great energy, Father Hidalgo set out to organize and strengthen the interim government while plans were made to convene the constitutional assembly in Guadalajara. He appointed a minister of justice, a secretary of state, and a treasurer. He named ambassadors to countries he thought might be sympathetic to the insurgent cause. Governors and judges were appointed throughout the land. Laws were passed outlawing the system of tribute, the *encomienda*, established by Hernán Cortés and the *conquistadores*. Lands were returned to the Indians. Royal monopolies were abolished so that anyone who wished to engage in commerce and agriculture could do so without restriction. These measures and others of a similar nature were referred to as the "Reconquest of Mexico."

A newspaper, *El Despertador Americano*, was founded. Its pages served Father Hidalgo to make clear his objectives to Mexico and to the world. He wrote: "We believe we are authorized by the Supreme Being, from whom we received the same natural rights as all other people, to openly aspire to independence." Therefore, for the first time, he openly and plainly proclaimed Mexico's independence from Spain.

In issue after issue of *El Despertador Americano*, Father Hidalgo explained the reasons for the insurrection. He said self-government was an idea impressed upon peoples' minds by God. He asked the Spanish how they could refuse the Mexican people the right to self-government when at that very moment they were themselves denied self-government in Spain by the French tyrant, Napoleon Bonaparte, whose brother occupied the throne only by force of arms. He wrote: "Three hundred years ago, you robbed us of the most estimable and precious thing which men and women may have: Liberty! The time is long past for its return."

News received from other parts of the country was encouraging, at least at first. Father Morelos sent word of success against the royalists in the south. He developed a strategy called guerrilla warfare, a way of fighting that involved harassment of the enemy by small bands of soldiers who were seldom seen before they struck. Using this approach, he was able to capture Acapulco and other cities on the Pacific coast. It seemed Father Hidalgo's plan might work. By demonstrating that a republican government had the support of a majority of the people, he hoped the Spanish would see the futility of continuing to fight.

But then news came that the viceroy's armies had recaptured Guanajuato; they had erected dozens of gallows and hung anyone suspected of having supported the insurgency. Town after town, village after village, was recaptured and supporters of the insurgency were hung, shot, or had their throats cut. The Spanish generals then consolidated their forces and began a slow advance on Guadalajara.

During the time Father Hidalgo was at work on the creation of a government, General Allende had attempted to fashion the men and women who had joined the insurgency into a disciplined army. Though many had gone home after the retreat from Mexico City, the army still numbered in the tens of thousands. Those remaining were eager to confront the royalists in battle. The problem continued to be a lack of weapons and gunpowder. Consequently, Allende was reluctant to commit to a single battle against a force vastly superior in field artillery. He advocated a series of surprise attacks and quick retreats, the guerrilla strategy so effectively employed in the south by

José Morelos. But Father Hidalgo sought an opportunity to settle the
matter once and for all in the open field, to prevent the massacre of
civilians caught in a battle. Finally, General Allende yielded to the
priest's arguments, and the insurgent army marched out of Guadalajara to meet the approaching royalist army.

✦

Twelve leagues east of the city near the Bridge of Calderón over
the Santiago River, the advance elements of the Spanish army were
sighted. I was anxious to learn who was in command. Since Don Esteban had directed the defense of the capital, I wondered if the viceroy
had selected him to lead the pursuit of the insurgents. It was not
long, however, before a reconnaissance party General Allende dispatched to scout the enemy's strength returned to report that the
gachupín forces were led by General Manuel de Flon. I supposed the
Marqués had, for some reason, remained in Mexico City. Perhaps he
was waiting for Cristóbal to return from Spain with King Fernando.

Using a telescope, General Allende scanned the enemy lines as
they advanced. I asked if I could take a look, and when I trained the
instrument at the assembly of royalist leaders, I saw the red-faced
Flon. I recognized several other officers including General Joaquín de
Arredondo, who had commanded the garrison at Guanajuato before
being promoted to command the armies of the northern provinces. He
had been a friend of Juan Riaño and in many ways reminded me of
the arrogant intendant.

At one point I was startled when I focused on one of the other
officers I knew viewing us through his telescope. I was certain that if
he saw me, he would recognize me. If he did see me, and there was no
reason he would not, he probably wondered what the daughter of
Baldemar Rangel, the man people in Guanajuato thought was my
father, was doing wearing the uniform of the army of insurrection. If
the Spanish were triumphant, there was no way I could return to the
life I had lived before. I did not try to hide. If I was recognized, so be
it. I was where I wanted to be.

As is often the case with major battles, the activity most crucial
to victory occurred before the first shot was fired. For hours, the gen-

erals on both sides shifted their soldiers and equipment time and again in an effort to obtain positions that set them at an advantage over the enemy. Units of infantry or cavalry would be moved by one side, and immediately the opposing general would withdraw a platoon of grenadiers and advance a contingent of dragoons. Such a response would then cause the other side to make adjustments, so that shortly afterwards with drums beating cadence, artillery pieces were pulled back or brought forward. It was like a deadly game of chess. The fate of a nation depended on the outcome of this battle. And many who awoke to this day would not live to see its end.

After Teresa, Coalter, and I helped the physicians establish a field hospital away from where the battle was likely to take place, I ventured up a hill closer to the armies. Now I could see how the forces had been deployed. It was not long before I understood General Allende's strategy, and it was masterful. He had somehow managed to draw the Spanish to the east side of the Santiago River while he occupied the west bank. By so doing, he had decreased the royalists' ability to use the many two- and four-pounder cannon they had brought from Mexico City. Light field artillery was designed to be moved rapidly from place to place in order to be able to break the advance of infantry, dragoons, or a cavalry charge. Outnumbered, the Spanish were assuredly counting on the use of their small cannon to wreak havoc on the insurgent army. That option was now severely handicapped by the river.

General de Flon must have realized that he had been outmaneuvered, because he signaled a withdrawal. It was then that General Allende ordered the firing of the siege guns that were still functional. From where I was located, I could see that Captain Guerra and Lebe Seru commanded those guns. Sailing across the river, thirty-pound balls slammed into the enemy retreat lines. If the royalists had known how limited was the insurgent supply of gunpowder and how few of the cannon aimed at them worked, they probably would have consummated their escape, but believing that their retreat had been cut off, they quickly returned to protected positions along the banks of the river. Allende had pinned them down. They would have to fight on his terms or surrender. When Teresa joined me on the hill after the guns were silenced, I pointed out what was happening.

"I hope they surrender," she said.

"They will not," I assured her, "until General de Flon is killed. The lives of his soldiers mean nothing to him. That is why he is called *El Carnicero*, the Butcher."

The sulphurous odor of gunpowder drifted to where we stood, and my stomach knotted. There was a time when I loved this smell. It made me think of the glorious battles Cristóbal and I had read about in the histories. But now it choked me and sickened me because I knew the suffering it caused. It made me quite nauseous, and to my great embarrassment, I found myself retching.

Teresa asked, "Carmen, are you ill?"

"A little," I said and explained to her about the gunpowder.

She smiled. "It is not the gunpowder that makes you feel that way."

I had suspected something but was unsure. I told her what was happening.

Teresa embraced me. "Have you told Coalter?"

"No, Teresa. I am not sure. It could be a false sign. Remember the things your mother told us?"

"I think you can be sure. When will you tell him?"

To that, I had no answer. Certainly, I could not go to him at the beginning of a great battle and tell him I thought it possible I was going to have a baby. He was preparing the wagons to take the wounded to the physicians. It was an important task, and he did not need to be thinking about this matter, especially since I was not yet certain.

When I looked back across the river, I saw that the Spanish were moving their artillery closer to the bank, near a place where the current ran shallow. They were preparing to give cover to a troop of cavalry about to attempt to ford the river. Insurgent musketeers were moving forward to prevent their crossing. If the cavalry managed to ford the river, they almost certainly would attack the siege guns. With those gone, the royalists could bring their artillery across the river and that would change everything. The battle would be over quickly and end in their favor.

Teresa smiled. "You will have a beautiful child, Carmen. Don Esteban will be very proud."

Her statement puzzled me. "Why should Don Esteban be proud? Why should he even care?"

"Because you will have his grandchild."

Somehow, I was not surprised that Teresa knew. "How long have you known he was my father?"

"Several years. My mother told me of the love Cata Valeria had for Don Esteban and his love for her. She told me you were their daughter." I guess my expression betrayed my thoughts because she continued: "Do not hate your father, Carmen. He loves you."

The Spanish began a cannonade of the west bank just as the cavalry commenced to charge. Direct hits were scored on the musketeers, killing many of them instantly. Seeing this, hundreds of insurgents, most of them armed only with machetes, rushed down the embankment to confront the horsemen. Dozens were felled by the barrage, but others made it to the banks, hacking at the riders and their mounts. The cavalrymen swung their swords at the men and women who were wading out to challenge them, and soon the river was red with blood.

Looking back to where Captain Guerra and Lebe Seru were in command of the siege guns, I cried out for them to aim for the Spanish artillery which continued to fire on the insurgents that raced down the embankment to replace their fallen comrades. I could not be heard over the noise, of course. I asked Teresa to return to the field hospital. Already the wounded were being loaded onto Coalter's wagons. I told her I would join them soon. Then I ran as fast as I could to where the big cannon sat idle and shouted, "Why aren't you firing? You must knock out the Spanish cannon! Hurry!"

"We cannot," Captain Guerra said.

"Why not?"

"We have only enough powder for two, perhaps three, more rounds. If we fire now, we will have nothing to use when the Spanish attempt to bring their artillery across the river."

I could see he spoke the truth about the powder. There was only one unopened keg, and it required twelve pounds of powder to fire one of the big guns. I watched in horror as wave after wave of men and women hurled themselves against the royalist cavalry. Fired upon by both artillery and musketeers, the insurgents were having to run over the dead bodies of their *compañeros*, but they were beating back the cavalry. They were not allowing the Spanish to ford the river. Those who ran down the embankment knew they would be killed. Their deaths were certain. They were sacrificing their own lives to keep the royalists from coming to our side of the river. Never had I witnessed such courage.

Lebe Seru said, "If we can hold them on the west bank of the river and draw their fire, they too will exhaust their supply of powder. When that happens, they are defeated."

The men and women of the army of insurrection, fighting only with their bare hands or the most primitive of weapons, were forcing the royalists to use up their powder knowing that this would deprive the enemy of their advantage. It was the only path to victory. They were dying so that others could be free.

I turned to Captain Guerra. "I will get my musket. I am a good shot. I can hit those manning the artillery."

"It would do no good. The Spanish are beyond the range of our muskets."

It was something I should have grasped. The Spanish artillery was well out of range of a musket. I remembered Barnet's long-rifles. The royalist cannoneers would be in easy range of anyone using such a weapon. Even the Spanish generals, watching the battle astride their horses on a hill well behind their artillery positions, could be hit with a rifle. General de Flon, in his red coat and gold epaulets, would be an easy target for a rifleman as would be Joaquín Arredondo and the others. For the first time, I understood what a difference long-rifles could make in a battle. But we had no rifles and our soldiers on the embankment were being slaughtered by round after deadly round of shot being fired by the Spanish cannon.

"I have to do something!" I cried. I realized the importance of those ready to fire the siege gun should the Spanish reach our bank and attempt to bring across their field artillery. But I was not necessary to the firing of the cannon. And I knew how to use a machete. "I'm going to the river!"

Captain Guerra said, "Carmen, go and help Coalter. Many who have been hurt can be saved. They need you."

Though I felt like a coward, I agreed to go. And I was needed. Throughout the afternoon, as the battle raged along the banks of the river, we worked unceasingly to transport the wounded to the physicians' camp. Most of the time, I drove the wagon back to the field hospital while Coalter ran alongside carrying someone in his arms because there simply was no more room on the bed of the cart. We would unload the wagon, carrying those who were still alive to the physicians who were working frantically to save lives; we deposited the dead away from the camp. Then we would race back to the banks of the river.

The fighting ended at dusk. Under the light of torches and lanterns, we continued to assist the physicians with the wounded. Coalter tried to get me to stop and rest. Neither of us had eaten anything all day. In the midst of such misery, who could have an appetite?

"You rest," I told him, enjoying the luxury of a moment in his arms. "You are exhausted."

He kissed me and then looked into my eyes. "I cannot, but you should stop for a while. I saw you earlier behind those bushes. You were ill."

"It is all of this death and suffering," I said, still unable to tell him what might be the nature of my illness. Now was not the time.

Before the first light of dawn, the fighting began anew on the banks of the river. It was only a matter of minutes before there were fresh casualties, and we were feverishly at work transporting them to the camp. After the third trip, one of the physicians asked that I stay and help hold down the wounded. Teresa and the women were helping, but they needed more people. Coalter continued with the wagon.

At midmorning, Captain Guerra came rushing into camp followed by a squad of soldiers, each carrying muskets and powder horns. "Carmen," he shouted, "some of the Spanish have crossed the river south of here! We have to stop them before they get behind our positions on the banks. There is no one to stop them except these few men with me. I've left Lebe Seru and two men with the cannon in case the Spanish break through below. I need you to go with me."

I ran to the wagon, retrieved my musket, and followed Captain Guerra and his men. We moved south along a ridge and up a hill.

"We'll wait for them here," Captain Guerra said. "Load your weapons."

I had poured the powder into the tube and was about to insert wadding when, looking up, I saw, next to me, my cousin.

"Teresa, what are you doing here?"

She was ramming a ball into the tube of an old brass-barreled musket.

"Teresa, go back!"

She withdrew the rod and smiled at me.

"You don't even know how to shoot a musket!"

"Yes, I do. Don't you remember? You taught me. You made me learn so you could beat me in the contests of marksmanship we used to have at the hacienda. I happen to be a very good shot."

I continued to beseech Teresa to return to camp until Captain Guerra broke us into two ranks and instructed us on how to pattern our fire so that we would not all aim at the same target or reload our weapons at the same time. While he talked, I finished packing the tube of my gun. Those of us in the front rank stretched out flat on the ground. My cousin was to my right. Again, I told her to go back to the field hospital.

"I know what I'm doing, Carmencita."

The musket she was holding was longer than she was tall. When fired, its recoil would probably break her shoulder.

"Here they come!" Captain Guerra warned.

Advancing up the embankment, muskets held at ready, a line of Spanish infantry was moving toward our position. They had not seen us. I cocked the flintlock on my gun and brought my finger to the trigger.

"Aim!" Captain Guerra said.

I framed my sights on the man at the far left of the formation. With each step they grew larger and would soon be in range. My target was becoming clearer through a haze of smoke. He was wearing a blue uniform with no insignia. I could see his face. He was a young man. Though tall, his face was that of a boy, a golden-haired boy whose locks were tossed by a strong breeze.

Slowly, I lowered the barrel. It could not be possible, I thought. I blinked my eyes. The soldier I was supposed to kill looked like Cristóbal! Had Cristóbal returned from Spain? I quickly calculated the months since he had left and realized that it was possible.

Behind me, Captain Guerra said, "Carmen, stay down!"

I had started to get up. My impulse was to run to Cristóbal. I wanted to throw my arms around him. He was my brother. How could I kill my own brother?

"Steady," Captain Guerra said. "They are almost within range. Hold steady."

And then I could see it was not Cristóbal, but a young man who looked like him. He was not as tall as Cristóbal. And I saw something in his face that I had never seen in Cristóbal's: fear. The boy coming up the hill was frightened. I looked at the soldier to his left, an older man. He too was afraid. All the soldiers were terrified. I could feel their fear as deeply as my own.

"Fire!"

I heard the crack of muskets as those in my rank obeyed Captain Guerra's command. But I could not squeeze the trigger. I watched the boy who was my target crouch and look at his fallen comrades, some of whom lay motionless on the ground. Others, wounded, screamed out in pain. I aimed again. The boy was raising his musket, taking aim. I knew I must fire or he would shoot one of those in my rank who had raised to reload their weapons.

I could not do it. He was just a boy, a frightened boy far from his home. At that very moment, there were probably people somewhere who were praying for his safe return; perhaps his mother, maybe a sister, or a sweetheart. They did not want him to die. It did not seem right that one so young should die. He had not yet had a chance to live.

Shifting my aim to the soldier next to the boy, I saw that he was older. There were lines in his face and a gleam of silver in his mustache drooping from perspiration. He had lived longer. He had seen life, so I decided I would kill him instead of the boy. The Spanish soldiers fired their weapons, and I heard the cries of those among us who had been hit. I still could not squeeze the trigger. I could not even feel my hand as I watched the man I had selected as my target commence to reload his musket.

"Fire!" Captain Guerra shouted, and those in the second rank discharged their weapons.

Though I did not fire my weapon, I watched through my sights as the older man dropped his weapon and clutched at his eye which had exploded in a burst of blood. Someone else's bullet had found its mark. The man fell to the ground next to the boy who looked like Cristóbal. He too had been hit. Neither man moved. None of the Spanish soldiers remained standing. For a moment, I watched the motionless bodies. All were dead.

When I became aware that the soldiers behind me were standing, I raised up and looked to my right.

"Teresa?" I said and then froze. She was slumped, face forward, on the ground. "Teresa!"

Captain Guerra rushed to my side and helped me turn my cousin over as I prayed not to see that horrible blank stare I had so come to dread. She was alive, but when she opened her mouth to speak and blood poured out, I knew what it meant. I had seen too many wounded not to realize that blood in the mouth was a very bad sign. Reluctantly, I let my gaze drop, and I saw where the bullet had entered. She had been shot in the stomach.

"We must get her to the physicians," I said. "Quickly!"

Captain Guerra lowered his head.

I knew what he was thinking, and I would not permit it. Teresa could not die. I would not let it happen.

"Carmen, let her die in peace."

I lifted Teresa into my arms and began to run toward the camp.

Halfway there, Teresa opened her eyes and smiled. "Carmencita?" she whispered. "Did you see him?"

My lungs were bursting. "Who, Teresa?"

"Rubén. He was there with me. Just a moment ago. It was Rubén. He has come to take me home."

Momentarily, I paused when I heard the noise of a loud blast. At first, I thought Lebe Seru had fired the siege gun, which meant the Spanish were trying to bring their artillery across the river. And then there was a second blast and a third. They were louder than the noise made by the siege gun. Much louder. It was a series of explosions. I ran into the camp and shoved through the people around one of the physicians. He helped me lay my cousin to the ground. I fell to my hands and knees and tried to catch my breath. When I looked up, the physician had turned from Teresa to me.

"There is nothing I can do."

"Help her," I begged. "Help her!"

Suddenly, the camp was filling with people. Many of them were not wounded. I saw Lebe Seru and his men. They had abandoned the siege gun. And I began to smell smoke. There was the strong aroma of burning grass and white smoke was streaming into the camp. The stench of sulphur that hung in the air was overpowering. Coalter drove the wagon, empty of any wounded, into camp. He jumped from the deck and ran to where I was kneeling.

"Coalter," I gasped, the smoke now choking me. "Teresa has been shot. We must help her."

Captain Guerra ran into the camp. I saw him sink to one knee. His shirt was bloodied. He too had been wounded. Lebe Seru rushed to his side just as General Allende rode in on a destrier and quickly dismounted. He ran to the physician in charge of the camp.

"The Spanish," he shouted, "scored a hit on one of our ammunition wagons. It ignited a grass fire which is coming this way. We will have to retreat."

"But General," the physician said, "the wounded cannot be moved!"

More officers rode into the camp. Everything was in disarray. The smoke was growing thicker, and I felt the heat of the fire. The wind was blowing it our way. Everyone was coughing. I stared at the thickening wall of smoke in disbelief. We had been on the verge of victory. We were defeating the Spanish, and now, suddenly, this disaster. Why was it happening? Had God taken the side of those who would slit the throats of children with their swords because they did not want to waste bullets? I had always believed that wars were won by those who were on the side of what was right. What was happening could not be possible.

General Allende rushed to Captain Guerra who, with Lebe Seru's help, had managed to get to his feet. Father Hidalgo ran into camp, and immediately, several officers tried to lift him on the back of a horse. He wanted to go to the wounded.

When I looked down, Teresa smiled. "Do you see him, Carmen?"

"Who, Teresa?" I gasped, choking on the smoke which was now so thick I could no longer see the river.

"Rubén is here. Don't you see him?"

After a hurried conference, General Allende issued the order for a retreat. Muskets were to be loaded and left with the wounded. Suddenly, it occurred to me what was happening. The wounded were to slow the royalists' pursuit. Their lives were to be forfeited so that the army could escape the Spanish who were now bringing their artillery across the river.

"No!" I cried, getting to my feet. Through the smoke, I could see Father Hidalgo was as opposed to the plan as I was, but he had been forced onto the horse and was being escorted from the camp behind General Allende.

Coalter was unharnessing the team to the wagon so that the mules could escape as best they could. It would be impossible to drive them through the smoke. He turned and shouted, "Carmen, hurry. We must go!"

"I cannot leave Teresa!"

Holding several muskets in his arms, Captain Guerra staggered to where we were and looked down at Teresa. He had been placed in command of those who would remain behind.

"I can use a musket, Captain," Teresa said and looked at me. "I had a good teacher."

Kneeling at her side, I said, "Teresa, I cannot leave you here!"

"Take care of her," Teresa whispered and nodded toward Lupita who was watching us. I had not noticed when the little girl had entered the camp. "Now off with you. Hurry!"

Lebe Seru picked up Lupita and carried her in his arms. He and Coalter guided me away from my cousin who looked so small lying there on the crest of that hill. Soon, I could no longer see her for the smoke. At the edge of camp, we stopped and Lebe Seru embraced Captain Guerra. The African was so overcome he was unable to speak.

"Do not grieve, my friend," Captain Guerra said. "I leave this world a free man. More than that, you cannot ask." He stepped back and saluted. "Long live liberty!"

"Long live liberty," Lebe Seru managed to respond weakly.

As we ran through the billows of swirling smoke, I tried to cover my face with my hands. Here and there, patches of dry grass had ignited. We made our way around them when we could and leapt over the flames when we could not. Suddenly, there was the unmistakable blast of two-pounders followed by the crack of musket fire. The Spanish had crossed the river and were mounting an attack. For a long while, the guns roared, the sound becoming ever more faint as we continued to run. And then there was silence.

VIII

Because of the sacrifice made by brave men and women like Teresa and Captain Guerra, the insurgent army was able to escape what would have been certain annihilation. Traveling day and night, we made our way to the mountainous terrain of the Sierra Madre where the royalists would find it difficult to follow with their artillery. Some urged that we stand and fight, for the Spanish had also been weakened. Indeed, General Allende's scouts discovered that the butcher, Flon, had been killed in the last stage of the battle. The royalists had suffered losses, and we still outnumbered them, but in the final analysis, what could not be ignored was our lack of gunpowder. To attack artillery armed with nothing but machetes and slingshots would be suicide.

The only advantage the insurgents had, and it was not a small one, was the support of the people in the villages and countryside. The activities of the royalist armies were monitored by these people who then sent runners to relay information to General Allende. Unfortunately, each report brought fresh news of how desperate our situation was. Fresh troops and supplies were arriving each day from Mexico City to reinforce the army that had defeated us at Calderón. One option was to flee south and link forces with Father Morelos. The Spanish, however, anticipated this strategy and concentrated their strength between our position and the south, effectively blocking our way.

210

Meeting at a secluded hacienda called Pabellón, the leaders of the insurgency considered a bold course of action put forward by Father Hidalgo. Although risky, if it met with success the impasse would break. The plan called for utilizing the sheer size and vast distances of New Spain as a weapon against the Spanish. Father Hidalgo proposed shifting the new government to the northern provinces where, hundreds of leagues from their armories in Mexico City and their ports on the gulf, the royalists would find it difficult to enforce their authority. Spanish power had proven ineffective against the *indios* to the north. Since the insurgency was made up largely of Indians, such people would be our natural allies. We would be able to accomplish in the isolation of the north what Father Morelos was doing in the remote south.

"What we need," Father Hidalgo said, "is time. We need time to prepare for what will be a long struggle. Going north will give us this time."

His plan was adopted, and it was decided that the seat of government would be moved to San Antonio de Béxar in Texas. We made our way into a flat, desert-like country that would have to be crossed before reaching Texas. Coalter, Lupita, and I were with the soldiers commanded by Lebe Seru whom General Allende had promoted to the rank of captain. We were the rear guard of a larger force assigned to protect Father Hidalgo and his government-in-transit. There were vast uninhabited spaces between villages, and from time to time we were met by bands of guerrilla fighters who would escort the insurgent government through their territory and provide us with food. They were always overjoyed to see Father Hidalgo, and despite the urgency of our flight, he would always take the time to visit with them and to talk about liberty, equality, and justice.

✦

The last town we entered before embarking on the final stage of the journey to Texas was Saltillo. Because Father Hidalgo's supporters still held it, he was received there with great enthusiasm. As always, when this happened, it reminded me of the fiestas we used to have at the Hacienda de Abrantes and of how Teresa so loved to sing on those occasions. As we sat on a sun-bleached stone bench and watched the dancing, I missed my cousin very much. Sensing my sadness, Coalter held my hand as we listened to the the laughing boys and girls who, thankfully, had not seen the horrors we had. Maybe, I told Coalter, in Texas there would be no more killing, no more dying. Maybe the worst was over.

"I hope that is the case," he said softly stroking my hair. The day before I had cut my hair very short because it was easier to keep clean when we traveled. Afterward, I had worried I had cut it too short and that Coalter might not approve of it because it might make me look like a boy. But he said he loved me no matter how short I cut my hair.

It was cold so I pulled my serape tight around my shoulders. In the flight from Calderón, I had lost my *rebozo*, and now I wore a serape made of a coarsely woven unbleached wool. It was the kind of pullover serape normally worn by men.

"Carmen," Coalter said smiling, "you are going to love Texas. There is a river there called the Brazos and another called the Colorado. Between them lie the most beautiful green valleys and fertile lands in the world. After we are married, I would like for us to go to a place I know on the Brazos. We can build a cabin. You will be happy there, Carmen. I promise you that."

Because we had been constantly on the run to elude the Spanish, I still had not told him I thought I was with child. And now that we were so close to this land he so loved, this Texas, I thought it best I should wait until we arrived there to tell him.

Squeezing his hand tightly, I said, "I will be happy wherever you are. It does not matter where we live. We could live at the top of the world or at the bottom. As long as I am with you, I will be happy."

He brought my hands to his lips and caressed them. His eyes sparkled.

Smiling, I tried to conceal my uncertainty. I continued to wonder what Coalter would think if he knew the truth about me. Would he still love me if he knew I was conceived in sin, that my father was not the man who had married my mother? Was I being dishonest not to disclose this terrible truth to the man who wanted me to be his wife?

It had occurred to me that if I told him, he may no longer wish for me to be his wife. I would not blame him. And, if in fact I was with child, what would it mean for that child if Coalter decided he no longer wished to marry me?

"Carmen?"

I looked up. He had been talking, and I had not been listening.

"Carmen, what's wrong?"

"Nothing," I lied.

There was such concern in his beautiful eyes. "Please do not worry. Everything will be fine from now on. I will take care of you. I love you. I will protect you."

We embraced, and I wished that everyone in the world could know the love that I felt at that moment. I loved Coalter so very, very much! I knew he would take care of me and I would take care of him. Everything would be well from then on.

✦

The next morning, Father Hidalgo and the other leaders of the government left Saltillo at daybreak. Some distance north of town they were to meet the escort that would guide the main body of General Allende's army to the Río Bravo, beyond which was our destination: Texas. The commander of the escort was to be Colonel Ignacio Elizondo, a *gachupín* who had joined the insurgency after the fall of the Alhóndiga in Guanajuato. There was something about this man I did not like. He was haughty and arrogant, but since those were qualities not unusual among people of his station, I tried to put aside my trepidation.

Lebe Seru waited until the caravan was out of sight before following. There had been unconfirmed sightings of a large royalist force to the south, one led by General Arredondo himself. If we saw Spanish troops, we would fire shots to alert those ahead. We carried extra pouches of water in addition to our other bags because the area we were to cross was reported to be exceptionally dry. The brown clouds of an approaching dust storm could be seen on the horizon.

Just before noon we heard the noise of musket fire in the distance. The sounds came from the north. We stared at each other, hoping someone would think of a reason we should not be alarmed. Maybe, one of the soldiers suggested, there was a celebration. Sometimes insurgent bands would fire a salute when they sighted Father Hidalgo. But the firing continued, and we all recognized the pattern of the shots. It was no celebration. It was a battle. Lebe Seru gave the order to advance.

Before leaving, Coalter said, "Carmen, stay here with Lupita."

Remaining behind was not something I wanted to do, but I knew we could not take Lupita to the scene of a battle nor could she be left alone because the Spanish might be behind us. They did not hesitate to kill insurgents' children. If I saw them coming, I could hide her.

For what seemed an eternity, I knelt beside Lupita and waited as the firing continued. Finally, I could not stand it any longer, and after concealing Lupita in some tall grasses and firmly instructing her to stay put, I raced ahead toward the sounds of battle.

By the time I got to the scene of the fighting, the shooting had stopped. It was difficult to determine what had happened because sand was blowing, reducing visibility to no more than a few feet. There were many men on horseback, far more than had been with Father Hidalgo's party. As I drew near, I was able to make out the red, blue and black colors beneath the dust covering the men's uniforms. They were not General Allende's soldiers. They were Royal Dragoons. Sabers drawn, they were walking their mounts among dozens of bodies on the ground.

And then, I froze as I saw Coalter on the ground, on his side, gripping his right arm. I ran to him and knelt. Blood was surging through his fingers in spurts.

"Carmen," he said hoarsely, "you should not have come."

All I could think was how I had seen many such wounds before, and how they were usually fatal. I had to find a physician. But as I looked about, I saw nothing but the dragoons and the bodies of our comrades on the ground, dead or dying. I had to find someone who would help or, very soon, Coalter would lose too much blood and die.

"Carmen" he whispered, his voice weakening. "It was a trap. Elizondo captured Father Miguel and General Allende."

I did not want to acknowledge the obvious. It was over. The Spanish had captured the leaders of the insurrection, so the revolution was over. It had ended as quickly as it had begun. We had been defeated not on the battlefield, but through an act of betrayal. I did not want to acknowledge it, nor did I want to admit that the man I loved was dying. I placed my hand over the terrible wound on his arm and tried to hold back the blood. There was absolutely nothing else I could do. The blood flowed over my fingers and into the sand. Coalter's body went limp and his eyes closed.

So intent was I in holding my hand to the wound, I did not even look up when one of the dragoons reined his horse to a halt near us and ordered, "You there, move away from that dog. Now!"

More dragoons surrounded us. One asked, "Do we kill them?"

"No," a sergeant said. "You heard the order. We must save some for execution in the villages. They will serve as a lesson of what happens to traitors to the king. Bind them."

Several soldiers dismounted and two jerked me to my feet. One bent over Coalter and then looked up at the sergeant. "This one is dead."

"Then leave him for the vultures and bind this one," the sergeant said, nodding toward me, "Place him with the others."

The man binding my wrists with leather cords laughed and said, "This fellow has the hands of a woman!"

Along with the thick serape, I was wearing a wide-brimmed sombrero, and with my face covered with sand, he did not notice I was a woman. My height, together with my short hair and the clothes I wore, led him and the others to think I was a man.

I was made to stand with a dozen or so others who had been captured. It is possible, I believe, that nature contrives ways to soften its cruel blows because, at that moment, all my thoughts stopped. Otherwise, how could I have refrained from screaming out my agony? Coalter's body was just yards away from where I stood. I could not bring myself to look at him. I stood silently, unthinking, unfeeling, for what seemed like an eternity as more prisoners, many bleeding from wounds, were led to stand with us.

When I heard my name whispered, I turned to my left and saw Lebe Seru, his hands bound behind his back, at my side.

"Carmen," he repeated. "Look."

I followed his gaze to a point some distance away at the edge of what had been the battlefield. It was difficult to see through the sand whipped by the wind, but I could make out a small form.

"Lupita," I whispered. The little girl had disobeyed me and followed. I knew that she, too, would die this day.

The whole world was dying. I no longer had the strength to question it. All I could do was trudge forward when the order to march was given. I forced myself to look back one last time and saw Lupita kneeling over Coalter's body.

✦

We were taken to the town of Bajan, and then, after several days, marched north to Monclova where we were herded into a stock pen with some of those who had been captured in the battle. We caught only a fleeting glimpse of Father Hidalgo and General Allende as they were transferred from one building to another. Both were manacled and in chains.

Though I no longer cared what happened to me, I was spared a particular horror due to the fact I had been mistaken for a man, for women prisoners were separated from the rest and taken to where the royalist soldiers were billeted. We heard their screams far into the night. Some of these women found ways to end their lives in order to avoid the degradation. Their bodies were thrown in a common grave with prisoners who had been executed.

To protect my identity Lebe Seru and other prisoners stood or sat in such a way to shield me from the view of the guards who, after a while, did not come close to our pens because of the horrible stench. It did not matter to me if I was discovered. I would do what the women before me had done, and I thought of doing it regardless of whether I was found out or not. I had no reason to go on living. Without Coalter, I had no reason to continue.

One night, with no advance warning, we were roused from our sleep, our hands bound, and marched out of town in single file. Near the middle of the column, under heavy guard, were Father Hidalgo and General Allende. Both were blindfolded, and no other prisoners were allowed near them. We seemed to be going south, and so I assumed we were to be taken to the capital for execution. Two days out, the caravan was met by a coach escorted by a cavalry regiment. On the coach was the crest of the House of Bourbon. After a hurried conference between the passengers of the coach and the officer in charge of our transport, the column turned abruptly to the northwest. Later, on the basis of conversations overheard among the guards, we learned that the viceroy was concerned that a rescue attempt might be made if Father Hidalgo was taken to Mexico City. We were to be taken to Chihuahua to await the arrival from the capital of high officials who were to certify the executions.

Many did not survive the arduous journey across the desert to Chihuahua. The dead and dying were left unburied on the side of the road, and the sky was thick with vultures. Father Hidalgo was so weakened he was carried on a stretcher the last few leagues. The Spanish officers were afraid he would die and deprive those coming from Mexico City the chance to witness his execution.

In Chihuahua we were incarcerated in a series of wire-fence pens set up in what had been a cow pasture behind a now-closed Jesuit seminary. To our surprise, Lebe Seru and I found that we were to be placed with Father Hidalgo among others.

Just before entering the pen, the corporal-of-the-guard, a bearded man with hard black eyes, stopped me and stared into my face. I suspected he had detected I was a woman. He looked familiar, and I thought possibly he was one of the soldiers from the garrison in Guanajuato that I used to visit with Captain Rangel. There were hundreds of soldiers there who would know me. Finally, the corporal nodded for me to enter. For the time being, I had gone unrecognized. In my pocket, however, I carried a sharp-edged stone, which I had found on the road. If they came for me, I would use it to slash my wrists.

After the gates were secured, Father Hidalgo rushed to us and took our hands in his. Smiling, he whispered, "Carmen! Lebe Seru!"

It was painful to see him the way he was. Though the cords binding us had been removed, he was still manacled. He had lost much
weight and was so frail it appeared the irons might slip off his arms
and legs. His clothes were in tatters exposing the sores made by the
chains on his wrists and ankles.

"Father Miguel!" Lebe Seru sobbed, unable to hold back his tears.

"Do not be distraught," Father Hidalgo said, patting Lebe Seru's
face. "We have finished the course. We have kept the faith. Be of good
cheer!"

Lebe Seru was beside himself. "Father Miguel, you must not die.
You must not die!"

After comforting Lebe Seru, Father Hidalgo looked at me and
asked, "Did Coalter escape?"

There was pain registered in those kind forest green eyes when I
shook my head to indicate that he had not. I saw that he understood I
could not utter the words that Coalter was dead. He embraced me
and held me for a long time. Over his shoulder, I saw that our pen
was situated next to a corral and beyond it was a hill on which a solitary tree grew. I looked at the gate and saw the corporal-of-the-guard
watching me.

Over the next several days, while we awaited the arrival of the
officials from the capital, I never ceased to be amazed at how Father
Hidalgo managed to remain cheerful in the wretched squalor in
which we were forced to exist. The food was virtually inedible, often
consisting of animal parts normally discarded such as chicken talons.
We were given rancid beans and moldy bread crawling with insects.
The water in the bucket placed daily in our pen was dirty and smelled
of urine. But Father Hidalgo told stories of when he was a student in
the seminary and played tricks on his teachers. He led some of the
other prisoners in song, and I could see that it made things easier for
those who were not lucky enough to have had their senses dulled like
mine.

As for me, it did not matter. At Father Hidalgo and Lebe Seru's
insistence, I always remained at the back of the pen so that my identify as a woman might not be revealed. I spent my time staring at the
ground or at that lonely old tree on the hill.

When the officials began to arrive in their elegant coaches drawn by high-stepping jobbers, I wondered if Don Esteban would be among them. Many came to stare at Father Hidalgo or General Allende who, along with other officers of the insurgent army, was kept chained in a stable a short distance from us. Bishops wearing silk hats and frock coats and generals in gold-braided uniforms, would edge warily up to the pen and whisper among themselves. Father Hidalgo would be made to stand at the gate, and they grew bolder when they saw how frail he was, how bent and broken. They would ask the guards if indeed this insignificant-looking old man was the leader of the revolution. Surely, many said, a mistake had been made. This was just a white-haired old man. Some spat on him and shouted obscenities in his face.

I pondered what I would do if the Marqués did come to Chihuahua. Would I ignore him, not speak to him, which is what I hoped I would do; or would I fall to my knees and beg him to arrange for my life to be spared because I was his daughter? I was not certain what I would do. Part of me wanted to die. Coalter was dead, and I wanted to follow him.

But, slowly I began to realize, there was someone else to consider. I was now certain that I was with child. There was, as yet, no outward sign, but I knew. There was no doubt. I was carrying Coalter's child. If I died, that child would die, and something in me did not want that to happen. The child in me was all that remained of the man I loved, and I did not want that to die. So I did not know what I would say to Don Esteban if he came. Would I implore him to spare my life? Would I plead for him to allow me to live until his grandchild was born?

It was not destined that I find out because Don Esteban was not among those sent by the viceroy to witness the executions. We wondered if the viceroy himself would come to Chihuahua. One of the guards told us he had heard the viceroy was not coming because of a rumor that Father Morelos was on his way to rescue his old teacher. The Spanish had come to greatly fear José Morelos. He was able to assemble a large number of soldiers out of nowhere, strike hard, and vanish without a trace. Some of the prisoners were hopeful that Father Morelos would come in time to save us.

There was a pretense of a trial for those of us who had participated in the insurrection. We were taken to a court convened in the adjoining corral, the same place in which the guards said we would be later stood before firing squads and shot. It was, of course, a sham because the judges were all *gachupines* and they had their minds made up.

Father Hidalgo spoke eloquently on the reasons for the actions he took. He detailed the injustices visited upon the people of Mexico for centuries and defended the legitimacy of a government established by the will of the people. He also challenged the viceroy's authority in view of the abdication of the Bourbons and the ascension to the throne in Madrid of Joseph Bonaparte. Finally, he argued that since he alone had proclaimed the cry for freedom, he was solely responsible for what had happened, therefore, no one should be executed except for himself. He pleaded for the court to accept his death as atonement for what was done and to let the rest of us live. His request was denied.

The first to be executed were the officers of the insurgent army. Each morning at dawn, beginning with those of lowest rank, officers were taken to the corral in groups of three or four. As was the custom with soldiers accused of treason, they were made to stand with their backs to the firing squad, usually ten men equipped with muskets. Many were so weak, they were unable to stand and had to be supported by their comrades while their executioners aimed their guns and fired.

Day after day, as each group was led to the corral, Father Hidalgo would stand at the gate of our pen and make the sign of the cross. Always, when they saw him, the officers would kneel, and then, heads held high, walk to the place where they would draw their final breath.

Because he was the supreme commander of the insurgent army, General Allende was the last officer to be brought to the corral. He knelt in the sand as Father Hidalgo made the sign of the cross. For an instant, the two men looked at each other, and I saw both smile. General Allende rose, strode boldly to the assigned spot, and faced the squad. The Spanish officers tried to force him to turn his back, but he refused.

As the sword was raised to signal the firing squad to aim, the general shouted, "*¡Viva Miguel Hidalgo! ¡Viva José Morelos! ¡Viva México!*"

There was the crackle of musket fire and he fell to his knees and then collapsed to the ground. His body was drug through the dirt to a chopping block and decapitated.

✦

Since the laws of Spain forbade the execution of a priest, Father Hidalgo was brought before a panel of bishops to be defrocked. After these legalities, he was made to remove his priestly garb. The wooden crucifix was jerked from the cord around his neck. He was given a shirt and pants made of unbleached cotton. When they brought him back to our pen, the corporal-of-the-guard announced that Father Hidalgo would be executed at dawn, after which, the rest of us would be shot. The soldier's dark eyes lingered on me before he withdrew. He did not seem gleeful at his assigned task. The same could not be said of the royalist officers who supervised the firing squads or the high officials from the capital who certified the deaths. After each day's executions, they held a celebration with music, dancing, and much drinking.

Father Hidalgo did not want our last night to be gloomy, so he told stories and led us in the singing of songs. Lebe Seru was especially distraught by what was to happen at dawn, and so, Father Hidalgo asked him to tell us about his youth in Africa. At first Lebe Seru was reluctant to talk, and his voice was filled with emotion. But as the priest gently encouraged him, he told us of his mother and father, his brothers and sisters, all the people he left behind when he was captured by the slave traders and made to leave his home. Father Hidalgo asked many questions, and I could tell Lebe Seru's sadness was lessened by memories of things he said he had not voiced to another person since he had been forced to leave Africa. He said he was now at peace and prepared to die.

After prayers, everyone settled into solitary meditation. I was neither at peace nor ready to die. All I felt was confusion and fear.

Father Hidalgo must have sensed this, because he sat next to me and took my hands in his. For a long time, he said nothing. Then he whispered, "You are going to have a beautiful child, Carmen."

Startled, I asked, "How did you know?" It was embarrassing to me that he knew, for even though he had been excommunicated, he was still, at least to me, a priest. He knew of my sin.

Smiling, he said, "It is in your eyes."

My throat grew tight. "Tomorrow I die, and my child will die with me, Father. I am glad my child will not be born into this world. This world took my child's father, and he was a good and decent man. It is a curse to be born into this ugly world. It is for the best that I die and that my child not be born."

"Your child will be born, Carmen. And you will not die; not for a while yet."

"I will die," I said, and thoughts which had been frozen in my mind since Coalter's death began to thaw. "What will happen at dawn is my punishment. I have sinned and therefore I must be punished. It is God's will."

For a moment, his lips shaped into a puzzled smile. "You think you are being punished by God?"

I nodded. It was what I believed, though I had been unable to put these thoughts into words.

"Why do you think that?"

Since I was going to die anyway, I reasoned I may as well speak what I had told no one, not even Coalter. I explained to Father Miguel that I had learned the Marqués de Abrantes, not the man who had married my mother, was my real father.

When I did not continue, he said, "This is your sin? This is why you are being punished?"

"My sins are great and so my punishment is severe, for me and for my child. This is why I lost Coalter, and this is why I must die before the firing squad."

Father Hidalgo turned his gaze to the star-encrusted sky. He remained silent. I was ashamed that I had picked this time to trouble him with something so personal. Everything he had tried to accomplish had collapsed. His dream of liberty, equality, and justice for the people of Mexico had been crushed. His friends and the members of his family were being murdered one by one. He was about to die, and here I was, pouring out the contents of my troubled heart, disturbing his final moments of repose. I started to get to my feet so he could at least have a little time alone, but he held my hand tightly. I looked into those clear green eyes.

"Carmen, our Master said, 'Call no one on earth your father; for one is your Father, who is in heaven.'"

I do not know what I had expected him to say, but this was not it.

He must have realized my confusion, because he continued: "Your father, Carmen, is not the Marqués de Abrantes. He did not create your life any more than you created the life of your child. No man or woman can create life. God is the source of life." He looked at Lebe Seru, who sat a few feet from us. "It matters not whether our skin happens to be black or white; we have the same father.

"When we come to know this truth, something wonderful happens, because we realize the life of our neighbor is the same life that is our life. It is then we can genuinely love our neighbor as ourselves. Knowing this is the only freedom. It is the only reason we struggle, to know this freedom. The only true revolution occurs in here." He pointed to the center of my chest. "It is in the heart that the battle must be waged. We must become soldiers of the heart in the only war that should be fought."

I cannot pretend I understood these words, but they did bring to me a measure of serenity. Maybe it was as much how he said them as what he said. He was without fear. Here was a man about to die, certain to die, and he was without fear, without anger, without hatred. He was at peace and some of that peace was conveyed to me. We sat in the silence of the night for a long time.

At dawn, the corporal-of-the-guard opened the gate. He seemed reluctant to speak. Finally, he said, "Father Hidalgo, it is time."

We knelt before Father Miguel to receive his blessings.

"I am sorry," he said, "I do not have a crucifix. They took away my crucifix."

Suddenly, I remembered the jade pendant. I unloosed the cord from around my neck and handed it to him. Since it was impossible for me to speak without crying, I pointed to the ancient symbol beneath the head of Chimalma, to the row of recessed dots that formed the outline of a cross.

"The Toltec Cross," he said and touched my face with his fingers. "Thank you, Carmen." He made the sign of the cross and gave us his blessing.

Lebe Seru whispered, "We will follow you soon, Father."

The priest smiled and shook his head. "No, Lebe Seru. You will follow; that is certain, but it will not be soon. All things happen as they must and in their time. You and Carmen have yet much to do before you follow me. There is no hurry. God is patient."

At the gate, the corporal handed Father Hidalgo a small sack and said, "I brought what you asked, Father."

"Thank you, my son."

"Father...would—" The corporal fell to his knees in the sand. Tears flowed from his eyes. "Bless me, Father!"

Father Hidalgo made the sign of the cross.

He was led to the corral and permitted to give each of the men of the firing squad a piece of candy from the sack. It was a way of demonstrating he bore no malice and forgave them for what they were required to do. In turn, he asked each to forgive him for the suffering he may have caused. He was then seated on a wooden chair facing the soldiers. Because the light was faint, he held his hand beneath his heart so the executioners could be accurate in their aim.

The men were nervous and all of their shots missed except for one ball that struck and lodged in Father Hidalgo's hand. Quickly, the men rammed powder, wadding and balls into the tubes of their muskets and took aim. Father Hidalgo held his bleeding hand steady beneath his heart. When the officer in charge of the execution brought down his sword, the soldiers fired again. Miguel Hidalgo y Costilla, the Father of Mexico, slumped in the chair and slowly collapsed to the ground.

✦

Following the execution of Father Hidalgo, there was a flurry of activity around the buildings where the high officials from Mexico City had been lodged. Teams of horses were led from the stables, hurriedly placed in harness, and hitched to the ornate coaches that were to return the notables to the capital. The generals and the bishops were anxious to convey to the viceroy the news that the leader of the insurrection had been put to death.

Judging from the number of dragoons riding escort, it was probably also correct to assume they had no strong desire to remain in a remote region where no one could be certain of the whereabouts of Father Morelos. Though not a tongue spoke his name, it was possible to sense the royalists' fear of the priest who had been like a son to Miguel Hidalgo. José Morelos was now the leader of the revolution, and even in his absence, he seemed to be present like the stillness in the air before a storm.

Because the soldiers comprising the firing squads were required to participate in hastily arranged ceremonies for the departing dignitaries, the execution of those of us remaining in the pens was delayed. Throughout the morning, we expected at any moment we would be led to the corral and shot. It was almost as if we had been forgotten or, at the least, ignored. No buckets of food or water were placed inside our pens. Of course, no one was in any mood to eat. We huddled together and waited.

By mid-afternoon, we had begun to wonder if our executions had been deferred until the following day. When we heard loud singing and laughter coming from the officers' quarters, our suspicions were confirmed. They were celebrating Father Hidalgo's death. Soon, they would be drunk. We settled back, convinced that we had one last night in this world.

The noise from the officers' barracks continued far into the night and then began to wane as the effect of the alcohol took its toll. I happened to be gazing toward the tree on the hill when, suddenly, just as the moon was hidden by a thick cloud, soldiers approached our pen. They were led by the corporal-of-the-guard.

"Lebe Seru," I whispered when one of the men unfastened the gate so the corporal could enter.

Taking my hand in his, Lebe Seru said, "We will die like our comrades, brave and with dignity."

Were we to be executed in the middle of the night like thieves, I wondered. The soldiers, entering the pen behind their corporal, gripped drawn sabers. They were not even going to bother to shoot us. To save bullets, our throats would be cut like animals in the slaughterhouse.

Getting to our feet, we braced for the end. The corporal-of-the-guard stopped in front of me. "Señora?"

As I had suspected since the beginning, he knew I was a woman. I was seized with panic when I realized they might have come for a purpose other than to kill us. Quickly, I slipped my hand into my pocket and grasped the sharp stone I had placed there for just this occasion. If I used it correctly, I would be dead by the time they took me to the barracks. My time to die had come, but I would leave this world on my terms.

And then, extending his hand, the corporal said, "Señora, I wish to return this to you."

It was quite dark, but I could see he was offering me my mother's jade pendant. I looked up at this bearded man who had known all along I was a woman and yet had not told the Spanish officers.

"Before his death the padre asked that I return it to you."

I studied the corporal's face as I retrieved the pendant from his hand and looped the cord over my head. This was the closest I had been to him and he looked familiar. Somewhere, I had met this man and, naturally, thought of the garrison in Guanajuato.

"Do you not remember me, Señora?"

"You are from the garrison in Guanajuato?"

""Mexico City, Señora," he said and smiled. "The night you came with your *niña*, I was the one who took you to the palace."

It was the beard that had fooled me. He did not have a beard that night. He was the soldier who had escorted me to the National Palace so I would not be mistakenly shot by Spanish soldiers. I had asked his name because I wanted to tell Don Esteban of his bravery. He must have known who I was from the moment we were placed in the pens, and certainly, he knew I was a woman. Why, I wondered, had he not told the officers.

"Yes," I said. "I remember you. Santiago Montemayor." I looked into his dark eyes. "And now you have come to take us to the corral. Yes? Or will you slit our throats here?" I nodded to their drawn swords.

"Neither, Señora. You are free to go. All prisoners are free to go." Lebe Seru glanced toward the officers' barracks.

The corporal read the question in the African's eyes. "The officers do not know we are releasing you, Captain. They lied to us. They have been lying to us from the beginning. They told us Father Hidalgo wanted to become Joseph Bonaparte's viceroy. We did not know that Father Hidalgo was seeking justice for the people of Mexico. Now we understand. We heard his words. We watched him die. A man who dies with such dignity does not lie." He stepped back and gestured with his hand toward the gate. "You may go whereever you wish. The officers will not miss you until morning. By then we, too, shall be gone."

"Where are you going?" I asked.

"To José Morelos, Señora. If he will lead us, we will follow." He lowered his head. "We shall ask his forgiveness for what we did to Father Hidalgo."

Lebe Seru put his hand on the corporal's shoulder. "He will forgive you, *compañero*. And if it is justice you seek, he will lead you."

We helped open the gates to the other pens and explained to the prisoners what the soldiers were doing. Together, we cautiously made our way to the edge of town.

Before leaving Chihuahua, Corporal Montemayor said, "You are welcome to come with us." His eyes fixed on mine. "It would be an honor to travel with brave soldados."

I looked at Lebe Seru. "It is necessary that I find someone and..."—I drew a deep breath—"...and see that he has received a proper burial."

The corporal's eyes saddened. "Your husband, Señora?"

I nodded. While we had not been married by a priest, I regarded Coalter as my husband. In my heart, Coalter was and would forever be my husband.

"I am sorry, Señora. And your niña? Where is she?"

I recalled how my life had been spared because the soldiers in Mexico City had assumed Lupita was my child. There was no need now to say otherwise. I looked at Lebe Seru and saw reflected my concern for the little girl we had last seen kneeling over Coalter's body. "I do not know, Corporal Montemayor. We were separated from her after Father Miguel was captured." I did not want to put words to the admission that Lupita, too, was dead.

"Perhaps," he shrugged, "she has made her way home. You said you were a servant at the Hacienda de Abrantes. She may have returned there."

"Perhaps," I said. It would have been too complicated to explain that I had not been a servant at the Hacienda de Abrantes and that there was no reason for Lupita to go there. I was too tired to put straight all of my lies, and furthermore, I could see the men with the corporal were anxious to be on their way. It was obvious they regarded Santiago Montemayor as their leader.

"Will you stay in Guanajuato?"

"I do not know what we will do, Corporal," I said truthfully. "Perhaps we will go to Texas. That is where Father Miguel planned to go. He was going to establish his government in Texas. And Texas is a place my... my husband loved."

"Texas?" His face brightened.

"I am from the province of Texas, Señora..."—he cocked his head—"...Señora, what is your name?"

I told him my name.

"I am from Texas," Santiago Montemayor repeated. "I was born in a small village called La Bahía. If you go to Texas I hope you will go to La Bahía, Señora Rangel. My parents live there. They will assist you."

Although I was dazed by all that had happened, I tried to manage a smile. Santiago Montemayor was a decent man. I owed him very much. He had saved our lives, mine and Lebe Seru's. And, it occurred to me, he had saved the life of Coalter's child who, it seemed, might come into this world after all. For that, I was grateful. He had saved the one thing that gave me a reason to continue living. When we parted, I returned his wish that we go with God and asked him to tell Father Morelos how his teacher faced the firing squad with dignity and with serenity.

✦

As we made our way south, we encountered other refugees from the insurgent army who generously shared their food and water and gave us clothes to replace the filthy rags we had worn in captivity. They were among those who had managed to elude the royalists and were now uncertain as to what to do. Some were intent on carrying out Father Hidalgo's plan to go to Texas, even though the northern provinces had been recaptured by the royalists. Others were on their way to join Father Morelos. Whatever their plans, they took into their care the children of our fallen brothers and sisters, and so each time we crossed paths with those who had been our *compañeros*, we visited the orphans, hoping that Lupita would be among them. She was not, and reluctantly, we concluded that if the little girl had not been slain by the Spanish soldiers, she had perished in the desert.

Finally, we came to the scene of the battle where Father Hidalgo had been betrayed. It was where I had last seen Coalter alive. Approaching that place was the most difficult thing I had ever had to do. We found several graves over which simple markers with no names had been placed. Undoubtedly, people like those we had met on the way had buried our fallen comrades. Using branches and cords, they had fashioned crosses. They had placed them on the graves of those whom they had never met in most cases but with whom they shared their dream of liberty, equality, and justice. The love and respect felt for those who had sacrificed their lives for this dream was evident in the way stones had been gathered from afar and neatly stacked over the graves. Somehow, it made it just a little easier to know that my feeling of loss was shared by others.

As I surveyed the graves, I knew that the man I loved, the man whose child was beginning to stir within me rested in one of them.

Holding his sombrero in hand, Lebe Seru stood beside me in silence, and then he offered a prayer in the language of his people. I thanked him for his words and told him I was ready to leave.

"Carmen," Lebe Seru asked, "what do you plan to do now?"

Looking up at this man who had remained a stalwart friend through so much, I said, "I think I would like to go to Texas, Lebe Seru. I am carrying Coalter's child. I would like for his child to be born in the land he loved."

He smiled. "I think he would like that."

Somehow, I had assumed Lebe Seru would go with me, but I now realized he might have plans of his own. "And you, Lebe Seru? Where will you go? Will you return to your people?"

There was sadness in his eyes as he surveyed the bleak desert surrounding us. "How can I do that, Carmen? My people are on the other side of a great ocean."

My impulse was to tell him I would obtain the gold from Don Esteban for his passage. If he wished to return to Africa, the Marqués could arrange it. And then I remembered that I had run away from Don Esteban. I could not go to him. "Come with me to Texas, Lebe Seru. It is what Father Miguel wanted us to do. We will join those who continue the struggle to win our independence from Spain. We will make Mexico a free land where no man can enslave another. Mexico is your home now, Lebe Seru. Come with me to Texas."

He nodded. "I have thought of what you are saying, Carmen. Thousands of my people are in bondage in the United States. I would like to find a way to help them escape. And if they do, there must be a place for them to go or they will be captured and forced back into slavery. I would like to help make Mexico a land where men and women can live in freedom. It was Father Miguel's dream."

"Then come with me. We will help to raise a new republican army in the north. We will continue the fight and will not rest until the Spanish grant Mexico her independence."

Something was troubling my friend. I could read it in his expression. "I will go to Texas, Carmen, but not now. For me, that will have to wait. There is something I must do first."

I realized what he was thinking. "You wish to stop Barnet from bringing his men with their long-rifles into Mexico. You want to prevent his opening New Spain to the slave trade."

"If Barnet is able to return to his country, Carmen, and organize an army to march on Mexico, Father Morelos will not succeed. Barnet will reopen the slave trade. I must try to stop him. He and Humberto must be stopped."

For the first time since Don Esteban told me he was my father, I grasped that Humberto was my brother. It had not occurred to me before. Maybe it was something I had not wanted to admit, even to myself. It was one thing for Cristóbal to be my brother; of that I was proud. But Humberto was something altogether different. I told Lebe Seru the truth about who my real father was. I felt he had a right to know.

"I suspected the Marqués was your father," he said when I finished. "I could see the love he has for you."

My path was clear. I knew what I had to do. Lebe Seru had helped me. He had saved my life, and so it was my turn to help him. But it was more than that. What the African had said was true. If Barnet was able to bring his men with their long-rifles into Mexico, what Father Hidalgo had begun, what Father Morelos was now struggling to achieve, would never be realized. Men like Humberto would rule New Spain and injustice would continue. The dream of liberty, equality, and justice would be lost. Thousands, including the man I loved, would have died in vain. I had no choice. Though, like Lebe Seru, I had no idea what we could do to stop Humberto and Barnet, I knew we had to try. We would have to return to Guanajuato.

Before departing, I gazed one last time at the graves, each marked with a cross. I closed my eyes and said a final farewell to the man I would forever love.

IX

Our journey south was arduous. We were forced to spend much of our time hiding from royalist patrols seeking to destroy the remnants of General Allende's army, so it required the better part of a month to travel the distance from Saltillo to Guanajuato. Finally, late one afternoon, we climbed to the crest of one of the hills adjoining the Hacienda de Abrantes. Peering across the way, I tried to determine who was there. In the corral were the Parisian barouche horses used to pull the Marqués's coach. As far as I could determine, the mounts ridden by Humberto and Barnet were not among the rest of the stock.

Lebe Seru said, "Barnet may have already left for the United States. If so, we are too late."

As we debated what to do, a large man stepped from the hacienda. It was some distance away, but I could tell he was not someone I knew. He was not a servant at the hacienda. The man carried a chair to the patio and placed it next to the fountain. After returning to the hacienda, he reemerged carrying a second man in his arms. The head of the man being carried drooped forward and he was covered with a blanket so I could not immediately make out who he was. The big fellow placed him in the chair and arranged the blanket over his shoulders. When the man in the chair raised his head slowly to look toward the fountain, I recognized him.

"Don Esteban," I whispered and looked at Lebe Seru. "It is Don Esteban!"

"Something is wrong with him."

"Yes," I said, suddenly alarmed. I could not ever remember seeing Don Esteban hurt or sick. He had always been so vigorous. Lebe Seru suggested we stay on the hill until we were certain Humberto and Barnet were not at the hacienda. We had no weapons, not even a knife or a sword.

"I must go and talk to Don Esteban," I insisted. "He will tell me where they are."

"If they are at the hacienda, they will harm you."

"Don Esteban would not let them harm me." Despite all that had happened, I was as certain of that as I had ever been. Don Esteban had always protected me. He would not allow anyone to harm me. Looking back down the hill, I saw Hortensia step from the hacienda. She went to the Marqués and held a cup to his lips. "It is my aunt. I must go to them."

"Then I will go with you."

We made our way down the hill and then walked up the gravel pathway that led to the place that had been my home for all but the past year of my life. My heart began to pound as I drew nearer the hacienda. And then I broke into a run. There was no longer any anger in my heart for Don Esteban. I wanted him to pick me up in his arms and hoist me to the sky as he had done when I was a little girl. I could not get to him fast enough. "Don Esteban," I cried when I came to the edge of the patio. "Don Esteban!"

When Hortensia saw me, her hands went to her mouth. I stopped when I saw the man in the chair by the fountain. Had I been mistaken? This could not be Don Esteban. The man slowly raising his head to look at me was an old man, his face twisted and gaunt.

"Don Esteban?" I looked at Hortensia whose eyes were filling with tears.

She ran to me and embraced me. "Carmencita!" she whispered again and again. "Oh, my Carmencita!"

"*Tía,*" I said. "Teresa..."—I did not know how to tell her Teresa had been killed—"Teresa is—"

"I know," she said as more tears flowed down her face. "Some of the people from Guanajuato returned after... after Calderón. They told me what happened."

"Tía," I said. "I am sorry. I am so sorry."

"She is with her father and Rubén, Carmen. They are with Jesus. Do not be sorry. They are happy."

I looked again at Don Esteban. He had yet to utter a word though he shaped his mouth as if he wanted to speak. I glanced at the big man who had carried the Marqués. He looked frightened as he stared first at Lebe Seru and then back to me.

"Hortensia," I said. "Who is this man?"

"He was hired in Mexico City to help Don Esteban when..."—she closed her eyes—"...when he received the news and became ill."

"News? What news?"

"Carmencita, Cristóbal is dead."

My heart sank. When I looked down at Don Esteban, I saw that he had managed to bring his hand to a pocket inside his jacket.

"The letter," Hortensia said. "He wants you to read the letter. He keeps it in his coat. It is from Captain Rangel."

The Marqués was having difficulty placing his hand into the pocket so I reached inside his jacket to retrieve it. In so doing, my hand brushed against the small pistol that he always carried in a shoulder holster. I secured the letter, unfolded it, and began to read. I was sickened by what it said.

Captain Rangel reported in his letter that he and Cristóbal had gone to the place where the royal family was held captive by the French. Cristóbal had managed to personally deliver his father's message to Fernando de Borbón. Unfortunately, they discovered too late that Fernando had taken an oath of loyalty to Joseph Bonaparte in return for a pension. Fernando told Joseph Bonaparte of the Marqués's proposal, and Spain's new king ordered Cristóbal's arrest and execution. Captain Rangel managed to escape and was now fighting alongside Spanish republicans who were attempting to drive the French from their country.

When I finished reading the letter, I saw Don Esteban was watching me.

"I killed Cristóbal," he whispered in a slurred, almost incomprehensible speech.

I wanted to comfort him, but I knew that if I said anything, I would burst into tears. Cristóbal was dead. It did not seem possible. My brother was dead.

"Carmen," Hortensia said. "You should not be here. It is dangerous! You must—"

She turned her head in the direction of a rumbling noise. Horsemen were approaching the hacienda. They were coming up the road from Guanajuato. I had let my guard down. Too late, I whirled about in time to see a dozen or so men on horseback coming through the wrought-iron gates that had been thrown open. In the lead were Humberto and Barnet.

I looked at Lebe Seru and saw that he, too, knew we had made a grave mistake. We were without weapons and there was no place to run.

"Oh, Carmen," Hortensia whispered. "You should not have come back. These men are evil. You should not have returned."

Seeing Lebe Seru and me, the men spurred their horses to an angry gallop and raced to the patio. I thought of the pistol in Don Esteban's jacket, but there was no time to pack a charge.

"Carmencita!" Humberto shouted as though he was glad to see me. He pulled from his head a wide-brimmed hat banded by a burgundy-colored silk sash. "Welcome home, Carmencita!"

Barnet remained on his horse. "Well, well," he said, "if it isn't old Jeb. What a surprise. How are you, Jeb?"

Several of the men who had arrived with Humberto and Barnet dismounted and drew long-rifles from the leather sheaths secured to their saddles. I did not know who they were but from their dress, dirty uniforms and unpolished military boots, I suspected they were deserters from the royalist army. Such men often banded together to operate as highwaymen and thieves. Apparently, they were now in the hire of Humberto and Barnet. The aroma of *pulque* was thick in the air.

Barnet then spoke words in English to Lebe Seru. I did not understand what he was saying, but when I heard Coalter's name, I assumed he was inquiring what had happened to him.

Lebe Seru did not look at me when, in Spanish, he said, "Coalter Owens was killed in battle. He died a brave man fighting for a just cause."

I was determined not to change my expression. I did not want to give either Humberto or Barnet the satisfaction of knowing that my heart was breaking at hearing those words.

Barnet laughed. "Coalter Owens died a fool fighting for a fool's cause."

Lebe Seru started forward as if intending to pull Barnet off his horse.

"No!" I cried and jumped in front of him when one of the men aimed his rifle at Lebe Seru.

Gently coaxing me aside with his hand, Lebe Seru said, "Carmen, stand back."

"Don't shoot old Jeb here, Reyes," Barnet said. He pulled a long cigar from inside his coat. "I paid more for him than that rifle you're holding. Jeb is valuable property."

"What do we do with him?" the one called Reyes asked, disappointed he had not been allowed to kill a man he had never, until that moment, even seen. This Reyes wore a lavender-colored silk scarf around his neck and appeared to be the kind of man who fancied himself as handsome. He kept glancing at me with a lewd expression on his face.

"Bind him and take him to the carriage house," Barnet said as he bit off the end of his cigar. "I'll decide what to do with him later."

"And the woman?" Reyes asked, grinning. "What do we do with the woman?"

Barnet spat a piece of tobacco. "If you don't know what to do with her, Reyes, then I must conclude you are even more stupid than you look."

The other men started to laugh but stopped suddenly when Reyes glared at them. He was larger than the others and seemed to be their leader. Then a sly grin snaked onto his lips and the cutthroats and thieves resumed laughing as several of them rushed forward to bind Lebe Seru's hands with leather straps. He resisted, but they quickly subdued him and then turned toward me.

"No!" Hortensia cried when they grabbed my arms. "Leave Carmen alone. No!"

Don Esteban made an attempt to get to his feet but sank back into the chair where he struggled to get his breath.

"Stop!" Humberto shouted as I fell to the ground after an unsuccessful attempt to kick my attackers. "Leave her!"

The men froze in place and looked up at Barnet who shrugged and said, "Do as he says. I guess he wants the wench for himself. Yes, Humberto? You want her all to yourself?"

I studied the face of the man who I now knew was my brother. Something was different about him. He was not acting the way he had on that night when he dragged me up the stairs and tried to rape me. He was not comfortable with these men surrounding us. Nor was he comfortable with Barnet. Something had happened between them.

"Yes," he said finally. "I want her to myself."

Barnet lit his cigar and blew a long stream of smoke between pursed lips. "Do you remember what happened the last time you wanted her all to yourself?"

Humberto swallowed hard. "It is different now."

"Yes," Barnet said. "It is different now. Now, señorita Rangel is a real soldier. Yes, Señorita? Before, you were a play soldier. But you became a real soldier in the army of Hidalgo and Allende." He grinned, the cruel grin of a man who would stab other men in the back and cut the throats of old men. "We have heard of you. There are many tales about how the daughter of Captain Rangel was seen fighting in the army of Hidalgo and Allende. Is it not true?"

I stared at him and said nothing.

"Yes," he continued. "You have become famous. So famous, the new intendant of Guanajuato has issued a reward for your capture. And a handsome reward it is, one that will make the man who apprehends you able to live comfortably the rest of his days. Were you aware of this? Did you know you had become famous, Señorita Rangel?"

I said nothing.

Barnet threw back his head and feigned a laugh. "No wonder Hidalgo and Allende failed so miserably. They had an army made up of women and Africans! Now we understand why they were defeated. They outnumbered the Spanish a hundred to one, and still they managed to lose."

The band of brigands joined his laughter.

"Yes," Barnet said. "Señorita Rangel and old Jeb were soldiers in the army of Hidalgo and Allende. Where is your army now, Señorita? Who leads it now? Who leads this motley army of *indios*, women, and Africans?"

Without hesitation, I said, "The army of the Republic of Mexico is led by José Morelos." I do not know why it came to me to say this. "And José Morelos will not be defeated. Never!"

Suddenly, the laughter stopped. Reyes and his sweaty-faced men blinked their eyes and looked up at Barnet. Several whispered the name of Morelos.

Barnet shook his head as if amused and dismounted. He ordered the men to take Lebe Seru to the stables, and then, without so much as glancing at Don Esteban, turned and walked to the hacienda.

Gesturing to the attendant, Humberto said, "Take my father to his room. It is hot out here. You can return him here later after the sun sets. In this patio, next to this fountain, is the only place where he wants to be." He looked at me. "Come with me to the library, Carmen. I would like to talk to you."

It was no easy thing to walk through the corridors of the hacienda. I could almost hear Cristóbal's peals of laughter when we were children running as fast as we could and then sliding in our hard-soled boots across the polished stone floors. From up and down the hallway echoed Alexander the Great's commands to his *compañeros* and Thalestris' orders to her legion of Amazons.

And in the library, the books stared down from the shelves as if to ask, "Where is Cristóbal? We miss him." How many happy hours had we spent in this room, reading to one another, or listening to the Marqués tell us some exciting adventure about the men of the House of Abrantes who had fought at the side of the great kings of Castile? How was it possible for such sweet memories to be so painful? Cristóbal was dead, and I would never see him again. I would never be able to tell my brother I loved him dearly.

Humberto asked, "Would you care for a glass of wine?"

"No," I said and watched as he poured red wine from a dark bottle into a gold goblet.

Why Humberto was acting this way with me, acting as though he had not tried to do something ugly to me, I had no idea. I detested him for what he had done, and I wanted to scream out my disgust, but I knew I must not. If I was to get Lebe Seru out of this alive, I had to subdue my anger. And it was not only Lebe Seru who was on my mind. I had to survive so that Coalter's child would live. If it had been just me, I think I would have found a way to hurt Humberto. Though it would likely mean my death, I did not care. But I did care what happened to my friend and to my child. I could not allow either to be harmed.

"I noticed you saw the letter from your father," Humberto said after downing the wine in the goblet. "You know that Cristóbal was killed."

I nodded. He had said "the letter from your father," which meant Don Esteban had not told him that he, not Captain Rangel, was my father. Therefore, Humberto did not yet know I was his sister.

"Poor Cristóbal," he said. "He must have been very surprised when Fernando turned him over to Joseph Bonaparte. He did not know that kings are no different from other men."

Hoping to induce Humberto to disclose something of what he and Barnet might be planning, I said, "At least Fernando will not become king of New Spain."

He rubbed his chin and looked at me. "I'm sorry. What did you say? I was not listening."

"You no longer intend to make Fernando king of New Spain and reopen the slave trade; not after what happened to Cristóbal. Fernando was responsible for what happened to your brother. You would not want this man to be king of New Spain."

"No," he said. "That is true. Fernando will not become king of New Spain."

An absurd thought sprang into my head. It could not be possible. Surely he was not about to say what I thought he was.

But he did. "I shall become king of New Spain."

I knew I must not laugh. Why I was not in the stable, under guard, with Lebe Seru, I did not know. All I knew was I dare not offend Humberto. I watched him walk to the table in the middle of the room upon which lay the map of the continent of North America.

"The greatest empire the world has ever known," Humberto said, gesturing with his hand to the map, "and I will be its ruler."

Scanning the room, I noticed the great broadsword mounted on the wall, the walloon that had been handed down from father to son by men of the House of Abrantes for generations. It was a sword so heavy I had never been able to lift it. For a moment, my attention was for some reason totally absorbed by that sword.

"Why do you not speak, Carmencita? Are you not surprised that I shall be king of New Spain?"

Looking back at him, I hesitated, unsure of what I might say without provoking him. "I suppose it is logical you would be the king of New Spain. The House of Abrantes is an old and honorable family of Castile. You have great wealth. Why should you not become king? It is—"

He raised his hand to cut off my words. "You need not lie, Carmen. I know what you think of me." He sat the empty goblet on the table near the map. "And I do not blame you. I have behaved badly toward you. I am ashamed of the way I treated you over the years." He grimaced. "Especially...especially that night. I am very ashamed of what I did that night. I understand why you had to run away. I was a beast."

What sort of trick, I wondered, was this. Never in his life had Humberto apologized for any of the disgusting things he had done, and there had been many.

He straightened up. "From now on, it will be different. I will treat you with respect. Everyone will treat you with respect. They will treat you with the respect due..."—he paused and smiled—"...their queen."

My stomach turned to stone. I looked at him, hoping I had not heard correctly.

"Their queen," he repeated. "My wife!"

My initial impulse was to tell him as rapidly as possible the reason I could not be his queen and certainly not his wife. I was his sister. But I had no idea how he would react. All I knew was I was not in the hands of Reyes and his band of vermin at that very moment only because Humberto had intervened. If he had done that because he had come to believe I could be his wife, I must do nothing to change his mind.

"I recall, Carmen, that you always dreamed of the glory of empire. You read about these things in the books in this room, and they were the things you wanted. Is it not so?"

"It is so," I answered truthfully.

"Then you shall have your dream. You will share in the rule of the greatest empire the world has yet to see. You know the great wealth of this land. You have heard my father speak of it. It is a rich land untouched by any save the *indios*. And we shall soon remove them. The primitive's days are numbered."

I refrained from reminding him that my mother was an Indian, though I am not sure it would have mattered. Humberto was believing only what he wanted to believe, and he would hear only that which pleased him.

He continued to speak of his empire, until he looked at me and said, "Share it with me, Carmen. Be my wife."

I wanted to ask how he could reconcile what he had tried to do to me that terrible night with what he was asking me to become, but I dared not. I could not risk his anger. All I could do was ask, "Why me?"

"Even when we were children, I was attracted to you. I know now I was attracted to you because you are strong. I need that strength, Carmen. Barnet thinks he can tell me what to do because of his men and their long-rifles. Once he brings his army into New Spain, he may think he no longer needs me. He may find some other man to be king of New Spain. There are many who will offer themselves. I need someone I can trust to help me control Barnet until I no longer need him. Will you do it, Carmen? Will you share my throne? Will you be my queen...my wife?"

When he started toward me with his hands extended, I instinctively took a step back.

He stopped. "I will not touch you, Carmencita. I promise. Not until you are my wife. I will never harm you again. Just say you will be my wife. Please, Carmen. Do you remember what my father always said? He said that the men of the House of Abrantes were always at the side of the king of Spain, and at their side, sword in hand, always stood a Rangel. Do you remember? Well Carmen, I will soon be the king of New Spain, and I want you at my side just as your father was at my father's side. I need you there. Tell me you will be my wife."

I made a slight shrug of my shoulders which could be interpreted as assent.

"I knew you would. You have made me the happiest man in the world!" He started for the door. "I must go now. I need to confer with Barnet. There are many details to which we must attend before we leave for the United States to assemble my army. But I will be back. Why don't you go to your room and rest. You look tired. And change your clothes! You look like a peasant's daughter in those rags and that old serape. Here, why don't you take it off now."

When he reached for me, I again backed away. I had begun to show the signs of my condition and the serape concealed them.

He smiled and raised his hands. "Now you are being modest. How charming. In any case, we will have ample time to talk. It is growing dark. Go and rest now."

I did go to my room on the second floor. I went as fast as I could, but it was not to rest or to change clothes. There was only one focus to my thought: the muskets in my gunrack. Frantically, I burst into the room, placed my hands on the rack and stared at the empty spaces where my guns had been. Why should I be surprised they were gone? The hacienda was swarming with thieves. Undoubtedly, one of them took my muskets. My sense of futility was tempered by a consideration of what I would have done if I had found the muskets in the rack. There were at least a dozen deserters in the stable, not to mention Humberto and Barnet.

I walked to the window, and as I stared toward the stable, a plan began to form in my mind. It would involve great risk, but I did not see that I had much choice. Suddenly, there was a noise at my door and I turned, expecting to see one of the brigands. It was my aunt.

Rushing across the room, she embraced me and then stood back and looked at me. A soft smile came to her lips.

"You are with child."

I nodded.

"The young *norteamericano*?" Her eyes saddened. "The one who was killed."

"Yes."

"Oh, Carmencita," she said and started to embrace me again.

Stepping back, I said, "Hortensia, why did you never tell me Don Esteban was my father?" I do not know why I would think of that at that particular moment. "Why did you not tell me?"

The little woman opened her mouth but was unable to say anything until, finally, she drew a deep breath. "When Cata Valeria was dying, she told me not to tell you until you were older. She made Anselmo and me promise not to tell you, just as she made the Marqués promise."

"My mother made Don Esteban promise not to tell me he was my father?"

"She did not think you would understand until you were older."

It was growing dark, and if the plan that was taking shape in my thought was to work, I would have to act quickly. I would have to act before the men in the stable had an opportunity to drink too much *pulque*. I turned to my aunt. "Hortensia, can Don Esteban walk?"

"I think he can. But he has lost the will to live, Carmen. He wants to die because he has no reason to live. That is why he does not walk."

I grasped Hortensia's arm to impress upon her the urgency of what I was going to say. "Hortensia, listen to me. I am going to the stable and—"

"No, Carmen! Those men are evil. You must not go there!"

"Listen to me! I am going to the stable. When I do, I want you to have the attendant take Don Esteban back to the patio. Tell him to make certain the Marqués is wearing his jacket, the one he wore earlier. Do you understand?"

She again attempted to dissuade me from going to the stable, but I hurried her off, and after a moment to marshal my courage, I left the room, raced down the stairs, and proceeded quietly to a door that would allow me to leave the hacienda without being seen by Humberto. He, I assumed, was in the library conferring with Barnet. Concealed by a hedge, I made my way past the corral and into the stable.

Inside, I was greeted by a dozen pair of leering eyes. At least they had not started drinking. Alcohol gave some men a false courage, and I was counting on these men to reason clearly.

I looked about until I saw Reyes, approached him, and in a strong voice, said, "Humberto said I could see the prisoner."

Reyes, who was cleaning his pistol, shrugged that it did not matter to him.

I rushed to where Lebe Seru was sitting on the straw in one of the stalls. His hands remained tightly bound behind him, and I saw bruises and cuts on his face where he had been beaten.

"Lebe Seru," I whispered when I entered the stall and knelt by his side. "Did they hurt you?"

"Carmen," he whispered, "you must get away from here! Go to Father Morelos. It is over for me. Save yourself."

"I will not leave without you."

"We must face the facts, Carmen. You—"

Hushing him, I explained as quickly as I could why I had not been bound and placed under guard. I told him what I planned to try to do. Before he could object, I rose and left the stall. I walked straight to Reyes, gathered myself up to my full stature, and looked into his eyes.

At first, he grinned, conveying with his manner the thoughts in his filthy head. And then, as I expected, he grew nervous that I did not say anything. I simply stared into his eyes as hard as I could. His smile faded and he glanced toward his comrades who, as I also anticipated, were beginning to take an interest in what was happening.

Angrily, Reyes demanded, "What is it you want, woman? You have seen the prisoner. Why do you look at me like this?"

Over the past few months, I had learned a few things about how some men behaved. I was counting on the predictability of such behavior. I said nothing, but continued to stare.

A flicker of a smile returned. "You want something from me, Señorita?" He was encouraged by the snickers of his men. "I would be glad to give you something." His expression quickly returned to anger when I said nothing. "If you were not Humberto's woman, I would give you plenty!"

"You," I said, surprised I could make my voice so deep, "are a dead man."

At first he laughed but stopped when he realized his men had remained silent. "A dead man? What do you mean, a dead man? Are you crazy in the head?"

"Why," I asked, "do you think my friend and I came to Guanajuato?"

"I do not know. Perhaps you are stupid! You were with Hidalgo and Allende, so you must be stupid!"

"We were with Hidalgo and Allende," I said. "But now we are with another army. We are with the army that is at this moment marching on Guanajuato and will attack the city at the first light of dawn." I waited until it appeared he had absorbed this information before I delivered what I hoped would be the death thrust. "It is the army led by José Morelos!"

Like an echo, the name Morelos was on the lips of the men gathered around us.

"Do you think we would come here alone?" I continued, stepping closer to the leader of this pit of snakes. "All of us who were with Hidalgo and Allende have been ordered by Morelos to converge on Guanajuato. In groups of two or three we have been arriving. We are coming by the thousands! José Morelos seeks vengeance for what was done to Miguel Hidalgo. Revenge! And he will have it. No one who has ever been in the Spanish army is to be spared!"

Drawing back, I crossed my arms and watched Reyes. Never had I met a man who enjoyed hurting others who was not a coward. This man was no exception. His eyes darted about at his *compañeros* who were busy telling each other stories they had heard about José Morelos. Morelos, they said, had never been defeated. He came when least expected and crushed his enemies. His followers did travel in small groups and came together quickly to strike. So, they concluded, I might be telling the truth.

Reyes asked, "When is Morelos coming to Guanajuato?"

"Tonight."

Suddenly, my existence was forgotten. Even when not in the grip of fear, a coward thinks only of himself. These men had one priority: the debate over what they should do to save their necks. However, I knew I dare not go to Lebe Seru to loosen his restraints. If I called attention to him at that instant, men such as these might lash out. For the moment, they had no interest in their captives, and my gamble was they would forget about the man out of their sight in the stall. Furthermore, it was best I remove myself from their midst. If I remained, they might question me and determine I was lying. My absence would unnerve them. I slipped out the door and headed for the hacienda where I hoped I would be as successful in the second phase of my plan as I seemed to have been in the first.

As I hoped, the attendant had returned Don Esteban to the patio. Everything was going according to plan. I rushed to where he sat in the chair by the fountain. The attendant and Hortensia stood behind him.

"Tía," I said, "I want you to leave the hacienda. You and this man go below to the city."

"Carmencita," Hortensia pleaded, "what is happening? What are you doing?"

"Do what I say, Hortensia. Now!" I felt terrible about speaking to my aunt this way, but I did not want her to be harmed if my plan failed. I looked at the attendant who appeared only too ready to obey my order. "Take my aunt to Guanajuato. Protect her, *hombre*, or you will answer to me! Do you understand?"

The man nodded, placed his arm around Hortensia and led her out of the patio and across the grounds to the gates of the estate.

When I knelt by the Marqués and looked up at him, I could see the confusion in his eyes.

"Carmencita," he whispered. His speech was still slurred, but his voice was stronger. "Why did you send Hortensia away?"

My eyes focused on the place on his jacket where I knew the holster pistol was concealed. It was this weapon that was the object of my having him returned to the patio. I knew I might not have time to go to his room and come back down.

"Don Esteban, I must have your pistol." I looked back at the stable. The brigands were still there. That was not good.

"Why do you want my pistol?"

I looked into those pale eyes, eyes the color of the sky, and for a moment I thought I was gazing into Cristóbal's eyes. There was the same boyish innocence. "I am going to fight Barnet."

He turned his head toward the stable. "But those men. They will—"

"They will soon leave. There will be only Barnet and Humberto. I need the pistol for Barnet."

His eyes grew wide in alarm. "No, Carmen. He will kill you! Life means nothing to Barnet. He will kill you!"

"I will not let him, Don Esteban. I will not allow him to kill me because if he kills me..."—I paused, not certain why I wanted to tell him this—"...if he kills me, he will kill your grandchild. I will not allow that to happen."

His brow wrinkled in puzzlement. And then a smile softened his gaunt face.

"I am with child, Don Esteban. The father was the young *norteamericano*, Coalter Owens. Do you remember him?"

"Yes." He continued to smile, but his eyes saddened. "He was a good man."

Knowing that I had to be strong, that I must not cry, I was compelled to look away. And then I heard a noise coming from the corral. It was Reyes and his rabble doing exactly what I had hoped. They were saddling their horses and leaving.

"What is happening?" the Marqués asked, peering toward the stable.

"Don Esteban!" I said. "Your pistol. I must have it!"

"No, Carmen. They will kill you!"

"Let me have it, Don Esteban!" This was the crucial moment. Everything hinged on what happened now. "Hurry!"

Barnet and Humberto came running from the hacienda, stopped briefly to look at us, and then headed for the corral.

"Don Esteban!" I shouted. "Give me the pistol!"

"Carmen, if they see you with a pistol, they will kill you. These are brutal men! You must not—"

I reached for his coat, but he grabbed my wrist and held it. For a man who was supposed to be ill, he was surprisingly strong. I tried to go for the weapon with my other hand, but he took that wrist as well.

"Don Esteban, please!" I cried. "Those men are leaving. There will only be Humberto and Barnet!"

"There are two of them, Carmen. I cannot let them hurt you. You are my daughter! I love you!"

Barnet and Humberto were now running from the corral trying to catch up with the cutthroats who had spurred their mounts to a gallop and were riding through the gates like rats scurrying off a sinking ship. And yet Don Esteban held me fast. I pleaded for him to release me as I saw Barnet and Humberto race back and enter the stable. The irony of it did not escape me. Thinking that he was protecting his daughter, Don Esteban was acting in a way that would surely mean my death and the death of his grandchild.

Finally I wrested my hands free and started again to reach for the gun, but it was too late. Barnet came running to the patio and in his hand was a pistol. He aimed it at me. Not wanting him to notice Don Esteban had a weapon in his jacket, I raised my hands and backed away.

"So," Barnet said, "José Morelos is coming. Is that so, Señorita Rangel? José Morelos is coming?"

I said nothing.

Emerging from the darkness, Lebe Seru, his hands still bound behind him, appeared, walking ahead of Humberto who held a pistol aimed at his back. It surprised me in that I had never so much as seen Humberto touch a gun. He had always been afraid of guns. As they drew near, Humberto shouted, "They said José Morelos is coming!"

"José Morelos is not coming, you fool!" Barnet said.

"We must get out of here!" Humberto insisted. "Let's get our horses and follow the others!"

"José Morelos is not coming," Barnet repeated, never once taking his eyes from me. "The wench made it up. It's a woman's trick. So, Señorita Rangel, what do you do now? Your trick worked. Those fools believed you and rode away. What do you do now?"

"Carmen," Humberto said, turning to me. "You made it up? You told the men José Morelos was coming to Guanajuato? I don't understand. Why?"

The plan had worked, at least in part. I saw no reason to retreat from it now. "Because it's true, Humberto. José Morelos's army is converging on the city at this very moment."

Humberto's handkerchief shone in the dark as he wiped his face. "It could be true," he said to Barnet. "It is said that Morelos strikes from all directions and at anytime of the day or night! We have to get out of here! We have to—"

"Calm yourself," Barnet said. "And keep that gun pointed at Jeb. Shoot him if he makes a false move." He looked back at me, the anger burning in his eyes. "I can't see out here! Let's take them where we can see. Take them to the library. We'll get to the bottom of this. Move, wench!"

Before I entered the hacienda, I looked back and saw the Marqués slumped in the chair. I had a terrible feeling that I would never see my father again.

In the library Lebe Seru obeyed Barnet's order to sit on the floor and Humberto stood over him nervously pointing the pistol which shook in his hand. I stood near the table on which lay the map of North America Humberto had unrolled earlier.

Barnet seated himself behind the desk where he laid his pistol and reached inside his coat for a cigar. "So," he said, "José Morelos is coming to Guanajuato."

My eyes focused on the pistol on the desk. If I could get to that pistol, I knew I could force Humberto to lay down his weapon.

"That is correct," I said and edged a little closer to the desk. "José Morelos is on his way here at this very moment. He seeks vengeance for what—"

"Enough!" Barnet exploded, cutting me off. "Do you think I am stupid? Do you think I am like those fools who ran away tonight without stopping to wonder why, if Morelos is coming, you and Jeb are here by yourselves? If Morelos is coming, why did you not wait for him? Did you decide to begin the invasion of Guanajuato before he arrived? An army of two? An Indian and an African? Please, Señorita. Do not insult my intelligence."

Barnet may not have been deceived by my lie, but I could tell that Humberto, wiping the perspiration that was flooding from his face, was not so sure. I had to try to keep them off balance until I could reach that pistol.

"Why should we not come here?" I asked, edging still closer to the desk. "We had no way of knowing you and your men were here. It was a mistake, I admit, but we merely came here to pass the time until José Morelos arrived. After all, this was my home."

"You came here, Señorita Rangel, to try to stop my return to the United States." He lit the cigar and looked at Lebe Seru. "Is that not right, Jeb? If Morelos is successful in his revolution, he will be able to enforce the law he and Hidalgo made against slavery. But he would stand no chance at all against an army of three or four thousand men armed with long-rifles. Am I correct, Jeb?"

Lebe Seru stared straight ahead and did not answer.

"Carmen," Humberto gasped. "Is that right? Is that why you came here?"

"No," I said, trying to conceal a sudden quiver in my voice. I looked at Humberto and forced a smile. "I want to marry you, Humberto. I want to be your queen. Together, we will rule New Spain." I was now almost within reach of the pistol. "Tell Colonel Barnet of our plans."

Humberto swallowed hard. "Carmen is going to be my wife."

Barnet laughed. "Are you blind, Humberto? Look at the wench. Look at her!"

Humberto looked at me, uncomprehending.

"She is with child!" Barnet shouted. He stood up suddenly and seized the pistol on the desk. "Can you not see it, you stupid fool? Your queen is going to have another man's child!"

Humberto almost dropped the pistol he held as his mouth fell open. He stared at my body.

Barnet continued, "Who is the father, wench? Was it Owens? Is that who it was?" He began to laugh. "Or maybe it's Jeb here. Is that it, Jeb? Are you the father? I'll wager you are, you rascal."

"Humberto, don't listen to him!" I pleaded. "I want to be your queen. I want to rule New Spain at your side. I want to be your wife!"

Humberto looked from me to Barnet and back to me again. "You are with child. I can see it." His eyes grew wild. "You played me for a fool!"

All trace of amusement vanished from Barnet's face. "We've wasted enough time with these two. We have more important things to do." He transferred his pistol to his left hand and reached inside his coat and drew forth the long-blade hunting knife. It was the same one he had used that night to stab Coalter, the one I assumed he had used to slit Anselmo's throat. "I'm not going to waste a bullet on you, Jeb. I'm going to gut you and watch you die real slow." He looked at me. "And then I'm going to gut your little wench."

As he moved toward Lebe Seru, all I could think of was that I could not allow it to happen. I would not allow Lebe Seru to be killed. I would not allow Coalter's child to be killed. But what could I do? Barnet was stooping down and preparing to thrust the knife into Lebe Seru.

From the corner of my eye, I saw mounted on the wall the great broadsword that had belonged to generations of men of the House of Abrantes. It was the sword of my ancestors. I was not a man, but I was an Abrantes as much as Don Esteban or Cristóbal. I did not have their name, but their blood was in my veins and in my soul. Reaching as high as I could, I grasped the hilt and drew it from the scabbard. I swung the sword in an arc and brought the blade down into the back of Barnet's neck. I raised it again, prepared to strike a second blow.

"Carmen!" Lebe Seru shouted. "He's dead! Watch Humberto!"

Indeed, Barnet was dead. His head had been severed from his body. Humberto, jolted by what had happened to Barnet, had yet to react but now he raised the pistol in his hand.

I knew there was no time to swing the sword again, so I braced to receive the charge and watched Humberto's finger tighten on the trigger. Nothing happened. He squeezed a second time and the weapon did not respond. He pulled the trigger several times, all with the same result. And then, I saw the reason. He had forgotten to cock the flintlock. Realizing his omission, Humberto lowered the pistol and awkwardly began to fumble with the mechanism.

Now I had a decision to make. Should I use the sword again? I stood close enough to deliver an effective blow. I could do to Humberto exactly what I had done to Barnet. As I watched him reason out how to cock the flintlock, I was at that moment aware that Humberto was, after all, my brother. Was I capable of killing my own brother?

My instant of hesitation rendered the question moot. Humberto had cocked the pistol and was raising it to aim at me a second time. The brief opportunity I had had to use the broadsword was gone. Humberto used both hands to steady his aim as he shouted obscenities at me. Again, I braced myself, hoping he would miss. At that range, however, it would be virtually impossible for anyone, even Humberto, to miss.

When I heard an exploding noise, I flinched. Strangely, I felt no pain, but I recalled how people who had been shot in battle often said they felt no pain.

When I opened my eyes, I saw Humberto sinking slowly to his knees. Blood trickled from a gaping wound in his temple. He was staring not at me, but at the doorway behind me. And then his eyes rolled back into his head and he collapsed next to where Barnet's body had fallen.

Quickly, I turned and saw Don Esteban. Smoke wafted from the barrel of the pistol in his hand. His grip relaxed and the weapon fell to the stone floor. I used the sword to cut the restraints binding Lebe Seru. And then I ran to my father and embraced him.

✦

Though Don Esteban made a rapid recovery from his illness, I was reluctant to leave until I was assured that his health was fully restored. Moreover, in the weeks that followed, I realized I was in no condition to travel. I finally accepted Lebe Seru's suggestion that we defer our plan to go to Texas until after my child was born.

As it turned out, I was fortunate in that decision because I do not know what I would have done had Hortensia not been with me. I had lived through battles, been shot at, and walked thousands of leagues across the face of Mexico, but nothing prepared me for that day when my daughter made her decision to enter this world. Hortensia was with me throughout the entire ordeal except for the brief moments it required for her to race to the next room to keep Don Esteban and Lebe Seru posted on what was happening.

Finally, it was over, and after a period of sleep, I awoke to see Don Esteban and Lebe Seru, both of them smiling at my bedside. Hortensia placed the little girl in my arms, and I looked at her for the first time. It was a strange mixture of joy and sadness for I immediately saw that she had her father's eyes.

"Carmen," Don Esteban asked softly, "what will be her name? What will you call her?"

I had not given it any thought, so I told him I did not know what to call the baby.

"May I make a suggestion?" he asked glancing at Hortensia. "Is it possible that she could be named after your mother?"

The little girl was grasping my finger firmly in her tiny hand. She was strong like her father. She seemed to look at me and respond when I said, "Cata Valeria."

Don Esteban saw it too. "Look!" he said eagerly. "She knows her name, Carmencita! Did you see the way she turned her head?"

"It is a pretty name," Lebe Seru agreed when I looked to him for his opinion. "A pretty name for a pretty little girl."

"Then that will be her name," I said. "Cata Valeria."

Hortensia wiped tears of joy as she repeated her sister's name, now the name of her grandniece also.

✦

In the days and weeks that followed, as I recovered my strength and was up and about, I thought more about the future and what I must do. Remembering what Barnet had said about the reward offered by the new intendant of Guanajuato for my capture, I knew I must be very careful. Not only was my life in jeopardy, but Cata Valeria's as well. Don Esteban had cautioned the few servants who remained in his employ not to tell anyone that I had returned to the hacienda. These were people who could be trusted, and since the estate was at some distance from the city, I felt reasonably secure as long as we remained there. We were careful to remain indoors except at night.

Nevertheless, I did not wish to remain in hiding for the rest of my life. Moreover, I shared with Lebe Seru the desire to join our *compañeros* in the field in the continuing fight for Mexico's independence from Spain. Servants who went into town for supplies returned almost daily with news of Father Morelos' efforts in the south against the royalist armies. Battles were fought, but none proved decisive for either side. Father Hidalgo's assessment that the struggle would take years was very likely going to be proven true. Lebe Seru and I wanted to be a part of this endeavor. I knew it was what Coalter would have done. I did not want his daughter to grow up in a land ruled by viceroys and intendants. I wanted her to live in a republic governed by a constitution that guaranteed liberty, equality, and justice. Coalter would have wanted this for his daughter.

Don Esteban now shared my goal. Cristóbal's death at the instigation of Fernando had opened his eyes to the truth that the kings were as corrupt as the viceroys they appointed. And he respected what Lebe Seru and I told him about Father Hidalgo and Father Morelos. We had many long conversations on these matters. Indeed, had it not been for the danger I knew my presence at the hacienda brought upon my family and friends, I would have wished to stay in the place of my birth, and now my daughter's birth, forever. It was my home.

But I knew it could not be. It would only be a matter of time before someone outside learned that the woman everyone had thought was Captain Rangel's daughter, the woman seen fighting in the republican army, was at the Hacienda de Abrantes. Soldiers would be dispatched to search the premises, something Don Esteban no longer had the power to prevent.

Lebe Seru and I knew we could go south to fight with Father Morelos but chose to carry through on our original plan to go to Texas. He wished to be closer to the land where so many of his people were in bondage. It was his hope to secure a safe haven for those who could escape. I wanted to help him in this, but I also yearned to go to the place Coalter had loved: Texas. Something deep within was drawing me there. It was as if going to Texas would somehow bring me closer to him.

We studied the maps and plotted a route we felt would afford the best chance to avoid royalist forces. Don Esteban, of course, begged us to stay. But in the end he recognized the threat posed by the new intendant in Guanajuato outweighed even the unknown risks to the north. And then, finally, came the issue upon which we were in agreement: the safety of Cata Valeria. If I remained in Guanajuato, she would be endangered. And, since we were going north to fight the Spanish, I dare not take her with me. A revolution was no place for a baby girl.

"Hortensia and I will care for Cata Valeria until you return," Don Esteban said. "I will raise her as my daughter and give her my name. She will be Cata Valeria de Abrantes. It will be written into the records of the church. If anyone should ask how she came to me, I will say she was left at the convent I support by a woman who never returned. Such things have happened."

Though he spoke these words in love, they struck cold in my heart when I heard him say "a woman who never returned." I knew, however, that his words conveyed what I knew to be the reality I must accept. It was likely it would be many years before I returned to my daughter. It was difficult to leave her, but I did not know what else to do. I was convinced that what I had chosen to do was best for her, both for her immediate safety as well as for her future well-being.

Before I left, I held my baby one last time, and after placing her in her grandfather's arms, I removed the jade pendant of the Mexican goddess Chimalma from around my neck and looped it around hers. Cata Valeria grasped it and held it tight in her little fist. What my mother had given me, and women in her family had given to their daughters for generations, I now gave to my daughter. Quickly, I turned and left so that my father would not see my tears.

X

We entered Texas at a shallow water crossing about a league upstream from where the Río Bravo empties into the Gulf of Mexico. At first Texas looked no different than the chaparral we had negotiated for weeks. However, as we continued up the coast, we did begin to notice changes. The vegetation, mostly mesquite and sage, grew thicker the farther north we advanced. In some places it became so impenetrable we were able to make progress only by following winding trails made by bands of javelinas. These thin-legged wild pigs strutted about fearlessly, confident their sharp tusks would protect them from anything. This included the wolves and big cats we saw on occasion and whose threat prompted us to keep our muskets loaded. More than once, a boar would menacingly raise the coarse hair on his back to warn us not to get too close to his harem of females and their piglets. We always yielded, for this was their home, not ours.

This rugged land of the gulf coastal plain was quite alien to someone who had grown up in the crisp, thin air of a mountain range. I was not accustomed to such unrelenting heat and humidity. The salt breeze dried my skin, and I longed for a fresh-water stream in which to bathe away the biting sand that accumulated after each day's sojourn. But there were no streams or rivers, no lakes or even ponds other than an occasional sinkhole containing brackish water. Fortunately, storms from the gulf provided us with intermittent rains, some of which were heavy. Like the wolves or the big cats, we would eagerly lap up water from rivulets before they were consumed by the parched earth. We would store as much as we could in our earthen jars, for when the storms had passed, the scorching sun would retrieve the moisture very quickly and there was no way of predicting when the rain might come again.

Food was more of a problem than water. We had, of course, stocked our packs with quantities of corn, rice, and beans, expecting, as we had always done in the past, to replenish those supplies along the way. Since we came across no villages or farms, we soon began to run low. Normally, we could forage in the countryside for wild grains, squash, melons, berries. But neither of us was familiar with the vegetation as we advanced farther north, and we were not certain what was, in fact, edible, and what poisonous. Moreover, we entered Texas in the winter and many of the plants were in dormancy. Mesquite trees were quite numerous but void of beans. What tunas remained on the prickly pears were pithy as were the fruit stalks on the yucca and sotol cacti. We sustained ourselves on the tasteless, but abundant, supply of acorns that fell from stands of gnarled, wind-bent scrub oaks that become thicker as we continued up the coast.

Though Lebe Seru shared my dislike against the killing of animals, we would have partaken of such sustenance if we had not been reluctant to fire our weapons. We did not know if a Spanish patrol was nearby ready to rush toward the sound of a gun's discharge. Rather than take a chance, we searched ever more diligently for other kinds of foods.

In the shallows of the bays between the mainland and a long line of narrow islands in the gulf, we found oyster beds. After much coaxing, I overcame my reluctance, accepting Lebe Seru's assurances that, despite their appearance, these creatures were edible. Lebe Seru even managed to scoop up small fish and shrimps with his hands, and so hungry were we at the time that we devoured them raw after beheading and gutting them with our machetes.

Since I had never before seen the sea, I was at times overwhelmed by the immensity of the bays. The pungent fragrance of the salt water and the incessant roar of the ocean beyond the offshore islands were a whole new world to me. Often at dusk, before retiring, we would watch the coming and going of the seabirds. Teeming flocks of gulls would screech and fight for each other's catch while the larger birds, some with wings as long as a man is tall, would glide over the water, dive, and effortlessly snare a fish. Often, at such times, I would notice Lebe Seru's gaze turn to the eastern horizon.

Once I asked, "Are you thinking of your home across the ocean?"

"Yes," he replied sadly. "If I had the strength, I could enter the sea right here and swim to my land. But I cannot. It is too far away." He turned his eyes to the sky. "My home might as well be on one of those stars. I can reach for them, but they will forever be beyond my grasp."

"We are both far from our place of birth," I said in an effort to console. "Perhaps this Texas can be our new home."

He drew a deep breath and shook his head. "I do not know if people like us will ever find a home, Carmen. Perhaps we can make one for those who come after us, a place where they can live in freedom."

My thoughts turned to Cata Valeria as I pondered Lebe Seru's words. Certainly, she was the reason I was in this strange and bewildering place, this Texas. I was not at all certain why her father had found it so fascinating, but I was here because I wanted his daughter to be able to live, as Lebe Seru said, in freedom. We would make Mexico such a place for those who came after us. It had been Father Hidalgo's dream. It had been Coalter's dream. It was for this dream that thousands of our sisters and brothers had given their lives. I knew I must do all I could to make that dream a reality. However hard it might become, there was no turning back. It was what I must do. It was all that was left for me to do.

✦

It was a wonderful day when we arrived at the next river after the Río Bravo that flowed into the gulf, and we were at last able to bathe away the sticky salt that was caked on our skin after months of travel. We found tall trees heavy with pecans, which is why, we assumed, the Spanish explorers had chosen to name the river "Nueces; and we were able to feast to our fill on these flavorful nuts along with ripe squashes and sweet melons we found growing in the rich soils north of the river. Indeed, the farther north we traveled, the

soils became darker and supported the growth of an enormous variety
of plants and trees. I began to understand what Coalter had meant
when he said the most productive land in the world was in Texas. I
was no rancher, but even I could see it was true.

Studying our maps, we plotted a direct route to San Antonio de
Béxar, where we hoped to link up with republican armies, but I
noticed that a slightly different course to the north would take us to
the only other settlement noted on the map other than San Antonio
de Béxar and Nacogdoches—the latter an outpost far to the northeast
almost on the border with Louisiana.

"Do you remember," I asked, "the corporal who freed us from the
prison in Chihuahua after Father Miguel was executed?"

"Santiago Montemayor," Lebe Seru responded. "I recall that he
said he was from Texas."

"He said he was from this place." I pointed to the map. "La
Bahía."

Since there were no other towns charted on the maps, we decided
it would be wise, even though it would take longer, to break our journey to San Antonio de Béxar with a stopover in La Bahía.

It required another month to reach the place near a narrow,
high-bank river where the map said the settlement should be. We
approached it cautiously because the map indicated the Spanish
maintained a presidio at La Bahía.

Because we arrived at dusk, we could see a glow in the night's
sky which we interpreted as the sign of fires being made for the
evening meal. We drew ever closer until we spied the white stone
walls of the presidio situated on a rise over the south side of the river.

And then, suddenly, we heard the sound of muskets being fired.
Throwing ourselves to the ground beneath tall stands of grass, we
looked at each other as the "crack" from the muskets was drowned
out by the roar of cannon. From the noise of the explosions, I judged
them to be nine-pounders. Naturally, we concluded that a battle was
being waged. Perhaps republican forces were attempting to storm the
presidio. The cadence of the firing of the cannon, however, indicated
the artillery was being used not in battle but as part of a ceremony.
When the barrage stopped, the sound of men cheering could be heard.

Realizing we may have carelessly drawn close enough to the fort to be spotted by lookouts, we began to crawl through the grass in the opposite direction.

We had not gone far when we both froze in place at the sound of a whispered voice: "Señora Rangel!"

Our muskets were loaded with charge, and only reflexively did we ready them. Immediately we knew who it was or at least we thought we recognized the voice.

Tentatively, I whispered, "Corporal Montemayor?"

Several dozen people raised to peer over the grass. They were all around us. It surprised me they were so close, and we had not heard them. They, in fact, had surrounded us. And then, I saw the corporal. He motioned for us to stay down but to follow them.

We traveled at a rapid clip about a league to the south and then turned west to the river, which we crossed on a makeshift bridge of several logs lashed together. The bridge was quickly retrieved and concealed in underbrush after the last person had crossed. I assumed this was done so the Spanish, if they followed, would not be able to cross after us.

As we continued northward past a large stone mission building on the north bank, I noticed there were both men and women in the group. Some of the men, despite the coldness of the night, wore nothing but loincloths. These men, whose long black hair was parted in the middle, had blue markings on their faces. Additionally, they carried bows and arrows. It seemed logical to conclude they were some of the people indigenous to Texas.

Only after the glow from the fires at the presidio could no longer be seen on the horizon did we stop. The corporal then approached us, shook Lebe Seru's hand, embraced him, and after some hesitation, awkwardly did the same with me.

"Corporal Montemayor," I said after he released me from a bear hug that almost took away my breath, "I thought you had gone south to fight with Father Morelos."

The beard he had worn while at Chihuahua was now gone, and I recalled how he had looked that night in Mexico City when he had escorted Lupita and me to the palace. He was a solidly built young man with strong, rugged features. From the appearance of the *indios* around us, I suspected he may have shared their heritage.

Smiling broadly, he said, "We did go to the south, Señora Rangel. And we met Father José. He ordered us to return to Texas and join with the Republican Army of the North led by Bernardo Gutiérrez."

Bernardo Gutiérrez de Lara was one of the men who had been an advisor to Father Hidalgo from the earliest days in Dolores. Though I had seen him with Father Hidalgo and the other leaders many times, I had never made his acquaintance. "Gutiérrez is in Texas?" I asked, happy that he had escaped the fate of so many of the other republican leaders.

"Yes," the corporal said. "He is at present assembling an army near Nacogdoches which he plans to occupy in the name of the Republic of Mexico. We will depart in a matter of days to join him. After Nacogdoches he plans to come south to capture San Antonio de Béxar."

Though we were now some distance from the presidio at La Bahía, we all crouched when we heard the muffled roar of the cannon once again being fired.

"Corporal Montemayor," I said. "Why are the—"

Smiling, he interrupted to say, "I am now a lieutenant, Señora Rangel. Father Morelos commissioned me an officer in the republican army." He smiled. "But please, call me Santiago."

Again, the cannon sounded.

"Santiago," I asked, "why are the cannon being fired at the presidio?"

His smile faded and he looked from me to Lebe Seru and back. "I guess you have not heard."

"Heard what?" Lebe Seru asked.

"Napoleon Bonaparte was defeated in a great battle. His brother was forced to flee Madrid. Fernando de Borbón is again the king of Spain. That is why the soldiers in the presidio are celebrating."

This news angered me. Fernando de Borbón was the man who had killed Cristóbal. He was the traitorous coward who had capitulated to the Bonapartes and lived in luxury while his people fought the invaders. He was the man whose viceroys ordered the slaughter of the children of Mexico. And now he was king of Spain. It was no use thinking about it. One could go crazy thinking about such things.

Santiago continued: "The soldiers in the presidio know that soon more soldiers will be coming from Spain. That is also why they are celebrating." He looked about at the people watching us. They were curious to know who we were. "Please allow me to introduce my friends."

Some of the men with Santiago had been with him that day in Chihuahua when we set off on our separate ways. Like their lieutenant, they had been soldiers in the Spanish army before realizing that Father Hidalgo's actions had been taken on behalf of justice for the people of Mexico. They all said they were happy to meet soldiers who had served Hidalgo and Allende.

Santiago stepped to one of the *indios* and said, "Allow me to present Meyei, Chief of the Emet Tonkawas. His people have joined our fight to win independence from Spain."

Chief Meyei, an older man with greying hair, nodded and said something I took to be a greeting in his Tonkawan language. Lebe Seru and I expressed our pleasure in meeting him and greeted each of the chief's warriors. Though slight in stature they were a well-proportioned people, slender and athletic in appearance. The facial paintings they wore, a series of chalk blue lines and geometric symbols, were quite striking and no two were identical. Each had a necklace made up of various shells that I suspected had been obtained from the gulf coast where we had been for the last several months.

While Lebe Seru was talking with Chief Meyei, I turned around because I sensed someone staring at me. I found myself looking into the eyes of a young woman.

Shyly, she said, "I am called Pilar Fuentes, Señora Rangel."

She was an attractive young woman, about my age. Her smile prompted me to request that she call me Carmen when I introduced myself.

"Santiago has told us much about you," Pilar said. She glanced at the lieutenant who was looking after one of his men who had sprained an ankle. The Tonkawas were using their machetes to cut branches to make a stretcher for the man who was unable to walk.

"He told us of your bravery." She smiled. "However, he did not tell us you were so beautiful."

It was not difficult to discern from the way Pilar looked at the lieutenant that she was his sweetheart. "Santiago," I said, "saved us from the firing squad. Lebe Seru and I owe him our lives."

Pilar was friendly but her awkwardness conveyed that she was not certain what to make of me. "Santiago said your husband was killed in the revolution. I am very sorry."

I saw no reason to explain that Coalter had not been my husband. As far as I was concerned, he had been and would forever be my husband.

"And your little girl?" Pilar asked. "Santiago said you had gone to look for her. Was she found?"

At first I thought of Cata Valeria but remembered that Santiago had thought Lupita was my child, and I had never corrected him. "No," I said. "We did not find her. I believe she perished in the desert." Though these people were friends, I was not inclined to tell anyone of Cata Valeria. If the intendant in Guanajuato ever learned that my daughter was at the Hacienda de Abrantes, he would undoubtedly do her harm. Only Lebe Seru knew of my daughter, and of course, he would tell no one. It would have to remain our secret.

Pilar said, "You have lost much. But you are among friends now, Carmen." There was warmth in her dark eyes. "I would like to be your friend."

Not since Teresa had I had a woman as a friend. Indeed, my cousin had been the only friend of my sex, so it was difficult to know what to say. I had spent most of my life with men.

"Come," Pilar said, taking my arm, "we are ready to leave. We are going to Meyei's camp. There we will find you some new clothes."

Looking down at the tattered rags I wore, I managed a smile, and when I looked at Lebe Seru, I saw that he, too, had found a new friend. He was attending closely to something Chief Meyei was detailing as we began to follow Santiago and his men along a narrow path in the darkness.

It was daybreak before we reached the Tonkawas' camp in a clearing several leagues north of La Bahía. We were greeted by many children, both Indian and Mexican. Pilar explained that the families of the men with Santiago, most of whom were from La Bahía, had left the settlement for fear of reprisal from the royalist soldiers in the presidio.

I met Santiago's parents, his brothers and sisters, his nieces and nephews, all of whom were friendly. I was introduced to Pilar's brothers and sisters and their families. Pilar seemed to be as much a leader as Santiago because she directed people, men and women, to tasks such as gathering wood for the fires over which the morning meal was being prepared.

It was a treat to eat tortillas, beans, rice, and *pan dulce*, sweet buns covered with honey, after what Lebe Seru and I had been forced to consume for so long. None of the feasts Hortensia had ever prepared for the highest notables of Guanajuato ever tasted so good. I ate my fill and washed it down with a tart juice made from white grapes. After I ate, Pilar led me to a stream where I was able to bathe in privacy. Then she brought me a cotton shirt, cotton pants, a pair of sandals, and a serape. It was wonderful to wear things that were fresh and clean even if the garments were too short in length. Pilar promised she would find something that would fit better.

"You are very tall," she said. "Are you *india*? Few *indios* are as tall as you."

"My mother was *india*," I said and, seeing her puzzlement, added, "my father is Spanish."

"My father, too, was from Spain. He was a sergeant at the presidio at La Bahía." Her eyes saddened. "He died when I was just a child. I do not remember him."

"And your mother?"

"She was Tonkawan. She was of Meyei's tribe, the Emets. Most of the people you see here are my aunts, uncles, and my cousins. My mother died of cholera when I was a girl. The diseases of the Europeans have killed many of my mother's people and have greatly reduced their numbers."

When we returned to camp, Pilar took me to one of the Tonkawan lodges. She said it would be my home, a gift from her people. It was a small, squat structure made of animal hides stretched over poles lashed together to form a cone. She gave me blankets and suggested I try to get some sleep because we would very soon be leaving to join Gutiérrez's army on their march on San Antonio de Béxar.

✦

Our movement north to rendezvous with Gutiérrez took us across several great river basins: the Colorado, the Brazos, and the Trinity. Much of it was an area inhabited by various Tonkawan clans which had different names such as Meyei's Emets. Other Tonkawan clan names were Cavas, Toxos, and Tohahas. Pilar explained that the clans were formed on a lineage of kinship to the mother's family. Unlike some of the tribes to the north, such as the Comanches who would trade the women like property, the Tonkawas regarded women as equal to men. They shared the work, and the men spent much time with the children. The Tonkawas lavished much affection on the children who were very well behaved. At no time did I ever witness a Tonkawan child being struck.

The Tonkawas were a democratic people who elected their chiefs. This was one of the reasons, Pilar said, they had chosen to answer Father Morelos' call to join the struggle for a Mexican republic independent of Spain. The viceroys of New Spain had often warred against the indigenous peoples of Texas because of their refusal to participate in the system of *encomiendas*. Also, the Spanish had failed in their promise to protect them from the warlike Comanches who greatly outnumbered the Tonkawas and their cousins in the neighboring tribes to the south and east, the Coahuiltecans and the Karankawas.

Establishing no permanent settlements, the Tonkawas were nomadic, moving from place to place, hunting, fishing the rivers or the coastal bays, and gathering the bountiful harvests to be found in the forests of the river basins. There was no lack of food for those who knew how to recognize it. I was amazed at how quickly the Tonkawas could disassemble their lodges and pack their belongings and provisions which they carried either on their backs or strapped to long poles pulled by dogs. The Tonkawas functioned very successfully in this land and seemed to be happy except for the incursions by the Spanish and the Comanches.

From what I could understand, the Comanches were not unlike the ancient Romans who conquered and dominated their neighbors. Even large and strong tribes, such as the Apaches in the western regions of Texas, would flee before the Comanches. These things were told to me by Pilar who, I could tell, was not fond of Comanches.

✦

The distances in Texas were vast. It took us almost two months to arrive in east Texas where Bernardo Gutiérrez was organizing the Republican Army of the North for an invasion of the provincial capital of San Antonio de Béxar. Though not mountainous or at a high elevation, this region reminded me somewhat of my home near Guanajuato because of the tall pine trees and the mild temperature. The soil was coarse and not as rich as the regions to the south through which the great rivers to the gulf flowed.

Bernardo Gutiérrez greeted us with great affection. He was anxious to hear of the directives issued by Father Morelos and the congress he had convened after the death of Father Hidalgo to reaffirm the Mexican republic and its constitution.

When we were introduced to him, Gutiérrez embraced Lebe Seru and me. His eyes filled with tears when we related to him the account of Father Hidalgo's execution.

Gutiérrez was a rather corpulent fellow of middle years with a round expressive face that revealed his friendliness and his love of conversation. My initial impression that he was not an astute military tactician was never contradicted in the days ahead. He was much more interested in food and drink than in planning battles and spent no small amount of his time preparing lavish meals from various game his men shot. He was particularly fond of wild turkeys and pheasants. He was the republican army's chief cook as well as its commander.

Gutiérrez's forces were not much larger than our band of some one hundred and twenty, which included the families of Santiago's men and Chief Meyei's warriors. We were perplexed as to how he

expected to defeat the garrison at San Antonio de Béxar, a professional army estimated to number between one to two thousand soldiers, including cavalry and dragoons. When Santiago queried
Gutiérrez on this point, he smiled and said, "Do not worry. We have
an ally and he has over seven hundred men. They will be joining us
very soon, and we will take Nacogdoches before going on to San Antonio."

"An ally?" Santiago asked.

"Recently, I had occasion to travel to New Orleans to sample
their cuisine," Gutiérrez explained. "Magnificent!" He touched his fingers to his lips. "During my stay, I met an officer in the army of the
norteamericanos, a lieutenant by the name of Augustus Magee. He
believes in our cause and said there are many like him who will join
us to help liberate Mexico from Spain."

Santiago was confused. "I do not understand. Do you mean to say
the army of the United States is coming to Texas to fight the Spanish."

"Oh, no!" Gutiérrez said and laughed. "Not their army. No. Lieutenant Magee has resigned his commission in his country's army. The
men he is bringing to Texas are volunteers. They are republicans like
us!"

✦

A few days later, Augustus Magee, a tight-lipped and determined
looking man of small stature, led eight hundred volunteers into our
camp. I, of course, had known only two *norteamericanos* in my life.
One was the man I loved, the father of my child; the other was the
man I had killed in order to protect my child. And so I was not at all
certain what to make of these solemn-faced men who briskly marched
into our camp, each carrying a long-rifle similar to the weapon Barnet
had had Coalter demonstrate to Don Esteban that day that now
seemed a lifetime ago. In addition to their rifles, most displayed a
wide assortment of other weapons including long-blade knives,
swords, and pistols.

Lebe Seru shared my misgivings. These men were from the country where he had been held in bondage for so many years. How many

of them owned slaves? How many, like Barnet, had been slave traders? We expressed these concerns to Gutiérrez, but he continued to insist that Magee's men were idealists who wanted nothing more than to help their neighbor to the south do what had been done in their own country: depose a king's tyrannical government and establish a republic.

By and large the *norteamericanos* kept to themselves. They looked at us with the same suspicion in their eyes as we looked at them. There were exceptions. Some of the men extended their hand in friendship. But because of the difference in language, it was difficult at best.

A number of the men watched Lebe Seru and Chief Meyei and his warriors with anything but friendliness in their countenance. Some eyed me, and I knew what was on their minds, but they kept their distance when Lebe Seru, Santiago, and Chief Meyei let it be known that the women in our contingent were to be left alone and respected. Most tended to their own affairs and spent their time endlessly sharpening their knives and swords or cleaning and recleaning their weapons and equipment, which included several six-pounder artillery pieces.

What really motivated these *norteamericanos* was uncertain. Some, especially those who made an effort to visit with those of us who had come with Santiago, were, I believe, sincere in wanting to help a people who had been abused by rulers they had not chosen. Others were adventurers seeking to make their fortune, and still others were on the run from the authorities. Some wore faded uniforms of past armies they had served which, judging by the insignias, included a number of European countries; others dressed like gentlemen of means; most preferred the garb of the backwoodsman, practical clothes made from homespun fabrics and animal skins. All in all, they were a motley bunch.

Their leader, Augustus Magee, was a man who had graduated from his country's military academy at a place called West Point. He was a thin, narrow-chested fellow, almost frail, with a persistent cough. Though courteous, he was reserved not only with us but with his own men, some of whom, I think, believed that they, not Magee or

Gutiérrez, should be in charge of the expedition. One fellow in particular, a Major Kemper, often challenged Magee's authority and disre-
garded his orders.

Indeed, one characteristic I noticed about these *norteamericanos*
was a tendency to argue about who was in charge of this or that and
who had what authority over whom. They would spend hours trying
to determine lines of authority and rank. Also, they continually
argued over how to proceed, even regarding inconsequential matters
such as the proper way to load ammunition on a caisson.

Once, I saw a group of them bickering over how to harness a
team of mules. I asked Lebe Seru to translate for me what one man
kept repeating over and over to another man.

"He is saying, 'That is not the right way to do it,'" Lebe Seru
explained.

"That is not the right way to do it" were the first words of English
that I learned, and I heard them spoken time and time again among
these men.

✦

After a few weeks of basic drill and an attempt to integrate the
various elements of our forces into a coherent fighting unit, Gutiérrez
and Magee decided to strike out for Nacogdoches which was not far
from our camp. At the head of our columns, a man on horseback carried a green banner, the battle flag of the Army of the Republic of
Mexico, Father Morelos' flag. We were met on the road by a patrol of
about two dozen dragoons who leveled their muskets at us and
mounted a charge. Foolishly, they fired even though we were well out
of their range.

Immediately, the *norteamericanos* aimed their long-rifles and
killed the dragoons with dispatch. They killed all of them. Most were
shot in the head, even though some were as far away as two hundred
yards.

Without a moment's delay, we double-timed to the fort, a small
structure made of logs which the Spanish had attempted to fortify
with bales of wool, taking up positions just beyond the range of the
defenders' muskets. The six-pounders were packed with charge, and

the rifles were aimed at the infantry who stood in plain view, apparently unaware they were within range of our weapons.

It was Major Kemper who orchestrated the deployment of our forces. He stood near the battery of cannon while Magee hung back with Gutiérrez, an act that did not go unnoticed by any of us who were in the front lines. I saw the looks of disgust on the faces of the *norteamericanos,* and though I was just beginning to learn their language, I knew the words they spoke were not complimentary. Some called Magee a coward.

Gutiérrez sent one of his sergeants under a flag of truce to direct the commander of the fort to surrender. The sergeant returned to convey the commander's query. He wanted to know under what authority Gutiérrez was acting. Gutiérrez told the sergeant to say they were the Republican Army of the North acting under the authority of José Morelos and the Congress of the Republic of Mexico. The commander ordered Gutiérrez's sergeant shot after he delivered his message; this in spite of the fact that he was carrying a white flag.

Infuriated, the *norteamericanos* shouted, "Treachery!"

Without so much as a glance back at Gutiérrez or Magee, Kemper ordered his men to open fire. Within moments, most of the defenders of the fort had been felled, and large portions of the walls had been leveled and were on fire.

A white flag of surrender was quickly raised by the Spanish. Many of us had not even had an opportunity to discharge our weapons. Moreover, not one from among our force had suffered as much as a scratch in this exercise which effectively netted for the Republic of Mexico the control of the northern and eastern portions of the province of Texas. It was abundantly clear that Spanish musketry was no match for the Pennsylvania long-rifles.

✦

Before marching south toward San Antonio de Béxar, Magee dispatched his prisoners to Louisiana under a guard of men who were told to broadcast the word of our victory and recruit more volunteers to join us on the way. Organization and planning were Augustus

Magee's strongpoint. Every night at camp, he spent much time studying detailed feature maps of Texas made by Santiago and his men.

   He also poured over drawings made by one of Gutiérrez's men,
Captain Antonio Delgado. Delgado's father had been beheaded by the
governor of Texas, Manuel de Salcedo, for leading the republicans in
their brief occupation of San Antonio de Béxar following Father
Hidalgo's proclamation. Captain Delgado reported how the Spanish
garrison in Béxar had fortified the old mission of San Antonio de
Valero, also known as the "Alamo."

   Magee never tired of hearing about battlefield tactics employed
by the Spanish. On this latter issue, I was able to supply information,
and it was in listening to Lebe Seru translate my words into English
for Magee that I daily increased my knowledge of that language. Lebe
Seru said I would soon be able to speak English as well as he.

   Of course there were some words that I overheard spoken by the
norteamericanos in their nightly drinking bouts that I knew it was
best I not learn. These men had brought with them a large supply of a
beverage they called "sourmash whiskey," and it was evident they
had a great fondness for it. Gutiérrez, who quickly acquired a taste
for whiskey and loved to talk and laugh, frequently joined Kemper
and the *norteamericanos* in celebrations that often lasted long into
the night. Magee avoided these festivities and became increasingly
isolated from the very men he was supposed to be leading.

   As we drew closer to San Antonio de Béxar, Chief Meyei's scouts
were able to provide Gutiérrez and Magee with information on what
the Spanish were doing to prepare for our arrival. The Tonkawas took
pride in their ability to run rapidly for long distances without tiring.
Using a system of relays, Meyei was able to know within hours the
movements of royalist troops even when we were still days from San
Antonio. When his scouts told us that Governor Salcedo was being
reinforced by hundreds of troops—presumably fresh troops from
Spain—everyone took pause. Based on Captain Delgado's drawings, it
was apparent it would be difficult to dislodge the royalists from their
fortifications behind the thick walls of the Alamo.

   Finally, Magee hit upon what I thought was an intelligent strategy. He proposed we veer away from San Antonio de Béxar and take

the presidio at La Bahía. If we did that, he said, we could expect Governor Salcedo to vacate San Antonio de Béxar and march on us for the purpose of retaking La Bahía. The artillery and the long-rifles were much more effective against an enemy in the open than one dug in behind walls several feet thick. Gutiérrez, after soliciting the advice of Santiago, Lebe Seru, and Meyei, agreed to the plan. Kemper, who had become the leader of the *norteamericanos* for all practical purposes, consulted with his lieutenants and agreed.

After we moved out to implement the plan, I told Magee, in his own language, that I thought he was a good strategist. I did this because by now almost none of the people he had brought from his country were talking to him. He thanked me for my courtesy, and when he did, I saw the fear in his eyes. I think he wanted to do great things and was able to plan for these things, but he was very frightened of dying. If he had been a general, entitled to stay behind the lines and away from the fighting, Magee might have been a great leader. His fear, which he could not conceal, cost him the respect of his men, most of whom seemed to relish the prospect of battle. They wanted to fight. They wanted to kill the Spanish, and the possibility that they might themselves be killed or wounded did not seem to enter their heads.

Like the soldiers at Nacogdoches, the royalists at the presidio in La Bahía grew nervous and opened fire when we were still beyond their range. At a distance of almost three hundred yards, Kemper's sharpshooters calmly used their long-rifles to pick off those unfortunates who peered over the walls.

Quickly, the white flag was run up, and in short order, it was brought down as Gutiérrez personally raised the green banner of José Morelos' Republican Army of Mexico. In the celebration that followed, there were some—both Mexicans and *norteamericanos*, who said that the green flag was the symbol of a new nation: not the Republic of Mexico, but the Republic of Texas.

There was very little time for celebration or argument as to what the green flag symbolized because, in a few days, Chief Meyei's scouts brought word that Governor Salcedo was personally leading a force of several thousand men from San Antonio de Béxar in the direction of La Bahía.

Upon hearing this report, Magee suggested it might be best if we withdrew toward Louisiana so that we would not be cut off from a retreat should the governor's force prove too much for us to handle. Kemper rejected this option immediately and, instead, endorsed Santiago's plan to stock the presidio with provisions so that we could withstand a siege. Gutiérrez, who looked almost as nervous as Magee, agreed that Santiago's idea was best, and everyone hurried to bring sacks of corn, beans, rice, and other provisions behind the stone walls of the fort.

When the advance elements of Salcedo's royalist force arrived, there was a small skirmish, and we abandoned the settlement of La Bahía and moved everyone, including the families, inside the presidio.

Over the next several days, approximately two thousand Spanish infantry surrounded us and placed some forty-eight artillery pieces, mostly nine- and twelve-pounders, out of range of Kemper's sharp-shooters. They had heard of what had happened at Nacogdoches, and they wisely respected the capabilities of men with long-rifles.

After offering us a chance to surrender, which Gutiérrez promptly refused, Governor Salcedo ordered a cannonade of the fort which lasted for two hours. To our relief, the walls held, and when the royalists, thinking their barrage had damaged our positions, launched an infantry charge, our own artillery, in concert with the firepower of some seven hundred rifles, took a heavy toll. The slopes of the hill upon which the fort sat were littered with the bodies of men, many of whom, only months before, were in Spain battling Napoleon's retreating army.

Following several days of this kind of give and take, Salcedo silenced his guns. The positions he set up were an indication that we were in for a long siege. Fortunately, the presidio was more than adequately supplied with food and water, so there was good reason to believe we could outlast the Spanish. Their provisions had to be transported from San Antonio de Béxar, some one hundred leagues to the north. Moreover, Chief Meyei's kinsmen of the Tonkawas clans were actively mounting ambushes on the supply trains as well as the encircling army itself. In the dark of night, the Tonkawas were able to approach the Spanish camps, launch a barrage of arrows, and vanish, before the soldiers who were still alive could respond.

✦

As the days turned into weeks, many grew anxious at the forced confinement. One morning, just before dawn, I sat with Pilar near a small fire and watched the changing of the lookouts on the ramparts. Santiago and his men were taking over from a squad of Kemper's men who had maintained the nightwatch.

"Carmen," Pilar asked, "how much longer can this continue?"

Pilar was brave, and I knew she feared not so much for herself as for Santiago. Just the day before, he had led a party outside the walls to fight a skirmish with a Spanish patrol over a milk cow that had wandered onto the field north of the fort. Our side had retrieved the animal, but one of Santiago's men was severely wounded.

Hoping to lift Pilar's spirits, I answered, "I am certain the Spanish will soon leave. Did you hear them firing into the darkness again last night? The Tonkawas are picking them off, one by one. Their morale must be very low."

At that moment, the back door to the presidio chapel opened, and stretching his head slightly, Magee surveyed the world outside before rushing to the latrine area. He carried a Bible in his hand.

"Look at that poor man," Pilar said. "He is so frightened. I feel sorry for him."

I watched Magee rush back and close behind him the door to the chapel where he spent each day and night in prayer. Several times I had taken him food, but he was too embarrassed at his own fear to say more than a few words before retreating to his self-imposed exile.

"Carmen," Pilar said. "Tell me about your husband. If it is not too painful I would like to know. What was his name?"

Of course it was painful, but I knew she asked not out of idle curiosity. "Coalter Owens."

"He was a *norteamericano*?"

"Yes," I said going on to confess to Pilar that, though Coalter was the man I loved, we had not married. I related the circumstance of our meeting, and how we had come to be a part of Father Hidalgo's revolution. I had never talked to anyone about what happened to Coalter, and though saddened, I also felt better after being able to relate to another person what I felt for him and how I missed him.

When I finished, Pilar said, "You did not see Coalter die."

"No. But it would have been impossible to recover from such a wound."

For a while she said nothing. Then she remarked, "I do not know what I would do if Santiago was killed." She lowered her head, unable to say more. Tears came to her eyes.

I moved closer and took her hands in mine. "Do you love Santiago?"

"Santiago and I grew up together, Carmen. We have always been together. I—"

"Do you love him?"

"Yes," she said firmly. "I love him. I love him very much."

"Then why have you not married?"

"We had planned to marry, but then came the revolution. We decided to wait until Mexico is independent of Spain. There will be time."

Gripping her hands tightly, I shook my head. "The struggle for independence could go on for years, Pilar. Do not postpone your happiness. You do not know what tomorrow will bring. Listen to me! Do not wait until it is too late and your life is over."

She dried her tears and looked at me. "There will come another man for you, Carmen. You are very beautiful. You have seen the way the men look at you."

"No, Pilar. There will never be another man for me. I loved Coalter with all my heart, and I love him still. I will always love him."

I started to tell her about Cata Valeria but stopped. Though I trusted Pilar, I could not risk the possibility that anyone in Guanajuato learn she was my daughter. It had now been almost two years since I had left my father's hacienda, and increasingly I realized my daughter was likely to grow up without me. I would not be there to protect her, and so I must do nothing to jeopardize her safety. It was a bitter irony that the best thing I could do for my child was to disappear from her life.

✦

The siege dragged on for months. Finally, Governor Salcedo sent word that he would like to meet with Magee. He had made it clear in previous communications that he did not recognize Gutiérrez's authority and denounced him, along with José Morelos, as a traitor to King Fernando. We all suspected some kind of treachery and urged Magee not to accept the governor's offer. After all, the Spanish were losing men to the Tonkawan raids, and we still had provisions to hold out for several more months if necessary. In fact Chief Meyei and his warriors routinely slipped in and out of the presidio at night and were able to replenish our supplies.

Magee, however, was bereft of all resolve, and so he rode out to a conference to be held across the river at the site of the mission. When he returned, he called an assembly in the yard of the presidio and announced that Governor Salcedo had offered the *norteamericanos* safe passage to Louisiana if they would lay down their arms and give up the fight. Those of us who were Mexican would be taken to San Antonio de Béxar to stand trial for treason.

Captain Delgado, whose father had been the first to lead the republicans in Texas, shouted, "If the *norteamericanos* wish to leave, let them! I will remain here and fight. I would rather die fighting for my freedom than kneel before pigs like Salcedo!"

Gutiérrez said he was not sure what to make of the governor's proposal. I think he was inclined to accept, but he did not want to lose his head.

Magee pleaded for acceptance of the offer. It was the first time in months he had been in the yard, and he was pale and gaunt. His hands trembled as he held a cloth to his mouth and coughed repeatedly. He said he wanted to go home. He had had enough of Texas. There was a long period of silence. Magee asked all those who agreed to accept Salcedo's offer to raise their weapons above their heads.

No one raised their weapon.

And then a strange thing occurred. Major Kemper gripped his long-rifle by the barrel, raised it a few inches and then brought the stock to the ground with a thud. He repeated this action and other of the *norteamericanos* joined him. Soon, seven hundred men were pounding the butts of their rifles on the ground. It made an ominous sound.

Delgado, recognizing that the *norteamericanos* were expressing their disapproval of the offer, began to do the same thing with his weapon and Gutiérrez's men joined him. I had never seen anything like this before. I felt sorry for Magee who must have known the men were demonstrating their rejection not only of Governor Salcedo's proposal but of his own leadership. More than that, they were rejecting him as a man. His hands began to shake more violently and he stumbled backwards before he staggered to his right, turned, and rushed back to the chapel.

The pounding of the rifles did not cease. Something about it made me sick to my stomach. The expressions on the faces of the men were ugly. Pilar, who was next to me, took my arm, and we looked at each other. This had turned into something horrible, and I wished the men would stop. They kept on pounding their rifle butts on the ground.

Suddenly, we heard a loud popping sound from the chapel. It was the noise of a pistol being discharged. As if on command, the pounding of the rifles on the ground stopped in unison. From where I was standing behind Santiago and his soldiers, I did not have a clear view of when Kemper had entered the chapel, but he appeared at the open door, stood there a moment, and then walked to stand before the assembly. He raised a pistol above his head and announced that Augustus Magee had committed suicide.

It was, I thought, a sad and cruel irony: the only way this poor, lonely man could escape his fear of death was to end his own life. I hoped he had found peace.

Without a word, the men broke ranks and climbed to the ramparts overlooking the hillside. Kemper ordered the cannon fired as a sign of our rejection of the governor's offer.

The following morning, a loud cheer broke out when we realized that the Spanish had lifted the siege and were withdrawing to San Antonio de Béxar. Running from the presidio, we embraced the Tonkawas who had remained outside to harass the royalists. We crossed over to the north bank, reclaimed the mission, and entered the town of La Bahía. All of Texas was now controlled by republican forces except for its capital, San Antonio de Béxar.

That night a great celebration was held with music and dance. Santiago stood before an assembly and proposed that La Bahía be renamed Goliad in honor of Father Hidalgo. Goliad was an anagram of Hidalgo. The people shouted their approval, even the *norteamericanos*, most of whom had no real idea as to who Miguel Hidalgo was. For my part, I was elated at the choice and told Santiago it was a wonderful tribute.

I then looked at Pilar and said, "I believe you two have some unfinished business. What better time than on this day."

Santiago was puzzled, looking from me to Pilar and back. But soon he understood, and our celebration turned into a marriage ceremony. The priest at the mission conducted the mass, and Pilar and Santiago became husband and wife in the town named that day after the man who was the father of our country.

✦

Within days, the cry of "On To San Antonio" resounded in the streets of Goliad. Gutiérrez met with Kemper whom, to no one's surprise, the *norteamericanos* elected as their new leader. Then they agreed that now would be a good time to strike Governor Salcedo while his forces were still retreating.

We caught up with the royalists near Salado Creek, some ten leagues from San Antonio de Béxar. Though outnumbered more than two to one, we prevailed decisively in a pitched battle that raged for almost two hours. Once again, Spanish muskets proved to be no match for the Pennsylvania long-rifles. Whether through confusion or inept leadership, I do not know which, the royalists failed to run up the flag of surrender until they had lost over half of their men. A total of one thousand were killed. The republican losses were ten dead.

When Governor Salcedo arrived at our camp headquarters to surrender, I witnessed yet another instance of *gachupín* arrogance. Salcedo tried to deliver his sword to Kemper who would have none of it.
Instead, the *norteamericano* directed him to surrender the sword to
Gutiérrez who, after all, had been appointed commander of the
Republican Army of the North by Father Morelos whom we Mexicans
regarded as our president. Rather than hand the sword to Gutiérrez
like a gentleman, the governor threw it to the ground.

Among those also surrendering on that day was Simón Herrera,
governor of Nuevo León, who had led a force from his province in support of Salcedo. With this victory, all of Texas, including its capital,
was now in the hands of the republicans! The green flag of the Republican Army of the North was hoisted. It waved gently in the breeze
above the Alamo mission.

In effect, Bernardo Gutiérrez was now the governor of Texas. He
was basically a fair and decent man. Despite the insulting behavior
directed against him by Salcedo, Gutiérrez arranged to send Salcedo,
Herrera, and their aides to Galveston. From that port they were to be
taken by commercial vessel to New Orleans to await the end of the
war for Mexico's independence from Spain. Gutiérrez was concerned
that the Spanish leaders might be harmed by the citizens of Texas
they had cruelly abused for so long.

Gutiérrez made the mistake of appointing Captain Delgado to
guard the prisoners. It was Salcedo who had given the order of
beheading Captain Delgado's father three years before. The craving
for vengeance is powerful and, on the way to Galveston, Delgado
beheaded the former governors of Texas and Nuevo León.

When Delgado, bearing the heads of his victims, returned to San
Antonio, Kemper and his lieutenants were exceedingly angry, as were
most of us—Mexican, *indio*, and *norteamericano* alike. Kemper held
Gutiérrez as much as Delgado responsible for the atrocity, and after
announcing that he had had enough of Texas, he packed up and left
with a substantial number of his volunteers. Kemper's place as the
leader of the force of *norteamericanos* who remained was taken by a
man named Captain Perry. After Kemper's departure, Gutiérrez, disturbed by what Delgado had done, yielded his position to a man

named José Toledo, a Cuban who possessed the administrative skills Gutiérrez admitted he himself lacked.

Less than two months after the fall of San Antonio, a force of some three thousand infantry was dispatched by Viceroy Venegas to recapture Texas. Meyei's scouts reported that this army was led by General Ignacio Elizondo, the very man who had betrayed Father Hidalgo and brought about his capture and execution. Therefore, it was with no small measure of enthusiasm that those of us who were Mexican marched forth with Perry and his *norteamericanos* to do battle with the royalists. And, though again outnumbered, we defeated Elizondo who, rather than surrender, led his men in a bloody retreat across the Río Bravo leaving a trail of some one thousand of his dead soldiers behind him.

Over the next several months, Toledo established a civil government in Texas, appointed *alcaldes* or mayors for each town. Communiques were received from Father Morelos congratulating us on our victories and reporting similar successes in the south, despite the continuing arrival of fresh troops from Spain.

It seemed at last that Father Hidalgo's dream was on the verge of becoming a reality. I began to dream of returning to Guanajuato to see Cata Valeria who by now would be walking and talking and, if I knew her grandfather, learning to ride a horse.

My hopes were dashed when Tonkawan runners arrived with the news that a new force of six thousand royalists, led by Joaquín de Arredondo himself, was crossing the Río Bravo. Toledo and Perry led the Republican Army out to meet the Spanish. A successful charge was mounted and the royalists retreated. Almost at the same time, Lebe Seru, Santiago, and I recognized that the retreat was feigned, a ploy to draw us into a trap. We warned Toledo and Perry. Perry did not agree with our assessment and pushed ahead. Too late we were proven correct, and the main body of our force was ambushed, entering a valley, by artillery concealed above us. All we could do was fight our way out, and in the process, hundreds of our people were killed including almost all of the *norteamericano* volunteers who had remained in Texas.

Our defeat was total. Those of us who escaped avoided Arredondo's campaign of savage terror against anyone even suspected of aiding the republican cause. Hundreds of men, women, and children were executed next to the graves they were ordered to dig for themselves. Others were crammed into windowless huts, the doors closed, and suffocated. So hideous was the unrelenting carnage that Ignacio Elizondo was murdered by one of his own men driven insane by the horrors against the people of Texas he had witnessed.

In charge of these massacres and responsible for them was one of Arredondo's officers, a lieutenant named Antonio López de Santa Anna. His was a name we swore we would never forget.

As if the bitterness of our defeat was not enough, we received word, soon after the fall of San Antonio de Béxar, that Father Morelos had been captured in the south and executed. He simply did not have the guns and the powder to withstand the legions of men and materials being poured into the Viceroyalty of New Spain by King Fernando. Many of the members of the Republican Congress had also been captured with Father Morelos and executed. Those few who had managed to escape had been forced to flee in disarray. Like those of us in Texas, they had retreated to the countryside in the hope that someday we would be able to rise again and fulfill Father Hidalgo's dream. For now, however, Mexico remained more firmly than ever under Spain's rule. And this meant I could not return to my home to see my father and my daughter. It possibly meant I would never see either again.

XI

The years following the execution of Father Morelos were difficult ones for the republican cause in Texas and, indeed, throughout Mexico. Though at no time did the congress created by Hidalgo and Morelos cease to function, it was often forced to move from place to place just one step ahead of royalist armies. New leaders emerged, men such as Vicente Guerrero in the south and Guadalupe Victoria in the north. But these patriots, dedicated as they were to the principles of liberty and equality, would be the first to admit they lacked Hidalgo's ability to inspire or the military genius of Morelos. Moreover, the young Mexican republic did not possess the guns and powder to mount an effective challenge to King Fernando's well-equipped army. Other than conducting harassing raids on royalist patrols that ventured forth to escort officials of the viceroy's government, there was little more we could do than survive and keep alive the dream.

Our small band, led by Santiago and Chief Meyei, retreated to the region north of the settlement we continued to call Goliad, now back held by the Spanish. They, of course, had restored its original name of La Bahía. Having grown up in Texas, Santiago knew the area and how to use the countryside to our advantage. Living in the forests with Chief Meyei and his warriors, we made it very difficult for the presidio to be supplied. In effect, we kept it under a state of continual siege, especially at night when the Spanish rarely ventured beyond the protection of their walls. They knew that at night their muskets were no match for the Tonkawas' bows and arrows.

283

While cities and towns were held by royalists, the countryside was republican. Runners, mostly *indios* like the Tonkawas, maintained almost instant communication throughout the Republic of Mexico from Texas to Panamá, from California to the Yucatán. From time to time, the congress would direct that delegates be sent to consult with Guerrero or Victoria, who were charged with coordinating all military efforts against the Spanish.

We elected Santiago to be our representative. He would make the long and arduous treks to meet with General Victoria despite his preference of staying with Pilar and their growing family. They had named their first son Miguel in honor of Father Hidalgo, and when two years later their first daughter arrived, they named her Josefa after Father Morelos.

I helped Pilar as much as I could, especially when Santiago was absent. Watching Miguel and Josefa grow and learn to play games with their cousins among the Tonkawas, I often thought of Cata Valeria. I wondered what she was doing and what she was learning. What games did she play and with whom? I wondered if she spent time in Don Esteban's library reading the very books that Cristóbal and I had so loved as children. Several times, I considered making the trip south to Guanajuato to see her. I also wanted to see my father and Hortensia. But I knew I must not take this risk. The hatred the royalists had for republicans grew deeper each day, and they did not hesitate to massacre our children when presented with the opportunity. As much as I longed to see my daughter, I knew I must remain in Texas.

✦

One hot afternoon, we were camped on the north bank of the Brazos. Pilar and I were watching over Miguelito and his friends as they played on the sandy banks and swam in the clear shallows of the river. I held Josefita in my lap while Pilar stitched together deer hides to be used as coverings for the lodges.

It was a lazy day, and my thoughts were a thousand leagues to the south with Cata Valeria when Pilar said, "Tell me about Lupita, Carmen. You never speak of your daughter."

It did not seem right to continue to lie to Pilar, not after all these years. She had come to be like a sister to me. Except for Teresa, I had never been so close to another woman. It served no purpose to conceal the truth from Pilar.

"Lupita was not my daughter," I confessed, and then I told her the story of how I had come to know the strange girl with the scar across her forehead.

When I finished, Pilar said, "I did not think Lupita was your daughter. At that time you were not old enough to have a child that age."

Josefa handed me a pecan she had found on the ground. I cracked it and picked out the meat for her to eat. She laughed and pointed to a bushy-tailed red squirrel that had run halfway down a tree to fuss at us for taking her pecans. A mockingbird landed on the topmost branch of a yellow-leafed sycamore not far from where we were sitting and began to rehearse his songs. From time to time he would leap from his perch and flap his wings while singing. These birds were fearless. A few days before, I had witnessed one of them as it attacked a rattlesnake. The serpent, about to pounce on a young mockingbird that had fallen to the ground while attempting to fly, was forced to retreat.

"When you first came to us," Pilar said, "and I asked about your daughter, I could see something in your eyes, and it was not the sadness a mother has for a child she has lost. It was the concern she has for one who is still alive. You do have a child, Carmen. Yes? You left behind a child you know is alive."

"Yes, Pilar. I have a daughter, Coalter's daughter. Her name is Cata Valeria."

"Cata Valeria. That is a pretty name."

"It was my mother's name."

Pilar put down her work. "Why did you not bring your child with you to Texas, Carmen? Is she with your mother's people in Guanajuato?"

"She is with my aunt, my mother's sister." I paused. "And with my father."

"I thought your father had returned to Spain to fight the French."

"My father is not in Spain, Pilar. My father is Don Esteban, the Marqués de Abrantes. I..."—it would be the first time I would say this, even to myself—"...I am his illegitimate child."

I no longer felt shame that my parents had not been married. There was no reason for shame. I was not conceived in sin, but in love. I went on to explain to Pilar how it had been arranged for Captain Rangel to marry my mother before I was born, which gave me the name of Rangel.

"And so," Pilar said, "Cata Valeria is with your father."

"Don Esteban is raising her as his daughter. The Spanish would kill her if they knew I was her mother, because officers who think I am Captain Rangel's daughter saw me with Allende's army. That is why I did not tell anyone of my daughter, not even you, Pilar. That is why I did not bring her with me to Texas."

For a long while nothing more was said, and we watched the dozen men and women who were casting their nets downstream to seine for perch. Members of a neighboring tribe to the south, the Karankawas, were visiting the Tonkawas. Highly skilled fishermen, the Karankawas were demonstrating a technique they used in the bays between the coast and the gulf islands where they often made their camps. They were a tall, dark-skinned people. I found them to be quite friendly though they had a reputation among the Spanish as fierce warriors. Some even said that they were cannibals, but this was not true. They were simply a people who had refused to submit to Spanish authority.

Presently, Pilar asked, "What will you do when the war is over, Carmen? Will you return to Guanajuato to live with your father and your daughter?"

It was not something I had considered. Certainly, I expected to return to see Cata Valeria and my father, if I survived the war. But where I would live and what I would do I did not know.

"When I was a little girl, Pilar, not much older than Josefita, I dreamed of being a soldier. I wanted to go to Europe and fight in the wars. It did not matter to me what the wars were about as long as I could fight. I wanted to serve my king. I thought there was glory in war. I suppose it was in my blood. My father's ancestors, the men of the House of Abrantes, had been warriors since before the days of the Cid."

"Well, you did become a soldier. Perhaps you can be a soldier in the army of the republic when the Spanish finally leave our shores."

"No," I said without hesitation. "I no longer wish to be a soldier, not even in the republic. I know what it is like to kill. I have killed and not a night passes that it does not haunt my dreams. I will not remain a soldier."

"Then what will you do?"

"I will go to Guanajuato to see my father and my daughter." Josefa handed me her hairbrush. I began to stroke her pretty, black hair. "And then perhaps I will return to Texas and live with the Tonkawas."

She laughed. "You were raised in a great hacienda. You are the daughter of a wealthy notable. Why would you wish to live the life of an *indio*?"

"My mother was an *india*," I said and stopped to watch the Karankawas pull their nets slowly through the green current of the Brazos. Lebe Seru was helping them. He was laughing and having a wonderful time. "Look at these people, Pilar. The Tonkawas. The Karankawas. They live in harmony with the land. I think this is the way my mother's people must have lived. I would like to live this way. Perhaps this, too, is in my blood. When I was a child, I was ashamed of being part Indian, but now I am proud that my mother was an *india*. I think I would like to live with the *indios* in Texas."

"It can be a hard life."

"Yes, but the people help each other. They share life's burdens." I lay back and inhaled the sweet fragrance of yellow clover blossoms. I listened to the soft sound of the water lapping at the river's bank. "I think I would also wish to live here because it makes me feel closer to Coalter. Sometimes, when I sit here by myself, alone, on the banks of the Brazos, I almost feel as if..."—it was a strange but recurring thought—"...I feel as if Coalter is still alive."

✦

Most of the fighting took place far to the south, under the leadership of Guerrero and Victoria. In the north, we continued to do what we could to harass the garrison at Goliad. Often, we would assist Juan Seguín and José Navarro, the two principal leaders of the republicans in San Antonio de Béxar, in their effort to disrupt the supplying of the garrison in that town.

Additionally, we gave support to another expedition led by a man named James Long. Long, a physician, tried to enlist the aid of Jean Lafitte, a French-born buccaneer who headquartered on Galveston Island and plundered Spanish shipping in the name of the Mexican Republic. Dr. Long even proclaimed Texas an independent republic, but he was captured and later murdered in a royalist prison. Lafitte continued to attack Spanish ships after moving his operation from Galveston to the Yucatán, but I do not think he had great interest in our republic.

Each year, we held a ceremony to mark the anniversary of the day when Father Hidalgo first called for an end to corrupt government in New Spain, September 16. And each year, we wondered if we were any closer to fulfilling the dream he proclaimed that night on the steps of the little church in Dolores. We had singing and dancing during our celebrations of the anniversary because that is what Father Hidalgo would have wanted.

For me, it was difficult to be festive because I remembered that night in Dolores. I remembered standing next to Coalter as we listened to Father Hidalgo's stirring words and his call for liberty, equality, and justice. It was good to note that occasion, especially for children such as Miguelito and Josefa who were now old enough to understand why we fought. But for me it was difficult because each anniversary marked yet another year of my separation from Cata Valeria. She was as much a stranger to me as had been my mother, the woman for whom she had been named.

Finally, almost twelve years after Father Hidalgo's proclamation, the viceroy, along with the officials of his government and most of the Spanish-born soldiers, boarded ships at Vera Cruz and set sail for Spain. This departure had little to do with what the republicans had struggled to achieve. The move was forced by *criollo* merchants in

Mexico City. They had grown tired of King Fernando's policies siphoning off the wealth of Mexico to pay for the monarch's costly effort to rebuild the army and navy of Spain. He was sapping the wealth of his colonies to insure that the Bourbons might never again be driven from the throne or humiliated by another Bonaparte.

High-ranking *criollo* officers, the colonels and the captains who had carried the fight over the years against Hidalgo and Morelos and their successors, were angry at the fact that only the Spanish-born officers received titles and great haciendas; that they, because they were not Spanish-born, could not even aspire to be generals. Because the *criollo* officers commanded the soldiers, when they called on the viceroy and told him it was time to leave, he and those few individuals who were still loyal to the King had little choice. After a few brief and inconsequential skirmishes, they boarded their ships and sailed away.

When the news arrived in Texas of the viceroy's departure and the lowering of the banner of the Spanish House of Bourbon in Mexico, we knew it was no cause for celebration. Juan Seguín, who had just returned from a conference with Guadalupe Victoria, traveled to Goliad to share with us the information. He told us that the head of the junta who had forced the viceroy out was Colonel Agustín Iturbide, a *criollo* officer. His name was etched in the minds of those of us who had fought at the Battle of Calderón. Iturbide had been one of General Flon's officers charged with the execution of republican prisoners after that battle had ended.

Another officer in Iturbide's junta was Antonio López de Santa Anna, the lieutenant who had massacred the families of republicans that had participated in the failed Gutiérrez-Magee expedition.

At first, Iturbide called for a reconciliation of all factions in Mexico. He said it was time to end the fighting. He extended the hand of friendship to both Guerrero and Victoria and even promised to include them in his new government. It was not long before he revealed his true colors, and we were not surprised when he repealed both the constitution proclaimed by Hidalgo and Morelos and the authority of the republican congress. After abolishing the congress, he created a "Committee of Notables" which in turn proclaimed Mexico to be an Empire and "demanded" that Colonel Iturbide be crowned Emperor Augustín I. Like Napoleon Bonaparte, who now languished on a desolate island in the south Atlantic, Emperor Augustín I placed with his own hands the imperial crown on his head.

Mexico's new emperor immediately issued orders to his armies to crush all opposition to his rule and execute any individual who advocated a constitution or republican government. We had exchanged a foreign king for a home-grown tyrant. Other than that, little had changed. We still harassed the soldiers in the presidios. They, in turn and for the most part, obeyed the same officers who had served the viceroy and continued to try to hunt us down. The struggle for liberty and equality continued, and as days and weeks and months dragged on, my hope of returning to Guanajuato to see Cata Valeria and my father seemed as far off as ever.

✦

One change instituted by Augustín I was the new policy of immigration to the northern provinces. The last viceroy had been deeply suspicious of the intentions of the United States toward the northern provinces of New Spain. He had had to contend with hostile forays into Texas by *norteamericanos* led by men like Magee, Kemper, and Long. Emperor Agustín had a different view. He welcomed colonists from the United States and Europe into the northern provinces. He wanted to make these lands productive so he could increase the wealth of Mexico and support an even bigger army.

In short order, colonists began to make their way from Louisiana into Texas. Though a few came in small groups, most arrived in contingents of several hundred families organized by entrepreneurs, called *empresarios*. They negotiated contracts with Agustín's government to issue land titles in exchange for monies. A number of the *empresarios* were dishonest men who stole from both their colonists and the Mexican government and were never seen again, but others were competent. The ones who were successful made certain their people came with adequate foodstuffs to survive until they could put in their crops. They made certain they brought mules and the tools required to become productive *rancheros*. And most important of all, they made certain that they brought their Pennsylvania long-rifles.

Soon, the silence of the countryside and forests was broken by the sound of the axe as farmers cleared the land to be plowed. Fallen trees were used to build cabins and animal shelters or they were burned because they were simply in the way. Settlements went up almost overnight, and merchants opened stores in which the farmers could purchase the various items they needed. Every settlement had a dry goods store, a smithy, a pharmacy, and offices for doctors, dentists and lawyers. For each one of these useful establishments in the town, there was usually one or more taverns. There was always an abundant demand for sourmash whiskey and no one ever went broke selling this commodity to the inhabitants of Texas. Those of us who viewed Agustín's government as simply the successor to Spanish tyranny and who continued to maintain allegiance to the government founded by Hidalgo and Morelos were uncertain as to what to think about this sudden influx of colonists from the north. In order to enter Texas, these people, under the supervision of their *empresarios*, had to take an oath of loyalty to the Mexican emperor. It was doubtful that most had ever heard of Hidalgo and Morelos, much less the constitution our elected delegates had written or the laws our congress had drafted. We watched them arrive and wondered what this all meant to our dreams for the Republic of Mexico.

✦

One morning, Chief Meyei's scouts returned to report that colonists had constructed a cabin upriver from our camp on the Brazos and were now clearing land. This in itself was not unusual. Not a day passed that the horizon was not stained by columns of smoke from trees and brush being burned to make way for the plow. What the scouts reported that was out of the ordinary was that among those stripping away the trees and vegetation were people different in appearance from the previous colonists.

"Different?" Meyei asked when his scouts hesitated to continue. "In what way, different?"

One of the men said, "They are like Lebe Seru."

Exchanging glances, Lebe Seru and I were of one mind as to what this meant.

Santiago had recently gone south with Juan Seguín and José Navarro for a meeting of the republican congress; therefore, except for Lebe Seru and myself, the party that set out to investigate the scouts' report was comprised exclusively of Tonkawas. As we approached the clearing where the colonists had settled, we saw that five of the people working to cut and burn the trees and brush were, in fact, African. Three were adults, two women and a man, and two were children, a girl and a boy, both about the ages of Miguel and Josefa. Three *norteamericanos*, two men and a boy, were standing at the edge of the field watching the Africans work. They were holding long-rifles.

The *norteamericanos* raised their weapons when Lebe Seru and I emerged from the cover of the forest and approached them. We were unarmed. The larger of the two men had heavy jowls and a massive stomach that protruded over a thick leather belt to which was attached a leather sheath containing a big, bone-handled knife not unlike the one I remembered Latham Barnet carrying. He eyed us menacingly as we stopped some twenty yards from where they were standing. The smaller was a hawk-faced man. He had a thick bulge in his cheek and tobacco juice seeped from the corner of his lips. The boy, a lad of about eight years, glanced nervously toward the log cabin structure behind them. I could see a woman and several girls peeking through the windows covered only with cloths.

"We come in peace," Lebe Seru said in Spanish.

Keeping the muzzle of his rifle aimed at Lebe Seru, the bigger man growled, "We don't speak no Mes'can."

"Let's kill 'em, J. W.," the smaller man said. "They look like some kind of Injuns."

The one called J. W. continued to eye Lebe Seru. "This one ain't no Injun. You ain't no Injun, are you, boy? Where you from and who is this here woman with you?"

In English, Lebe Seru said, "My name is Lebe Seru and this is Señorita Carmen Rangel. We are citizens of the Republic of Mexico."

"We gonna kill 'em, '?" the smaller man asked spitting a big wad of tobacco juice in our direction. "I say we kill 'em and—"

"Shut up, Leeper!" the big man snapped, causing the boy behind him to jump. The boy's hair was the same rusty color as the one called J. W., so I assumed he was his son. "Gonna find out what they're up to before we do anythin', so you keep yoar mouth shut and I'll do the talkin'. You understand?"

"Whatever you say, J. W.," Leeper responded quickly.

The Africans who had been working in the field huddled around a white-haired woman and stared in our direction.

Continuing to look at Lebe Seru, the big man said, "My name is Mr. Keane, boy. This here is Mr. Leeper. We's citizens of the United States." He thrust out his jaw. "And you look to me like you mighten be a runaway. Is that right, boy? You run 'way from yoar master and done went and found you a squaw woman?" He looked at me for the first time. "Is that right, boy?"

The English I had learned from listening to the *norteamericanos* on the Gutiérrez-Magee expedition was limited, but I could follow what this Keane was saying, and it annoyed me that he referred to Lebe Seru as a 'boy.' Lebe Seru was old enough to be this man's father.

"Lebe Seru is not a boy," I said in English. "He is a captain in the army of the Republic of Mexico."

"Well, well," Keane said and looked at Leeper whose grin revealed dirty tobacco-stained teeth. Apparently satisfied that we constituted no threat, they lowered their rifles. "The squaw woman can talk!" He looked back at Lebe Seru. "Went and got you a squaw that can talk, did you, boy? She ain't a bad lookin' one neither. For an Injun, that is."

The woman came rushing from the house. She wore a long-sleeved, ankle-length calico dress and a starched bonnet which covered most of her face.

"J. W.?" she called when she neared us. "What's wrong, J. W.? What do they want?"

Quickly, Keane's sneer turned to anger as he turned and yelled, "Git back in that house, woman! Who tol' you to come out he'ar?"

The woman drew closer and looked at me. Her face was drawn and haggard but there was something resembling a smile on her thin, wind-dried lips. "Are they hungry, J. W.? Is that why they come here? We have some food in the cellar and—"

Keane stepped to the woman and slapped her face. "I tol' you to git back to the house! Gawdammit, woman. Do what I tol' you. Don't make me have to hit you 'gin! Is that what you want? You want me to hit you 'gin? Is that what you want?"

The boy started to move toward them when Keane drew back his thick hand a second time but froze in place when his father saw him. Leeper stared at the ground, but I could see he was smiling. He thought it was all very amusing.

Lowering her head like a whipped puppy, the woman scurried back to the cabin.

When Keane turned back, Lebe Seru nodded toward the field and asked, "Are these people in your employ?"

"My employ?" Keane said and burst out laughing. "Did you hear that, Leeper? This ol' buck wants to know ifen the darkies are in my employ!" The feigned laughter stopped abruptly. "Them thar darkies are my slaves, boy! They belong to me, just like you belonged to some stupid sonavabitch who let you sneak off and go find you a squaw woman. I won't make that mistake. You belong to me now, boy. And ifen you try runnin' away from me I'll fix you so you can't never 'gin breed with squaw woman here. I'll turn you into a gawdamn mule! You understand what I'm a saying to you, boy?"

This man disgusted me. I drew myself to my full height and said, "Slavery is not allowed in the Republic of Mexico, Señor. The people working in that field are free to go where they wish. They no longer have to work for you."

Keane's eyes narrowed into a squint. "What the hell did you say, squaw woman?"

I recognized my words meant nothing to a man like this, but I explained: "Under the Constitution written by Miguel Hidalgo and José Morelos, slavery is forbidden in Mexico."

He stared at me as if trying to decide whether to spit on me or laugh. "You're mighty brave to come walkin' in here makin' noises like that, squaw woman. Mighty brave!"

"I am not so brave, Señor. You cannot do anything to hurt me, so it is not brave that I come walking in here and make noises."

"I can't do anything to hurt you? Maybe you don't know what a Kentucky rifle can do to your head. Why, I'll bet you ain't never even seen a rifle, have you, squaw woman?"

"Yes, Señor. I have seen many rifles, and I know what they can do to your head. I also know what a dozen arrows will do to your fat stomach if you so much as raise that rifle in your hands and point it at either of us."

Lebe Seru lifted his right hand to signal Chief Meyei.

"Gawdamn, J. W.!" Leeper gasped. "Injuns! Must be a hunderd of 'em! We're dead men!"

Keane's mouth dropped as he surveyed the Tonkawan warriors who had stepped from their places of concealment in the surrounding forest. Each held his bow string taut, ready to launch an arrow at the two men.

"Place your weapons on the ground," Lebe Seru said quietly, "and you will not be harmed."

Leeper quickly complied and looked at Keane who was hesitating. "Do it, J. W.! Don't be a damn fool!"

After the men backed away from their weapons, Meyei's warriors guarded them as Lebe Seru went to talk to the Africans in the field.

I approached the cabin and looked inside until I saw Keane's wife. She was clutching several girls to her.

"Please," she whispered. "Don't hurt my babies. Please!"

"Señora," I said. "My name is María del Carmen Rangel. I am a soldier in the Army of the North of the Republic of Mexico. You will not be harmed." I looked at the ugly cut on her lip made by Keane's blow. Blood from the cut had splattered on the front of her dress. "Do you wish to come with us, Señora? You do not have to stay here."

She closed her eyes and drew a deep breath. "I must stay here. He would not care if I left with the girls, but he would never let Doyle go. I must stay to protect my son. Do you understand?"

Returning to the clearing, I was surprised that not all of the Africans had decided to go with us. The young man had chosen to remain and was retreating toward the house as the two women and children followed several of the Tonkawan women to the forest. Before leaving with the Africans, we discharged Keane's and Leeper's rifles and removed the flints. When we entered the forest, I looked back and saw the two men had returned to the cabin. Loud noises and shouts could be heard. The boy, Doyle, remained outside. He sat on the ground and put his head between his knees. He looked so alone and forlorn I hated to leave him at that place.

✦

Very soon Pilar and I became good friends with the African women and children. The name of the older woman with the white hair was Maudie. Her calloused hands betrayed a hard life, though this is something she would never say. Maudie immediately began to help with the chores in camp and would not stop when, because of our respect for her age, we suggested that she rest. Unlike Lebe Seru, Maudie had not been born in Africa but had been the child of slaves.

When I asked why the young man with them had elected not to come with us, she said, "Sometimes, Carmen, when you're born a slave and your parents were slaves, you begin to think like a slave. Instead of you thinking the thoughts, the thoughts start thinking you. Thomas stayed behind because he thinks like a slave. He is a slave and his master is fear."

The younger woman, Marva, who was very pretty and, like me, tall in stature, explained that before coming to Texas the slaves were told that the *indios* in Texas were cannibals and that they would be eaten if they ran away from their masters and were caught.

"Why then," I asked, "did you come with us, Marva? We are *indios*."

At first she would not answer and hung her head. When Lebe Seru and Meyei and the other men had gone, she told Pilar and me that she came because Keane had said he was going to force her to have children with him, children which he would then sell for money to others who wanted slaves so he could purchase more land. She said she knew nothing about the *indios* of Texas, but that she would rather be killed than be subjected to what Keane was planning.

"What did his wife think of this?" Pilar asked.

Marva shook her head. "You saw what he did to her. He beats her often. He even beat her because she only gave him one son and the others were girls. He beat her so much she can no longer have children. J. W. Keane is an evil man."

"And the man with Keane?" I asked.

"His name is Ellis Leeper," Maudie said. "He came to be the overseer of Keane's slaves. Keane hopes to someday have a great plantation with hundreds of slaves. He hates the men who own the big plantations in places like Virginia and the Carolinas where we came from, but he wants to be like them."

Neither the boy nor the girl who had followed us belonged to either Maudie or Marva. They were children Keane and Leeper had bought from other slaveholders before coming to Texas. They had been taken from their parents as babies and sold. When Maudie told us this, tears came to her eyes. She disclosed that her own children had been taken from her years before and sold. She took care of the ones who were with us as if they were her own. The boy had been given the name Jim by the slavers and the girl was called Beulah. Lebe Seru changed the boy's name to Binu and called the girl Amma. They were handsome children and, in a day or two, were playing games with Miguel, Josefa, and the children of the Tonkawas.

Sometimes, while sitting with Maudie on the banks of the river and watching Lebe Seru teach the children to swim, I wished Cata Valeria were with them. I was certain she would be jumping in the water to see who would be the first to swim to the other side. That is what I would have done when I was a little girl. I always wanted to be the first at everything. Of course, Cata Valeria might be beyond that now. She might now be of the age that she would not want to play with the younger children. She might want to stay only with girls her age and talk about boys. So much time had passed, I would never know what my daughter was like as a baby or even as a little girl.

✦

About two weeks after our visit to Keane's farm, Meyei's scouts arrived in camp to report that three men were riding in our direction. Two of them were Keane and Leeper, but the scouts did not recognize the third. Though the approach of only three men did not represent a threat, Meyei told his scouts to return to their stations and be on the alert for others who might be following.

As Keane and Leeper entered our camp and dismounted, they looked about nervously though they must certainly have known they were in no danger. If we had wished to harm them we could have done so at the farm. Keane glared at me and Lebe Seru as we stood at the chief's side.

The third man did not appear to be ill-at-ease. He approached Meyei and, seeing me, removed his wide-brimmed hat in a gesture of civility. He was a well-dressed man, somewhat small in stature and pleasant of face. He had large grey blue eyes and was clean shaven though his sideburns grew down his jaw and his reddish brown hair was long. His knee-high riding boots were a freshly polished black. In his hands, which were small and delicate, he held a leather pouch, the kind used to hold important documents.

Raising his hand in friendship, Meyei said, "I am Meyei, chief of the Emet Tonkawas. I bid you welcome to our camp."

Bowing slightly, the man smiled and, speaking in an accented Spanish, he said, "My name is Stephen Fuller Austin. I am the *empresario* of the lands between the Colorado and the Trinity. If I may, I would like to have a word with you. I—"

"It's them two thar!" Keane interrupted and pointed to Lebe Seru and me. "They's the ones that stole my darkies. Do your duty, Austin! Tell 'em they ain't got no right to steal a man's property! No right a'tall!"

In English, Austin said, "That is enough, Mr. Keane. I am certain this misunderstanding can be resolved to everyone's satisfaction. Be patient and please do not interrupt me."

Keane muttered something under his breath which I suspected was a curse.

Turning to face us again, Austin smiled and said, "I apologize for this man's behavior." He looked from Meyei to Lebe Seru then to me and back to the chief. "He did, however, recently come to me with a disturbing story. He claims that individuals from this tribe did enter his property uninvited and..."—he stopped as if searching for the correct word—"...appropriated...certain properties belonging to him, namely, two negro women and two negro children." He cleared his throat and looked over our shoulders where Maudie, Marva, Binu, and Amma stood in full view. "Did this in fact occur?"

Though this Stephen Fuller Austin had the face of a poet, he chose his words as if reading from a book of codes. Lebe Seru explained that we had informed those working for Keane that they had the option of going where they wished and all, except one, had chosen to leave.

After Lebe Seru spoke, Austin opened the leather case he had been holding and withdrew documents which, he explained, confirmed his authority as *empresario* of the lands on which we were standing. He said that, as *empresario*, he had been assigned executive, legislative, and judicial responsibilities over all peoples inhabiting these lands.

I could see that he had, in fact, been given a very great power over an enormous area of Texas, certainly the area most suitable to agricultural enterprise. It surprised me that Iturbide's government would delegate so much power to a man who, until recently, was a citizen of another country.

It was obvious Austin was comfortable with documents and legalities. Apparently, he believed that once we understood the extent and source of his authority, we would return Maudie, Marva, and the children to Keane.

"Señor Austin," I said. "We do not dispute that you have been given great authority by the illegal government of Agustín de Iturbide. But what does this have to do with the issue that has brought you here today?"

His expression registered puzzlement when I used the word 'illegal.' "Señora?" he asked by way of inquiring if I was married.

I told him my name.

"Señorita Rangel, the authority granted me by the government of Emperor Agustín I includes the responsibility of resolving civil disputes. If a party on the lands I oversee claims another party has illegally appropriated his property, I am charged with adjudicating the conflict and rendering a just verdict."

"You seek justice?"

"Yes, Señorita. I seek justice."

"And how do you do that, Señor Austin?"

He started to speak but checked himself. There was a smile on his lips as if anticipating I might be leading him into a verbal trap. Finally, he said, "I do so by attempting to follow the law."

"Whose law, Señor?"

"Why, the law established by properly constituted authorities, of course."

"Who are the properly constituted authorities in Mexico?"

Austin looked at Lebe Seru and back to me. "The Emperor Agustín I," he said without much conviction.

Something in this man's expression conveyed that he knew very well where my inquiry was leading. I had never seen this man, Stephen Fuller Austin, before, but I knew he understood that Agustín de Iturbide's government was illegal. He was an intelligent man, an educated man, so most certainly he understood this. I decided to make our position clear to him.

"Señor Austin, some years ago the elected representatives of the people of Mexico established a republic and the first law enacted under the authority of that republic's government was one prohibiting slavery. In the Republic of Mexico, people are not property that can be bought and sold."

"The Republic of Mexico?"

"Yes, Señor. The Republic of Mexico. Those of us standing before you are soldiers in the republic's Army of the North, under the command of General Guadalupe Victoria. We have been charged with the authority to uphold the constitution of the Republic of Mexico, and that is what we intend to do. There will be no slavery in Texas."

Slowly, Austin returned his documents to the leather satchel, and as he did, he seemed to study what I had said.

Finally, he looked at me and asked, "I gather you people were the followers of Miguel Hidalgo and José Morelos."

"Yes, Señor Austin," I said and nodded. "We were the followers of Father Hidalgo and Father Morelos."

"I have heard of them. In fact, I—"

"Austin!" Keane bellowed. "Thar's been 'nough talk. You gonna git my darkies back or not?"

Stepping closer to me, Austin said, "You are obviously an educated woman, Señorita Rangel. I hope you can understand my position. I am personally opposed to slavery as was my father who began this colony shortly before his death. My father was from Connecticut, and he despised the institution of slavery in the southern states of our union. Unfortunately, many of the people I have sponsored as participants in my colony come from that region where slavery has long been an accepted practice. At a later date, I hope to bring more people to Texas from the northern states and from countries in Europe. It is my expectation these people will help establish a climate in which we can dissolve the foul practice of slavery.

"However, until such a time, Señorita Rangel, we must be flexible because without their slaves these people will not be able to bring this land to heel and make it productive. All things must happen in due course, Señorita. I am certain you understand."

Stephen Austin may have been a newcomer to Mexico, but he already understood something of Spanish customs. There was a charm about him, an ability to soften hard edges and make the path smooth.

"Señor Austin," I said as straightforward as I could manage, "there can be no slavery in Mexico, not now nor ten years from now. It is against our constitution, the one written by Father Hidalgo and Father Morelos. Too many good people have died for that constitution for us to abandon any of the principles behind it. We believe in liberty and equality, Señor. On this we cannot compromise or wait until tomorrow."

His disappointment at my intransigence was tempered, I believe, by the natural inclinations he had for republican government. In a courteous manner, he said he would study this matter further and must now take his leave. He said he would be pleased if I would visit

him at some future date at his headquarters settlement of San Felipe
de Austin. He then walked to his horse and mounted.

Keane, of course, was livid that he did not leave with what he
regarded as his property, but neither he nor Leeper dallied in following Austin out of our camp. I knew we had not seen the last of these
men. Certainly, I knew what to expect from Keane and Leeper. As for
Austin, I was not so certain.

✦

When Santiago returned from the meeting of the congress, and
we told him what had happened, he said the republican leaders,
including Guerrero and Victoria were disturbed by the reports that
colonists from the north were bringing slaves into Texas. Juan Seguín
shared my uncertainty concerning Stephen Austin. He had met
Austin in San Antonio de Béxar and had at first believed the *empresario* shared our commitment to republican principles and would be
an ally. But he was later disappointed to learn that Austin himself
owned a slave though he had subsequently sold the man on a trip to
the United States.

Both Seguín and José Navarro had befriended a number of the
recently arrived *norteamericanos* and hoped they would be our allies
against Iturbide and Santa Anna. Navarro spoke of a man he had
taken into his home named James Bowie, who had become famous in
his own country as a duelist. Bowie spoke openly of his desire to see a
Mexican republic, but not only had he owned slaves in Louisiana, he
had, years before, been a slave trader.

We agreed to continue to inform the slaves who were brought
into Texas that the Mexican republic had a law against involuntary
servitude. Word began to spread, and before long, some of these people were abandoning their so-called masters in order to seek refuge
with our small band. Lebe Seru, Maudie, and Marva helped them
adjust to our way of life in the forests with the various Tonkawan
tribes and the Karankawas.

Initially, the number of colonists who brought slaves was small.
Those few colonists who owned slaves took measures, including the
use of armed guards, to insulate their homesteads from us. Rather

than confront them and risk the loss of life on both sides, Lebe Seru, Maudie, Marva, and other of the people they had helped to liberate initiated a clandestine effort to contact their people and help them escape. In the meantime we hoped that Iturbide would soon be toppled so that we could establish governmental institutions to enforce our laws.

✦

Returning one evening from a meeting with Juan Seguín in San Antonio de Béxar, we were hurrying to arrive at our camp before dusk when we heard a woman's cry for help. Since we were not a great distance from J. W. Keane's farm, and the call had been made in English, my first assumption was that Keane's wife was in need of assistance. I suspected Keane might be beating her, so we rushed toward the sound of the voice which issued from the direction of a creek bed that was usually dry except during the rainy season. Coming over a rise, we saw a woman with a child in her arms, and I realized that she was not Señora Keane. When the woman saw us approaching, she cried out and started for us but fell to her knees on some rocks.

Meyei's younger warriors reached the woman first, and by the time the rest of us arrived, they were able to report to their chief that the woman's child, a boy of about four or five years, had been bitten on the leg by a rattlesnake.

Peering over the shoulders of the men around the child, I could see the leg had already begun to swell and discolor. The fang-marks were about an inch apart, an indication the deadly serpent had been a large one. Unless it had recently bitten an animal, it would have injected a large amount of venom into the child's leg.

Understandably, the boy's mother was distraught and pleaded with us to do something to save her son. She was dressed in clothing similar to Señora Keane's and had something of the same haggard look to her features. Her flaxen-colored hair was pulled back in a tight bun at the back of her head. At one point I took her arm to prevent her from falling and was struck by how fragile she was.

"Señora," I said, "do not worry. We will help you."

There was great relief in her expression when she looked up at me and, in a strained voice, said, "You...you speak English?"

"A little, Señora." I looked about, thinking there must be someone else with this woman. Surely she would not be in such a place all alone. "Señora, where is your husband?"

"My husband had to go to San Felipe de Austin this morning. He told me to stay near our cabin. I thought it would do no harm to come up here to pick berries. That is where..."—she began to sob—"... the snake...Please, do something! Please help my little Christopher. He must not die!"

I looked down at the little boy she had called Christopher. His eyes flickered open briefly, and I saw they were blue. I did not want to tell this poor woman that the chances for her son's survival were not very good.

Chief Meyei decided that the only useful thing we could do was have his runners rush the child ahead to the camp where the tribal *curandera*, healer, could administer herbs the Tonkawas had found effective against snakebites if administered in time. Speed was of the essence. I explained the chief's suggestions to the woman, and she immediately concurred. Very quickly, the runners lifted the boy and disappeared from our view in the direction of the camp. When we began to follow, the woman stumbled and fell several times, so I held her hand and arm to steady her and guide her along the path in the darkness.

At the camp, we found that the *curandera* had already applied a poultice to the leg to draw out the poison. So limp did the child lay on the blankets, I was uncertain as to whether the little fellow had not already perished. His mother must have thought the same thing because she sobbed uncontrollably. Maudie gently led her to sit at a place near a fire, wrapped her in a blanket, and coaxed her to drink a broth she had prepared.

The Tonkawas then did something I had witnessed before when a member of the tribe had fallen gravely ill. Sitting on the ground in a circle around Christopher, twelve men and women placed their hands on the boy. Around these, another larger circle was formed and they placed their hands on the shoulders of those in front of them. A third

larger circle was formed and these individuals laid their hands on the
backs of those in the second circle in turn. Everyone began to sway to
a chant recited by the *curandera* who knelt to cradle her young
patient's head in her lap.

At first the boy's mother appeared alarmed at this unusual sight
visible only in the soft light of flickering campfires, but Maudie
assured her the Tonkawas were doing all they could to help her son.
Soon, she settled back, and began to doze in Maudie's arms. Maudie
was not herself unfamiliar with herbs. Because she believed in the
curative power of sleep, I suspected she had added something in the
broth to induce drowsiness.

I sat across from them and studied this *norteamericana's* face.
There was something about this frail woman I liked. This was someone who, while she may have experienced adversity in life, had not
broken or become embittered. Her features expressed a deep inner
selflessness.

The Tonkawas in the circle swayed to the *curandera's* chant
through the night. At precisely the moment the first edge of the sun's
arc appeared on the eastern horizon to silhouette a line of trees on a
hill, the *curandera* raised her arms to the sky to offer a silent prayer.
Then she gathered the boy into her arms and stood up.

From the smiles on the faces of the people in the circles, I could
tell little Christopher had survived the serpent's bite. Rising, the people made way for the mother to rush forward and receive her child
from the *curandera*. She then proceeded to prepare an herb tea for
the boy to drink. Now wide awake, he looked about at all the smiling
faces, brought his chubby little hand to his mouth and managed a
weak grin that wrinkled his freckled nose. His dark blue eyes
sparkled.

Even though the mother knew only English, she expressed her
gratitude again and again to the *curandera* and then sought me out
and asked me to tell all the people in the tribe how grateful she was
to them for saving her son's life.

When we returned to sit by the fire where Maudie and Lebe Seru
were preparing breakfast, I asked, "Is Christopher your only child,
Señora?"

"He was the only one I was able to carry to term. And he will be my only child. The physicians in New Orleans said I must never attempt to have another child. My health will not permit it."

"You are from Louisiana?"

"Yes. We arrived in Texas only recently. My husband has long wanted to settle in Texas, ever since he was a boy and used to come here on trading missions with his father. We could not come until now because of my illnesses."

Santiago and his children came to the fire with food Pilar had sent to share with our guests. Christopher's eyes grew wide with excitement when Miguel, Josefa, Binu, Amma, and Tonkawan children presented him with gifts of wooden animals they had carved from mesquite limbs.

He was even strong enough to consume a little food, and after breakfast, his mother insisted on helping to clean the utensils. And then she said they had better get back to their cabin because her husband would be returning and would be worried if he found them gone.

"I do not think it would be good for the boy to walk," Maudie advised. "It would best if he stays off that leg for a few days."

I suggested that Christopher could ride on a pole stretcher attached to one of the ponies, and that I would go with them to guide the animal and return him to our camp. Lebe Seru said he would go with us.

"I would be obliged," the woman said, "but I do not wish to put you to so much trouble. You have helped us so much already. You saved my son's life. And"—her hazel eyes sparkled—"I do not even know your names. In all of the excitement, I did not ask your names or give you mine."

I introduced myself and everyone at Maudie's camp.

Smiling warmly, she said, "My name is Mrs. Coalter Owens, but I would be pleased if you would call me Rhoda."

XII

It was as if the sky had suddenly changed from blue to red; such was the effect of the words this woman uttered so casually. Somehow, I managed to retain my composure as she continued to talk with the people around her. For a long while, I stared at her, unsure that I had heard correctly or that perhaps her husband was another man who happened to bear the name Coalter Owens. Some people had the same name. Such a name may have been quite common among *norteamericanos*. How should I know? But deep within, I knew I had not misunderstood her words, even though my ear was not accustomed to her language; nor was it likely that her husband was a different Coalter Owens than the man who was the father of my daughter. What she had said could only mean one thing, one wonderful and magnificent thing: the man I loved was alive! Coalter was alive!

When I looked around, it took a moment for it to register on my awareness that Lebe Seru was standing next to me.

"Carmen," he said softly. "Are you all right?"

I nodded that I was and watched several of the Tonkawas prepare the pole stretcher and lift Christopher onto it. Miguel, Josefa, Binu, Amma, and many of the Tonkawa children were with their new friend, and despite problems of language, they had no trouble communicating their happiness and excitement. Maudie and Marva were talking with Rhoda about the herbs the *curandera* had packed for use on the boy's leg. Everywhere I looked, life had returned to normal.

People were going about their daily routines, and children were playing as if they did not know that a miracle had occurred. The world,
after lying cold and still for so long, had begun to breathe again. It
had color and warmth and beauty. The very air was fresh and sweet.
Was I the only one who noticed?

"Carmen," Lebe Seru asked, "Did you hear what she said?"

"Yes," I whispered and bit my lip so my voice would not waver.
"Yes!"

"What are you going to do?"

Pilar approached us. From the neighboring campsite, she had
been quick to recognize that something had profoundly affected me.

"Carmen," she said anxiously and glanced at Lebe Seru. "What's
wrong? What happened?"

After relating to Pilar what Rhoda had just said, I looked at my
friends, the only two people in Texas that knew about Coalter and
me. "Tell no one."

"But Carmen," Pilar began, "you must explain to this woman
that—"

"No!" I said firmly. "I will tell her nothing."

"But why?"

I did not know why. I did not know anything except that Coalter
was alive. That was all that mattered and, for the moment, that was
all I could assimilate. I knew Pilar meant well and that perhaps she
was right. But for now, I wanted nothing to be said, and I asked my
friends to promise they would honor my wish.

On the return trip, Lebe Seru, aware of my state of confusion,
talked with Rhoda and answered her many questions about who we
were and what we were doing with the Tonkawas. I, of course, was in
no mood for talk. My thoughts had traveled back to that day so many
years ago when I had been forced to leave Coalter in that desolate
place. As though it had happened yesterday, I could distinctly recall
one of the royalist dragoons tell his sergeant that Coalter was dead.
How had he managed to survive? And if he had survived, why had he
not come for me? Why had he married this woman?

Several times, Rhoda tried to engage me in conversation. I did
not want to be rude; she seemed to be a most sincere and gracious

woman. But I found it difficult to even look at her. She was married to the man I loved. She was the mother of his son.

Perhaps sensing my abrupt change of behavior toward her, she asked, "Carmen, are you ill? Please, if you are ill, let us return to the Tonkawa camp."

"I am not ill," I said trying to think of what I could say to her. "I just do not feel well."

Lebe Seru, the true friend that he was, came to my rescue and began to point out the trees and other vegetation, telling Rhoda the names and what bloomed at which time of year and other such information to absorb her attention. She was, however, a perceptive woman, and several times, I caught her watching me. I suspected she may have begun to wonder if she had said something to provoke my silence, or perhaps, she even intuited my deeper feelings of antagonism, feelings I was trying very hard to conceal.

We stopped several times to allow Christopher to drink water and answer nature's call. The *curandera* had said it would be good if he consumed large quantities of water to accelerate the purge of the snake venom from his body. He was a shy boy and did not at first say much. As he grew accustomed to our company, he began to ask questions about the Tonkawas. At one point, he looked at me and asked, "Are you a Tonkawa?"

I studied those eyes which were exactly the same color as Coalter's. They were the same color as Cata Valeria's. It came to me that he was in fact my daughter's brother. He was her half-brother.

"No, Christopher," I said. "I am not a Tonkawa."

"Are you from another tribe? Are you an Indian? Are you—"

"Christopher, please," Rhoda said. "Do not annoy Señora Rangel." She looked at me and smiled. "I am sorry, Carmen. I called you Señora and I do not know if you are married."

"I am not married," I said more curtly than I intended.

"Are you an Indian?" Christopher repeated.

"My mother was an Indian," I said before Rhoda could scold him. He was a pleasant boy and meant no harm. "But she was not a Tonkawa. Her people lived far south of here, and they did not call themselves Indians. That is what the Spanish called them."

"Where are you from, Carmen?" Rhoda asked.

"I am from a place called Guanajuato. I am sure you have never heard of it."

"Oh, but I have! My husband went to Guanajuato many years ago, before we were married." Her smile faded. "He went to New Spain with a terrible man, Latham Barnet. While there, Coalter became a follower of Miguel Hidalgo and was gravely wounded. He almost died. Perhaps you knew him. If you are from Guanajuato and fought in Father Hidalgo's revolution then—"

"We are almost at the creek bed," Lebe Seru interrupted, "and had better watch our step. The snakes come to dry creek beds on warm days like this."

"Oh, yes," Rhoda said. "We must be very careful. Is there a way we can go around the creek?"

I knew, of course, why Lebe Seru had deflected Rhoda's query and began to wonder how long I could postpone her learning about Coalter and me. Moreover, why should I care if she knew? As we made our way around the creek bed, I realized that we were drawing ever closer to their cabin, and Coalter likely would have returned from his trip to San Felipe de Austin. My heart beat faster. Soon I would see him. Was it best, I wondered, that I see him. After all these years, what would he think? What would he say? And what would I tell him? Should I tell him that he had a daughter? These questions overwhelmed me. Suddenly, seeing Coalter again did not seem to be such a good idea.

Just as I was on the verge of suggesting that Lebe Seru take Rhoda and the boy on ahead while I returned to the Tonkawa camp because of my illness, Rhoda sank to her knees.

"Mama!" Christopher yelled.

We rushed to her side. She looked at me and said, "I'm sorry. I guess I don't feel very well either."

"Are you in pain?" I asked.

She took several deep breaths. "No," she said, placing her hand to her head. "It's just that sometimes I get dizzy. I'll be all right. May I have some water?"

Because we had been encouraging Christopher to drink so much water, our jugs were almost empty. I knew the Brazos was not far away so I said I would go for water.

"I'll go with you," Lebe Seru said. "If I recall correctly the bank is quite steep along here, and I may have to hold you while you fill the jugs."

"We'll be fine," Rhoda said when I looked at her. Her face was drenched with perspiration and she was pale. "Be careful. Watch for snakes!"

The river was a little farther than I had remembered, and we had to go over a rise, blocking our view of where we had left Rhoda and Christopher with the pony. Of course, as soon as we got beyond the woman's hearing, we began to talk about her revelation.

"Lebe Seru," I exclaimed, "I thought Coalter was dead! I even heard a soldier tell his sergeant that he was dead."

"I remember that day, Carmen. There was a great dust storm. It was difficult to see. The soldier must not have noticed that Coalter was still breathing, or possibly he did not want to kill a wounded man, and he lied to his sergeant."

We reached the bank of the Brazos, and because it was so steep, it was necessary for Lebe Seru to hold my left hand as I stretched down to submerge the clay jug in the current. After I filled it, we climbed back up and started to get to our feet when I heard the sound of a flintlock being cocked.

Looking up, we were staring almost directly into the muzzles of two long-rifles. They were being aimed by Keane and Leeper.

"Well, well," Keane said, grinning. "Looky what we got here."

Tobacco juice drooled out of Leeper's mouth as he eagerly asked, "We gonna kill 'em, J. W.? Let's kill 'em!"

"Damn, Leeper," Keane said and used his rifle to gesture us on up the bank. "Is that all you can think about?"

"Well, hell! They stole our darkies, didn't they? Why we been followin' 'em if we ain't gonna kill 'em? If we take 'em to that sonavabitch, Austin, you know he ain't gonna do nothin' but talk about it from now to judgement day. And ifen we don't do nothin', the word'll get 'round that the darkies in Texas can come and go as they please. It'll turn the good ones bad."

"Did I say we warn't gonna do nothin'?" Keane asked. "Go back to the animals and get them ropes. You two, git down on your bellies. Now!"

Foolishly, we had left our muskets in their sheaths strapped to the pony used to transport Christopher, so there was nothing we could do but comply. Leeper hurried back to their mounts which had been concealed behind a stand of mesquites, retrieved several lengths of rope and gleefully bound our wrists and ankles. He took especial delight in making the knot so tight it cut off the blood. Very soon, my hands and feet were throbbing.

With both of us bound and no longer a threat, the two men leaned their weapons against a nearby oak tree and stood over us as though surveying game they had just killed. Keane withdrew the long-blade hunting knife from the scabbard on his belt.

"Wha'cha gonna do, J. W.?" The small man nervously danced back and forth from one foot to the other and his hands made involuntary contortions. "You gonna cut 'em? Is that what you gonna do, J. W.? You gonna cut 'em?"

"Well, I don't rightly know," Keane drawled slowly. "Think I might cut the buck here. Yeah. Reckon I'm gonna have to cut the buck 'cause I promised him I'd make him a mule if he crossed me. And after that, I think I might cut the squaw woman but..."—he grinned at Leeper—"...I shore as hell don't plan to do it with no gawd-damned knife!"

Leeper found this vile assertion quite amusing. The tobacco juice flowed onto his dirty shirt as he howled with laughter.

Keane started to bend over Lebe Seru. "I ain't never castrated me a buck as old as you, boy. You so old, you probably already a mule! I'll wager—"

He stopped because of the sound of a flintlock being pulled, the same sound that only moments before had seemed to seal our fate.

It was Rhoda. Some eight feet from us, she stood with my musket. She had it aimed dead square for Keane's enormous stomach which swayed and bounced like the belly of a pregnant hog as he slowly raised and stared at the weapon pointed at him.

"Drop the knife and move back," she said.

"What the hell?" Keane gasped as the knife slipped from his hand. "I know yew. Yo'ar the Owens woman."

"Back away, Mr. Keane," she ordered as she kept the musket trained on the big man. "I don't like you. I've seen what you do to your wife. It won't be hard for me to blow you to hell where you belong."

Snarling, Keane yelled, "Gawddammit, Leeper! Do somethin'!"

"Don't try it, Mr. Leeper," Rhoda said, still keeping the musket aimed at Keane. "I'll shoot him. He's a hard target to miss, and I happen to be a very good shot."

Leeper's hands were trembling. "She says she'll shoot you, J. W., ifen I—"

"I heered what she said, you damn fool!"

I managed to scoot across the sand and grasp the knife in my hands which were now almost too numb to feel. Lebe Seru positioned his wrists so I could began to cut the cords binding them.

Seeing what we were doing, Keane grew frantic. "Damnation, woman! Don't let that buck get loose. He's got a knife!"

"Don't try it, Mr. Keane," she warned when the big man started to stoop down.

Straightening, Keane swallowed hard and said, "Come to your senses, woman. Why you doing this? What we got here is nothin' but a nigger buck and an Injun squaw. That's all they are! For gawd's sake, yo'ar a white woman! You'd kill a white man over some runaway darkie and a squaw woman? That ain't right, woman! It just ain't right. What's wrong with you?"

"This man and woman helped to save my child's life, Mr. Keane. What do you think? If I have to choose between a wife beater's life and the lives of people who saved my son, whose do you think it will be?"

Finally, the cords gave way around Lebe Seru's wrists. He quickly cut the ones on his ankles, the ones binding me, and we got to our feet. When I rushed to Rhoda and took my musket from her trembling hands, I realized the weapon had not even been packed with a charge. There had not been time. Lebe Seru went to the tree where the rifles had been placed and retrieved them.

Leeper started making a gurgling noise. He looked at Keane and moaned, "J. W., we're dead men."

Keane's eyes were wide as he watched Lebe Seru approach him with the rifles. "W-what you gonna do?" he stammered. "Please don't do nothin' to hurt me. I warn't gonna hurt you. We was just havin' some fun. Jus' gonna scare you a little. I warn't gonna do nothin' to you. Please. Please don't hurt me. I've got a wife and babies!"

"We take nothing that does not belong to us," Lebe Seru said. "If you want these back"—he hurled both rifles into the Brazos— "you know where to find them."

I held the empty musket at the ready.

When Lebe Seru drew back Keane's knife to throw it, Keane raised his arms to his face. The knife made a loud plopping noise when it hit the muddy current near a whirlpool.

Keane wet his lips with his tongue and looked at me. "Please don't shoot me, lady. I don't wanna die."

Both Leeper and Keane continued to back away.

Lebe Seru ordered, "Get out of here. Both of you."

The men began to run. We watched as several times they fell down and quickly got to their feet to run.

When they were no longer in view, I turned to Rhoda who was standing beside me with her head bowed and her eyes shut. "You are a brave woman, Señora."

She looked at me and started to smile, but her knees buckled. I caught her before she fell. Hoisting her up into my arms, I carried her back to where Christopher was still with the pony. She was as light as a feather. Lebe Seru followed with the jug, and we helped her to take a sip of water when she opened her eyes. Before leaving, Lebe Seru untied Keane's and Leeper's horses and gave each a swat on the rump to send them home.

It took another hour before we reached the cabin. As we drew near, I could feel Coalter's presence. I looked at the logs making up the walls of the small structure and realized that he had cut them, notched them, and carefully stacked them so they came together to make a home. Much hard work had gone into this little cabin. It was impossible not to think of the times he had told me he would make such a cabin for me. This place could well have been our home. It would have been ours if so many terrible things had not happened. Instead, it now belonged to this frail woman Lebe Seru carried into the austere but neat little pine log one-room house and placed on a bed. I carried Christopher to his bed on the other side of the room.

"I guess Coalter's not back from San Felipe de Austin," Rhoda said after I returned to spread a checkered red and green quilt over her. She was shaking, and when I placed my hand to her forehead, I could feel that she was warm. "I hope he did not encounter any problems."

"Señora," I began, "you are—"

"Please call me Rhoda," she said and took my hand in hers. "I hope we can be friends, Carmen. There are not many women on the frontier. Coalter and I went to the Keane's place for a visit when we first came, but that poor woman..."—she shook her head—"...that awful man beats her, and I think she is too embarrassed for anyone to see her. I want us to be friends, Carmen. Can we be friends? Can we visit often?"

Not knowing what else to say, I shrugged, "Of course...Rhoda. But we need to get you to a physician. Immediately. You are very sick. We need—"

"No," she interrupted, squeezing my hand. "This is not uncommon for me, I'm afraid. It will pass in time. I just need to rest. I—"

She stopped and cocked her head to the sound of a rider approaching at a gallop. At first, I thought of Keane and Leeper and looked at Lebe Seru who went for the rifle mounted over the stone fireplace.

"It's Coalter!" Rhoda cried and raised her head from the goose-down pillow.

For a moment, I felt as though my heart had stopped and I could not breathe. I wanted to get away from this place. I did not want Coalter to see me. I did and I did not. I did not know what I wanted. At that moment I was certain of only one thing: I had to get away.

But there was no other door to the cabin and Rhoda was clasping my
hand tightly in hers.

Before I could do anything, Coalter was at the door. I watched
those beautiful dark blue eyes grow wide when he saw me. He was
more handsome than I remembered. His mouth opened and silently
shaped my name. He was trying to say my name!

And then he took a step inside and staggered backward. I suppose the shock of seeing me scrambled his senses. He put his hand to
his head. His hair was longer, almost to his shoulders, and though he
was still cleanshaven, his sideburns now came below his ears to the
corner of his jaws.

"Coalter," Rhoda said. "What's wrong?"

Quickly, I withdrew my hand from Rhoda's and moved toward
Lebe Seru who was standing near Christopher's bed.

"*Papá!*" Christopher cried out. "I got bit by a rattlesnake!"

Coalter was struggling to reclaim his breath. He looked from me
to Lebe Seru and again tried to speak, but could not. And then he
stepped toward us and looked down at the boy who was proudly holding up his leg so his father could see where he had been bitten by the
serpent.

"He's fine now," Rhoda said and began to explain what had happened and how we had helped Christopher after he had suffered the
snakebite. At the same time, Christopher started talking about the
Tonkawas and displaying the carvings the children had given him as
presents.

I desperately wanted to run to Coalter, to throw myself into his
arms and hold him tightly. I wanted to tell him that, yes, I was alive.
I was not a ghost. I wanted to tell him that I loved him, that I had
never stopped loving him and that not a day had passed that I had
not thought of him or a night that he had not been in my dreams. I
loved him! Oh, how I loved him! And I wanted to tell him.

But I could not do it. It would destroy this woman who was lying
on the bed, this woman who had saved my life and Lebe Seru's life at
great risk to her own. Rhoda Owens was a brave woman, a good
woman, and I did not want to hurt her; I could not. I walked toward
the door.

Rhoda started to rise from the bed. "Carmen," she said, puzzled. "Please. Don't go. I want you to meet my husband. Lebe Seru? Please stay." She fell back, exhausted by this simple effort. "Please."

Turning, I looked in Coalter's direction and said, *"Buenos días, Señor."* I avoided his eyes. "Please forgive us, but we must return to our camp. It is getting late."

Coalter was trembling. When he raised his hand toward me, I saw the expression of bafflement on Rhoda's face. She looked from him to me and back to her husband. Quickly, I stepped outside and began to walk as fast as I could. Lebe Seru was behind me.

Catching up, he said, "Carmen, this is wrong. You must go back. You must talk to Coalter!"

"I cannot, Lebe Seru. I cannot!"

I had walked only a few feet more when I heard what my soul had for so many years ached to hear: Coalter calling my name. He was running after us. And then his hand gripped my arm to stop me. I could not look up at him. I knew I must not or I would lose all control.

"Carmen," he whispered. "Carmen!"

"No," I said and pulled away. "Go back to your wife. She needs you. She is ill."

Lebe Seru said, "I will look after her and the boy." He ran quickly to the cabin leaving Coalter and me alone next to a single redbud tree heavy with tiny white and maroon blossoms.

"Carmen, please!" He spoke in Spanish. "Please look at me. Carmen!"

Folding my arms tight against my body so he could not again grasp me, I backed away and faced him. There were tears flowing down his face. It was so difficult not to go to him and wipe them away and hold him and kiss him. Though, like me, he was older, there was still that boyish look of innocence in those blue eyes, eyes behind which was the same flame of love that had ignited my heart so many years before. That flame still burned and my soul was on fire.

"Carmen," he said, extending his hand palms up. "I thought you were dead! I-I was told that all those who had been captured with

Father Miguel had been executed. Oh, Carmen! You're alive. Thank God, you're alive! You're alive!"

It was the hardest thing I had ever done in my life to continue to back away until he stopped reaching for me. At first my voice failed, but finally I managed to say, "I thought you were dead! That day... that...awful day you were wounded so badly and were losing so much blood. What happened? How did you survive?"

"I don't know." He shrugged. "When I woke up, I was in a different place. I had been taken to a place in the mountains. Many days had passed since I saw you."

"Taken to a place in the mountains?" I asked, shaking my head in bafflement. "Who took you to this place?"

"Lupita."

"Lupita?"

"Yes. She was with me when I woke up. She fed me. She took care of me until some of the people who had been in General Allende's army found us. They were the ones who told me the news that Father Miguel and General Allende had been executed and that all those who had been captured with them had been killed."

"How could Lupita have taken you to a place in the mountains?" It seemed impossible. "She is just a little girl."

"I don't know. She never said anything. You do remember that she never talked? She could not—"

"I remember," I said, now impatient to learn more. "Where is she now? Is she with you?" I looked about, half expecting to see her. She had always been so quiet. She may have been watching me with those dark eyes all the time and I would not have known. "What happened to her? Where is she?"

"I don't know what happened to Lupita," he said and his smile faded. "The people from General Allende's army took me north with them. I was very ill. For a long time, I was too weak to even walk.

"And then, on the very day we crossed the Río Bravo, Lupita disappeared. Everyone searched for her. Some even went back across the river to look for her. They looked as long as they dared, because the royalist army was behind us. The Spanish did not want anyone from General Allende's army to cross into Texas. Months later, when I was able to travel, I could not return because, by then, the royalists had concentrated their forces along the Río Bravo.

"I wanted to look for Lupita. I wanted to find you!" His eyes teared again. "Even if it was just to find your place of rest, I wanted to go back. But there was no way I could return. And as time passed, I did not want to return south because it would remind me of you. It would remind me of us! It was too painful, and so I went on to Louisiana."

Again, I wanted to comfort him, to tell him I understood. I recalled the time Lebe Seru and I returned to the place where Father Hidalgo and General Allende had been captured. I remembered standing over those graves, wondering which contained my beloved's remains. I knew the pain. But I knew that if I uttered a word of any of this, it would be impossible not to embrace him and if I did that— just one wonderful, embrace!—I would never part from him again.

"And you, Carmen," he whispered. "How...What happened? You were not executed with Father Miguel."

In a simple statement of the facts, I told him what had happened after we had been captured by the royalists. I told him of the executions of Father Hidalgo and General Allende and how Santiago Montemayor had freed us.

"And then?" he urged when I did not continue.

"I returned to..."—I paused, remembering that I had never told Coalter that Don Esteban was my father—"...to the Marqués's hacienda."

He smiled. "How is Don Esteban?"

"He is fine," I said and, of course, thought of Cata Valeria. I so desperately wanted to tell him we had a daughter, a daughter who was by now a young woman. I wanted to tell him we had a daughter who had his eyes, his lovely eyes the color of a deep mountain lake. "The Marqués is fine."

His face hardened. "And Barnet? Barnet and Humberto? Were they at the hacienda when you returned? Barnet never returned to Louisiana. No one ever heard of him again."

What could I say? Could I tell him that I had killed Barnet? I had slain Barnet in order to save our daughter's life. I could not tell him this so, quietly and simply, I said, "Barnet and Humberto are dead."

He seemed to realize that if I wanted to say more about what happened to Barnet and Humberto, I would. "And so you came to Texas?"

I explained that Lebe Seru and I had come to join the Army of the North of the Republic of Mexico and told him how we had become part of Santiago's band and his allies, the Tonkawas, led by Chief Meyei.

"Oh, Carmen," he said when I finished. "I... I still love you! I never stopped loving you over all these years. I think of you constantly and—"

"No," I said and put my hands to my ears as if that could shut out the words I so wanted to hear. "You have a wife and a son, Coalter. I... I must go now. Please tell Lebe Seru we must go. We must return to the Tonkawa camp."

"Carmen, I did not marry Rhoda until seven years after I thought you had been killed. Please understand! I...Carmen—!"

I had turned and begun to run. I had to get away as fast as I could or I would go mad. I could not be near him and not take him into my arms. When Coalter followed, I shouted at him to leave me alone, to go back to his wife and son. At the edge of the clearing, before entering the forest, I glanced back and saw him standing by that solitary tree.

✦

Never in my life had I been so confused. I was both happy and sad. Coalter was alive and that filled me with a joy that was wondrous and sublime. The whole world seemed once again bright and vibrant, the way it had been when I was a child and Cristóbal and I had played our games on the grounds of the Hacienda de Abrantes. I was aware of things I had ignored for years, things such as the gentle whisper of the wind through tall trees and the way the early morning dew on the grass would sparkle like diamonds when the sun rose. The world was at each moment new and fresh and alive. And why not? Coalter was alive! He was alive!

At the same time I also felt the deep ache that gripped me when I first thought Coalter was dead and I no longer wanted to go on living. He was not mine. He belonged to another. I loved him more than before, and he said he still loved me. But he could never be mine. I would never hold him in my arms. We could never share a life together. I could not tell him of our daughter, the child who was the product of our love, our joy. I truly thought that my heart would break.

Pilar and Maudie made daily trips with Lebe Seru to the cabin to look after Rhoda and Christopher and administer the herbs sent by the Tonkawas' *curandera*. Santiago went with them when Lebe Seru told him that Coalter had fought with us in General Allende's army. A friendship developed between the two men, and Santiago told me that Coalter said he wanted to help in the republican cause.

Coalter began to assist in the clandestine effort to inform those being held in bondage by Stephen Austin's colonists that slavery was against the law in Mexico. It was possible for him to go to the farms and settlements where slaves were forced to labor and talk to them. The owners did not suspect him; after all, he was *norteamericano*. And so he was able to direct the slaves to Lebe Seru if they decided to run away.

Sometimes, Coalter rode to the Tonkawa camp to confer with Santiago, Lebe Seru, and Meyei, or with Juan Seguín and José Navarro when they came from San Antonio de Béxar. I would always leave before he arrived and spend the day in the forest. My actions, of course, puzzled Santiago who, Pilar said, wondered why I avoided Coalter especially since he invariably asked for me. She honored her pledge to say nothing, even to her husband, and apparently Coalter said nothing to him about us. But I think Santiago realized the truth. He knew we had been much more than just friends.

I had no idea what Coalter said to his wife, but Maudie, and Pilar, after each trip to the cabin, always reported that Rhoda asked about me and requested that I come for a visit. Her health prevented her from coming to our camp, though Christopher, once healed from the snakebite and anxious to see his new friends, returned often with his father and he, too, always asked for me.

Hearing about Coalter second-hand, sneaking about to avoid him, and seeing him from a distance with his son worsened my state of mind, so I decided to go to the coast with Lebe Seru, Maudie, and Marva on one of their visits to the Karankawas who were accepting into their tribe the Africans who had decided to escape from bondage.

The Karankawas lived in an area far from the colonists. This made it less likely that the armed parties dispatched by Stephen Austin to search for the runaway slaves would be successful. Lebe Seru, Maudie, Marva, and sometimes Binu and Amma, would go to the Karankawa camps to assist the runaways in their adjustment to their new lives. I reasoned that a change of surroundings might help me regain my bearings and decide what, if anything, I should do now that I knew Coalter was alive.

Something about the steady roar of the ocean crashing against the barrier islands between the gulf and the mainland did seem to clear my mind. The salty fragrance of the sea breezes and the cries of the birds that lived in the estuaries along the coast made it almost possible to step outside of time itself. I would sit for hours and watch the endless lines of geese flying in formation toward their winter nesting grounds to the south. And there were huge cranes, their outstretched wings as long as a man is tall, riding the wind currents and uttering a haunting "whooping" noise. The pure freedom of these magnificent birds that so effortlessly traversed the skies made it possible, if only for a while, to escape the prison constructed by the web of memory and the dream of what might have been.

It also helped me to work with Lebe Seru, Maudie, and Marva as they cared for the ex-slaves. The dilemma I faced did not seem all that large when I saw these people who had fled the vicious nightmare that was slavery. Many bore the scars of the whip and other signs of the savage treatment received at the hands of people who felt it was their right to own other human beings. I saw people whose fingers and toes had been chopped off as punishment for attempting to escape. Some had been branded and others beaten so badly, their bodies were misshapen and twisted. One poor man had had his eyes gouged from his head. Often, the deepest scars were those not visible on the body. It was especially horrible to see the little children who had been taken from their parents as babies. Things had been done to some of these children that were unspeakable abominations against the laws of God.

Up until this time, slavery had been an abstraction to me. Now I saw the reality of it. It was unimaginably cruel. Thousands upon thousands of lives were being destroyed. One people's prosperity was being purchased through another people's pain and ruination. How such a thing could be done by those who claimed to be Christians was beyond my comprehension. How anyone could witness such injustice and not ache to see it ended was a mystery I could not fathom. More than ever, I understood the courage and compassion of the man who had begun the revolution to prevent this horror in Mexico. Miguel Hidalgo had given his life to end this blight upon all of humanity.

It angered me that day after day more slaves were being brought into Mexico by Austin's colonists. Father Hidalgo and Father Morelos had made laws against this atrocity, and those laws, I felt, must be respected. Whatever I decided about Coalter, I knew that I must go on with my effort to realize the two priests' dream.

Now that Coalter was helping Santiago and Lebe Seru, it occurred to me that once again, just as we had so many years before in those days after Father Hidalgo's proclamation in Dolores, Coalter and I were in the same army. We were both still following Father Hidalgo, our fallen leader. I only wished it could be as before when the two of us shared the struggle, side by side and in each other's arms. I looked back upon those days with great fondness. They were gone, but the love I felt for Coalter at that time burned deeper in my heart than ever before.

+

Upon our return to the Tonkawa camp, we were greeted with the news that Agustín de Iturbide had been forced to flee Mexico. A new constitution had been written based on the principles first proclaimed by Miguel Hidalgo and José Morelos. Their prohibition of the institution of slavery had been written into the new constitution. Guadalupe

Victoria had been elected the first president of the Republic of Mexico. The new constitution established a federation of states. Texas was combined with its neighboring province to the south, Coahuila, to form a single state with the capital in Saltillo. A vice-governor would reside in San Antonio de Béxar.

Santiago and Pilar had just returned from Saltillo where the newly formed state legislature had convened. I asked how the republicans had managed to depose Iturbide who had an established army at least as powerful as the Spanish.

Santiago said, "It was not the republicans, Carmen, who turned out Iturbide."

Lebe Seru shared my confusion. "If not the republicans, then who?"

I saw the expression of concern on Pilar's face. Neither she nor Santiago seemed to be especially happy that Father Hidalgo's dream of a republic had been realized. We should be celebrating, but no one was happy. Something was amiss.

Santiago said, "Agustín de Iturbide was overthrown by General Antonio López de Santa Anna."

"Santa Anna?" Lebe Seru exclaimed. "Santa Anna is no republican."

"He says he is," Santiago said without conviction. "It was his army that defeated Iturbide. He was present at the writing of the new constitution and endorsed the selection of Guadalupe Victoria as president of the republic."

"But why?" I asked, still unable to fathom what had happened. This made no sense. Santa Anna had fought with Spain against the republicans. He had massacred republicans—men, women, and children—after our defeat in San Antonio.

"Iturbide did not give Santa Anna the estates and honors he thought he deserved, so Santa Anna stabbed the emperor in the back."

"And," Pilar added, "he will do the same to Guadalupe Victoria and Vicente Guerrero. He claims to be a republican only because most of the people are republican. He will claim to be anything if it serves his interests. I do not trust him."

Seldom had I seen Pilar so bitter.

"I'm afraid Pilar is right," Santiago said. "I met Santa Anna at the constituent assembly in the capital. He is a charming man and a great orator, but I don't think he believes in anything except Santa Anna. After all these years of war, Mexico is divided into many factions. Santa Anna will play one against the other. As long as he acquires land and wealth, he is content to remain the power behind the scenes. I do not trust him or his supporters. There are many today who call themselves republicans, but yesterday they were supporters of Iturbide, and before that, they served Spain."

"But we now have a republican government," Lebe Seru said and looked from Pilar to Santiago. "It will enforce the law against slavery. The colonists from the United States will have to free their slaves. They will no longer be able to bring slaves to Texas. Is it not true?"

"It is true," Santiago said, "that President Victoria is against slavery, but others, calling themselves republicans, are not so quick to take action against it because if the colonists prosper, they prosper."

"If there is a law against slavery," Lebe Seru exploded, "it must be enforced!" There was anger in his eyes. "Father Hidalgo began our revolution to end slavery and injustice. Thousands, tens of thousands, have died to end slavery and injustice! A republic that allows slavery to exist is no republic. It... it is a lie! A lie!"

"I agree," Santiago said and placed his hand on Lebe Seru's shoulder. He looked at Maudie and Marva. "But Stephen Austin was at the constituent assembly and he says there are no slaves in Texas."

"How can he say that?" Marva asked. "Each day, more slaves arrive. We have just received word that a man named James Fannin has landed over one hundred fifty slaves at Galveston and sold them at the auction block. He purchased them from North Americans who have reopened the trade in slaves from Africa. How can Austin say there are no slaves in Texas? How can he say that?"

Pilar said, "He says the slaves are not really slaves, Marva. He calls them indentured servants. He says they are the same as servants who contracted to work for people in the English colonies in exchange for their passage to America."

"The indentured servants," Maudie said, "served for a limited time and they were then released from their obligation to serve. Did Austin say these so-called indentured servants in Texas will be released after a period of time?"

Santiago shook his head sadly. "He says the obligations of the indentured servants is for a period of ninety-nine years and that children born to them must also serve for that period of time. I'm afraid there are supporters for Austin's position in both Saltillo and Mexico City, and they have managed to exempt his colony from the laws against slavery."

This news was a blow to us all. I assured Lebe Seru we would continue to do what was necessary to end slavery in Texas, but I could see that his spirit had been wounded. In some respects, our long struggle seemed for naught. Our victory, which should have been cause for great rejoicing, was a hollow one. We had our Republic of Mexico and a man who had long fought for the republican cause was our president, but we all knew it was not the fulfillment of Father Hidalgo's dream. We still had a long way to go, and we were weary.

That night, Pilar took me aside and told me that while we had been to the coast, Coalter had come to her many times to ask about me.

"How is Coalter?"

"He is well, Carmen. Coalter is a hard worker and his farm is productive. He shares what he grows to help feed those we release from slavery. He is a good man."

"Did Christopher fully recover from the snakebite?"

"Oh, yes. He is growing fast. Christopher and Miguel and Josefa are great friends."

When she did not continue, I asked, "And Rhoda? How is Rhoda?"

"Rhoda is very sick, Carmen. She always asks about you and wishes you would come to see her." For a moment Pilar was quiet and then she said, "I think Rhoda knows about you and Coalter. I think he told her."

"He should not have done that."

"What was he to do? He loves you, Carmen."

Folding my arms tight against my body to ward off the night chill, I walked away from the campfire and stared into the darkness. From the direction of the river came the croaking sounds of countless frogs, punctuated from time to time by the trill of an owl.

"What are you going to do?"

"I don't know, Pilar. Maybe I should return to Guanajuato. I have not seen my daughter since she was a baby. And I would like to see my father. He is growing old and I want to see him before he dies. The revolution is over. Mexico is a republic. I am no longer a danger to Cata Valeria. Perhaps I should go home. Guanajuato is a thousand leagues from Texas. Maybe there, I will forget Coalter."

"Will a thousand leagues make you forget him?"

A falling star traced an arc across the sky. As I followed its silent flight and watched its dying glow vanish into a nothingness as dark as my thoughts, I knew that if I were to go to the other side of the world, I would be unable to forget Coalter. If I could somehow ride a star to the very edge of the universe, I would not forget him. Though he could not be mine, never for one moment would he cease to be the very life of my soul. Though I remained silent, Pilar knew the answer to her question as did I. I would never forget Coalter. And I still did not know what to do.

✦

Not long after our return from the gulf coast, I accepted an invitation to go with Pilar and Santiago to San Antonio de Béxar. Santiago wanted to meet with Juan Veramendi, the new vice-governor of the combined state of Coahuila and Texas. Veramendi had been one of the first to answer Father Hidalgo's proclamation. Santiago was convinced there must be some way to have the judiciary overturn the exemption given to Stephen Austin regarding the constitutional provisions against slavery. He also wanted to talk with the vice-governor about guaranteeing the rights of the Indians to the lands they had lived on for generations. It was not the custom of the Indians to settle in one place, and some of Austin's colonists had begun to push them off their ancestral lands.

San Antonio de Béxar had changed little since that brief period we occupied it during the Gutiérrez-Magee expedition. Its dirt streets and simple wooden structures made it little more than a sleepy village that had grown up in a haphazard way around the Alamo, the San Fernando cathedral, and the governor's palace. There was, however, a thriving marketplace where farmers sold their produce and the workers of crafts displayed their wares. Having lived in the countryside for so long, I was captivated by the sights, sounds, and fragrant aromas of the market which we passed on the way to the house of José Navarro. He graciously extended his hospitality and was our host during our stay. His family, along with the Sequíns and the Veramendis, had all been loyal supporters of Miguel Hidalgo.

The morning we arrived, there were red, white, and green ribbons and banners decorating almost all the buildings. Piñatas in the shape of animals were hanging from tree limbs, and children were playing games while people sang and danced to music played by strolling musicians. A great celebration was in progress, and when we reached José Navarro's house, not far from the governor's palace, he told us the festivities were in honor of the marriage of Vice-Governor Veramendis' daughter, Ursula, to James Bowie.

Expecting our arrival, the vice-governor had sent word to the Navarros that he would be pleased if we would attend the wedding to be held that afternoon at the cathedral. I was reluctant to go because of the stories that Bowie had been a slave trader. Pilar, who was a friend of Ursula Veramendi, prevailed on me to attend, and finally I agreed since I knew the issues Santiago had come to discuss with the vice-governor might be likely to come up at the reception to be held at the palace. I wanted an opportunity to speak on behalf of the Indians and against slavery.

It had been years since I had bathed in a tub filled with hot water. Señora Navarro, the kind of cheerful woman whose greatest pleasure in life was giving to others, insisted that I accept as a present a beautiful, white cotton dress. On the sleeves and collar of the dress were flowers and birds elaborately embroidered in green and red threads. I did not feel comfortable in such attire. I was still a soldier, and our work was far from complete. But, at least, I was not dressed at variance with the other women who drew lace shawls over their heads as we entered the San Fernando Cathedral to witness the marriage sacrament administered to Ursula Veramendi and James Bowie.

At the reception in the governor's palace, I made my way outside to a patio next to a grape arbor. The crowd of people, laughing and celebrating in the palace, had only served to strengthen in me the feeling that my life was empty. I wanted to get away from them, but even in the patio, I could hear the noise of their happiness, and it somehow seemed to mock my own despair. I was on the verge of returning to the Navarros' house when Pilar came out to the patio with Ursula and rushed over to introduce me to the bride. Ursula was a lovely young woman, and it was easy to see she was very happy. Not wishing to appear rude, I could not very well leave while Ursula and Pilar joyfully described for me events and experiences they had shared when they were girls.

Before I could make a gracious exit, James Bowie came out to the patio, spotted us, and walked to where we were standing. Pilar introduced us, and reluctantly, I accepted his hand. Though not a particularly big fellow, Bowie was an imposing figure. There was danger in those broadly set grey eyes. It was easy to believe the stories about his having fought many duels with knives. More than any man I had ever met before, he impressed me as being a cold-blooded killer. Nevertheless, he smiled at me, and when he looked at his bride, I saw happiness.

"Señorita Rangel," he said in perfect Spanish, "I have heard of your bravery. I was told that you fought in the army of Ignacio Allende. He was a great general."

"I fought in the republican army of Ignacio Allende," I said coolly, stressing the word "republican" which I assumed meant little to a man like Bowie. It was impossible for me to ignore that this man had been a slave trader. I could not pretend I did not feel a profound contempt for him, and certainly, I did not need his compliments.

For some reason, Pilar began to talk about some recent skirmishes that had occurred between Austin's colonists and the

Tonkawas and the Karankawas over the issue of the colonists' clearing of forests.

Bowie shook his head, and his expression became grim. "Steve Austin," he said, "will not be happy until not a tree is standing between the Red River and the Río Bravo. His idea of progress is to place every square inch of land under cultivation and to have a settlement every ten leagues. If the Indians are an obstacle, he will remove them just as a farmer clears tree stumps and rocks from his field. He is going to turn Texas into a desert."

Though I suspected Bowie's characterization of Stephen Austin was accurate, I did not see where he had room to criticize anyone else. I told myself that my ire was due to his background as a trafficker in the slave trade, but in truth, I was also annoyed that a person such as Bowie had found happiness and I had not. There were times when I thought I deserved my fate. I had, after all, taken human lives, the greatest of sins, and so the unsatisfactory nature of my existence may have been a just and deserved punishment. But James Bowie had ended far more lives than I, and here he stood before me, a happy man, married to the person he loved, while I had to live alone, separated forever from the only person who could make me happy. It did not seem fair, and that irritated me even though I had long ago realized there was little fair about life in this world.

Bowie had continued to talk about Austin, but I interrupted him to say, "Stephen Austin does clear away the forests and make the land bare like the desert, but he does so, Señor Bowie, through the use of the forced labor of men and women whose liberty has been stolen from them by evil men like you. If what is being done in Texas offends you, then perhaps you must share the blame."

Ursula was, of course, distressed that her day of happiness had been marred by my hard words. I had insulted her husband of less than an hour. She politely excused herself and returned to the main hall of the palace. Pilar, while I am certain she agreed with my remarks, gave me a look that clearly conveyed her wish that I had chosen a more appropriate time for my outburst. She rushed after Ursula.

Bowie remained alone with me in the patio. Perhaps, I thought, he would like to challenge me to a duel. I had insulted him. We could go at it with knifes. Certainly, he would be able to kill me in short order; he was a professional killer. But I had little to live for, and he would know he had been in a fight.

I was feeling somewhat pleased with myself until he cleared his throat and asked, "Have you never done anything in your life that you regretted, Señorita Rangel? Did you not, when young, have a craving for fame and fortune that sometimes made you do things you knew were wrong?"

Naturally, my memory chose that moment to dredge forth the recollection of how I had, so many years before, urged Don Esteban to accept Barnet's offer of men and Pennsylvania long-rifles in exchange for permission to reopen the slave trade in New Spain. Because I had so wanted to play a role in making Fernando the first king of New Spain, and because I yearned to exalt my name, I had been willing to ignore my conscience which told me slavery was wrong.

When I did not answer, Bowie continued, "I did many things as a young man that I now profoundly regret. I wish I could change those things, but I cannot. In part I came to Texas to escape my past. I could not. It followed me. But when I met Ursula, my whole life was transformed. Her love has lifted me out of the hell into which I had descended. I tell you this, Señorita Rangel, because I have a great respect for you. I would like for us to be friends."

It was not easy to continue to hate a man who admitted he was flawed. I could not forgive what Bowie had done, neither did he ask it of me. I found myself extending my hand not necessarily in friendship nor in respect. It was more of a kind of grudging admission that we might have more in common, this Bowie and I, than I cared to acknowledge. Furthermore, who was I to say that he had not changed? It was obvious he loved Ursula deeply, and I very much knew what love could do to change a person's entire life.

Bowie and I spent some time on the patio talking about what was occurring in Mexico City. He was very well informed about events in the capital, and when I told him of Pilar's doubts that Santa Anna was a true republican, he said he agreed with her assessment. He believed Santa Anna to be a tyrant.

After a while, we stepped outside to get away from the noise of the celebrants, and when we did, Bowie waved at a man approaching the palace on horseback.

"Over here, Sam!" he yelled in English. "I have someone here I want you to meet!"

The man waved back and reined his mount, a small Spanish pony, toward where we stood. He was a big man, and his feet, encased in a handsome pair of black leather boots, almost dragged on the ground.

"That crazy *hombre* there," Bowie said, nodding his head, "is Sam Houston, the former governor of Tennessee. He was Andy Jackson's fair-haired boy, and if he hadn't of spent the last five years of his life stone drunk, he might today be president of the United States."

When Houston dismounted, he quickly removed the wide-brimmed hat from his large head and bowed as Bowie introduced us. He was a tall and broad-shouldered man of impressive appearance, and it was not difficult to understand that other men might turn to him for leadership. An ivory-hilted sword in a red leather scabbard hung from his side beneath a buff-colored frock coat. The coat was open revealing an orange and black vest fashioned from leopard skin. Here was a man not afraid to draw attention to himself.

"Damnation, Houston!" Bowie said loudly. "Why don't you just get yourself a smaller horse and then you can carry him 'round on your back." He glanced at me and grinned. "The governor likes to ride a small horse so he'll look bigger than God." He looked at Houston and tried to keep a straight face. "I've got a jackass, Sam, that I could let you have real cheap. 'Course then, nobody'd know ifen it was you doing the ridin' or ifen it was you doin' the carryin'!"

"What brings you to Texas, Señor Houston?" I asked in English when Bowie's laughter subsided.

"I have friends in the Cherokee nation who have recently come to Texas, Señorita Rangel. They are hoping to persuade the Mexican government to allow them to establish a colony in Texas. I wanted to see for myself if all the things they've been telling me about Texas are true." Straightening to his full stature, he towered over me. "Bowie, too, has been telling me about Texas, but you can't believe him 'cause he's such a liar. When he was a boy, back in the bayous of Louisiana, he used to go out and catch crawdads for his dinner, but after he done finished tellin' 'bout it, he had half the people in the territory thinking them little ol' crawdads was sixteen foot alligators, and he et 'em raw, seasoned only with cottonmouth venom!"

The two men swapped insults and stories, progressively employing a dialect I found hard to follow, until Bowie happened to mention I had lived many years with the Tonkawas.

Houston became very serious and began to ask me questions about the Texas Indians and their way of life. He appeared to be a friend of the Indians in his country. When he learned I had been with Allende's army, his queries expanded to include solicitation of information about Spanish battle tactics. It was evident that this was a man of keen intellect, and his interest in Texas was not as casual as he had tried to lead me to believe. He intrigued me and so I decided to ask him his views on slavery.

"It is a terrible thing, Señorita Rangel," he said. "I am sorry that Steve Austin has allowed it to be established in his colony. Slavery will not endure, either here or in the United States, though in the latter, I fear it will require armed conflict to bring it to an end. A terrible struggle will come on this issue, and when it does, I hope the union will survive."

We continued to talk until Vice-Governor Veramendi came to the street outside the patio, and after greeting Governor Houston, turned to me and said, "Señorita Rangel, please forgive me, but there is someone in the reception hall to see you." He smiled. "Someone from Guanajuato."

XIII

As I made my way from the patio, edged through the crowd of celebrants, and rushed to the reception hall near the front entrance to the palace, I realized that I had not taken the time to ask the vice-governor if the person seeking me was a man or a woman. My first thought had been of Don Esteban. It was logical that he would come. The long struggle was over, Mexico was a republic, and no longer did I pose a threat to my own child; therefore, my father had come to take me home and, soon, I would see my daughter. Or, perhaps, Cata Valeria had come with him!

I looked about frantically in the hall for the Marqués. When I did not see him, I realized he might not be as I remembered. The years often changed people's appearance and so I focused on men with white hair and beards. I saw smiling faces, but none of the men were as tall as my father. I looked at young women who would be Cata Valeria's age. They, too, smiled, but none came to greet me. It surprised me how much I wanted to see my daughter. I wanted very much to see Don Esteban, but I desperately wanted to see Cata Valeria.

And then I became aware that a little *comadre* was staring at me. She was a small woman, bent, and with thin wisps of white hair. She stepped toward me.

"Hortensia?" It did not seem possible. "Hortensia!"

"Carmencita," she said softly. "My Carmencita!"

334

I rushed to my aunt and embraced her. She was now a fragile little thing, but there was still strength in her arms and for a long while, she did not release me.

Finally, grasping her hands, I stepped back to look down into her eyes. "Hortensia," I said. "You came all the way from Guanajuato? That is a long journey. You must be very tired."

"I came in a carriage. It was most comfortable."

"Not by yourself!"

Her eyes grew wide. "I cannot drive a carriage, Carmencita!" She laughed. "I had a driver, a very good driver."

She began to tell me about her driver who, it turned out, had been one of the coachmen's sons at the Hacienda de Abrantes before I left. I remembered him as just a tiny boy. I could sense she might go on about the driver and her carriage for some time, so I gently interrupted and asked, "Hortensia, my father? Did he not come with you? He sent you here alone? My father..."

When her smile faded, I intuited at once the reason for her trip. It saddened me, of course, but I suppose that somehow I expected it. Even before I left, his health had begun to fail. It did not catch me entirely by surprise.

"Your father," she said, "he—"

I put my fingers to her lips. I did not want to hear the words. Closing my eyes, I drew a deep breath and asked, "When, Hortensia?"

"Almost a year. I would have come sooner, but there were many matters to attend to. The Marqués made many arrangements so that the titles to his lands and to his mines would transfer to Cata Valeria. He wanted all of this to be completed as soon as he was gone. He made me promise to see that everything was in order before I came to you."

My thoughts were on the Marqués as she was talking, and only gradually did it register that she had spoken my daughter's name. "Cata Valeria?" I said, my eyes looking about to find her. My heart began to race. "Did she come with you? Where is she? Is she well? How—"

Her bright smile halted my queries. "Cata Valeria is fine, Carmen. She did not come with me."

That struck me as odd, though I was not sure what to make of it. "She... she is in Guanajuato?"

"No, Carmencita. She is not in Guanajuato. Cata Valeria is in Mexico City. That is where she lives."

"Mexico City?" I tried to collect my wits. "Why would she live in Mexico City? I do not understand."

As her smiled broadened, my aunt seemed to become younger, reminding me of Teresa. There was the same serenity in her expression that I had witnessed in Teresa on the day she died. "She lives in Mexico City, Carmen, because that is where her husband lives."

My head was light and I thought perhaps I had not heard correctly. "Her husband?"

"Lieutenant Arturo de Sestos. He is an officer in the army of Generalísimo Santa Anna. He is a fine boy, the youngest son of the Conde de Sestos, and very handsome!"

I was totally unprepared for such a revelation. "Cata Valeria has a husband? She is married? But she is just...a baby."

Hortensia's eyes sparkled. "She is older than you were when you gave birth to her, Carmencita."

Though I had many questions, I could see that my aunt was tired. It was a long and arduous journey from Guanajuato to San Antonio de Béxar. I decided to take her to the Navarros' house. And as I expected, Señora Navarro was more than happy to provide a room for Hortensia and accommodations for the coachman in the carriage house.

I helped the coachman stable the horses which, I could tell, descended from the Marqués's team of silver-maned Parisian barouche horses. I fondly remembered how both Don Esteban and Cristóbal had loved these animals. It made me sad that they were both dead: my brother and my father. They had been such vital men, so full of life, and now they were gone, and even though so many years had passed since our last time together, I was deeply grieved. For a long time, I remained in the Navarros' stable, groomed the horses, and thought of my brother and my father. A part of me, a part deep within me, was gone forever. It was as if something inside me had died with them, and I felt so alone.

That evening, after Hortensia had had a chance to rest and to eat, I sat with her on the veranda overlooking the gently rolling hill country to the north and west of San Antonio de Béxar. There were so many things I wanted to know about my daughter, I hardly knew where to begin. Finally, I asked about the things she liked to do.

"Oh, Carmencita!" Hortensia said beaming. "Cata Valeria is just like you. She pretends she is a soldier, and she loves to ride the horses! Her *papá* taught her how to ride and—"

"Her *papá*?"

My query confused my aunt. "Don Esteban raised her as if she were his daughter. That was your wish. Yes?"

Of course it was my wish, but it did not sound right to refer to Don Esteban as my daughter's father. Coalter was Cata Valeria's father, not Don Esteban. Don Esteban was her grandfather. However, it had been precisely my wish that she be raised as the Marqués's daughter, and I tried to reassure Hortensia with a smile.

"And so," I said, "Cata Valeria is healthy. That is good."

"Very healthy!" Hortensia said, shaking her head for emphasis, and then her eyes narrowed. "Of course, we did not think so at first. As a baby, she was very sickly. In fact, soon after you left for Texas, we thought Cata Valeria would die."

"Die?"

"Yes. The Marqués had the best physicians in all of New Spain tend to her. Still Cata Valeria did not get better. We had almost given up hope when Doña Lupe came to the hacienda. Doña Lupe saved Cata Valeria's life. She cared for her, and from that time forward she became Cata Valeria's constant companion. She went with her to Mexico City when she married Arturo."

Surely, I thought, what came to my mind was not possible. I searched my aunt's eyes and asked, "Doña Lupe? Do you mean Lupita, the little girl who was with me when I returned from Dolores with Father Hidalgo?"

"Yes!" she said and vigorously nodding her head. "The same! Doña Lupe came to the hacienda and Cata Valeria lived. Don Esteban said she saved his little girl's life and he was very grateful."

It was incomprehensible to me how Lupita had found her way back to the Hacienda de Abrantes. According to Coalter's account it was right before they entered Texas, at the Río Bravo, that she had disappeared. It did not seem possible that a tiny child could cross the desert alone with no one to look after her or protect her. It was not possible.

I thought about this for a while, and then without any fore-thought I asked, "Did Don Esteban tell Cata Valeria about me?"

"No, Carmen," she said softly. "The Marqués told her she had been left as a baby in one of the convents to whose support he con-tributed. That he had adopted her. He understood that this is what you wished the child be told. He knew you did not want anyone to suspect she was your daughter so that no harm would come to her."

My daughter did not know I was her mother. She did not know Coalter was her father. My plan had worked very well. Cata Valeria had not been harmed. Apparently, she had had a happy childhood and was now a happily married woman. Everything had gone as it should, so why did I suddenly feel so empty?

"Carmen? What is wrong?"

I shrugged pretending that nothing was wrong. But something felt very wrong. As a matter of fact, never had anything felt quite so wrong before.

Taking my hand, Hortensia smiled and said, "You can go to Cata Valeria in Mexico City. You can tell her you are her mother. I will go with you. It is safe now. That is why I came for you. We will go to the capital. There, you can—"

"No," I said impulsively. "There is no need for Cata Valeria to know I am her mother. She has done very well without having me in her life. You said her husband is the son of the Conde de Sestos? It is true?"

"Yes."

My thoughts were disordered, but I thought I detected some logic in the words taking shape in my head. "The House of Abrantes and the House of Sestos..."—I waited for more words, not at all certain what I wanted to say—"...Cata Valeria is a very wealthy woman. What need has she of me?"

"You are her mother."

"No, Hortensia. You are her mother. You raised her and took care of her while I went to Texas. You go to Cata Valeria in Mexico City. It is time for her to take care of you."

Distraught, Hortensia repeated, "You are her mother!"

I took my aunt's tiny hands in mine and looked into her eyes. "I am a soldier, *Tía*. That is all I have ever wished to be. When I was a child, I told you I would be a soldier. Well, a soldier I am, a soldier against tyranny, and my place is here in Texas. Go to Cata Valeria in Mexico City. Tell her nothing of me. It is for the best. It is what..."—hoping to conceal my lie, I smiled—"...it is what I want. Please honor my wish."

Hortensia remained in San Antonio de Béxar until I was certain she was rested and strong enough to make the long journey to Guanajuato. On the day of her departure, as I waved my farewell, I felt I would never again see my aunt. My father was dead and my daughter, who did not even know I existed, had a life of her own, and I could never bring anything to her except embarrassment and shame. What did I have to offer? Nothing. Therefore, there was no reason for me to return to the place of my birth. There was no one waiting for me there. No one. I would never see the Hacienda de Abrantes again. It was no longer my home.

✦

For several months after Hortensia left, I remained in San Antonio de Béxar. Meanwhile, Santiago met and conferred almost daily with José Navarro, Juan Seguín, James Bowie, Sam Houston, Lorenzo de Zavala, and other leaders of the republicans in Texas.

Day after day, I listened to these men debate the problems created by Texas having been joined with Coahuila into a single state governed from Saltillo. Since the populace of Coahuila far outnumbered that of Texas, certain powerful landowners and merchants in Coahuila were able to pass laws that benefited their interests at the expense of the interests and well-being of the people of Texas. I listened to men, like Seguín and Navarro, who had spent their lives battling Spanish tyranny first and later Iturbide's dictatorship. Still their dreams of living in a republic remained unfulfilled.

I listened, also, to Stephen Austin who arrived in San Antonio de Béxar to report that his colonists were enraged at having their rights trampled by the government in Saltillo. When I asked about the rights of the Africans held in bondage by his colonists, he explained that no one in his colony was kept in bondage. Rather, some people were under obligation as indentured servants.

This absurdity angered me, and I shouted, "The man called James Fannin has brought to Texas hundreds of people forced from their homes in Africa. He has sold many of them to your colonists, Señor Austin. These people are not under obligation as indentured servants. They are slaves! You may call it what you wish, but it is still slavery!"

Even in the face of my outburst, Austin remained calm and logical. He was no different than on our first meeting when he arrived at our camp in an effort to return Maudie, Marva, and the children to J. W. Keane. "Señorita Rangel," he said softly, "as I have explained to you previously, we need the Africans to work the land, to make it productive so we can establish liberty in Texas. It is necessary that—"

"Liberty?" I cried. "How can you speak of liberty?"

Without batting an eye, Austin said, "Liberty is perhaps an arduous concept for someone unfamiliar with the Anglo-Saxon tradition of representative government. This tradition is alien to Spain and unpracticed in her colonies. I know it must be difficult for you, Señorita Rangel, to understand why we are forced to follow certain measures in order to achieve our objectives, but I assure you, liberty is our ultimate goal."

"Liberty," I said sternly, "was the goal of Father Hidalgo. He sought to achieve that goal by ending slavery in all its forms, Señor Austin. You are correct; I do not know anything about Anglo-Saxon traditions, but I do know that no one is truly free as long as even one single person remains enslaved. This I learned from Miguel Hidalgo."

Austin thanked me for my observation and assured me that the matter of African slaves would be satisfactorily resolved, and that once Texas was restored as a state in the Mexican republic on equal footing with the other states, a goal he said he was on his way to pursue with the authorities in Mexico City, it would all come to pass.

After my exchange with Austin, my participation in the discussion of events that were arousing deep anger and resentment among Texans was limited. Although both Santiago and Pilar urged me to make my views known, I continued to feel a strange hollowness within since Hortensia's visit. All that was happening, all that was being said, all the anger, no longer seemed to concern me. There were times when I did not care about much of anything. When the meetings were called and the inevitable arguments commenced, I would more often than not slip away and find a place where I could be alone.

As usual, Pilar was able to read my mood and finally she took me aside and insisted that I tell her why I was so troubled. It was on a day when we had gone to a corral outside of San Antonio de Béxar to look at mules. Santiago and some of the soldiers he had led from their time with Morelos had decided to form a commercial enterprise. They would transport goods between San Antonio, Goliad, and Galveston. Since I was supposed to know something about animals, they had asked me to participate in their venture, and on that day, I was helping to select mules suitable for draying carts.

"Carmen," Pilar said when I walked away from her, "we are worried about you. Tell me what is wrong."

"There is nothing wrong," I said as I ran my hand over the flanks of an old grey. My heart was not in what I was doing.

Pilar led me away from the corral to the shade of a thick-trunked pecan tree. Once we sat down she asked, "Do you still grieve for your father?"

"Yes Pilar, I grieve. It is only natural. But my father had a full life."

"Then it is what your aunt said about your daughter," she ventured. "Why do you not go to Mexico City as she suggested? Go to Cata Valeria. Tell her you are her mother. It is—"

"No!" I said before she could continue. I had begun to regret I had confided to Pilar what Hortensia had told me. Many times I had explained my reasons for not wanting to enter Cata Valeria's life, and

I wanted Pilar to respect my decision. "I do not wish to discuss this anymore."

Being the friend she was, Pilar complied, but it was not long before she said, "Then go to Coalter, Carmen. Tell him that he has a daughter and that she is married. He has a right to know this. It would bring him great happiness. He—"

"No," I said firmly.

Pilar closed her eyes and leaned back against the tree. She had hoped to relieve my troubled soul, and now she was the one who was bereft. "I am sorry, Carmen. I wish there was something I could do."

"There is nothing anyone can do, Pilar, because...because there is nothing for me in this life. My life is over."

My remark, born from nothing but self-pity, angered Pilar. "That is a terrible thing to say, Carmen! You are a beautiful woman, and many men would—"

"What difference does it make," I exploded, "whether I am a beautiful woman or what many men think of me!" It was my turn to be angry. "Do you think I could ever love a man other than Coalter? He may not be mine, but no man could ever take his place in my heart! Why can you not understand this? If Santiago were to die, would you seek another man to take his place? Tell me!"

Pilar lowered her head.

My anger quickly subsided. Pilar was my friend and I might have lost my mind if I did not have her to share my confused and troubled thoughts. I moved closer to where she sat and put my hand on hers. "I am sorry, Pilar. It is just that..."—I hesitated, unwilling to say to another what I had been unable to admit to myself—"...I am afraid."

She received my hand in hers. "Afraid? Of what?"

For a moment, I watched Santiago and his men leading the mules they had selected from the corral. "Pilar, do you remember Augustus Magee, the *norteamericano* who headed the expedition with Gutiérrez?" She nodded. "He had such a great fear of death."

Pilar's eyes narrowed.

"For me," I continued, "it is not death that I fear but life. I have nothing to live for. My brother and my father are dead. All ties to my past are severed. My daughter has no need for me. Coalter is married and has a son. I do not know why I should go on living. I think death might...I think death might be a friend. For Augustus Magee it was. Perhaps I should—"

"No!" Pilar said, gripping my hand until it hurt. "No, Carmen! Do not think of such a thing!"

From the expression on Pilar's face, I immediately wished I had not said what I had. It was, of course, the kind of thing one should keep to one's self, and I vowed never to voice it again. Nevertheless, it was something that continued to weigh on my thoughts, and despite an effort to resist it, I did sometimes think of what Augustus Magee had done.

✦

After purchasing the mules and making contracts with persons who wished to arrange for the transport of their goods, we set out for Goliad where we had arranged for Lebe Seru to meet us. He and the people he was freeing from bondage were to be partners in this newly formed enterprise that had long been Santiago's dream. Before reaching Goliad, however, we were met by Chief Meyei. He informed us that his scouts had just arrived with the news that Lebe Seru, Coalter, and a number of our people had been captured in Karankawa country on the gulf coast by a large party of men armed with rifles. The men were led by J. W. Keane and Ellis Leeper.

The thought of Coalter and Lebe Seru in the hands of Keane and Leeper terrified me. Without delay, we secured our weapons, unharnessed the mules from the wagons and headed for where Meyei's scouts had last sighted Keane's party.

Two-days hard riding brought us to the Colorado, which we forded at a low water point. We then proceeded north. Before reaching the Brazos, Chief Meyei's scouts brought word that Mexican soldiers had forced Keane to relinquish Lebe Seru's people. Shortly afterwards, a party of armed slaveholders had reinforced Keane's group, and the Mexican soldiers had retreated to a fort on the coast at Anahuac. Keane and his men had followed and were attempting to regain their captives.

When we arrived at Anahuac, we discovered that the conflict was now a standoff. The Mexican soldiers had barricaded themselves inside a small wooden fort at one end of the small village, while Keane and his men had withdrawn to a tavern. From this vantage point, their rifles at the ready, they kept watch on the fort.

When we identified ourselves at the gates of the fort and Santiago explained that we had come as friends, I looked down the dirt street and saw Mrs. Keane and her daughters seated in an open-topped landau hitched to a team of brougham jobbers. Such a team would cost a small fortune. Keane, who stood with Leeper and other men on the front porch of the tavern, was dressed in a fine suit of clothes. He had obviously prospered since last I saw him on the banks of the Brazos. Staring straight ahead, Mrs. Keane appeared most uncomfortable.

The *comandante* of the fort was Captain John Bradburn. He, we soon learned, had been part of the Gutiérrez-Magee expedition. After the defeat at San Antonio de Béxar, Bradburn had gone south to fight with Victoria and Guerrero. Recently he had been commissioned by the new government with seeing that his former countrymen in Texas obeyed the laws of the republic, especially those against slavery. It was for this reason that he had intercepted Keane and taken his prisoners.

We spoke for a few minutes with Bradburn in his office, and when I anxiously asked where our people were, his expression told me something was wrong. He led us down to the end of the hallway and opened a door. The first person I saw was Coalter, who was sitting on a chair next to a bed.

Coalter quickly got to his feet, but before either of us had a chance to say anything, I looked beyond him at the person on the bed and, involuntarily, my hand went to my mouth.

Lebe Seru was face down on the bed. The flesh on his back had been torn and shredded to the extent that his ribs were exposed. It was a horrible sight, and only gradually did I become aware that Maudie and Marva were seated on chairs on the other side of the bed, opposite to where Coalter had been sitting. Maudie's eyes were swollen from crying. Binu and Amma were attempting to comfort her.

My stomach tightened and for a moment I thought I might fall. Rushing to where I stood, Coalter took my arm and steadied me. I looked into his face and saw an ugly bruise formed around a deep gash over his left eye.

"Coalter," I whispered, "is Lebe Seru...is he..." I could not finish my question.

"He is still alive," Coalter said. "But he has been very badly hurt."

After glancing again at my old *compañero* whose eyes were shut and did not move, I turned my head away. I could not bear to see him this way. "What did they do to him?"

Gently, Coalter guided me outside to the hallway and back to Bradburn's office. He helped me sit down on a wooden, straw bottomed chair and kneeled at my side.

"We were taking a group of runaways to the Karankawa camp," he explained, "when Keane ambushed us. We tried to fight our way out, but there were too many. We—"

He stopped because I had touched the bruise on his face with my fingers. I could not help myself. He took my hand in his and held it. I was too stunned by what I had seen to pull away. I could not resist allowing my hand to tighten around his.

"We were beaten," Coalter continued. He lowered his eyes. And then Keane tied Lebe Seru to a tree and bullwhipped him. If Captain Bradburn had not arrived, he would have killed him."

"How could he do it, Coalter? How could anyone do such a thing?"

Coalter, of course, could not answer my query. There was no answer. He sat on the floor next to the chair and continued to hold my hand. I looked into his eyes and saw the sadness, the weariness, the confusion. It would have been the most natural thing in the world to move to his side, to hold him, to wrap my arms around him and give him comfort and draw strength from him. I needed that strength as much as I needed the air in my lungs. I yearned to hold him, but I knew if I did, I would never again be able to let him go. Slowly, gently, I slid my hand from his.

Coalter was about to speak when we heard a commotion on the street outside the fort. We got to our feet. A sergeant ran inside and reported to Captain Bradburn that Keane and his men wanted to see the *comandante* and they had brought an attorney with them.

Bradburn looked through his window. "It's Travis."

"Who?" Coalter asked.

"William Barret Travis. He's an attorney, recently arrived from Virginia. He makes no secret of the fact that he would like to see Texas become a part of the United States."

Santiago and his men joined Bradburn's soldiers on the street as the captain went outside to confront Keane and his attorney. Coalter and I followed, standing together behind the rest.

Travis was a tall, lanky man who was wearing the same sort of expensively tailored clothes as Keane and Leeper. Unlike the profusely sweating Keane and Leeper, however, Travis looked at ease, as though he was used to wearing long-tailed frock coats and riding breeches. He doffed his wide-brimmed panama hat when he saw me. Then he bowed.

"Buenos días, Señorita," he said in correct Spanish.

I did not return his greeting. I was in no mood for civilities from well-dressed attorneys who defended slave-owners. I stared coldly at Keane and Leeper who, in turn, kept a weary eye on the muskets held by Bradburn's soldiers and Santiago's men. Behind and to either side of Keane and Leeper there were about three dozen men carrying rifles.

"Captain Bradburn," Travis began, "I have been retained by these gentlemen to obtain the release of certain of their properties you illegally appropriated."

"I hold the property of no man here, Mr. Travis," Bradburn said.

"Well, sir," Travis drawled with a smile and retrieved a number of papers from a pocket inside his coat, "I happen to have here the bills of sale for that property. I believe you will find the instruments in order. I have a bill of sale held by Mr. J. W. Keane for two negresses and—"

"These instruments," Bradburn interrupted, stressing the word, "may be valid in the United States, Mr. Travis, but they are not recognized in the Republic of Mexico. As you well know, slavery is forbidden by the constitution of the Republic of Mexico."

Behind Travis, Keane and the men with him began to make menacing noises.

Travis said, "Perhaps you are unfamiliar, Captain Bradburn, with the exemptions to the laws on slavery granted to individuals who are members of the colony established by Stephen Austin. If you are, I have a copy of the particulars of those exemptions that I would be happy to share with you."

Bradford waved aside the papers Travis thrust toward him. "I am familiar with these exemptions, Mr. Travis. However, I believe that if you read them, you will discover the exemptions apply only within the boundaries of Austin's colony. Anahuac is outside the boundaries of his colony."

Before Travis could make his retort, Keane shouted, "Enough of these fancy words, Travis! We demand you hand over our darkies, Bradburn!"

Turning to the crowd behind them, Leeper yelled, "I say we show these here Mes'cans they can't just come in and take a man's property. They's just a bunch of thieves, these Mes'cans, the same as Injuns. Texas won't be a fit place for a man to raise his family 'til we get rid of 'em all, Injuns and Mes'cans alike! I say, kill 'em! Kill all Injuns and Mes'cans!"

Some in the crowd raised their rifles but most seemed aware that they were still outnumbered by Bradburn's soldiers, now augmented by Santiago's force.

While the men grumbled, Travis drew close to Captain Bradburn and in a low voice said, "I feel it is my duty, as an officer of the court, to inform you that, even as we speak, men are on their way here from Louisiana. You will soon be outnumbered."

"It is my duty to inform you, Mr. Travis," Bradburn said, "that any man who violates the laws of the Republic of Mexico will be arrested."

Smiling, Travis again doffed his hat to me and turned to walk with a slow, deliberate gait back to the tavern. Keane and his men fell in behind, and when they reached the tavern, Keane, whose anger had not subsided, began shouting at his wife who had asked if she and her daughters could get out of the carriage. The sun was beating down mercilessly hot. Keane slapped her, and for the first time that day, I saw their son, Doyle, at the edge of the tavern. He was no longer a boy. He was a young man with that same forlorn look about him I remembered from the day when we visited their farm.

Back inside the captain's office, Santiago asked, "Is it true what Travis says about men coming from Louisiana?"

"Probably," Bradburn replied shaking his head. "But that is not the worst problem we face." He looked toward Coalter, who stood at my side. "We have recently received information that General Santa Anna is planning to overthrow the government in Mexico City. He plans to suspend the constitution and rule Mexico by decree."

"What?" Santiago gasped.

"It is true," Coalter said. "Before you arrived, we received the news. Santa Anna is supported by many of the men who arranged to grant the exemptions to the laws against slavery to Stephen Austin's colony."

"If Santa Anna comes to power," Bradburn added, "those of us in the army who support the Republic will lose our commissions. We will not be able to put down slavery nor obtain justice for the *indios*."

Coalter looked at me and said, "Everything Father Hidalgo and Father Morelos struggled for will be lost."

We returned to the room where Lebe Seru continued to battle for his life. I tried, as I could, to comfort Maudie. She was disconsolate. I was glad she had Binu and Amma to comfort her. Though now grown, a young man and a young woman, they were like her children.

As the afternoon passed, we kept a vigil in Lebe Seru's room. I sat on one side of the bed and Coalter on the other. Several times, he lowered his head to whisper a prayer for our friend. When our eyes met, I would look away. We exchanged no words, though I longed to tell him of Cata Valeria. I wanted to tell him what Hortensia had said. We had a beautiful and free-spirited daughter who loved to ride horses. And now she was married to a young officer and lived in Mexico City. I so wanted to tell him this and all the things Hortensia had said. Perhaps, I considered, Pilar had been correct in what she said. Coalter had a right to know he had a daughter. It would make him happy. I wanted him to be happy. I wanted that very much. He looked so sad, so weary. But I could not tell him. I could not tell him and it broke my heart.

At sundown, we again heard noises in the street. Thinking that the reinforcements from Louisiana had arrived, Captain Bradburn led us, fully armed, outside to face them.

What we discovered was Keane in front of the tavern urging his men to attack the fort. Leeper was at his side, echoing his every word. Even from where we stood and in the fading light of day, we could see that both men were drunk. When he saw us in the street, Keane unleashed a string of vulgarities and curses. After a while, he seemed to lose interest, and with Leeper behind him, he staggered back toward the tavern where many of the men had already retreated after growing tired of his harangue.

When her husband walked by the carriage, Mrs. Keane again pleaded for her and her daughters to be allowed to get down. Suddenly, like a crazed bull, Keane charged the carriage and nearly knocked it over as he seized his wife and dragged her by the hair from the carriage. He threw her to the ground and began to savagely kick her. None of the men at the tavern did a thing except watch. Some of them were laughing as if what was happening was no more important than an altercation between a couple of stray dogs. That a woman was being brutalized was nothing more than casual entertainment to these men.

Just as Coalter and I started down the street ahead of Bradburn and Santiago, a shot rang out and Keane reeled backwards and fell.

Freezing in place, I looked up and saw Doyle at the corner of the tavern. Smoke issued from the octagon barrel of the long-rifle he had used to shoot his father.

"J. W.!" Leeper screamed as he sank to his knees over Keane's motionless body. He looked up at the men around him. "He's dead! J. W.'s dead!"

Mrs. Keane, still on her hands and knees, crawled slowly to her husband's body.

Jumping to his feet, Leeper pointed at Doyle and howled, "He done it! He killed J. W.! Killed his own daddy!" He drew a pistol from a holster at his side and aimed it at the young man who did not seem to understand what was happening. "Prepare yourself for hell, boy!"

Before anyone could make a move, Mrs. Keane had withdrawn the big hunting knife from the sheath secured to the belt around her dead husband's bloated waist. She leapt to her feet and slashed the blade deep across Leeper's neck.

Blood gushed from the gaping wound and continued to pour into the dirt after the little man sank to his knees and then collapsed on the street next to his companion.

Mrs. Keane dropped the knife and began to sob. No one made a move to do anything, not even Travis who, clenching a long cigar between his teeth, had come to the door of the tavern to witness the events.

I went to Mrs. Keane and helped her into the carriage. "Señora," I said, "leave this place." I gestured for Doyle to mount the deck and take the reins.

Breathing heavily, the poor woman looked at me. "Where will we go?"

"Where are you from?"

"Alabama."

"Then return to Alabama, Señora. Leave Texas. Go at once and do not stop until you cross the Sabine. These men will not follow you. They're drunk." I turned to Doyle. "Take your mother home."

Mrs. Keane looked at me and for just an instant, I saw a smile. I squeezed her hand and then slapped the lead jobber on the rump to send the team on the way.

No one seemed to want to touch Keane or Leeper, but finally, Travis ordered them dragged off the street to a place behind a privy house where, I supposed, they would lay until someone bothered to dig a hole in the ground to bury them.

We returned to the fort and listened as the men in the tavern shouted and cursed and fought long into the night.

Toward dawn, long after the noise in the tavern had ceased, Captain Bradburn came to the room where we were keeping watch over Lebe Seru. He motioned for Santiago, Coalter, and me to join him in the hallway. Then he informed us, "My scouts have verified that men are on their way from Louisiana. I'm concerned that if we wait much longer, we will be forced to hand over your people."

"We can't do that!" I said, alarmed at what this would mean. We could not allow Maudie and Marva or any of the people Lebe Seru had freed to be returned to slavery.

"I know," Captain Bradburn said. "That is why I think it best that you leave now. It is still dark and the men in the tavern are sleeping off their drunk. Take Lebe Seru and his people and go south to Goliad. I know the *comandante* there, and he has more men than I do. He will protect you. Plácido Benavides has established a new colony in Victoria just south of Goliad. He, too, will offer protection."

"But what if the men in the tavern follow us?" Santiago asked. "We will not be able to travel rapidly. Lebe Seru is badly hurt and it would kill him if we go too fast."

"That's right," Coalter added. "When they discover we have fled, they will come after us."

Bradburn rubbed his chin. "I think I might have a way to keep them in Anahuac for a few days, long enough for you to reach Goliad."

"How?" I asked. "What can you do?"

"I will arrest Travis. The men in the tavern will forget about everything else until Travis is released. I'll hold him as long as I can."

"You are running a great risk," Santiago said. "In a day or two you will be outnumbered. They will try to take the fort."

"I can bluff them for a couple of days. By then, it will make no difference. Several of my officers are secret supporters of Santa Anna. I have a boat waiting for me at Galveston. As soon as I release Travis, I will go to Veracruz and join those who are taking a stand against Santa Anna. There is a man in Oaxaca named Benito Juárez who is opposed to Santa Anna and all he stands for. He will be our leader."

"I have met this Juárez," Santiago said. "He is a man of vision and courage. Like Morelos, he is an *indio*."

"Mexico will never be free," Bradburn said, "until Santa Anna no longer commands an army."

Under the cover of darkness, we carried Lebe Seru from the fort and placed him on a stretcher drawn by one of the mules. It hurt to

see the pain on his face as we moved him. But by the first light of
dawn we were well on our way and almost at the Brazos river.

A day after reaching the Brazos, we arrived at the point where
Coalter would veer north to his farm and we turned south for Goliad.
It was the moment I had been dreading. While Maudie and Marva
tended to Lebe Seru, and Santiago and his men watered the mules, I
walked a way up the trail with Coalter.

We stopped at the top of a rise that afforded a view of the Brazos
river valley and gazed across the green expanse of tall trees, their
massive limbs swaying in the brisk wind. The seasons were changing
and shimmering waves of yellow, orange, and red leaves whirled
about. Coalter looked at me. "Do you remember the time, Carmen,
when we were with Father Miguel, and I would speak to you about
this place?"

I nodded, afraid that my voice would fail me if I tried to tell him
that not a day passed that I did not recall that time, the time that
was the happiest of my life.

"This is where I wanted for us to live. This is where I wanted to
build our home, Carmen. Right over there is where I wanted to build
a cabin, a place where we could live in peace and raise a family. This
is—"

"Coalter," I interrupted. "Do not speak of this. You have a home
here now. And a family. What happened years ago..."—I tried to think
of how to make him understand—"...is over. We have our own lives
now. You have yours and I have mine. The past is over, gone forever.
Do not think about it. I do not think about it."

He looked at me, and I prayed that he could not see that I was
lying. "Have you forgotten what happened between us, Carmen?"

I shrugged my shoulders as if his question was a silly one and
what had happened too insignificant to remember. I tried to maintain
my nonchalance even though I could see the pain in his face at my
response to his question.

For a while he said nothing. Then, without looking at me, he
asked, "Why did you never marry, Carmen?"

I reached for some small pieces of blue flint that had flaked off an
outcrop at the edge of the rise. "There was not time," I said, matter-of-

factly, and began to toss bits of the flint toward the valley. "After Father Miguel was...gone, I wanted to continue his struggle against Spain. Those of us who had been in Allende's army were hunted by the Spanish. We came to Texas, beyond their reach, so we could continue what Father Miguel and Father José began. And we had to fight Iturbide when the Spanish left Mexico. There has been little time for anything else. I have lived the life of a soldier and..." I stopped because a smile had crept into his face. "What? What is it?"

"Nothing," he said after scooping up more pieces of flint to hand to me. "It is just that I remember so well how you had dreamed of being a soldier, of how you wanted to conquer Texas for your king, you and Cristóbal. You did not plan to become a revolutionary. You were not a republican."

Seeing his smile warmed me, and it was impossible for me not to respond in kind. What he spoke of seemed so long ago, and it was as if he were remembering someone I did not know, this girl who wanted to be a soldier. I looked across the valley and saw tall columns of dark clouds on the northern horizon. "Your son," I said, "his name is Christopher. Did you—"

"Yes," he said. "I knew how much Cristóbal meant to you, and so I named my son for him." His eyes narrowed. "Did Cristóbal return from Spain?"

"Cristóbal was killed in Spain," I said, and before he could offer his sympathy, I added, "Your son is a fine boy, Coalter. Very brave. You must be proud of him. When we found him after he had been bitten by the snake, he—"

"Carmen," he whispered and touched my arm. "Are you happy? Are you truly happy?"

I backed away a step, startled by the abruptness of his query. "Yes, Coalter. I am happy. I have many friends here in Texas. Santiago and Pilar and their children. Lebe Seru. Maudie. Marva. Binu and Amma. The Tonkawas. They have made me a part of their families. We work very hard and—"

"But are you happy?" he repeated. There was a quiver in his voice. "Do you not feel...alone."

Certainly, I knew what he was truly asking, but to deflect his query, I said, "I am seldom alone."

"Carmen," he whispered, closing his eyes. "Sometimes, I...I feel very alone."

It would have taken very little for me to rush to his arms and tell him that he need never be alone again, so I looked back toward the others and said, "I think they are ready to go. I had better return."

"Carmen, I cannot go on like this. I think of you every moment of every day. Every single moment of the day and night I think of you! How can I continue without you?"

"You must continue," I said trying to appear happy. And I was happy. I had been granted a few precious hours with the man I loved. I well knew there might be no more. For a brief while we had been together. I was grateful. "For Rhoda and Christopher, you must continue."

"Carmen, I love you."

I so wanted to offer those same words to him in return. My heart was bursting to shout them. Instead, I pretended I did not hear what he had said and looked to the horizon. "It is best you go, Coalter. There is a storm coming. You will be at your farm before it arrives if you leave now."

He held out his hand, and it reminded me of our first meeting, of the time on the firing range at my father's hacienda when he had awkwardly offered his hand in greeting. I took his hand in mine and smiled even though I had the most awful sense that this would be the last time I would see Coalter. I think he must have felt the same way because there were tears in his eyes, and upon releasing my hand, he quickly turned, mounted, and rode his horse away without looking back.

For a long time I watched him until he disappeared over a rise. "Oh, Coalter," I whispered. "I love you. I love you so very much."

✦

It was some time before Lebe Seru was able to walk again, but gradually his strength returned, and after a while, he was anxious to resume his efforts to free more of his people held in bondage. It was only with great persuasion that we were able to convince him that Binu and Amma, along with their friends Miguel and Josefa, were able to guide runaways to safety. He spent most of his days talking with the children, teaching them about their heritage and telling them of the dream of Father Hidalgo and Father Morelos that all people were equal and deserved to live free and with dignity.

On a day of great celebration, Lebe Seru and Maudie were joined in marriage in a ceremony that also united Binu and Amma. An old priest at the Mission La Bahía in Goliad conducted the mass, and Chief Meyei performed the Tonkawan wedding ritual. Afterward, there was music, dancing, all kinds of foods to enjoy, and the children played games and ran races.

The only thing to mar this day of happiness was when Pilar received news that her childhood friend, Ursula Veramendi, the daughter of the vice-governor and James Bowie's wife, had died in a cholera outbreak. The Bowies' young son had also died. It saddened me because I remembered how happy both had been on their wedding day.

Not long after the weddings, we received more bad news. Captain Bradburn's information about Santa Anna's plans proved accurate because the Generalísimo proclaimed himself El Poder Conservador, the supreme executive power responsible to no one. In short order he dissolved the National Congress and declared null and void the Constitution of 1824. This charter followed the guidelines of the constitution written by Miguel Hidalgo and José Morelos.

Immediately, republicans throughout Mexico took up arms to defend the constitution, but Santa Anna's armies were ruthless in putting down all opposition. The people of the state of Zacatecas rose up in rebellion, only to be brutally crushed, and Santa Anna, as he had done when a lieutenant in the Spanish army, ordered all prisoners put to the sword. Some republican leaders, such as Benito Juárez, barely escaped with their lives, and others were stood before the firing squads. The leaders who survived led their forces to the mountains to begin guerrilla warfare against the tyrant.

The reaction in Texas was, at first, cautious. Stephen Austin, who had been in Mexico City during much of the turmoil, had been for a period of time imprisoned, and his colonists did not wish to do anything that might get him killed. Upon his return, however, he urged that Texans proceed with the creation of a state government separate from Coahuila. Meetings were held, a constitution was written, and a state government was born. A military force was organized under the command of Sam Houston.

In the meantime, men such as Seguín, Bowie, and Navarro prepared to take on Santa Anna in order to restore the Constitution of 1824. They were ready for a fight and Santa Anna did not disappoint them. He sent advance elements of his army across the Río Bravo and, before long, the rumor grew that the Poder Conservador himself was leading an army to punish the Texans, especially those of us who were Mexican, for disloyalty.

In the course of these events, Santiago's teamster enterprise was proving to be much in demand. Despite the political uncertainties, there was an active and growing commerce in Texas, and so there was much need for our mules and wagons. Because Lebe Seru, Santiago, and his men were increasingly involved with what Seguín and Bowie were doing in San Antonio, Pilar, Maudie, Marva, and I drove the mule teams that pulled the wagons filled with goods.

✦

One day, about a league south of the ferry crossing at Washington-on-the-Brazos, I reined my team to a halt because I heard a voice in the forest calling my name. I climbed down and asked Pilar, who was driving one of the other wagons in our train, if she had heard something too. I was about to continue on after Pilar gave me a negative answer, when a gangly, long-legged boy emerged from the woods.

It had been some time since I had seen him, but I recognized it was Christopher. He obviously had been running very hard and appeared quite distraught.

"Christopher, what's wrong?" I said taking his arm as he staggered to keep him from falling.

"It's my mother! She's very sick. Please help her, Carmen. Please!"

By this time Pilar and Maudie, driving the third wagon, climbed down to join us. "Where is your father? Has he gone for a physician?" I asked, turning back to Christopher.

"My father went to San Antonio to meet with Juan Seguín and Jim Bowie. My mother was fine when he left. But all of a sudden, she became very sick!"

While Pilar and Maudie followed with the teams, I raced ahead with Christopher to the farm.

Inside the little log cabin, I found Rhoda on her bed. Though it was a warm day, she was wrapped in quilts and blankets, and yet she was still shivering.

When she saw me, she smiled and whispered, "Carmen, you've come. My prayer has been answered."

Placing my hand to her head, I resisted an impulse to pull away, not only because she was so hot, but because she looked so very sick. There was no color in her gaunt face, and her eyes, though smiling, were flat and unfocused.

"Rhoda," I asked, "are you in pain?"

She smiled at Christopher, who was anxiously standing behind us. "Son, could I please talk to Carmen in private?"

The confusion in Christopher's eyes reminded me of his father. Though no longer a little boy, he still had the innocence of a child. He looked at me and then left the room. I could hear the wagons outside and was glad Pilar and Maudie were with me. I started to get up so I could summon them and together we could devise some way of helping Rhoda, but when I did, Rhoda grasped my hand.

"Carmen, please. Stay with me."

"I'll go for a physician," I said urgently. "There's one at Washington-on-the-Brazos."

"No, Carmen, please. A physician cannot help me. Please stay with me and talk to me for a while. You never came to visit me. I so wanted you to come, but you would not."

"Rhoda, please," I implored, "let me go for a physician!"

She was weak, and I could have pulled away, but there was something in her eyes that compelled me to remain with her.

"I want to thank you, Carmen."

"Thank me? Why?"

She smiled. "I know why you did not come to see me. I know that you avoided Coalter all these years. You allowed me to keep my husband."

Of course, this made me most uncomfortable and I wanted to pull away. I could not.

"Rhoda," I said and tried to think of something to alter her train of thought. "You should rest."

"I know Coalter is in love with you."

"Rhoda, please."

"Do not be ashamed, Carmen. It is wonderful. I want you to be happy that he loves you and that you love him."

"He loves you, Rhoda. You are his wife."

"I know he does, Carmen," she said and raised her head slightly. Quickly, I adjusted the pillow so she could be more comfortable. "I know he loves me, but not in the way he loves you. I knew something had happened when he returned from New Spain after he had been wounded. I suspected he had met someone. He never spoke of anyone; he never spoke of you, and so I assumed that person had died."

Through the small window near her bed, I could see that Pilar and Maudie were consoling Christopher.

"Coalter and I grew up together. We thought we were in love, but when Coalter went to New Spain, I met another young man and realized that what Coalter and I had was a deep friendship, not love."

What Rhoda was telling me seemed very private, and I started to tell her it was not something she should be sharing with me.

But she raised her hand to silence me. "I was in love with this young man, Carmen, just as you and Coalter are in love. And I would have married him except..."—her smile faded—"...he was like me. He was suited for another time, another place. Louisiana was too much for him, just as Texas has been too much for me, and he died.

"When Coalter came back from New Spain, I was in mourning for my young man. I was happy to be Coalter's friend, and for several years, that is what we were, friends, pure and simple. With the passing of time, I think we began to feel that we were fated to marry. We were lonely and there was an affection between us. I knew I did not love him like I did my young man, and he never spoke of you, Carmen."

I cleared my throat. "He thought I was dead, just as I thought he had been killed."

"I see," she said and nodded. "Now I understand. And when you came to Texas and discovered him, neither of you knew what to do. Coalter was married to me, and he had a son."

All I could do was shrug. My voice failed me.

Squeezing my hand even harder, she said, "I wish we could have been friends, Carmen. I liked you from the very beginning." Her eyes wandered to the window, "This land, this...this Texas, it is a hard place and can be cruel. It has defeated me, but it cannot defeat you. You are too strong for it! You are at home here just like that mockingbird in the tree out there."

"Rhoda, it is your home too."

"No, dear Carmen," she said, shaking her head. "I am going to my home now. I am—"

"No!" I said firmly, realizing what she was saying. I did not want her to die, and I think, perhaps, I thought I could prevent it through an act of will. "You must—"

"Carmen," she interrupted and, with great effort, raised herself forward. "Listen to me. Listen! Coalter is in great danger. I want you to go to him. I want you to..."—she coughed and struggled for breath— "I want you to remove him from this danger."

"Danger? What do you mean?"

"He has gone to San Antonio de Béxar. Seguín and Bowie are planning to hold the Alamo against Santa Anna. It cannot be done."

"No," I said, alarmed at what she was revealing. "It cannot be done. They cannot hold the Alamo! Santa Anna's army will be far too big."

"Go there, Carmen. Convince them of the futility of what they are trying to do. And"—she held my arm, as I had begun to rise from the bed—"promise me, Carmen. Promise me you will marry Coalter and protect him." Her voice was growing weaker. "Protect him and...and protect my son. Protect my son."

"Rhoda, you will get better. You will—"

"Promise me," she insisted, pulling me to her. "Christopher will soon be a young man, but in many ways, he is still a boy. Because of my illnesses, I have kept him at my side over the years and he is not strong. There are many things about the cruelty of this world he does not understand, and it may be hard for him to survive. I want you to think of him as your son."

I did not know what to say to this. I wanted to argue with her, but I could see that she was dying. I had seen too many people die, not to realize what was happening.

"Promise me," she whispered. "Dear Carmen, promise me."

"I promise," I managed to say.

There was a smile on her face as she embraced me and then relaxed back on the pillow. "And now, please, ask my son to come in. I must...I must tell him to be a good boy."

After Christopher returned to the cabin, I told Pilar and Maudie what Rhoda had said about Coalter. Both were distraught at the news of what was happening in San Antonio de Béxar. Lebe Seru and Santiago had gone there with Coalter.

Presently, Christopher came to the porch, and I knew from his expression his mother was gone. We comforted him.

Pilar and Maudie prepared the body for burial, while I helped Christopher dig a grave near the redbud tree in the yard. Maudie read from the Bible, and we all recited the Our Father.

Christopher, of course, was devastated, but he wanted to go with me to San Antonio de Béxar when I told him I was going for his father. Rhoda had asked me to protect her son, and I was determined to do just that, so I insisted that he stay. Pilar and Maudie said they would remain with him until I returned.

I selected a mare from the corral, a jennet like the one I had owned as a girl, and saddled her. It was the first time in many years that I had ridden anything but a mule. Everything depended on this little horse. It was over a hundred leagues to San Antonio de Béxar. I prayed I would get there before Santa Anna's army, for I knew it would be impossible for a few hundred men, however brave or able, to hold out for long in the old mission called the Alamo.

XIV

Before reaching San Antonio de Béxar, I could hear the unmistakable sounds of an army being positioned for battle: the movement of horses, the creak and groan of caissons being maneuvered from place to place, the bugle's urgent blast, the dirgelike music of military bands played to advance or retreat infantry, grenadiers and dragoons. And when I urged my tired little jennet to the crest of a hill that afforded a view of the city, I was able to see that the walled mission, the Alamo, was already under siege by a force of at least five thousand men deployed in the streets, behind buildings and houses, and in the fields that had, only days before, been tranquil pastures for cows, goats, and sheep.

Smoke from hundreds of campfires hung over the city like a burial shroud. Gazing down, I saw gun emplacements, including several 18-pounders, in the yard behind the stone walls of the mission where the republicans had chosen to make their stand. Hanging from a flagstaff mounted over the chapel was the red, white, and green banner of the Mexican republic on which had been printed, in the white field, the date "1824." It was a way of announcing to Santa Anna that the men who were barricaded behind the mission's brooding walls were there for the purpose of defending the Constitution of 1824. All I could think of at that moment was that behind those walls was the man I loved and that I must take him from this place.

Knowing that a person on horseback might draw attention, I freed the winded horse and made my way on foot toward the mission.

Among the soldiers were a good many townspeople of San Antonio—
some vending food and beverages, others simply curious onlookers—
and, since I was dressed in my usual white cotton pants and shirt,
indistinguishable from what most were wearing, it was not difficult to
mingle with them. I simply walked straight ahead through the ranks.

The soldiers, for the most part, were standing about like soldiers
in all armies: smoking tobacco while awaiting orders to again move to
another position where they would wait some more and speculate on
who would or would not live to see another day. Several glanced at
me as I walked by, and if their gaze lingered too long, I would crane
my neck, shade my eyes with my hand, and pretend I was looking for
someone just ahead.

The front lines, facing the mission walls, were beyond the range
of the republicans' long-rifles I could now see on the ramparts. This
meant I had to cross a stretch of field in the open. How was I going to
negotiate this feat without being shot by Santa Anna's soldiers or the
republicans at the mission I did not know. And then I saw a flock of
chickens near the base of a section of wall not over five feet high, a
wall which I thought I might be able to vault without much trouble.
Oblivious to the commotion around them, the chickens were scratch-
ing in the dirt for insects and bits of shell and gravel. This gave me an
idea.

I had gone only a few feet when I heard a voice behind me shout:
"You! Stop!"

Turning, I saw a burly fellow with a corporal's stripes on the
frayed sleeves of his dirt-caked uniform fashioned from unbleached
cotton.

"Where do you think you're going?" the corporal demanded.

Gesturing toward the wall, I said, "My chickens, Señor. I must
get my chickens."

"Your chickens?" the corporal asked and looked at several of his
comrades who, busy rolling tobacco, were taking but casual notice of
what was happening.

"Yes, Señor," I said in a tone that might indicate I was none too
bright. "I must get my chickens and take them home so they can lay

their eggs and my husband will not beat me. The chickens will only lay their eggs in our yard and—"

The men started laughing.

The corporal, who did not laugh, seemed suspicious. "Get back over here!"

"But my chickens, Señor," I said and again began moving toward the Alamo. "I must get my chickens. They do not know where to lay their eggs. *Pobrecitas*, poor little things, they are very confused."

"You fool!" the corporal shouted. "The Texicanos will shoot you!"

This was exactly my next worry as I quickened my pace and continued toward the wall. Soon, I was out of range of the soldiers' muskets, but within range of the more powerful long-rifles that were now trained on me as I drew ever closer to the wall. I could see the men holding them, and I searched their faces, hoping I would see Coalter, Santiago, or Lebe Seru.

But the men on this low wall were an unfamiliar lot. Most were bewhiskered and dressed in animal skin clothing. They were rough-looking men, but they held their fire as I raised my hands to signal I carried no weapon. I walked right up to the wall.

"Who are you and what do you want?" a tall, hawk-nosed fellow asked in English. Though the eyes beneath his bushy brows were fierce, I detected a slight smile on his lips as if he were just a little amused to see someone simply walk up to their heavily defended position.

"My name," I said in English, "is María del Carmen Rangel. I have come to speak with Coalter Owens."

"Coalter Owens?" the tall man asked. He looked to his right at a man dressed in similar garb and with a racoon skin cap on his head. "Do we know a Coalter Owens?"

The man replied, "I believe he was one of the boys who came in with Juan Seguín, Colonel Crockett."

Crockett looked at me and asked, "Is this Coalter Owens with Juan Seguín?"

"Yes," I replied. When no one said anything more, I glanced behind at the soldiers who were probably now wondering why I was talking to the Texans rather than herding my flock of chickens away from the wall. I looked at the tall man. "Can I come over the wall? I need to speak with Coalter Owens. It is urgent."

Crockett's smile broadened and his eyes softened. This was the face of a man who was used to smiling, though it was also the face of a man who had faced adversity. He extended his arm and said, "All right by me, Señorita. Come on over. The more the merrier."

I took his hand, which was strong and calloused, and swung myself over the wall. At the exact moment I landed on the other side, I heard the sound of muskets being fired. Looking back over the wall, I saw that the burly corporal had ordered his men to fire. Instinctively, I lowered my head.

"Don't bother, ma'am," Crockett said as he leaned on the rifle that was almost as long as I am tall. "We're out of their range. They're just wasting ammunition." And then, as if he had just remembered his manners, he removed his narrow-brimmed straw sombrero and bowed. "My name is David Crockett, Señorita Rangel. Me and the boys here"—he gestured to the men stationed along the wall—"hail from Tennessee."

I scanned this motley crew, all of whom had magnificent rifles, and then I looked at Crockett. "You are from Tennessee? Why are you in Texas?"

"Well, ma'am," Crockett said and scratched at his scraggly beard streaked with lines of grey. "We were on our way to Californy to hunt b'ars, but we took a wrong turn up at the Sabine and wound up down here with the wrong Béxar."

One of the men said, "You never could read a map, Davy."

This evoked a round of laughter and when it died, Crockett shouted, "Hell boys, what do you expect? I served almost a full term in the Congress. By the time I escaped out of there, I damn near couldn't read my own name!" He looked at me and said, "Pardon my language, ma'am."

"Davy?" one of the men drawled, "I think I can hit that feller over thar."

We all looked over the wall, and I could see the corporal had foolishly led his men within range of the long-rifles, though we were still way beyond the range of their muskets.

"Yep," Crockett said matter-of-factly, "I do believe you could hit that ol' boy, Jeremiah."

"Want me to shoot 'im, Davy?" Jeremiah said and slowly raised his rifle to aim.

Crockett appeared to study the situation, and then he shrugged and said, "Naw, don't shoot 'im. Hell, in a couple days, we'll probably be over at one of them cantinas 'cross the river there, and that feller'll buy us a drink of some of that thar distilled cactus water. And then we'll buy him a drink of Tennessee sippin' whiskey. You can't go 'round shootin' a feller you plan to drink spirits with, can you, Jeremiah? Wouldn't be Christian, would it?"

"Reckon not, Davy," Jeremiah said and lowered his rifle.

Looking at me, Crockett said, "As you can see, Señorita Rangel, old Santy Anny's pert' much got us outnumbered. Couple more days and we'll probably surrender, shake hands, and go swap a few lies down at the cantina." His smile was genuine. It was the smile of a kind and decent man. "That's what I figure is going to happen here. What do you think?"

I sensed that, behind his casual demeanor, this Crockett was worried and he was asking me, a stranger, for my assessment of the situation. Desperate men will grasp at any new perspective. I saw no reason to lie. Pointing beyond the mission, across the river at the San Fernando cathedral, I drew the men's attention to a long, blood red banner that had been raised on a pole at the top of the tall church structure. It had been the first thing I had noticed upon arrival in the city.

"Do you know what that flag means, Señor Crockett?"

He ventured, "Santy Anny's battle flag?"

"It is not a battle flag," I explained. "In medieval times, when the Spanish were at war with the Moors, the red flag meant that no surrender would be accepted and no prisoners were to be taken."

The expression on Crockett's face turned somber.

"Many years ago," I continued, "the republicans fought a Spanish army south of Béxar. We lost. Santa Anna was a young officer in the Spanish army, and he was given the task of killing all prisoners. It was a task he accomplished with dispatch." I surveyed the faces around me. No one was laughing now. "I do not know who made the decision to defend this place, Señor Crockett, but it was not a wise decision."

At that moment, several men came running toward us. At first, I thought I must be mistaken because I was certain I recognized the man in the lead as William Travis, the attorney we had encountered at Anahuac, the same man John Bradburn had placed under arrest in order to facilitate our escape.

"Crockett!" Travis yelled. "What the hell is going on here? What was that gunfire about? Is this another one of your barnyard jokes? I've warned you about that."

The Tennessean's bemused smile returned to his lips. As he explained what had happened, I suspected that he was not an admirer of Travis. I was astounded, when Crockett introduced us, to learn that Travis was in command of the Alamo.

Turning to me, Travis doffed his hat, started to speak, and then narrowed his eyes. "Do I know you, Señorita?" he asked in English. "You look familiar."

I refreshed his memory.

For a moment, he appeared to be puzzled, but his attention was elsewhere. "Have you just arrived in San Antonio? From where did you come?" When I told him, he anxiously inquired, "Have you seen Sam Houston's army? Is he on the way here?"

I told him I had seen no army.

Travis glanced at Crockett and then back at me. "What about Seguín? Did you encounter Juan Seguín on your way here?"

"I thought Juan Seguín was here." Knowing that Coalter would be with Seguín and Santiago, I was suddenly hopeful that he was not in this place after all. "Is he not here?"

"No," Travis said "I sent Seguín to look for Houston. It is imperative that we be reinforced."

"Damn it to hell, Travis!" Crockett exploded. "You knew Houston sent orders to Bowie not to try to defend the Alamo! Houston wanted us to leave here before Santa Anna arrived in Béxar. Nobody's coming here to reinforce us. Not Houston, not Fannin, not nobody!"

An argument ensued between Travis and Crockett. There was apparent between them a marked difference of opinion as to the object of their mission. Travis thought he was to hold the Alamo until Sam Houston could arrive and engage Santa Anna's army. Crockett believed Houston planned to draw Santa Anna deeper into Texas and fight a war of attrition with the assistance of volunteers from the United States. Crockett's mention of Bowie returned my focus to why I had come.

"Did Bowie go with Seguín?" I asked, looking from Travis to Crockett and back. I knew Seguín and Bowie were friends, and it seemed logical that Santiago, Coalter, and Lebe Seru would go with Seguín and Bowie to look for Houston.

"Colonel Bowie is ill, Señorita," Travis said. "He is in the chapel."

Looking toward the chapel, my hopes were dashed because, at that moment, emerging from the side-door of the chapel, came Santiago, followed by Coalter and Lebe Seru. They had not gone with Juan Seguín. Travis and Crockett continued to argue as I rushed toward the chapel. My heart was heavy. How was I to tell the man I loved that his wife was dead? More than that, I was sickened by the realization that he had not left with Seguín but had remained in this doomed place.

From the instant Coalter saw me, he seemed to sense the reason I was there. He came to me and whispered my name. Lebe Seru and Santiago, too, must have suspected I brought bad news because they greeted me quietly and asked no questions. Taking Coalter by the arm, I led him to the mission garden on the north side of the chapel. We stopped near a lattice bearing the weight of twisting bougainvillaea vines, some of which were sprouting shiny new buds.

"It's Rhoda," Coalter said softly and lowered his eyes. "She's—"

I touched my fingers to his lips so that he would not have to say the words. For a moment, I tried to hold back, to do nothing but be there for him in this time of grief, but when he looked at me and I saw the tears in his eyes, I embraced him and held him tightly in my arms. I placed my head against his chest and could feel his heart beat. For a moment I thought I might melt in the warmth of my happiness at finally being held by the man whose life was my joy, my reason for being.

He whispered, "Christopher?"

Drawing back, I explained that Christopher was with Pilar and Maudie. They would care for him. I noticed Crockett and Travis, who were still in heated debate, walk across the yard and enter the chapel, presumably to confer with James Bowie.

Coalter said hoarsely, "I was not a good husband to Rhoda."

"That is not true," I said quickly. "I talked with her before she....She said you were a very good husband."

"What else did she say, Carmen?"

It did not seem appropriate to tell him everything Rhoda had said. There was, however, one thing she had requested that I had every intention of honoring. "She wanted me to take you home, Coalter. That is why I have come. I am going to take you back to your son. We will leave when it darkens." I looked to the sky. It was late in the afternoon. Already, I had formulated a plan of escape. While on the rise above Béxar, I had seen how Santa Anna's troops were deployed and had studied the lay of the land. "I think Santa Anna will attack tonight."

I started to explain how I had derived this conclusion when I noticed a peculiar expression in Coalter's eyes.

"What?" I asked. "What's wrong?"

"You will leave, Carmen. But I must stay."

"Stay?" I asked, thinking perhaps I had misunderstood. We were speaking in English, and there were times when I could not decipher certain words in this still unfamiliar language. "You cannot stay. You will be killed. Everyone in this terrible place will be killed!"

His silence and the way he looked at me confirmed that he understood the truth of what I had said.

"Coalter!" I said, suddenly frightened by what I suspected. "No! I will not allow it. I will not let you stay here and be killed. I will not allow it!"

"It has to be, Carmen. Santa Anna is destroying everything we struggled for, everything Father Hidalgo began that night in Dolores. We must hold out as long as we can. Houston is raising an army to the east and he needs time. We must give him that time, and we must weaken Santa Anna's army so that he will be defeated when he meets Houston."

Though I grasped the logic of such a strategy, I knew the sacrifice it entailed. "No," I repeated. "I will not let you die. I..."—it was now possible for me to say what I had longed to tell him since I had discovered he was alive—"...I love you, Coalter! I've never stopped loving you. I cannot lose you now! I cannot lose you again! I love you!"

"And I love you, Carmen," he said, taking my hands in his. "I always have." He lowered his eyes. "But you could not respect me if I did not fight for what is right."

"Fight for what is right? Coalter, there are men here, men like Travis and Bowie who have bought and sold slaves! What is happening here has nothing to do with what Father Hidalgo began in Dolores. He opposed slavery. He believed in freedom and equality! How can you fight here? How can Santiago and Lebe Seru fight here?"

"We are not fighting for Travis or Bowie, Carmen. We are fighting for the Constitution of 1824." His eyes drifted to the banner over the chapel on which had been crudely written the date "1824." "There are many men here like Santiago and Lebe Seru who fought the Spanish and, later, Iturbide. They have struggled many years for what Hidalgo and Morelos believed. Our brothers in Zacatecas fought Santa Anna and thousands were killed. We can not let men like Juárez carry the fight alone. If we are ever to have a chance to realize Father Miguel's dream, we must defeat this tyrant."

For a moment, I could not marshall my thoughts and then something occurred to me that might change his mind. I had to change his mind. "Coalter," I asked, "do you remember when we were at Mexico City with Father Miguel? The time when we surrounded the capital, and it looked as though a great battle would be waged. Do you remember?"

"I remember."

"What did Father Miguel do?"

He was puzzled, unable to fathom what I was asking.

"He withdrew from Mexico City without a fight," I said in answer to my own query. "Father Miguel withdrew in order that lives would be spared. He retreated from a victory so that people would live, not die. General Allende could have won the battle and taken Mexico City. Father Miguel would have presided over the greatest empire the world has ever known. But for it to happen many people would have been killed as happened at Guanajuato. Do you not recall? I was angry that Father Miguel withdrew, but now I understand." I gripped both of his hands tightly. "He retreated without a fight because what he began at Dolores that night was about more than liberty and equality. It was about more than independence for Mexico. It was about those things, but also about much more.

"Don't you see, Coalter? Father Miguel's revolution was about something far more precious." For a moment, I closed my eyes, and I could see the priest's smiling face when we were prisoners together in the corral during those days after the defeat of Allende's army. "Coalter, just before Father Miguel was killed, he told me that we should call no man on this earth father. We have only one father. We have the same father. He said that when we accept that as the truth, we can no longer enslave one another or hate one another. That is what Father Miguel wanted us to realize."

Coalter smiled, but I could see he was not convinced.

"Our army," I continued, "Father Miguel's army, did not march under that banner." I pointed to the flag above the Alamo chapel. "Do you remember? Our banner did not represent liberty or equality. It did not represent Mexico. Do you remember our banner? Do you remember the banner that was carried ahead of our army from one end of Mexico to the other?"

"It was the banner of the *Virgen de Guadalupe*."

"Yes. The banner of total and complete surrender to Divine Providence. The banner of love. I believe Father Miguel chose that banner because he wanted us to understand that we all have only one father, the same father. That is why he withdrew from Mexico City. His revolution cannot be won by killing our brothers and sisters. Nothing can be achieved by killing. We must leave this place, Coalter. To win

Father Miguel's revolution, we must live, not die. Do you understand?"

Gently, he touched my face with his fingers. He shook his head and lowered his eyes. "I want to leave here with you, Carmen. I do. I want to spend my life with you. I've never wanted anything more than that. But I cannot leave here. I cannot. Please forgive me."

My words were to no avail. I could see there was nothing I could say to dissuade him. His resolve was firm. I drew a deep breath and said, "Very well, Coalter." I tried to force a smile. "If that is the way it must be, we will stay. We will die together."

Now, it was his turn to be alarmed. "No, Carmen. You must leave! There is a way that you can escape. I know a man who can help. He will be able to..."

Coalter's voiced trailed when Travis and Crockett emerged from the chapel and approached us. Travis looked at me and said, "Señorita Rangel, Colonel Bowie would like to see you."

Surprised that Bowie would wish to see me at a time such as this, I looked at Coalter and then got to my feet.

At the doorway to the chapel Coalter said, "Bowie is distraught, Carmen. He lost his wife and son recently."

"I know that," I remarked, then I added, "Are you not coming with me?"

Coalter looked toward Santiago and Lebe Seru, who had rejoined us. "No. There is...something we must take care of."

Bowie was on a cot inside a small thick-walled room in the chapel. When I entered, he raised himself slightly, and I drew back at the sight. The first time I met him I thought he had the coldest eyes I had ever seen, but at least then, he was happy; he had just married. Now he looked angry, and he had the eyes of a killer. There was an open bottle of liquor on a small table to the right of his cot. Also on the table was a long-blade knife next to a flickering beeswax candle and a worn leather-bound copy of the Bible. It was dark in the small room and as damp as the inside of a mausoleum. And it was cold, the coldness of death.

"Who is it?" Bowie demanded.

Stepping closer into the faint candlelight, I said, "It's me, Bowie. Carmen Rangel."

At once, the eyes softened. "Carmen!" he said, pronouncing my name in a way that indicated he was genuinely happy to see me. "Please, come closer. My eyes, I'm afraid they are no longer so good."

His eyes were swollen and bloodshot, the eyes I had seen of men who drank too much alcohol. I extended my hand when he offered his. It was moist and hot, and his grip was weak like that of an old man.

Holding onto my hand, he began to tremble. "Carmen, I lost my wife. Did you know? Did you hear? I lost Ursula."

"Yes, Bowie. I know. I am sorry."

He was struggling for his breath, and he looked aimlessly about the bare chamber, which had but a simple wooden crucifix mounted on the wall above the bed.

"I loved her so much. Why did she have to die? Is it because I am an evil man? Is that why she died?" He fastened his gaze on me. "I remember how you told me I was evil because I sold slaves. Is that why Ursula had to die? It is because I am evil? I am being punished because I am evil?"

"I do not know, Bowie. I am not a priest."

Exhausted, he fell back on the pillow which was soaking wet with perspiration. "I am being punished," he said with a sigh of resignation as he let go of my hand. "And soon I will die. We are all going to die in here."

"Yes," I said as much to myself as to this broken man. The prospect did not frighten me. As long as I died with the man I loved, it did not matter. "We will all die here."

"That fool Travis!" Bowie shouted. "Houston ordered us out of this place. Travis ignored the order, and now we are all going to die!"

I hated to see him so agitated, and hoping to calm him down, I said, "Sooner or later, Bowie, all people die."

"That fool Travis," Bowie repeated, ignoring me. "He dreams of the glory of being the one to defeat Santa Anna. It's his vanity that got us in this hopeless situation!" He looked at me and began to laugh, a cynical, bitter laugh. "And Santa Anna, it's his vanity that has kept him here. If he did not have the need to defeat us, he would have gone around us days ago and engaged Houston before he had time to build his army. He knows better than to think we could stop him. We are barely a hundred men. We could do nothing in the open field to an army of six thousand men!" He laughed harder. "Travis and Santa Anna, they're two vain roosters, and they are both going to be defeated because of their vanity. They are two of a kind: two vain roosters! *¡Dos gallos!*"

I smiled at the image that came to mind of two strutting roosters. I recalled the time Teresa had called me a *juana gallo* and I had chased her with a pitchfork. It occurred to me that very soon I would see my cousin again. I would see Teresa and Rubén. It was a pleasant thought.

"King David spoke the truth," Bowie whispered, becoming serious again, his eyes distant. "Every man at his best state is altogether vanity." He then focused on me as if he had just become aware I was in the room. "You should not be here! You must leave. Everybody in this place will die!"

I tried to think of something to say to ease this troubled man's mind.

Staring vacantly at the walls again, Bowie asked, "Did you know that my Ursula died? Did you know? Did you hear?"

"Yes, Bowie. You told me."

"Why did Ursula have to die? For the first time in my life, I was happy. Why did she have to die? Why?"

Why indeed, I thought. Why did Ursula have to die? Why did Rhoda die? Why did Teresa and Rubén die? Anselmo? Alamar? Captain Guerra? Why did a gentle and compassionate man, a man of greatness, like Miguel Hidalgo, have to die? Why did Allende and Morelos die? Why did any of these people have to die, and why were many good people about to die in this place, probably within hours? People had been asking Bowie's question since the dawn of time. I did not have an answer, but I saw that he was watching me, waiting for me to say something. I tried to smile and then I said, "What I think, Bowie, is..."—my smile became genuine—"...I think that soon you will see Ursula again."

He raised his head. "I will see Ursula?"

"I think you will, Bowie. She's waiting for you. Ursula is waiting for you. She is waiting with your son."

Somehow, my words seemed to help. He lay back on the cot and closed his eyes. When I thought he had fallen asleep, I crept out of the room and left the chapel.

The moment I stepped outside, I felt hands on my arms. I was immobilized, unable to defend myself, before I could even see who was doing this or why. I thought perhaps Santa Anna had already taken the mission. Finally, twisting about, I saw that my attackers were Coalter, Santiago, and Lebe Seru. At once, I knew what they were doing as they gently, but firmly, began to lead me toward the east wall.

At the wall, Coalter embraced me. "Carmen," he said, "I am sorry we have to do this, but I cannot allow you to be killed. We are going to turn you over to a man I trust. He is a good man. You will stay with him until..."—he glanced at Lebe Seru and Santiago— "...until the battle is over."

The shock of what was happening tightened my throat and stole away my voice. I tried to convey with my expression that I did not want this. I wanted to stay with him. My life meant nothing if I could not be with him. He was the only reason I wanted to live. If he had to die, I wanted to die with the man I loved. I could not lose him again.

Coalter kissed my lips gently and looked into my eyes. He smiled that boyish smile of his, but there was sorrow in his expression, great sorrow. "Please remember that I have always loved you, Carmen."

Santiago drew near. "Carmen," he said, "Please convey my love to Pilar. Tell Miguel and Josefa I am proud of them." He drew a deep breath. "You are a brave soldier, María del Carmen Rangel. I am glad we were in the same army." He stepped back. "Viva Hidalgo!"

And then Lebe Seru was at my side. If anyone would understand, I thought, it would be my old friend, the man who had saved my life and guided me to Texas. But he did not offer to help. He said, "Tell Maudie that I love her, Carmen. Tell Binu and Amma, my son and my daughter, that I love them." He smiled. "Farewell, Carmen, my friend, my dear and true friend." His eyes welled with tears. "Viva Hidalgo!"

"Lebe Seru," I managed to whisper hoarsely. "Please, Lebe Seru. I beg you! I must stay. You know I must stay!"

They lifted me over the wall, and I could feel hands grasping me on the other side. I had one final glimpse of Coalter, and then I was being hurried away across the field. Looking to the left and to the right, I saw three men, all of whom were dressed in the uniforms of Santa Anna's army. One had a sergeant's stripes on his sleeve. Incredibly, Coalter had turned me over to soldiers in Santa Anna's army!

It all happened so quickly I was disoriented. Very soon, we were behind the lines, and I saw soldiers watching me as I was half-carried by the sergeant toward the river. Somehow, an arrangement had been made to allow my escape. Men who would soon be killing one another had managed to cooperate to allow a woman to be removed from the field of battle. If they could cooperate to do such a thing, why could they not find a way to avoid killing each other.

We crossed a bridge over the river and soon were near the tents which, because they were surrounded with banners and flags, I assumed were the headquarters of Santa Anna and his general staff. The sergeant, a round-faced and balding man, thanked the two men who had assisted him and they left us alone.

"I am sorry," the sergeant said, "if we hurt you. It was not our intention."

Looking back in the direction we had come, I saw the Alamo in the distance, and immediately I began to calculate how I would make it back. I was not going spend the battle in Santa Anna's camp. I knew that Coalter had arranged for me to be taken away because he loved me, but he did not understand that I could not go on without him. I would find a way to go back. This sergeant could not watch me all the time, and soon it would be dark. I would find a way to go back before the battle began.

"Do you not remember me?" the sergeant asked.

The man did look vaguely familiar. "Why should I remember you?"

He smiled. "When we were children, I was in love with you, Carmen Rangel. But you never noticed me. Do you not remember? When the fiestas were held at the Hacienda de Abrantes, I would come with the other servants from the Hacienda de Sestos. Several times, your cousin, Teresa, asked if you would go with me to—"

"Héctor Sandoval!" I said. He had certainly changed, but I could see the eager smile of the young man who played the guitar when Teresa sang. "You were Héctor Sandoval!"

He laughed. "I still am!"

It had been many years since I had seen this man who, of course, was a boy then. "Héctor, you...you are in Santa Anna's army?"

He explained that he had fought with Father Morelos and then Guerrero. I recalled how Santa Anna had played a role in overthrowing his mentor, Iturbide, and opened the way for the republican Victoria to serve as president and, later for Guerrero. It was all very complicated, but Héctor spoke as if he admired Santa Anna.

While he talked, I looked toward the ornate tents where many guards were stationed near the colorful battle flags whipping in the wind. A plan began to take shape in my mind.

"Héctor," I said, "is that Santa Anna's tent?"

Glancing back, he said, "Yes, it is the general's tent."

"Then I must talk to him," I said and started toward the tent.

Quickly, he blocked my way. "The general is asleep."

"Asleep?"

"Yes. He always takes a nap before a battle begins. It is his custom. Why would you wish to see him?"

"I must talk to Santa Anna, Héctor. I must convince him to give up this war and talk with the men in the Alamo. And then he must talk with Sam Houston. There will be great bloodshed if they do not talk. He must make a compromise with men like Seguín and Houston. He must talk with Navarro, Zavala, and Austin. There need not be bloodshed. Moreover..."—I paused to give my words greater effect— "...if Santa Anna meets Houston in battle, he will be defeated."

Héctor's eyes narrowed. "What do you mean? Our army is bigger. How could we be defeated?"

"Héctor," I said and drew closer. "Sam Houston will defeat Santa Anna. Houston has men with long-rifles, men who have used those rifles since they were boys. And look at your soldiers." I gestured toward the infantry around us. "Most are boys. They are farmboys armed with muskets left behind by the Spanish. And they are far away from home. They don't know Texas. Men like Juan Seguín know this land and how to make it their ally. Their fathers and their grandfathers lived here. They will defeat Santa Anna if he goes deeper into Texas."

For a moment, I thought Héctor might be weighing my words and would go to his sleeping general. But then his smile returned. "We will not be defeated, Carmen." He shrugged. "Besides, it is too late. Once the Presidente has made up his mind, it cannot be changed."

"Let me talk to him."

Gently, he took my arm and led me away from the tents. "I cannot, Carmen. He might have you shot. He thinks the *mexicanos* in Texas who side with the *norteamericanos* are traitors. I promised Coalter Owens that I would protect you. I cannot let you be shot."

"You know Coalter?"

"When Bowie asked the Presidente that the women in the Alamo be allowed to leave, Coalter was one of those who met with us to make the arrangements. He and the man called Crockett. They are good men. There are many good men in the Alamo. It is a shame they have to die."

We had proceeded away from the main camp and were nearing another. I heard the voices of men cheering in the camp we were approaching. I strained to see what was causing the commotion. When I looked back at Héctor, he was smiling more broadly than ever. There was an oddness in his expression.

"Héctor, why are you looking at me like that?"

"I think there is someone here that you should meet."

His tone was cryptic. "Someone I should meet? I do not understand. Who?"

Ignoring my query, he led me closer to the camp and, soon, I was able to see that the soldiers, some two or three hundred of them, had formed a large circle and were cheering a rider who was in the process of showing off his equestrian skills.

At first, my attention was not on the rider. I assumed that it was a case of soldiers trying to find a way to take their minds off the impending battle. Waiting for the battle to begin was always the hardest thing for a soldier. Anything was better than spending endless hours wondering if you were about to die or if you were going to disgrace yourself and be a coward in battle. Since the beginning of time, soldiers had found such ways to pass their time before the fighting began.

However, as I watched this rider, I began to have a very strange feeling. The rider was good, extraordinarily good. Folding his arms to his chest, he was guiding a galloping horse through a series of complex maneuvers by flexing the muscles of his long legs. Only the most accomplished of horsemen could do such a thing. The soldiers were cheering their admiration and respect for the rider's skills. I, too, appreciated what I was seeing. In fact, I could not take my eyes off this rider.

"He and the horse are of one mind," I whispered and then I remembered the only time I had ever seen a horse ridden with such skill and precision. "Truly, he is a dragoon."

"No," Héctor said. "Not a dragoon. And not a he."

Without taking my eyes from the magnificent sight of rare perfection being demonstrated with such eloquence before our eyes, I asked, "What are you saying? I do not understand."

"The rider, Carmen, is not a man."

I looked closer and could see that, indeed, the rider was not a man. The person riding the horse was a woman, a tall and slender woman, her hair tucked inside the crown of a black, flat-brimmed sombrero. And then I saw the color of her hair. Her hair was the golden red tint of the morning sun. I had only known two people who had hair that color. Stunned by what came to my mind, I brought my hand to my mouth.

"Yes," Héctor said to my unasked question when I turned to him. "It is her."

I felt dizzy, as though I might fall. "It cannot be!"

"Do you wish to know her name?"

My voice was gone, but I nodded.

"Cata Valeria." He pointed at a young officer standing not far from us. "And there is her husband, Lieutenant Arturo de Sestos."

I glanced at the handsome young officer who was cheering louder than any of the soldiers around him as Cata Valeria brought the horse, a magnificent black destrier, to an abrupt halt and leapt from its back. She landed gracefully and ran to the lieutenant who swept her off her feet and swung her through the air while executing a brisk dance step. She was laughing and telling her husband all about the ride. When I heard the sound of her voice, I was reminded immediately of Teresa. She had the same lovely voice as my cousin.

"When I returned to Guanajuato," Héctor said, "and went to visit your aunt at the Hacienda de Abrantes, I knew from the moment I saw Cata Valeria, even when she was a little girl, that she was Carmen Rangel's daughter. No one told me. They did not have to betray the secret. I knew she was your daughter."

I bit my lip. What was happening seemed like a dream. It could not be real.

"As the years passed," he continued, "and I watched her grow, I realized you were not the daughter of Baldemar Rangel. You were Don Esteban's daughter. No one told me, but this, also, I knew."

Even had I been inclined to prolong the lie, I could not. It was too apparent. I could not believe how much she looked like Cristóbal. She was, of course, a woman, and she was beautiful, as beautiful as any woman I had ever seen, but she had Cristóbal's coloring. More than that, she carried herself like him. She had his grace of movement, the kind of easy agility that sometimes made it seem that he was about to slip the restraints that bound mere mortals to the earth. To me, he had been like a Greek god, invincible and majestic. He had been the great Alexander. And now, before me, was a proud and enigmatic goddess. Before me was Thalestris.

It was frightening how she reminded me of my brother. She even wore a Prussian blue uniform, an unadorned uniform, the same cut and style Cristóbal had worn on the last day I had seen him before he left our father's house for Spain.

Héctor started to escort me toward where Cata Valeria and her husband were standing. Most of the soldiers had begun to drift away toward their campfires, and the two of them were alone, talking happily about her ride.

"No," I said as we drew nearer. "She knows nothing of me."

"She is your daughter."

Never in my life had I so much wanted to run away. Even in the most horrible battles, I had not wanted so desperately to flee. But my thoughts were racing ahead, and I knew I could not. This lovely young woman who was my daughter,was married to a young man whose influence was far greater than his military rank would indicate. He was a son of the House of Sestos. Such a man, even a young man, might have the ear of Santa Anna. Men like Santa Anna secured and maintained their positions through the support of wealthy men like the Conde de Sestos. I was at the end of my rope. I had to do something to save Coalter.

"Yes," I said finally. "Take me to her."

We were almost upon them before Cata Valeria looked away from her husband. There was a smile of recognition on her face for Héctor Sandoval, and then I saw her expression change. The beautiful face became anxious. She sensed my presence even before looking at me. And finally, when she did turn her eyes to mine, I saw she perceived a threat.

"Bravo, Cata Valeria," Héctor said. "As usual, you rode magnificently. Bravo!"

Without taking her gaze from me, she said, "Thank you, Sergeant Sandoval."

Her voice was lovely, hauntingly so, and I was reminded of what Don Esteban had said of my mother's voice. But what overwhelmed me and took away my breath were her eyes. They were the same eyes I had seen just a short while before. They were Coalter's eyes, blue, like a mountain stream. There was a wildness in those eyes that did not flinch from mine. There was great courage in those eyes.

"Cata Valeria," Héctor said and glanced at me. "There is someone here you will wish to meet."

She did not even realize she was drawing closer to her husband and gripping his arm. I saw the puzzlement in Arturo's face. He knew something was troubling his wife, and he looked from Héctor to me and back again.

"Cata Valeria," Héctor said, "this woman..."—he smiled— "...this woman is your mother."

"No," Cata Valeria said, almost before Héctor could finish. "It is not true."

Like a high-strung thoroughbred, she wanted to bound away. And if Arturo had not held her, I think she would have. From his expression, from the wide-eyed way he was looking at me, he must have sensed Héctor spoke the truth.

Somehow, I found my voice. "It is true, Cata Valeria," I whispered, my voice breaking on her name. "I am your mother."

"Who is this woman?" Cata Valeria cried and looked from Héctor to Arturo.

Straightening himself up, Arturo asked, "Who are you? Why do you say you are my wife's mother?"

"Because I am," I said firmly. I knew I had to convince them if I was going to make any progress in finding a way to save Coalter. There was no time to beat around the bush. "I am María del Carmen Rangel, the illegitimate daughter of Don Esteban, the Marqués de Abrantes. My mother was a servant at the Hacienda de Abrantes. It was kept a secret. When Cata Valeria was born, my father wished to raise her as his daughter. He promised never to tell anyone I was her mother because the Spanish regarded me as a traitor, and they might have harmed her."

Tears were flowing from Cata Valeria's eyes, and her effort to pull away from Arturo's grasp grew feeble. I wanted to go to her, but I knew I dare not.

"You," Arturo asked tentatively, "are the daughter of the Marqués de Abrantes? You...you are Don Esteban's daughter?"

"I am."

His eyes searched the ground, and then they narrowed as he looked at me. "If you are Cata Valeria's mother, who is her father?"

I took a deep breath. It had to be said. "Cata Valeria's father is a *norteamericano* named Coalter Owens. He and I followed Father Miguel Hidalgo. We were soldiers in the army of General Ignacio

Allende. The circumstances are too complex for me to relate at this
time, but Cata Valeria's father is at this moment in the Alamo." I
pointed in the direction of the mission, and as I did, I noticed that the
sky was growing darker. It was dusk. "If we do not find a way to stop
this madness, he will be killed. We must—"

"No!" Cata Valeria shouted and wrenched free of Arturo's grasp.
"It is all a lie! I will listen no more!"

She staggered away a few steps, and then began to run. I started
to go after her but realized Héctor was correct when he gently
touched my arm and told me with his expression I should let her go. I
watched as she ran past several groups of soldiers leaning against
their muskets. Soon, I lost sight of her.

It had gone as badly as I might have expected. My daughter had
rejected me. She had not believed me, and I could not say I blamed
her. But I did not have time for second thoughts. I looked at Arturo
and began to explain why I thought he might be able to persuade
Santa Anna to call a halt to the battle and agree to meet with Juan
Seguín and Sam Houston. I could sense he was dazed by my unexpected revelation. Unlike Cata Valeria, he believed me. I could see it
in his eyes. He trusted Héctor and so he believed me.

Finally, Arturo said, "Señora—"

"My name is Carmen."

"Carmen." He shook his head slowly. "I have no influence with
the Presidente. No one can tell him what to do. There are members of
his own family who have told him that this expedition is doomed, but
he will not listen. He is..."—he brought his hand to his head—"...he is a
little crazy."

I started to press the issue, to insist that the young lieutenant at
least make an attempt to talk to Santa Anna, but at that moment the
sound of bugles pierced the air, and a band near the headquarters
tents began to play the Degüello. My heart sank because I knew that,
like the blood red banner over the cathedral, the dirgelike march, the
Degüello, was a way of announcing that the battle about to be fought
would be one in which no prisoners would be taken. It also meant the
attack was to commence at once.

Glancing first at Héctor and then at me, Arturo said, "I must go to my men."

After he had departed, Héctor said, "Carmen, I, too, must return to my unit. The battle is about to begin. May I trust you not to attempt to return to the mission?"

I closed my eyes. I knew it was too late. It would be impossible for me to try to reach the Alamo. The army had already begun to advance. Soon, the Texans would be firing at anyone they saw coming toward them. There was no longer anything I could do. I nodded my promise, and Héctor rushed away.

To my left, I saw the generals assemble around several tables on which papers and maps depicting the deployments and battle plans were spread. In the middle of the generals was a small man in a lavish uniform covered with epaulets, brightly colored ribbons, medals, and gold braids. On his head was a large two-cornered hat bedecked with plumes. Since this man was directing the action, I assumed he was Santa Anna.

Watching him, I knew it would be futile to approach him with a plea to end the attack. He was enjoying himself. Far out of range of the long-rifles and the artillery, he was not threatened. His mind was filled with visions of glory and his place in history. I recalled what Bowie had said about vanity. Vanity was the most powerful force on earth. All I had to offer was reason. Reason would never defeat vanity. Not in this world.

I watched as the young soldiers marched forward toward the walls of the Alamo. Most of the young men were no more than fifteen or sixteen years old; many were younger. They were *rancheros*. Until a few weeks before, they had been tending goats and cows or tilling the earth. Now they were carrying old muskets they did not really know how to use, and they were advancing on men they had been told were evil. They were frightened, but they could not turn back. None of them realized their generals were marching them straight within the range of the republicans' artillery knowing full well that many of them would be killed. When the cannon roared, the generals would return to their papers, make adjustments and send another rank forward.

The republicans' eighteen-pounders belched forth their charge and the boys fell. The lucky ones died instantly, and the others screamed at the pain of having their bodies torn apart by shards of metal.

As I watched the carnage, I could not help but think that somewhere to the south, at that very moment, there were women—mothers, sisters, wives, sweethearts—who were praying that their boys be protected. I wondered if they could feel in their hearts the pain of those who had just been killed or were dying. Could they feel the pain and fear of those boys who would never see another daybreak, who would never again plow the soil, tend to their cattle, laugh, or cry?

And there were women, far to the north, in places with names like Tennessee and Connecticut, who were praying for their boys. As Santa Anna gave the order for his cannonade to commence, the republicans fell from their ramparts as walls collapsed beneath their feet. Their bodies were brutally torn apart. Did the women to the north feel their boys' pain?

I thought, too, of Pilar and Maudie, and of the women on the farms and in the villages across the Texas wilderness. Could they hear the cries of pain and anguish I heard? I suspected they could. I recalled when I was a child and some of the maids in Don Esteban's household said it was a curse to be born a woman in Mexico. Now I understood the truth of what they had said. It was a curse to be born a woman in Mexico. Perhaps it was a curse to be born a woman anywhere.

✦

The battle raged far into the night. Rank after rank was hurled against the walls by Santa Anna and his generals, but they were killed or driven back. At times, the guns would fall silent and the quiet was broken only by the unrelenting screams of the wounded and the dying. And then the cannon would be fired again, and in the flash of light made by their hellish explosions, flashes that turned the night to day, I could see the soldiers running again toward the walls with scaling ladders. After a while, the sound of cannon fire from the Alamo ceased. The republicans had run out of powder. But they continued to drive back Santa Anna's soldiers with their deadly long-rifles. The pattern was repeated over and over as though it would never end.

Sometime after midnight, I turned and began to walk away from the battle. I did not know where I was headed nor did I care; it was impossible for anyone in the Alamo to survive. I just started walking and soon I was some distance from the city, far from the encampments, I began to climb a low hill. What my intention was, I do not know. Mercifully, my thoughts had simply stopped. It would have pleased me greatly if I had been able to walk off the face of the earth and enter the abyss beyond the edge of creation. I wanted to vanish like the stars that streaked across the sky only to disappear into nothingness.

At the top of the hill, I stopped. For a moment, it did not register in my awareness that someone was standing before me. Gradually, my eyes adjusted to the dark, and I saw that a woman was watching me. It startled me that someone would be in such a place all alone. It frightened me in a most curious way that she did not move but that she stood, steady, motionless, watching me, and said not a word. I started to run away, but something drew me closer, and when I did, the woman's features became clear. It was someone familiar, someone I knew.

"Lupita?" I ventured.

She was older, of course—no longer a little girl—though not greatly changed in appearance from when I first saw her that day, so long ago, at the edge of a field of maize outside Dolores and she led Lebe Seru and me to Father Hidalgo. What I recognized were those dark eyes, those silent fathomless eyes that penetrated right through mine to the very depths of my soul. And above those eyes was the deep scar across her forehead.

"Lupita," I repeated louder and stepped closer. "Is it you, Lupita?"

She said nothing. There was not even the slightest hint of recognition, but strangely, it seemed as though it had been only minutes and not years that had elapsed since we had last been together on that dusty field I mistakenly thought had claimed the life of my beloved.

"Oh, Lupita!" I said, smiling in spite of the fury and madness of the battle raging below. "Lupita!"

And then I became aware that someone was behind us, approaching us, and looking into Lupita's eyes, I saw that she was watching this person. I turned.

Cata Valeria stopped and did not move, perhaps hoping I would not see her in the darkness. She stood for a long time that way and finally, whispered, "You...you knew Doña Lupe?"

"Lupita? Yes. I knew Lupita. She was a little girl in Dolores when I met her."

Around my daughter's slender waist was a wide red leather dragoon's belt to which was coupled a scabbard containing a broadsword. My eyes were drawn to the ornate hilt, and I realized it was the walloon that had been passed down from father to son through generations of men of the House of Abrantes from the time of the Cid. It was the sword I had used to slay Latham Barnet in order to save the life of my unborn child. And now this sword hung at that child's side as she continued to stare at me and I at her.

"Dolores?" she whispered. "Doña Lupe is from Dolores?"

"She was taken to Dolores when her parents were killed. Father Hidalgo took care of her as he did many of the children whose parents were killed by the viceroy's soldiers."

My daughter's brow wrinkled, and again I marveled at her beauty. There was an energy in her that radiated to me like the life-giving substance from the sun itself. I drank in that energy. It filled a place within that had for so long been empty. In her I had seen my brother. And now, strangely, I saw the mother I never knew.

In truth I could not even recall my mother's features; I was just a baby when she died, but somehow I could see her in this young woman watching me with such confusion in her lovely eyes, her father's eyes. I had carried this woman in my body. I had given her birth. I had killed that she might live. But she was a stranger to me just like the woman who had given me life. It was as though both

Cata Valerias—my mother and my daughter—were before me, and I did not know what to do. I did not know what to say.

"Doña Lupe..." Cata Valeria began and hesitated, groping for words, "...Doña Lupe knew Miguel Hidalgo?"

"You did not know?"

"No," Cata Valeria said quickly. "Doña Lupe was always at the Hacienda de Abrantes. I knew nothing about her. She does not talk. Did you know she does not talk?"

I nodded and glanced down at the contest below. Never had I seen a battle of such ferocity.

Following my gaze, Cata Valeria said, "I do not understand why you would be on the side of those men in the Alamo. You are a Mexican. Those men in the Alamo have invaded our country and seek to steal Texas from us."

Without taking my eyes from the battle, I said, "Many of the men in the Alamo are Mexicans, Cata Valeria. Many were born in Texas like their fathers and grandfathers before them. Most have fought for years for the republic, and some, men like your father, were with Father Hidalgo or Father Morelos from the beginning."

"My father," she said sternly, "is not in the Alamo! And you are not my mother!"

I lowered my eyes. There was nothing I could say to persuade her. And I no longer saw that it made a great difference. No power on earth could stop this battle.

"Those men," she continued and raised her hand to point toward the fighting, "may kill my husband! They are vicious men. They bring slaves into our land and refuse to obey our laws."

"Do you think Santa Anna will obey the laws?" I asked without conviction.

"Santa Anna has brought order to Mexico!" Now she reminded me of my father. "Everyone was fighting everyone. It was anarchy! Santa Anna was able to—"

She stopped because Lupita had approached her and was reaching for the collar of her jacket. Cata Valeria was puzzled but did not move as Lupita undid the top brass button of the military jacket and reached around Cata Valeria's neck.

I, too, was puzzled until Lupita stepped back, and in her hand, I saw the pendant she had unlatched and removed. She stepped toward me and extended her hand.

Looking down, I recognized the jade pendant I had so many years ago placed around my baby's neck before Lebe Seru and I left for Texas. Since it seemed to be Lupita's wish, I took the stone from her hand. I looked at Cata Valeria and saw that she was stunned by what Lupita had done. Her hand was at her throat as if trying to grasp the missing pendant.

"Why," she asked, "did she give you my pendant?"

The stone provoked so many thoughts in my mind. I recalled when Hortensia had tried to give it to me, and I had rejected it because I was ashamed that my mother was an *india*. I remembered how Father Hidalgo had admired it and explained its significance to me. And there was the time I gave it to him as he was being led to his execution. Gingerly, I touched the Toltec Cross beneath the head of the Mexican goddess.

"Why?" Cata Valeria insisted. "Why did she give it to you? It belongs to me!"

"Yes," I said. "It is yours. It was given to me when I was a little girl. My mother gave it to me before she died. Her name was Cata Valeria. That is why Don Esteban asked me to give to you the name Cata Valeria. He loved my mother. He loved her very much. And so I gave the pendant to you when you were a baby because she had given it to me."

She staggered back a step or two, and I worried that she might fall. "No," she whispered. "It cannot be true."

"The stone is carved," I continued, "to represent the head of Chimalma, mother of the Toltecs. Chimalma means 'shield hand.' For generations, the women in our family have passed this stone to their daughters for protection."

Cata Valeria brought her hands to her face. "No," she whispered. "No!"

When she turned to run down the mountain and into the darkness, I started after her, but Lupita touched my arm. She did not want me to follow. I looked again at the pendant and then handed it to Lupita.

"Please," I said, "give this to her. It belongs to her."

The battle below had begun to subside. Many fires were burning, and from the glow of their light, I detected that the walls had been breached. Santa Anna's soldiers were entering the Alamo, and so his artillery was now silent. It would not be long before all fighting ceased.

The futility of it all suddenly fell upon me like a great weight on my shoulders. Slowly, I sank to my knees and lowered my head. Most certainly, Coalter was dead. He was gone just as my father, Cristóbal, and Teresa were gone. Lebe Seru and Santiago were dead. Father Hidalgo. Captain Guerra. So many people I loved were gone. Rubén. Anselmo. Now, my daughter had left me. She had rejected me and left me alone. I had no one. I had nothing.

For the first time since I was a girl tears came to my eyes. I began to cry. It no longer mattered, I supposed. My father had told me that soldiers do not cry. But I was a soldier no longer. I had been broken and defeated. I had nothing and I was nothing. María del Carmen Rangel had been made to surrender.

I felt a hand on my face and when I looked up, I saw Lupita standing above me. Her soft fingers wiped the tears streaming down my cheeks. Though the night was cold, her hands were warm. I embraced her and buried my head against her chest. Without looking up, I reached for her face and inadvertently touched the scar on her forehead.

Briefly, I thought she spoke, that she said something, but I realized it could not be. Lupita could not talk. It must have been the sound of a bird, an owl in the darkness perhaps.

I cried until there were no more tears and a numbness gripped my body. Presently, I allowed my gaze to return to the Alamo. "Lupita," I said weakly, "the battle is over. It is finished."

It occurred to me to go below to claim Coalter's body. I would take it back to the Brazos valley that he so loved. Christopher would wish for his father to be buried next to his mother. I would take Lebe

Seru to Maudie and Santiago to Pilar. They would want me to do that. Slowly, and with Lupita's help, I got to my feet.

Before I departed from the hill, I looked at Lupita one last time and said, "Take care of Cata Valeria, Lupita. Watch after her. Protect her."

By the time I reached the field, the soldiers were already about the task of removing the dead and the wounded. Hundreds had been killed, and it was difficult to find a place to walk without stepping on their corpses. Here and there, soldiers knelt over their fallen comrades. Many sobbed, and others stared vacantly at the blood-soaked earth and the carnage.

Hearing loud voices behind me, I turned and saw, less than twenty paces from where I stood, Santa Anna receiving the congratulations of his generals. They were laughing, and I could smell the aroma of alcohol. How was it possible, I wondered, to celebrate amidst so much misery, amidst so many broken bodies and broken dreams. I wondered, too, if Santa Anna, strutting about with his gold-braided sycophants, knew that at that moment Sam Houston was rapidly assembling an army that would not allow him to stand beyond harm's way. By taking the time to dislodge little more than a hundred men at the cost of hundreds of his own and considerable amount of gunpowder, Santa Anna had insured his ultimate defeat.

I continued to walk slowly toward the mission. Several times I stopped so as not to block the passage of men who were carrying the wounded back to the tents where surgeons were working frantically to save lives.

And then, almost at the west wall, much of which lay in rubble, one of the soldiers obviously given up for dead moved. He was very young. At first I thought they must not have noticed him. Very soon, however, I saw why he had been left. Both of his legs had been severed. It was unbelievable that he was still alive and conscious. It was a terrible sight, and I started around him but stopped when I saw him raise his hand toward me. He was moving his mouth, trying to say something.

Bracing myself at the awfulness of his wounds, I drew closer and knelt beside him. I took his hand in mine and he grasped it tightly.

His mouth continued to move so I leaned closer to make out what he was whispering.

He thought I was his mother.

What else could I do? I put my lips to his ear and said, "I am with you, little son. Do not fear. I am with you." I kissed his brow. "I love you."

This seemed to bring some comfort because he closed his eyes and smiled. His grip relaxed, and I knew he had died.

Getting to my feet, I started walking in the wrong direction before turning and heading for a break in the wall that allowed me to climb over the rubble and enter the mission grounds.

Inside, the scene was no different. Dead men were clumped together in piles like corded wood. In the darkness, they looked no different from the men outside. I saw the long-rifles, many of them broken, probably used as clubs when the walls had been breached. At one point, I looked down and recognized the body of William Travis, his hand still gripping the hilt of a broken-bladed saber.

As I started toward the chapel, I halted when a tall man emerged through the door. Several soldiers were marching him out with his hands bound. I started toward them, thinking, praying, that this man was Coalter. But when I was almost upon them, I stopped. It was David Crockett.

The Tennessean recognized me, but with just a slight shake of his head, he conveyed that I should not let on to the soldiers that I knew him. As he walked by, I saw a slight smile on his lips. There was no doubt that he was being taken to his execution, but he was not afraid. Though he was about to die, he still had the compassion to think of my safety. That he was still alive to be executed meant that many of Santa Anna's soldiers could not bring themselves to obey the order to take no prisoners. There were decent and good men on both sides. Unfortunately, decent and good men seldom determine the course of events in this world.

Without thinking, I wandered into the chapel and went to the room where last I saw Bowie. Inside, I saw his body on the stone floor. He was surrounded by the bodies of soldiers who had died in ending his life. Maybe, I thought, he was at last with his beloved Ursula.

Stumbling out the back door of the chapel, I suddenly had a strange feeling. Before I looked up, I knew what I was going to see and did not know whether to be happy or sad. Slowly, I raised my gaze and standing before me, his hands bound behind his back, was Coalter. Behind him were Lebe Seru and Santiago, their hands also tied. Around them were soldiers preparing to take him to where it must have been decided the prisoners were to be executed.

Like Crockett, Coalter tried to warn me with his eyes. He did not want me to acknowledge him in front of these men who were charged with carrying out Santa Anna's orders. Of course, I did not hesitate to rush to him and embrace him. I looked at Lebe Seru and Santiago, both of whom stared straight ahead in an effort to make it appear they did not know me.

Attempting to pull away, Coalter looked at the soldiers and, speaking in Spanish, said, "This woman has mistaken me for someone else. I do not know her."

Several of the men grabbed me, but they could not break my grasp. No force on earth could pull me away from Coalter. I was going with him, and if they killed him, they would have to kill me as well.

Looking up into his eyes, now frantic with his fear for my safety, I smiled and whispered, "I love you."

"Send her away!" Coalter yelled. "She has nothing to do with me or any of us! Take her to the priests!"

"It is no use," I said. "We will die together. Please accept it."

The soldiers shoved us forward and toward a gate at the north wall. It seemed so foolish to open the gate and go through it when most of the wall had been blasted down. But it did not matter. All that mattered was that at last I was with Coalter and we would never again be parted. In my heart, I thanked the soldiers who had spared him so we could die in each other's arms.

Outside of the mission grounds, we walked toward the river and I surmised we were being taken to Santa Anna's headquarters. Perhaps the Presidente himself wanted to witness the executions. He had been too far away to see the death of those killed in battle.

Just before reaching the bridge, however, the men stopped and one of them, a corporal, alerted the others that an officer was approaching. I buried my face against Coalter's chest and paid no attention to who it was.

I heard a man say, "We will take the prisoners, Corporal."

It was a familiar voice and I looked up.

"We were told to take them to the Presidente," the corporal explained.

"I will take them to the Presidente."

It was Arturo. Behind him stood Héctor Sandoval. I looked up at Coalter and glanced back at Lebe Seru and Santiago. They were as puzzled as I.

The corporal continued to insist he should follow his original orders until Arturo shouted, "I told you I will take the prisoners from here! Do you wish for me to have you shot too?"

Héctor aimed his musket at us and used it to gesture us to cross the bridge.

"Return to the mission," Arturo said to the corporal. "Look for our wounded and bring them to the surgeons' tents. Now!"

"Yes, Lieutenant!" the corporal said, saluted, and quickly herded his men back in the direction of the Alamo.

Across the bridge, we veered to the left and moved down the embankment to the river's edge.

Suddenly, Cata Valeria stood before us. She stared at her father and he at her.

"Quickly!" Arturo said. "We must hurry while it is still dark." He looked at his wife. "Are you certain this is what you wish to do?"

Her eyes shifted to mine. She bit her lip and nodded her head.

"And you?" Arturo said to Héctor. "There can be no going back. We will be shot when it is discovered what we have done."

"I did not join the army to shoot prisoners," Héctor said. "Let us hurry."

"Keep your musket trained on them," Arturo said, nodding at Coalter, Lebe Seru, and Santiago. "We must make it appear they are our prisoners if we are stopped."

Rapidly, we followed the river south. When we came across soldiers, we simply went around them. Héctor kept the musket aimed at us, and Arturo carried his saber in his right hand. Cata Valeria raced ahead a few paces, turning back frequently to see why we were not moving faster. She appeared to know exactly where she was headed. It seemed to take forever to move beyond the encampments but when we did, Héctor cut the cords binding Coalter, Lebe Seru, and Santiago, and running, we continued to follow the narrow river on its course to the south.

After about an hour had passed and the sun had made a complete ascent above the horizon, we stopped. Looking back, all we could see were thin columns of smoke rising from the ruins of the Alamo and the funeral pyres. We were far beyond the reach of Santa Anna's army, and it would be days before that army was able to resume the march in search of Sam Houston's army.

I led Coalter to the river's edge and cupped my hand to bring water to his mouth. He was almost too exhausted to move. When we got to our feet, Cata Valeria stood behind us. Arturo and Héctor sat on the embankment and talked with Lebe Seru and Santiago.

"Coalter?" I said and took his hand in mine. "This is Cata Valeria de Sestos. She is..."—I looked up at him—"Cata Valeria is your daughter."

Cata Valeria drew closer. She appeared to be less apprehensive of her father than of me. After a brief hesitation, they embraced.

Releasing her father, Cata Valeria stepped to me and extended her hand, palm up. Softly, she said, "This is yours."

It was the jade pendant. I smiled and shook my head. "It is yours, Cata Valeria. I gave it to you. Perhaps some day you will have a little girl and you can give it to her. Until then, I would like for you to wear it."

She came closer, hesitated, and then awkwardly put her arms around me and we embraced.

"Carmen!" Lebe Seru shouted from the embankment. "Coalter! Look!"

My first impulse was to think he was warning us of Santa Anna's soldiers approaching. Following his gaze, I saw Lupita coming toward

us from a stand of oak trees. Cata Valeria had guided us to her. Lebe
Seru ran to greet this woman he had known as the girl who had
found us by the field of maize so many years ago and had often been
Father Hidalgo's silent companion when he was at prayer. Santiago
remembered her as the child I had carried in my arms in Mexico City,
the girl he had thought was my daughter. When Coalter came to
Lupita, he knelt, and embracing her, he placed his head against her
chest. Tears flowed down his face. He took my hand in his, and I
knelt beside him.

✦

We continued south along the river until we found a crossing,
and then made our way east to Coalter's farm in the valley of the Brazos where Cata Valeria met her brother. Maudie and Pilar thanked
me for bringing their husbands safely home, but I explained I had
nothing to do with it. The men wanted to continue east to be with
Sam Houston when he confronted Santa Anna. I persuaded them
there was much for us to do elsewhere. I knew that Santa Anna's
defeat, which was inevitable, would not mean the end of slavery. The
struggle to end slavery would continue for many years.

Nor would Santa Anna's defeat bring about the realization of
Father Hidalgo's dream of liberty, equality, and justice. People like
Benito Juárez were now sounding forth Miguel Hidalgo's vision anew.
Father Hidalgo's dream would require a continuing revolution, a revolution that, as he had explained to me on that night so many years
before, would have to take place in each person's heart. The battles of
this revolution were the only ones I was now prepared to fight. Soon,
with my husband at my side, together with our daughter and her
husband, our son and our friends, I would at last become a real soldier, a soldier in the only war that should be waged.